continued . . .

ACCIDENTALLY CATTY

DAKOTA CASSIDY

BERKLEY SENSATION, NEW YORK

THE BERKLEY PUBLISHING GROUP
Published by the Penguin Group
Penguin Group (USA) Inc.
375 Hudson Street, New York, New York 10014, USA
Penguin Group (Canada), 90 Eglinton Avenue East, Suite 700, Toronto, Ontario M4P 2Y3, Canada
(a division of Pearson Penguin Canada Inc.)
Penguin Books Ltd., 80 Strand, London WC2R 0RL, England
Penguin Group Ireland, 25 St. Stephen's Green, Dublin 2, Ireland (a division of Penguin Books Ltd.)
Penguin Group (Australia), 250 Camberwell Road, Camberwell, Victoria 3124, Australia
(a division of Pearson Australia Group Pty. Ltd.)
Penguin Books India Pvt. Ltd., 11 Community Centre, Panchsheel Park, New Delhi—110 017, India
Penguin Group (NZ), 67 Apollo Drive, Rosedale, North Shore 0632, New Zealand
(a division of Pearson New Zealand Ltd.)
Penguin Books (South Africa) (Pty.) Ltd., 24 Sturdee Avenue, Rosebank, Johannesburg 2196,
South Africa

Penguin Books Ltd., Registered Offices: 80 Strand, London WC2R 0RL, England

This book is an original publication of The Berkley Publishing Group.

This is a work of fiction. Names, characters, places, and incidents either are the product of the author's imagination or are used fictitiously, and any resemblance to actual persons, living or dead, business establishments, events, or locales is entirely coincidental. The publisher does not have any control over and does not assume any responsibility for author or third-party websites or their content.

Copyright © 2011 by Dakota Cassidy.
Cover illustration by Katie Wood.
Cover design by Diana Kolsky.
Interior text design by Kristin del Rosario.

PRINTING HISTORY
Berkley Sensation trade paperback edition / March 2011

Library of Congress Cataloging-in-Publication Data

Cassidy, Dakota.
    Accidentally catty / Dakota Cassidy.
        p.   cm.—(An accidental series; 5)
    ISBN: 978-0-425-23960-5 (pbk.)
    1. Women veterinarians—Fiction. 2. Upstate New York (N.Y.)—Fiction. 3. Shapeshifting—Fiction.
I. Title.
    PS3603.A8685A655   2011
    813'.6—dc22   2010046659

PRINTED IN THE UNITED STATES OF AMERICA

10   9   8   7   6   5   4   3   2   1

Acknowledgments

In honor of Katie Wood, who creates the most fabulous covers that, even in this author's wildest dreams, are more than I could have ever hoped for. I don't know how I got so damned lucky, but I'm all kinds of grateful for your genius. You, my friend, rocketh!

Also to Terri, who came up with a pearl of pure funny now contained within these pages. To Kate Pearce, who was a huge help with my Britishisms.

And, as always, this is with love and gratitude to the love of my life, Rob, my family, and especially to my father, Robert. I really miss you, Dad.

Huge thanks to the League of Reluctant Adults for more ROFLMAO moments than a marathon of *Last Comic Standing*.

And to the fans, bloggers, and booksellers—your emails, your support, your Facebook posts, your tweets, your hard work, and your devotion to this series are a joy to experience.

To my pets—every last seven of you. Thank you for having more health afflictions than *War and Peace* has pages. Those very health issues, and the 2,002 trips to the vet, came in very handy when writing about medical procedures and prescriptions. I love you each because of, and in spite of, your incontinence, hyperthyroidism, one-eyed-ness, un-potty-trainable-ness, diabetes, enlarged heart, blind-and-suddenly-deaf-only-when-it's-time-to-get-in-your-crate-edness. My nights just wouldn't be the same if I didn't have to sleep on a mere two inches of mattress in a king-sized bed while I burrow beside your beastly, stanky goodness. Truly, I adore you.

Last, but most certainly not least, to Nat in Canada (where some serious readers rule!). Seriously, dude, how could I have ever written a book without the word "homeslice" in it? Thanks for putting me back on the path of the righteous—you aiiight.

www.tshirthell.com/hell.shtml
wdfw.wa.gov/wlm/living/cougars.htm

Dakota ☺

AUTHOR'S NOTE

Please note, while I researched cougars as thoroughly as possible, I've obviously taken some artistic license due to the nature of my humor. If I've inaccurately portrayed any of the facts I've used in the book, please consider any and all mistakes mine.

CHAPTER
1

"Uh, Dr. Woods?"

"Ingrid?"

"You do see that, don't you? I mean, that's not just the buttery nipple shots I had after dinner talking, right? Because, like, *oh, my effin' God.*"

Katherine Woods, DVM, inhaled deep, then released with a whoosh of breath made visible by the chilly country air. "No. I didn't have anything even remotely buttery or nipply and I see what you see." She ran a hand over her forehead in thought.

What to do? What to do?

Ingrid Lawson, her faithful though often scatterbrained receptionist, clung to her arm, moving behind Katie. "This is a problem, right? I mean . . . you know, all on the front steps to the clinic, just out—out . . . in—in the open. Who knows what could happen? This could attract all sorts of . . . well . . ." Ingrid, too, breathed deeply, her thoughts clearly slowing with her shaky words. "Yes, bad things. It could attract very bad things. Just baaaad."

Katie nodded with a distracted smile, her mind sorting through her shock to search for a solution. "We definitely don't want to attract *the bad.* You wait here—"

"Oh, hell to the no!" Ingrid shouted, the echo of her response resonating throughout the woods surrounding the veterinary clinic. "I am *not* staying here with—with . . . *that.* Nuh-uh." Her multicolored black, green, and pink head shook a very definitive "not on your life" when she backed away.

"Calm down, Ingrid. I'll tell you what," Katie said, crouching on the steps. "You go get Kaih. I think he's still inside with Mrs. Krupkowski's Chi, getting her settled. We need some brawn. I'll wait . . . here." She pointed to the cement steps.

Ingrid was up the stairs in a shot, fueled by her fear and a couple of buttery nipples.

Katie eyed the steps, yawning with a shiver after a long day at the clinic.

She was getting too old for these kinds of hours.

She was definitely getting too old for these kinds of surprises.

Maybe she should just turn right around and head back down the hill to Ed's and have a buttery nipple—or five.

"THANK you for calling OOPS. This is Wanda Schwartz Jefferson, here to service all your paranormal needs. How may I help you?"

There was a pause—a long one—before Wanda gasped, then slammed down the phone with a huff, narrowing her eyes.

Casey and Marty exchanged wincing glances.

Marty bit her lip, sliding her pen back into its holder with care so as not to jar Wanda, who was very clearly on edge.

Casey fiddled with her stack of Post-it pads. Very pink. Very blank.

Nina, on the other hand, rose from her office chair and snorted. "Another crank that needs an ass kickin', pal?" she asked Wanda. "Do that frickin' caller ID thing and I'll call the shit stain back. He'll wish he'd thought twice before picking up the phone and smack talking us after I wrap his dick around his neck."

Wanda's lips trembled to a thin line when she pointed at Nina with the familiarly universal gesture for her to still her mouth. "That isn't the way we want to introduce ourselves to society at large, Nina. It's unseemly. We all knew crank calls would be a part of the deal when we decided to do this. You don't think the Ghost Hunters didn't take a potshot or two before they got their own show, do you? But they're not out there threatening to pull people's diaphragms through their belly buttons because much of society doesn't believe in ghosts, now, are they?"

She paused, flicking the ballpoint pen Heath had given her to celebrate the beginning of this venture. "There are people who need our help. That's our focus, not the nincompoops who call to ask if you can use your superhuman strength to kick their science teacher's ass for giving them a D-minus on their class project."

Casey leaned back in her chair, propping her ballet-slippered feet up on the edge of her desk. "Yeah. You know, I've been giving some thought to the nonbelievers. Maybe we should put an ad in the newspaper and invite those punks to a central location, then offer them Giants tickets as incentive to show up. Like a paranormal sting or something." She cocked her dark head with a sly smile. "Then I'll fry their asses while you guys hiss and shed. Whaddya think?"

Marty rolled her eyes, scooping Muffin up to set her in her lap. She twisted her poodle's lavender rhinestone-studded collar to straighten it. "I think you ain't seen nuthin' till you've seen scared

humans en masse with wooden stakes and a rope of garlic. We may
be bigger in numbers than most of the human population thinks,
but this isn't 'We Are the World,' Casey. The humans will always
outnumber us, unfortunately. While it would be LOL funny to
see the expressions on their faces when we shift or Nina gives them
the best display evah of a vampire behaving badly, that's sort of not
the goal here."

Nina made a face at Marty, tucking her arms under her breasts
and leaning back in her chair. "Remind me again just what the fuck
the goal *is* here, Marty? Why am I spending three nights a week,
volunteering time I could be spending with my man, answering
bullshit calls from whacks who actually believe *we're* the nuts?"

"It was your idea, Nina," Wanda offered dryly, gnawing on the
tip of her pen.

"This"—she spread her arms wide to encompass the small
space they'd rented for their venture—"was my idea how, Wanda?"

"Oh, please. To quote you loosely, I distinctly remember it was
you who said at Naomi's sweet sixteen party, 'There must be some
other poor chicks whose boyfriends have, I dunno, iguanas maybe,
that have accidentally bitten them and turned them into, like, Puff,
the Magic Dragon. If it happened to us, and we all know each
other, then there could be others like us.' Loose quote, unquote.
Remember that, Elvira?" Wanda asked on a neck roll.

Nina flicked her lean fingers in Wanda's direction. "Yeah, I said
it. But I didn't mean we should don our paranormal capes and
save the world Superman style. This is bullshit, Wanda. Nobody
is taking this seriously. We should have never taken out that ad in
that kooky alternative magazine or opened Twitter and Facebook
accounts. You should see the shit people say. They're all flakes."

Wanda heaved a sigh, letting her head fall to her arms. "Maybe
you're right, Nina." Her words held resignation.

Nina sat upright, her lean spine ramrod straight beneath her loose-fitting sweatshirt. "What? Did you say I'm *right*? Casey, Marty, prepare to meet your maker."

"I just mean that maybe this really was a stupid idea. Maybe we really are the only people in the world who've been accidentally bitten. I thought we could help people in supernatural distress. If I hadn't had you and Marty to guide me about what was happening to my body, I don't know what I would've done when I was turned. The more I thought about what you said, Nina, the more I thought we had valid reason to start up OOPS. But it's been three months and nothing but cranks and oh, surprise!—*more cranks*."

Marty stroked Muffin with a light hand. "I did say maybe the whole Out in the Open Paranormal Support wasn't the right name for us. Maybe it's just too weird and it freaked people out."

"No, it just freaked our husbands out," Casey reminded her. "Do you remember the look on Clay's face when we all told our Neanderthal mates that we were going to go live with this OOPS thing? I think if Clay could still die of a heart attack, he'd have done it right there in front of everyone. They weren't in love with this idea from the get-go. All that nonsense they spewed about living peacefully with humans and not making waves or drawing attention to ourselves when those men know perfectly well, if we all hadn't known each other, Nina would have ended up staked through that cold, black heart of hers within twenty-four hours of turning. Ditching it all would just prove them right. I don't know about all of you, but I don't much like being wrong. Besides, I like to tweet with the people who ask me stupid things like where my pitchfork is."

Nina's chair scraped against the cement floor, her arms rigid when she latched onto the edge of her desk. "My cold, black heart? You do know I can kill you, right?" she asked Casey.

Casey's eyebrow lifted in a scornful arch, unperturbed. "You do know I'll set your skinny ass on fire first, don't you?"

Wanda whacked a rolled-up issue of the very kooky paranormal magazine Nina spoke of against her desk, making everyone still. "This! *This* is exactly why I bought into doing this in the first place. Because I just couldn't bear the thought that someone might be suffering the effects of a Nina-like person who's cranky enough already without the supernatural ability to take on the entire NFL single-handedly. Or someone like you, Casey!" Wanda pointed to her sister with a pink fingernail. "Someone who still needs to get not only her anger and levitation under control but her wise cracking mouth. But really, what was I thinking? How could we possibly hope to help someone if they called anyway? The way you two behave, it'd be like the blind leading the blind." She threw the magazine on her desk with a disgusted grunt for emphasis.

Nina stood with a satisfied smile. "So does that mean this is a wrap?"

Marty jumped up from her chair, shoving Muffin under her arm. The jingle of her bracelets clanked together with a tinkle. "Jesus, Nina! You're so damned insensitive. Sit down and shut it. Please." The sigh she let go was colored with her aggravation. "Look, Wanda, maybe we should just have the calls rerouted to our cell phones or something? This way, if someone does call who needs our help, we can still aid and abet, we just won't have to sit around staring at four empty, very drab walls, I might add, while we do it."

"I hung up a poster to brighten the place up," Casey muttered. "Isn't it in your color wheel, *Marty*?"

"Dude, it's a poster for Just Say No to Drugs. Not so colorful. Just fucking stupid," Nina remarked with her trademark dry sarcasm.

"It was the only thing I could find from my teaching days, you wretched wench. I don't recall you offering to decorate and brighten things up," Casey shot back.

"What dungeon do you know of that needs decorating?" Nina waved a hand around the dark space they'd rented—the space with one grimy window and no heat.

They each fell silent again.

Wanda was the first to rise, smoothing her pencil-slim skirt and straightening the bow on the collar of her prim mango-hued silk shirt. "You're right, Marty. I think that's exactly what we should do. I have a book to write. Casey's got classes to attend and a teenager. You have little Hollis and Bobbie-Sue, and Nina . . . well, Nina has innocent people to brutalize. So let's scram," she said, defeat clear in her tone.

Chairs scraped against the cement flooring as they all rose in unison to file out.

The phone rang with a shrill cry. Each woman stopped short at the door where Wanda's hand rested on the door handle.

Wanda let go of the rusted handle with a purse of her lips. She looked over her shoulder at her sister and friends with a question in her gaze.

"Oh, c'mon, Wanda," Nina crowed. "It's probably just another ass-a-holic crank call. I wanna go the hell home and watch reruns of *Matlock* with my man."

Marty's eyes grew wary. "But what if it isn't and we leave, and someone's breathing fire as we speak but doesn't know why? Alone and terrified. Remember that feeling, Nina? Oh, wait. No, you don't because you weren't alone! Wouldn't you feel like the mean shit you are if that happened to some innocent?"

Casey let her shoulders flop with a tired sigh. "I hate to ever admit Nina's right about anything, but seriously, do we want to beat our heads against the wall just one more time for old time's sake? Not me, people. I'm tired of having questionably sane people call to ask me if I'll light their stupid barbeques."

Wanda's low ponytail shook. "But what if . . ."

Nina threw up her hands. "Fine, for Christ's sake—I'll get it, and I'm warning you, Wanda. If it's another stupid ass who wants to watch me drink blood and flap my bat wings, I'm gonna hunt his ass down and knock him from here to next year. Deal?"

Wanda's head hung low, letting her chin drop to her chest. She waved a hand at Nina. "Fine. You answer."

Nina groaned while she made her way to the desk and snatched up the receiver to the matching phones they'd all bought as an OOPS team at Costco. "This is Nina Statleon and you've reached OOPS. Which I thought was a totally stupid name for this crazy venture, too, but I was voted down by my pansy-ass waffler of a friend, Marty. I'm a goddamned vampire. If you called to razz me about that shit—c'mon over and I'll show you my fangs while I beat your head against this stupid, cheap, piece-of-shit desk I was talked into buying at Wal-Mart as part of my show of good faith. Really, it just means I was bamboozled into doing something I didn't want to do in the first place, but my friend Wanda the Werewolf used pretty words and stupid friendship euphemisms to steamroll me into this. So name your paranormal emergency and it better be good. I live in a castle. That takes a buttload of time to clean. Now spew, and make it fast." She finished with a smug smile in Wanda's aghast direction.

The voice on the other end of the line stuttered momentarily, then blurted out, "I think I—we—us, uh, we have a paranormal emergency . . . I mean, I *know* we do. Please. We need help. Fast! Yes, we need fast help. Like, super fast!"

INGRID eyed her boss from across the room while she tried to explain what had happened to the grumpy beast who'd answered the phone at the number she'd gotten from her favorite magazine *Vive La Paranormal*. "Yes. No. Oh, geez, I dunno. I just know we're in a serious pickle here. No. It's not me. It's my boss. No, I can't explain the symptoms. It's not me who has them. It's my boss!" she cried, pressure situations never having been her strong suit.

She paced the floor in front of the examining table, scrunching her eyes shut, running a trembling, ring-covered hand over her forehead. "You want to talk to her? I don't know if she can talk-talk. You know? She's had a serious incident here. I mean, she has—has . . ." Ingrid stumbled over her words, clearly unable to express what her boss "had."

Skirting the metal examining table, Ingrid scurried past it as though she'd never seen anything in her life like what was lying on the table.

Katie had to wonder, though the wondering was vague and distorted by vision so clear it made everything almost magnified, if her trusty receptionist had ever been to the zoo.

Ingrid approached her with obvious caution, holding the phone at arm's length. "The lady"—she held her hand over the earpiece—"and I use that term a bit loosely because she swears like a Navy SEAL—"

"Sailor," Katie corrected, surprised she still had the capability to think with any remote precision.

Ingrid's head bobbed in furious confirmation, the multicolors of her hair in pink and stripes of green, flashing painfully before Katie's sensitive eyes. "Yes. Like a sailor. She said she wants to talk to you, the person who's experiencing the paranormal phenomenon. So that's you, Boss, the paranormal-ee."

Apparently, that would be her. Katie eyed the phone with huge amounts of skepticism when Ingrid put it back to her ear, listened for a moment, then said, "Ohhh. I'm sorry I said you weren't very ladylike." She paused. "Absolutely. I swear I'll be more respectful in the future." There was another pause as a worried look flitted across Ingrid's face. "Look, lady! What do you want, a major organ?" Ingrid stopped short, her face going from mildly agitated to complete disbelief. "What do you mean an organ's useless to you?" There was another hitch in her breath, and then she said, "I'm sorry I asked, and I already apologized!" More silence and then, "Sorry, sorry, sorry. You're right. I'm just a little edgy right now. Okay, so here's my boss. Her name's Katherine Woods. Dr. Katherine Woods. Noooo, no, no, no. She's a veterinarian—like DVM, not a doctor-doctor."

Katie frowned at the irony of Ingrid's statement. Funny, her mother had said the same thing when she'd told her parents she was going to veterinary school. Looking back now, proctology didn't seem at all as boring as it had when she was twenty. In fact, a field of hairy, white butts wouldn't at all upset her right now.

Ingrid practically threw the phone at her, backing away with wide eyes. "The lady, and I do mean *lady*, wants to talk to you." In her rush to get away from Katie as though she'd contract the cooties just by virtue of osmosis, she bumped into the examining table, letting out a horrified squeak she attempted to hide by covering her mouth with her hand.

Katie's sigh didn't come out like the sighs of old. It sounded more like a low grumble. And it was resonant, if nothing else. Resonant and rumbly-tumbly. "Hello? Yes, this is Dr. Katherine Woods. Yes, it's true. I'm experiencing something, though I can't, with any amount of certainty, say it's of a *paranormal* nature." The fight to keep her professional decorum intact was punctured with fractured stabs of sheer terror.

"Can, too," her intern Kaih chimed in with bored disinterest from his desk in the corner. "I was raised by people who talk about this stuff all the time, Doc, but I didn't ever believe it until now. You got a problem, Dr. Swims in the River of Denial." His eyes zeroed in on her with a critical glance. "A *big* one."

Katie waved him off with a shake of her head while she listened to the list of symptoms the woman on the other end rambled off. "Did you say blood?" She blanched, fighting back the turn of her overly sensitive stomach. "No. I don't want to drink blood. And might I add, though I'm not a medical doctor of the human variety, certainly drinking another's blood can't be good for your immune system."

Now she, too, was pacing, hot and uncomfortable in her heavy sweater with the organdy lace around the cuffs—even with the big hole in it right under her breasts. "No. Forgive me. I didn't mean to lecture or declare I know any such thing about being a fuc . . . a vampire. Call it a hazard of my profession to spew unwarranted advice. Please, continue."

The next words out of the woman's mouth made her stop cold in her tracks. Okay. This had gone from slim hope to decidedly certifiable. End conversation. She clicked off the phone, placing it at the edge of Kaih's desk.

"Boss?" Ingrid asked. "What happened?"

"She asked me if I could shoot fireballs from my fingertips or," Katie cleared her throat, "float like one of those big *fucking* balloons in the Macy's parade. Then there was a bit of a scuffle on the other end—which I imagine had to do with her mother taking the phone from her. A mother I'm hoping had the common sense to ground her for life, so I hung up."

Ingrid's eyes took on that wide, terrified look again. "Oh, Dr. Woods! Why would you do that? Who else can we turn to for—for—help?"

Help. How odd that she was the one who needed the help, when typically, she was the helper. Physician, heal thyself. Or was that sentiment reserved for *real* doctors?

The harsh glare of the lights in examining room one, coupled with, well, with her issue, or issues, depending on how many hairs you wanted to split, began to make her head swim.

The world was falling away from her, right out from under her feet—or was she falling into it? She stumbled, tripping over Yancey, her office cat and one of many strays she'd collected over the years.

Ingrid ran to her side, reaching out to her, then snatching her hands back to shove them into the pockets of her oversized lab coat. Her petite frame came in and out of focus when she heard Kaih yell, "Ingrid! She's going to hit that floor like a ton of bricks! Stop acting like she has the plague and grab her, you spaz!"

There was a loud shuffle of feet, the wheels of her examination table scurrying against the cold tile of the floor, and then there was the floor.

Cool and refreshing against her cheek.

Okay, so the crash to the floor and the subsequent bruising blow she took to her cheek wasn't pleasant, but the black void of nothingness was A-okay.

CHAPTER
2

"Oh, I'm so glad you came! Thank the universe you're here!" Ingrid cried, her excited voice screaming through Katie's ears.

Katie heard a door open and shut. She saw two pairs of shoes, completely different in fashion statements, pass before her eyes. One set, a ratty pair of red sneakers, the other, a high-end open-toed heel in classically basic black. She clung to the edge of the couch she felt beneath her and fought to keep her powers of observation focused.

There were strangers in the room. It wasn't just that she clearly heard them, either. It was that she sensed them. *Smelled* them. And their scents couldn't just be attributed to perfumes and body lotions. Literally, Katie noted their gender, the blood coursing through their veins, the odd mixture of the scent of a human and something else . . .

Next she filed away their gasps in the disbelief category of her brain, assessed them as incredulous, and really, if they were seeing what she thought they were seeing, incredulous was perfectly acceptable.

"This is the subject?" a woman with soothing tones and perfect diction asked.

"Ye—yes. That's Dr. Woods," Ingrid stammered.

"Well, duh, Wanda. Look at her. Of course *she's* the subject," a scathing, husky voice, one much like the one Katie had heard on the phone, chastised.

"Oh. My." The sweeter of the two women exhaled the words.

Though her head swam and her limbs felt like tree trunks, Katie fought to sit up. Kaih rushed to her side, sliding to position her on the couch. "Doc, don't get up. Take it nice and slow."

"But the patient . . ." She shook her head. "I mean, you know the thing, uh, *cougar*, on the examining table. It *needs* me." Duty first and all.

Kaih patted her arm. "Oh, it needs something, but you took a pretty hard fall. Stay put, and stop worrying. I gave it another couple of cc's of that stuff you knocked it out with before. It's sleeping like a baby."

"Is that what we're calling what we just saw in that room? I don't know about you, but I ain't never seen a *baby* like that," the sarcastic woman from her earlier phone call remarked.

Brushing aside Kaih, Katie ran her good thumb over her eye. The thumb that wasn't . . . Oh, Hail Mary. She stopped herself mid-thought. Determination made her grit her teeth. Sort of. Her teeth and the ability to grit them were a work in progress. A glance upward, one that allowed her a panoramic view of each woman's pores, gave her the chance to give them the once-over. "Who are these people, Ingrid?"

Ingrid backed away, still in a state of perpetual horrification. She situated herself behind one of the most beautiful, enhanced by nothing but soap and water, dark-haired women she'd ever seen. "They're the OOPS people. The people you talked to on the phone. They're here to help."

The other woman, dressed in simple clothes with a tailored, elegant cut, moved toward her with measured steps. Her face, not as exotic as the other woman's, though just as lovely, had a Grace Kelly air to it. Cool, calm, serene. "I'm Wanda Jefferson. We're from OOPS. Your receptionist told us you were experiencing a paranormal phenomenon. We can help."

Short and to the point. Katie admired that. Yes. She was experiencing . . . Something paranormal? Not likely. "Thank you for coming. I know Ingrid asked you to come, but there's obviously nothing you can do for me." Though who *could* do something for her was out of her medical scope. "I hope we didn't make you go out of your way."

The dark-haired woman snorted, leaving the residual tremble of her tonsils ringing in Katie's ears. "Lady, we drove three freakin' hours to get here from the island. You live in a place right outta *Deliverance*, and you obviously got some shit goin' down. Me and Wanda here, we've seen shit. We've lived shit. You need help with that shit. If we go home, your ass is as good as the *Titanic*."

Katie's eyes shuttered, her thoughts piecemeal. *"Titanic?"*

"Sunk," she replied. "Oh, and I'm Nina Statleon. I'd say it's a pleasure, but I'm thinkin' you feel anything but pleasurable right now."

Katie nodded her head in agreement as she took in the irony of Nina's T-shirt that read "Don't Curse." "The vampire, right? Wasn't that what you called yourself on the phone?"

"That's what *I am*, lady. I know, I know. I've been through this a time or two. You don't believe. Hang on for a second, and I'll make you a believer."

Wanda reached out, snaring Nina's slender arm in her long, tapered fingers. "Do. Not. I'm warning you, Nina. *Do. Not.*" Her jaw clamped shut so tight, a tic began to pulse.

Nina shrugged her off. "Don't be such a tard, Wanda. If I don't show her, then we're gonna go a few rounds with the 'oh, my God, I can't believe it' bullshit. I'm just not up to the game, dude. It's the same old song. I've done it three solid times now, not counting myself. So I say we just get it on, let the weeping and wailing commence, and then get to the biz at hand, which is figuring out what the fuck happened to her."

The rational doctor in Katie's brain, the one who functioned like clockwork, considered a diagnosis of impulse control for the brunette Nina. The thwarted, freethinking side of her brain admired this woman's foul mouth and direct nature.

But that still didn't mean they could help.

Katie Woods didn't need their particular brand of help.

She needed an orthopedic surgeon and maybe some maxillofacial tweakage.

"Dr. Woods?" Kaih's soulful black eyes sought hers. "I'll say it again, where I come from, you know, like my tribe, beliefs like these aren't uncommon, but the one with the dark hair, uh, Nina," he whispered low. "I have to be honest. She scares the shit out of me. Plus, she thinks she's a vampire. Scared shitless plus vampire equals I wanna go home."

"Hey, Runs with Mouth," Nina poked Kaih's burly arm. "You shoulda listened to your tribe. I am a vampire, and if you don't shut your trap, I'll show you exactly what that means without so much as a heads-up. Feel me?"

Wanda threw her hands up, her black purse sliding to the crook of her elbow. "Why, for the love of Jesus and all twelve, didn't I ride with Casey and Marty? Oh, wait, I know. Because no one wants to spend three minutes in a car with you, let alone three hours. Nina! Back off or you'll be on phone duty until your ears fall off. Now, don't make me say it again—back up, and let me do the talking. Can your impatience this instant."

Wanda knelt before Katie, placing a hand on her knee. It was warm, reassuring, allowing her to let at least two inches of her vertebrae relax. "I know all the crazy thoughts running through your head right now, Dr. Woods, but I promise you, we can help. As this unfolds, you'll need people like us with experience in this phenomenon. I don't mean the kind of experience someone who's read a bunch of books on the subject or watched some paranormal movies has, but the kind of experience that can only be garnered by living it."

Wanda's pause, the one Katie regarded as a moment to allow her to let that information sink in, only served to re-create the tension in her spine. Clearly, this woman, though quieter, sweeter, all round less crass than the other, was in need of psychiatric attention, too.

Katie snatched her hand back, tucking it under her thigh, absorbing the cool leather of her office couch against her overheated skin. "You have to go." Yes. They had to go. She was good at giving instructions. Surely these women would follow them if she used her doctor voice. All of her patients' owners did . . .

Wanda's slender shoulders lifted then slumped in a sigh of "she'd heard this before." "Dr. Woods, you're disoriented due to the changes in your body's chemistry, and if we go, you'll go through the rest of the changes alone."

"There's more?" Ingrid squeaked, still tucked behind Nina.

"Shit, yeah. This is nuthin'," Nina said over her shoulder. "Wait. Didn't you say that the doc's incident happened earlier tonight?" she asked Ingrid.

Ingrid's lower lip trembled, her face pale. "Yes, just after *it* happened."

Nina shook her dark head in clear wonder. "Damn, that was fast. Usually takes at least twenty-four hours before shit starts happening."

Ingrid's breathing hitched. "So there might be more . . . uh, changes . . ."

Wanda nodded. "Yes, there could be more physical changes. Dr. Woods's turn was the quickest I've ever seen. That could be due to her . . . um, species. But there's also more in the way of emotional issues. So much more. Now, I think it's time for some realism. I hate to do it, but being a doctor, I'd bet you've been trying to put this all into some kind of medical file in your brain. You're a logical woman. That stands to reason due to your profession. However, what's happened to you defies logic and the science you think you know. I'm going to give you that first dose of the unreal with me as your support. So I'll need you to trust me just a little. Ingrid and Kaih can come with us, but I'd like it if you'd give me your hand and come with me."

Katie shrunk back against the couch.

"Oh, hellz no. I'm not going in there with you!" Ingrid yelped from around Nina's arm.

Exactly, Katie thought. She wasn't going anywhere with these women. They were unstable.

Kaih gave her receptionist a disgusted look. "Ingrid, the big kitty's asleep. Don't be such a coward. Suck it up, already. Can't you see Dr. Woods needs us? If it weren't for her, you'd have nowhere to live. The least you can do is be there for her in her time of . . . whatever time it is."When he turned to Katie, his dark eyes pleaded. "You really need to at least see what's in the other room, Doc. I'll go with."

Her perpetual state of disorientation cleared for a brief second. "Wait. What's in the other room that wasn't in the other room to begin with?"

Wanda held her hand back out. "Come. I'll show you."

"You've seen it?" Katie asked, allowing herself to be hoisted up by Wanda's unusually strong grip.

Wanda tucked her hand under her arm reminiscent of the nurturing way a grandmother would. "Oh, the things I've seen. You'd laugh and laugh if you weren't so fragile right now. I'm hoping, someday when all is said and done, we'll have a cup of coffee and do that laughing. That is, if you still drink coffee after . . ." She shook her head as if to clear it. "Never you mind. That's neither here nor there. Yes, I've seen what's in the other room, and apparently, things have changed drastically since you last saw it. But no worries," she assured. "It's all fine. Or at least it will be."

Wanda used her shoulder to push open the heavy oak-stained door a crack. "Okay, now, take a deep breath."

Katie complied, ignoring the rumbly growl from just beyond the door.

Wanda's smile was pleased and warm. "Good. Now here goes. First, look at your left pa . . . uh, hand." She reached for it, holding it up with her delicate fingers, and relieving Katie of the incredible weight of it. "Do you see what I see, Katie?"

Oh, Jesus, oh, Jesus, oh, Jesus! Her wince was riddled with painful acknowledgment. "I—" She cleared her throat. "I see." She saw. Oh. Lord. She saw.

Wanda's smooth complexion and clear eyes wrinkled at the corners. "That's not a hand, is it, Katie?"

Her stomach lurched. "N—no."

"It's a paw, Katie."

Well, now that she'd said it out loud, fine—it was a paw. She knew a paw when she saw one. She'd treated all sorts of paws in her fifteen years of practice. Infected paws, torn paw pads, paws, paws, paws.

Here a paw, there a paw, everywhere a paw-paw.

And it was a heavy one, too. Each time she lifted it, it fell back to her side like some sad, limp brick.

Wanda tilted her chin up, and Katie supposed it was to refocus her straying thoughts. "Katie?"

"Yes. It's a paw."

Her smile acknowledged her pleasure. "Good job! Now, I want you to use your non-pawed hand to run a finger over your teeth. Can you do that?"

Instantly, Katie's fingers went to the source of the trouble she'd had clamping her jaw. A tentative finger ran along the lower set of teeth in her mouth. Had she already called the Lord's name in vain? She didn't want to abuse the privilege, but *Jesus*!

"Do you feel that, Katie?"

She did. She felt the elongation of two of her bottom teeth. "I do."

"That's not normal, is it, Katie? I mean, when you woke up today, you didn't have those, did you?"

No. No, and no. These were a magically delicious surprise as of early this evening. Katie shook her head in confirmation.

Wanda's smile was of approval—the kind you gave small children when they said "please" or "thank you" appropriately. "Good. Okay, now we're going to go into this examining room. We'll talk about all the other things that have occurred in due time, but for now, I think we need to talk about the potential source of your troubles. You good with that?"

No. Yet, stoic reserve took over. "Okay," was all she managed.

Wanda gave her a tug, a gentle one she refused to lean into. "It's okay, Katie. I promise. Nothing will hurt you. Trust me when I tell you, Nina and I can handle whatever might arise. Now c'mon," she coaxed. Wanda's tug was harder this time, making Katie, whose legs were like soft-serve ice cream, cave. Kaih was right behind her, bracing a hand against her waist.

Katie's eyes grew wide, her mouth falling open. Which was

okay, considering all that extra enamel between her lips had become a lot to manage without drooling.

"Do you see what I see, Katie?"

Well, sure. "Yes."

"What do you see?"

Nina knocked Wanda in the arm, her impatience obviously getting the better of her. "Lay off the show-and-tell, Wanda."

Katie reflected on what she saw. When this had all gone down earlier this evening, the animal she and her two loyal employees had all but dragged into her clinic and hoisted into a large cage with much grunting and moaning had been . . . Oh. My. Hell.

"Nina," Wanda said in a strained warning. "Clamp it. Tell me, Katie, when you helped the animal outside your clinic earlier this evening, did it look like this?"

"No!" Ingrid shouted, jolting Katie's nerves from head to toe. "We helped a cougar. We thought he was an injured cougar. He was unconscious, but otherwise unharmed. Dr. Woods had us haul him in here so she could examine him because she thought he looked malnourished. We were sure he came from the exotic animal park down the road. They're horrible people—horrible! They mistreat those animals. I know it!" She gave them all a quick, vehement glance before saying, "Anyway, we managed to get him up on the table, and when Dr. Woods was helping by holding up his front paws, he jerked and she nicked herself on her arm. After that, everything went kaplooey."

Nina and Wanda gave each other knowing glances.

Glances Katie didn't much cotton.

"Is that true, Katie?" Wanda inquired.

Her nod was slow—words were something she was incapable of as the reality of what had come to pass began to worm its way deep into her brain. Yes. Everything Ingrid had told them was true.

She'd thought surely he'd somehow escaped from the exotic animal farm four miles down the road. Katie had always been suspicious about the kind of care animals, who in her opinion should be free to roam the wild, received there. She'd made her position on such clear to anyone who would listen in the small town of Piney Creek where she'd set up her practice in the hopes of rebuilding her now-tarnished career.

So she'd made the executive decision to give him a thorough examination before contacting anyone, even though large breeds and exotics weren't her specialty. If she could find proof the animals were undernourished and mistreated, maybe she could have the place shut down for good. Katie Woods wasn't afraid of a good fight when it came to an animal's right to humane care.

Just ask her ex-husband, George . . .

However, what slept so soundly in a tight ball in the biggest cage Katie had was, most assuredly, not what she, Ingrid, and Kaih had dragged into the clinic.

On the contrary. This was a whole different breed of animal than the one from earlier this evening.

A long, lanky, muscled, *naked* breed of animal.

Hysteria rose like cream in her morning coffee.

He was naked.

He was a he.

He was a full-grown man.

CHAPTER 3

Katie wobbled, but Wanda held her firm. Her strength was uncannily male and in stark contrast to her very feminine appearance. "I don't understand . . . he was a . . . and now he's a . . ."

"A man," Nina crowed with some sort of sick delight. "A big, hunky, not to mention naked, tigerlicious—"

"Cougar, brainiac," Wanda corrected with a wrinkle of her nose.

Nina waved a dismissive hand at her. "Fine, *cougar*licious man. So nom-nom, Doggie Doctor. You done good. We'll knuck up your coup later after you fully shift back to your human form and when that thing on the end of your arm . . . uh, your paw isn't such an eyesore."

Katie's eyes glassed over as did her mental ability to add yet another entry to her paranormal glossary. However, she steamrolled ahead in search of clarification anyway. "Shift?"

Wanda narrowed her eyes in Nina's direction while she held a near-hyperventilating Katie upright as though she was lighter than a feather. Her lips pouted in a sour form of disapproval. "Thank you for trampling all over what was, up until this very moment, a rather calm approach to a frightening situation, and turning it into Paranormals Behaving Badly, Nina. How about you don't say another word? In fact, I have a job for you. Why don't you get on that snazzy BlackBerry you text your husband with until it vibrates like some seedy sex toy in need of fresh batteries and create the beginnings of a *Ten Things You Should Never Do in a Paranormal Emergency* pamphlet?"

Nina narrowed her eyes at Wanda. "How the hell am I supposed to know what kind of crap we should put in something like that?"

Wanda cocked a lovely arched eyebrow. "Here's a clue, and this should be easy, Nina. Just write down every stupid, insensitive, in-your-face comment you've ever made or considered making when we've been in a situation just like this, and we'll label them the ten things you should *never* do when in paranormal crisis. Now be quiet. Don't say another word. Don't even breathe."

"I already *don't* do that, Wanda," was her reply in that tone laced with devilish delight intentionally meant to poke at Wanda.

In that moment, in the midst of all this chaos, Katie made a strange, completely unwarranted, totally unexpected observation. Often, due to her love of animals, she matched human personalities with the traits found in dogs. Nina was a Rottweiler. Just looking at one could inspire bone-chilling fear for some. Yet they were loyal, fiercely so, and incredibly loving once they knew they could trust you.

Nina, in your face and totally without inhibition, didn't know how to be anything other than truthful to the point of excruciating. She was what she was, and she owned it. She enjoyed pushing your hottest button, but she didn't do it to hide some insecurity. She didn't do it to deflect her own faults. She did it from a place that was as honest and, while painfully brutal, cut to the chase.

For a moment, Katie admired that gem of a quality. If only she'd spent more of her life using brutal honesty as her armor . . .

Then she frowned, capturing Nina's black, fiery eyes with her own, undoubtedly, panicked ones. "You don't do what?"

"Breathe," Nina said with satisfaction, dragging a chair from the corner of the examining room and straddling it backward with a casual lift of her long, shapely leg. She pulled out her BlackBerry and chuckled to herself.

Katie looked to Wanda. "She doesn't breathe? That's impossible . . ." Yes. That was definitely an impossibility. You couldn't be vertical and not be breathing.

Nina never glanced up from her BlackBerry when she said, "Just you wait until you find out how possible your impossible really is, Doc. Hoo boy, you don't know, but you will."

"Oh, look, Marty. Nina's already welcoming poor Dr. Woods into the paranormal fold with her usual grace and elegance." Yet another woman, short, curvy, with medium brown hair pushed back with a stylish hair band, poked her head around the door, glaring at the top of Nina's head. Katie was able to note, she bore a striking, if not fuller in the face, resemblance to Wanda. "Did you remember to shake her up real good and show her your fangs, Mistress of the Dark? Maybe you decided to take the gentler approach and just uproot a skyscraper with your pinky finger instead, huh?"

Nina's eyes lifted to meet the smaller woman's, menace lurking in them. "You wanna go?"

"You wanna be bald?" the shorter Wanda look-alike challenged.

"You both wanna be my lunch?" a pretty blonde with a small, white poodle tucked under her arm asked. "Both of you, just this once, let Wanda do the talking. No fighting, no interruptions, no insensitive comments if we're not moving at a pace that satisfies your lust for full-on hysteria, Nina. Please. I'm exhausted, my feet are killing me in these new shoes, and my Spanx are too tight. Now quiet."

She sauntered into the already packed examining room and held out her hand to Katie. "I'm Marty Flaherty. This is my dog, Muffin, and the missing link that came in before me is Casey Gunnersson, Wanda's sister. It's nice to meet you, even if the circumstances are difficult. And lovely area, by the way. Very rural and quaint."

When Nina and Casey remained quiet under the watchful blue eyes of Marty, Wanda turned back to Katie, her eyes filled with concern. "So where were we?"

"Shifting," Kaih chimed in, a gleam of anticipation in his eyes. "I'm so totally down with that, too. I can't even believe all those crazy stories I was raised on at the reservation are true."

No. They weren't true. The half of Katie that was still a veterinarian, a woman who believed in science, resurfaced. She shook her head with a vehement no. She didn't understand what was happening, but this was not true. "They're not true, Kaih." Not true. It was all myth, folklore, and in general, superstition. Not fact.

Kaih nodded at her disfigured hand and popped his lips. "Oh, yeah. Your sudden onset of elephantiasis says different." His confirmation landed in the pit of her stomach.

Ingrid whimpered, stuffing a fist into her mouth.

Wanda grabbed hold of Katie's shoulders and turned her, forcing her to look into her tastefully made-up brown eyes. "Katie, they're true. Now listen to me. I'm going to go all businesslike on you because we, as a paranormal whole, have found if you linger on the ledge of disbelief for long, you try to talk yourself out of what's right in front of your eyes. So it's cold-turkey time. What we'll show you will shock you, amaze you even, and yes, horrify you all in the same breath, but we need to get you to the point of acceptance, and then find a way to help you get situated. We know absolutely nothing about being a cat—"

"Werecat. She'd be a werecougar, more specifically," Casey stated again.

"Priceless," Kaih muttered.

Wanda nodded her acknowledgment. "Yes. Casey's right. You'd be a werecougar. We don't know the specifics about your new condition. We do know about what's called the shift. In that way, we're all almost fundamentally alike. You are now officially a shapeshifter. That means you can essentially shed your human skin and don the shape of a cat, er, cougar."

Yay!

Wanda looked as though she were allowing Katie the opportunity to let that sink in by her pensive gaze and pursed lips.

And sank it did.

Right to the bottom of her pit of despair.

"A werecougar . . ." Katie murmured.

"Yeah. Irony, huh, Doc? We haz it. We have so much of it, we own that bitch." Nina snorted, cracking her neck from side to side. Marty flicked Nina's hair, making a face of disapproval. "Nina, not now." She approached Katie with cautious steps. "I bet once you shift you'll be beautiful with all that platinum blond hair you've worked so hard to contain in that braid that does nothing for your facial features, FYI."

Wanda took a firm grip on Katie's slack, unchanged hand and pulled her out of the examining room. "Now come with me. We'll show you what we're talking about, but we need more room. Let's go out into your waiting area. Kaih? Will anyone interrupt this late at night, or are we fairly safe?"

He nodded his slick black head. "I'll keep an eye out."

Everyone filed out into the waiting area while Katie watched Marty move her sparse furnishings to one side of the room as though it hadn't taken two fully grown men and Kaih to get them in here in the first place. And she did it in heels and Spanx, no less. Bravo.

Ingrid's eyes grew wide and watery. The shiver of her multitude of bangle bracelets in neon colors of pink and green along her forearm gave way to her lower lip trembling. Kaih took her by the hand and sat her on the battered red vinyl couch. "You okay?"

"What did I do?" she squeaked, her eyes darting to the women.

"You did the right thing, Ingrid. That's what you did," Casey reassured with an easy smile. "We really can help. Promise."

As Katie watched each woman move in unison with one another, preparing for whatever this shift thing was, her almost-removed and distant haze began to lift. Whatever these women thought they were going to prove to her, they were going about it with conviction.

"Katie?" Wanda said, pointing to the far corner of the room. "Sit over there."

She moved on sluggish legs to the left corner of her waiting room and sat on the edge of the metal folding chair without a word, tucking her torn sweater around her.

"Kaih? Towels. We need towels, please," Wanda instructed.

Katie gulped. "For?" Was this a messy affair? Would skin and bones fly like so much confetti when they did whatever it was they did to get to their other shapes? She wasn't squeamish. She saw blood, innards, and any number of unpleasant things Ingrid called icky every day. But this . . . the thought . . . Oh, hell's bells.

Nina clamped a hand on Katie's shoulder. "It's not gory, if that's what you're thinking. Marty and Wanda need them because they turn into dogs. You know, just like those pesky little motherfuckers you charge a hundred bucks an office visit for? They'll rip their clothes if they don't take them off first. They need towels so you won't see Marty's saggy ass buck naked."

Marty hummed a low growl and gave Nina the finger.

Nina snickered. "But no worries, Doc. Casey and me keep our human forms. We do other stuff."

Other. Stuff.

Katie focused on her breathing and scrunched her eyes shut. "Kaih, can you get some towels, please?"

When Kaih returned with the towels, he handed them to each woman, his expression a mixture of stoicism and curiosity.

Wanda's gaze returned to Katie's, filled with warmth and the undertones of sympathy. "You ready?"

Ready-schmeady. If she was nothing else, Katie Woods wasn't a coward. Hadn't she faced down the biggest divorce attorney only the best money could hire not nine months ago?

Besides, really, how many people in her profession wouldn't give up a major organ to bear witness to what these women said they could do? How many of her colleagues wouldn't invite someone to bare their lunacy so they could someday write a paper on it? Her eyes narrowed with skepticism, ignoring her hand, her resolve was firm. "Bring it."

HAD she said, "bring it" just before all out parageddon had erupted in tufts of hair, tusklike teeth, and fire-breathing fingers?

Had she said it like she was some badass carbon-copy of Nina?

Yep. Katie remembered it clearly. She also remembered half thinking she'd simply humor these women so in the end of their supposed shifts, she'd come out the victor. Then she'd spew scientific improbabilities and mock their outrageous statements while beginning the search for some remote remedy to rectify her strange affliction that was surely hidden in a dusty medical journal.

Oh, what a difference a shift made.

Now, after seeing what she'd just seen, while Kaih sat with his jaw dusting the floor, and Ingrid huddled in a tight ball on top of the back of the couch, attempting to push herself through the wall and disappear, Katie was considering.

Or reconsidering.

As each woman had unveiled their proper title in the paranormal world and how they'd come to be, they'd shown her what they said was true.

Casey had created the most spectacular light show via her fingertips Katie had seen, barring even the fireworks show Macy's put on every year on the Fourth of July. To further convince Katie, she'd then levitated and crawled along the rippled, cracked walls of her waiting room.

And it had been so James Cameron by way of Dean Koontz.

Casey then went about explaining. In a freak accident, demon blood had been spilled on her by her now mate, Clayton. Clayton the former Viking who was older than dirt, because, Casey said, he wasn't just any old Viking. He was a *vampire* Viking.

Aha. Clearly, he was the super-deluxe, blue-plate-special version of paranormal, and she was his demonic bride. She had a teenaged stepdaughter named Naomi, who was also a vampire, and according to Casey, an eternal bundle of hormones and bipolar-like teenaged vampiric behavior.

Fascinating.

Nina's revelation might not have been as festive and entertaining as Casey's, but it was done with such maniacal glee, when she'd lifted up the couch Kaih and Ingrid sat on with one finger while sporting fangs, it had been the exact opposite of unimpressive. Nina's vampiric origins stemmed from her vampire husband, Greg, who'd bitten her quite by accident, while having dental work. Because surely, every vampire sought minty-fresh breath.

Wanda, now clothed once more, had shed her body like ice melting in the hot August sun. She'd rippled and squirmed until she'd turned into a wolf, er, werewolf that had the longest incisors Katie'd ever witnessed in her twelve-plus years as a veterinarian. Marty followed suit while Casey recited their stories as if she were reading a script.

Marty, the first of the fab four to have been accidentally bitten while walking her cute poodle, Muffy, uh, Muffin, was a werewolf. A cosmetic-company-owning werewolf. She had a husband named Keegan, aka the biter, who was the alpha male of his pack and also owned a cosmetics company. She was also mother to little Hollis, the child whose name brought genuine warmth to Auntie Nina's eyes.

Not to be outdone by Marty, Wanda, once dying of ovarian cancer, allowed Nina and Marty to purposely bite her in order to save her from certain death. Her onetime vampire-turned-into-a-human-then-turned-back-into-a-werevamp beau, Heath, was almost killed when he made the ultimate sacrifice and tried to save her by letting her bite his human flesh. Now Wanda, lovely, cured, and alive, was a werevamp, too. Who had a husband. Who had a manservant. Who . . .

Wanda's tale had grown vague then. Katie had zoned out when Nina, with yet more devilish glee, rambled on about some mishap when she and Marty had first tried to change Wanda in order to save her life.

Everything had gone all wrong and Wanda turned into some sort of "freaky-deaky" beast, as Nina'd said, with another maniacal cackle. Then she'd used the words rabid and slobbering and something about poor Heath, deader than a crack whore who'd OD'd. Yet, if Katie'd heard right, Heath was now alive. Not technically, but for all intents and purposes still roaming the earth.

Upright.

Even though he was dead.

Words like "dead" were maybe a little heavy at this stage in

Katie's state of mind. But it was when Wanda nudged her hand, staring at her eye level with a familiarity in her eerie wolf eyes that had been the tuning out point in this fantastical adventure.

Kaih patted her hand. "Doc Woods? You okay?"

As Nina held up the towels to shield the women while they dressed, she snickered. "No, she's not okay. She just saw some crazy shit. That she's not sniveling over in the corner like Braveheart here"—she hitched her jaw in the direction of Ingrid—"is a fucking miracle. Good for you, Doc. I like tough in a chick. I'll like it even better if you save the whine for after we leave. Because there'll be whining. Trust me. I've been to the land of whine. I've heard more whining in this lifetime than twelve vampires courtesy of the trio from hell here."

Katie dragged a shivering Ingrid down to the cushion of the couch, running her good hand over her forearm in a soothing motion. She regarded Nina with no venom when she assessed, "You can be exceptionally rude in your outspokenness."

Nina grinned. "Yep."

Wanda retied the bow at her collar with a final flick of her fingers. "That's our Nina. Rude." Smoothing her skirt over her hips, she eyeballed Katie with clear concern. "So, now that you've seen—we determine where you go from here."

"That was exactly my thought," Katie responded, dry and almost apathetic.

Marty cocked her head while running fresh lipstick over her lips. "It was?"

Katie nodded. "It was." There was no denying what she'd seen. Vampires, demons, and werewolves existed. They were also available in a combo pack. They had children, stepchildren, dogs, hamsters, and the occasional manservant named Archibald.

Casey popped her glossy-peach lips when she looked at her sister. "Denial," she stated.

Wanda sighed her agreement. "Yep."

Nina scowled. "Oh, the hell you say. She's not in denial. Look at her. She gets it, which is more than I can say for the three of you after you were turned. She'll be fine. That dude in the cage will wake up, tell her how to shift, fur will fly, teeth'll gnash, and maybe she'll even cry a little. Though from the looks of her, that doesn't seem like her bag. Then she'll adjust, eat some Fancy Feast, and turn into a big-assed kitty cat. We'll make sure she knows where her kitty comb and some hairball formula in a tube are on our way out. It's good. So c'mon, let's hit it. Peace out."

"Right," Marty chided, narrowed of eye. "Because that's how it worked for you, Elvira. We made a commitment when we decided to do this OOPS thing. *All of us.* We're not just going to up and leave her with instructions for "how to be a paranormal" on an impersonal, pink sticky note, you dimwit. Besides, Wanda's right. She's in denial. It's the calm before the monsoon."

Katie rose, her legs ironically steady even if her hand slapped around at her side like a dead fish. "No. I'm not in denial. I saw it with my own two eyes. I understand. I believe."

Wanda bit her lower lip, her glance at Katie tentative. "I'm not buying it. You're in shock. We know the signs. We've lived the signs. This paranormal thing—it's like the five stages of grief—"

"Wait," Casey held up a hand, shooting Katie a knowing smile. "I got this one, Wanda. Okay, so the five stages of grief—"

"No," Katie interrupted with her good hand. "I know the five stages of grief. I'm a veterinarian. I deal with grief every day."

"Yeah, but this isn't about some pet, lady. This is about how your life's going to change. Your body. Everything. Will. Change," Nina said pointedly. "It's not about boohooing over some damn dog."

Marty rolled her eyes. "Says the woman who called every last one of us in complete hysteria when she thought her hamster

Larry'd been sucked up by her new central vacuum system only to find she'd forgotten he was in his exercise ball in the basement of her dungeon?"

Nina clamped her fingers together under Marty's nose. "Oh, shut up, Marty. That was some scary shit. Leave my Larry the fuck out of this."

Nina turned to Katie, and this time there was no devilish glint to her black eyes. They were hard and clear. "So, on second thought, I kind of have to agree with Wanda. I don't like it, and it doesn't happen often, but here's the thing, lady. You've got some big-ass shit comin' your way, and it has to do with more than just the physical crap that's going to happen to you. I just fucking know it involves some lunatic cougar chick that hot dude in there belongs to—is mated to—should be mated to. I don't know. I only know it'll be like *Mutual of Omaha* extreme fighting style. She'll wanna scratch your eyes out because you have her man—or something. It's *always* something with this crazy paranormal bullshit. And it always means I'm going to have to save someone's ass. Always. Count on it."

Katie's eyes went wide, her one human hand shot to the tip of her braid to twist the fringed ends in an old nervous habit she'd never been able to break. "A woman?"

Wanda clamped a hand over Nina's mouth, her teeth clenched, jaw tight. "Nina, I will personally pull your tongue from your head if you speak when not spoken to again. Don't complicate matters with anything else. Stick to the business at hand." Marty and Casey giggled when she gave a grunting Nina a shove to the corner of the waiting area.

Turning back to Katie, Wanda smiled. "Ignore Nina. It's easy. We do it often and well. What we need to do now, Katie, is talk to the man in the cage. He's the one who holds the key to the specifics of what happens next for you. None of us can advise you on much other than general information about the paranormal and the emotions you'll experience as these enormous changes take place in your body. That's what we hoped to accomplish when we set out on this mission—to offer information and support in paranormal crises."

Katie folded her arms across her chest. "So what happened to each of you after you—you . . . were changed? Why does anything have to change for me? You all still live your lives, unconventional as they are. I know blood drinking and raw meat eating are a part of that. So what? There are plenty of cults and the like who call themselves vampires and do the same things you do. Okay, so they don't really have the restrictions imposed on them the way you do . . . but . . . What could possibly change other than my physical appearance?" Yeah. Big deal. She had a paw and some bitchin' teeth. And? Oh, indeed and.

How very minimalist she'd suddenly become.

Nina snorted, jamming her hands into the pockets of her jeans. "Listen, homeslice, that's optimism, if I ever heard it. I'm telling you, shit always goes down on top of your entire chemistry changing. If we have anything, we have drama. Count on it. Nothing's ever as simple as it first seems. With Marty, it was the beef over her stealing the alpha male of her accidental pack and a power-hungry blonde who wanted her dead because Marty's mate Keegan didn't like said blonde. The one his pack had picked out for him to mate with. He liked Cover Girl here better." She thumbed a finger in Marty's direction with a roll of her black eyes. "Throw in a kidnapping, a certifiable brother she didn't even know she had, and that about sums up the bullshit that went down with Marty. And that's only the beginning, lady. We all had trouble. There's always some history with these kooks, and it almost always means we have to kick some ass. Don't get me wrong. I like a good balls to the wall as much as any other girl, but you deserve to be prepared."

Katie held up her hand to thwart any further tales, but just as quickly let it fall to her side when she caught sight of her claws, thick and black. Shit, shit, shit. This really put a crimp in her pending manicure. "Maybe it's better I don't know anything about your personal histories, and instead we focus on what's next?"

Nina nudged her shoulder, making Katie's legs buckle a little. "I like you. You're no pansy."

Katie gave her a thoughtful glance. "Should I take that as a compliment?"

Marty barked a laugh. "Not unless you consider Attila the Hun's compliments flattering."

Nina threw an arm around Katie's shoulders and tightened her grip around her neck. "Ignore the imitation blonde. Let's go see how brave you really are and wake the hottie up so we can beat the shit out of him until he coughs it up."

"Do you mean his intestines, Nina?" Casey taunted from behind.

As Nina directed her toward the examining room, she shot her middle finger upward at Casey. "Intestines, information. They both begin with the letter *i*. Makes no diff to me what he hacks up first. Whatever it takes, is my motto."

The moment they entered the room, Katie's bravado fled, trickling away like sand through her fingers.

He was so big all huddled in a ball in the cage they kept for their largest breeds like Saint Bernards and mastiffs. He was also, undeniably, incredibly beautiful in the roughest of ways.

It was just that simple. His long thighs and calves, sprinkled with black hair, were sculpted and lean. Hard shoulders, broad and thick with sinew, lifted in a bronzed shrug of skin when he stirred. The thick fall of his hair, black with the most unusual deep chocolate highlights, was matted in places and raggedly cut at his jawline. He had a Harley-Davidson bad-boy appeal to him, all rigid edges and sharp lines. Big, gruff, and unkempt in a hard-sexy package.

He was also very, very naked.

And young. Maybe twenty-two tops?

"Wow, he's just a baby," Casey whispered after a low whistle.

Katie nodded, averting her eyes to avoid the clear path they wanted to take to his southerly parts. She decidedly ignored the twang of her womanly needs reacting to his manly bits and instead, focused on willing him to wake up.

His deep snore startled even Nina, who reacted by curling her strong fingers into the edge of Katie's shoulder and squeezing.

Marty sighed from behind them. "So what's next, Nina-nator? You wanna poke him with a stick? Razz him a little?"

"He should be waking soon," Kaih said as he came to stand with his boss and Nina, a glazed-eyed Ingrid clinging to his arm. "We gave him that last shot a couple of hours ago. He just needs a little nudge."

Katie inhaled to steady her breathing, forcing herself to follow the procedures she used when an animal was coming out of seda-tion. Under normal circumstances, she'd open the cage door and stroke their fur, cuddle them, speaking in soft whispers to encour-age them to rouse. Cuddling probably wasn't an option when the animal wasn't an animal, but a man. Who was an animal.

Oh-oh-ohhhh, God.

She shook off her fear, bracing herself. Running her nail across the bars of the cage, she said, "Time to wake up now . . ." Her new kitty ears cringed at the groan contained within the cage. It made her eardrums scream in protest. "C'mon now, um . . ."

"Spanky. His name's Spanky," Kaih offered with the clearing of his throat.

Katie's eyebrow rose. "How do you know what his name is?"

"It was on his collar. He was wearing a collar when he came in, and it said Spanky, remember? I took it off him just before we put him in the cage. See?" He pointed to the thick collar that was now lying by the sink with small, blunt spikes on the backside of it and a copper medallion hanging from the center.

Wanda muffled a giggle.

Nina leaned into Katie. "Tell Spanky Buckwheat that the gang's waitin' on him, and we need to get this show on the road. Daylight happens. Every day. It burns. You don't want to see me pissed off because I have a third-degree burn."

Katie turned back to the cage, her stomach a nervous nest of fear. "Spankyyyy," she cooed in a soft drawl, letting a tentative finger skim his shoulder, fighting the surprising pleasure touching his ruddy male skin brought. "Time to wake up now, kitty . . . uh, man . . . um." She sighed and whispered with a clench of her teeth. "Just wake up!"

Spanky stirred momentarily, then nodded off again, his head falling with abandon against the back of the cage, his mouth unhinged at his jaw.

"Oh, for the love of Jesus and all twelve. Move," Nina ordered with a snarl. Latching her fingers between the bars of the cage, she lifted it high over her head before Katie had the chance to react, shaking it up and down as though she were picking up nothing more than an empty cardboard box.

Spanky's muscled body banged against the sides in a mess of inert limbs. "Dude! Wake the fuck up, would you? I have shit to do. I don't have time to wait around until you feel like moving your bootylicious ass, Lion King."

"Nina!" Three women howled in unison. Wanda grabbed at her hands, slapping them away while Marty yanked the cage from her in a two-fisted grasp, plunking Spanky back down on the edge of the examining table with a jarring crash. "Knock it off! Jesus, Nina. The man's helpless in there, and you're slamming him around like he's a box of malted milk balls. Christ, you're so impatient!"

Katie fell back against Kaih in the commotion, her head swimming with the loud scrape of metal just as the cage tipped over the edge of the shiny table and took a dive for the floor, skidding into the far wall with a harsh crack.

The cage door popped open from the force of the impact, hanging with a lopsided slant to it.

Upon landing, Spanky's head and shoulders slid from the wire enclosure, lying at an awkward angle. His thighs spread wide.

Oh, yes.

They were spread—*wide*.

Casey rushed to his side, scooping his head into her lap to keep him from the cold floor of the examining room.

Nina whistled a catcall. "Oh, dude. That's a whole lotta man, huh?"

Wanda came up behind Nina, clamping her hands over Nina's eyes. "Pipe down, perv. He's a child, Nina. He couldn't be more than twenty, which, I might add, makes you almost young enough, in some regions of the country where women are forced into early marriages, to be his mother."

Nina flicked at Wanda's hands, slipping away from her grasp and eyeballing Katie. "Hey, Doc—question?"

Katie's eyes never left poor Spanky's prone form when she answered, "Yes?"

"How old are you?"

She frowned. "Forty-one."

"No way!" Marty gasped. "I gotta give it up to you, Dr. Woods. You look fabulous. I'd have never guessed a day over thirty. You have terrific skin, all berries and cream, and I suppose, if this cougar thing works the way it does with the rest of us, you'll have that skin for eternity. Damn. Why couldn't I have been turned at twenty?" she joked.

Eternity?

Nina rolled her tongue along the inside of her cheek and snorted. "A thought just occurred to me."

Casey grunted with a roll of her brown eyes. "Really? Huh. I thought the smell of burning flesh was just my fingertips cooling down."

Nina ignored Casey's jibe and turned back to Katie. "Know what this means—the age difference between you and Spanky here, don't you?"

"We'll have to find the nearest skateboarding park to drop him off at?" Katie returned dryly.

Nina chuckled, giving Katie her infamous devilish grin. "It means you aren't just a werecougar, lady. You're a cougar-cougar. You took stereotyping to a whole 'nother level. You're like one of those 'doesn't look her age' chicks who hits on young dudes because they got the zoom in their boom still happening. You're a total label. Hot. Niiiice work, Mrs. Robinson."

Katie bristled, her onetime surge of admiration for Nina's forward nature turning to frustrated impatience. "I most definitely have no plans to hit or even lightly nudge a twenty-year-old *boy*. You can believe that."

"You know," a gravelly voice, filled with sin and a husky British timbre, commented from below, stunning everyone into complete silence. "I wouldn't be opposed to someone like you hitting on me. But we can begin with just a nudge, if that's what makes you more comfortable. Maybe get to know each other first? You know, all the things people do when they're in the beginning stages of a relationship? You ask questions about me. I ask questions about you. As a for instance, and definitely not in any way a deciding factor to a future whirlwind courtship between us, what exactly has happened with your hand?" Spanky asked, blue, blue eyes dotted in a heavy fringe of lash, sparkling up at her with innocence.

Katie clucked her tongue, her control but a frayed thread.

Maybe it was the tension, the fear of the unknown. Maybe it was all the fantastical, mystical, crazy things she'd just witnessed. Maybe the final vestiges of the bizarre cloudy haze of disbelief had lifted. Probably, it was the audacity of his question. No matter. Whatever it was, she had but one instinct, and it wasn't nurturing or doctorish.

Glancing Nina's way, Katie growled and logically, as someone who'd studied animals and their patterns in great depth, she realized it held a distinct warning.

Were someone to ask her if she cared that she knew she was going to lose it—she'd have to say fat chance.

Out of all of the women, the raving lunatic hovering directly below Nina's surface would best understand what led Katie to where she ended up next.

Straddling Spanky's wide chest.

But not before she hissed, yes, hissed her fury with a feral scream, virtually leaping across the room with the grace only a prima ballerina possessed, knocking Casey across the room. The only thing missing was a pink tutu and the strains of Tchaikovsky's *Swan Lake*.

Latching onto Spanky's chest hair, Katie met his startled gaze. "I will kill you!"

CHAPTER 4

"Whooooa, okay, okay." Spanky held up a large hand as a sign of submission. "But one last request from the dead man not walking?"

Katie ran her tongue over her elongated teeth in predatory fashion, her anger, swift and rife, began to cool at the sound of his reasonable tone. "What's that?"

"If you decide to do that, and I don't see why you would. I don't even know you well enough to be killed by you, leaving me puzzled as to what I've done to bring the word 'kill' into our conversation with such haste and, dare I venture to say, venom. It's a little over the top and very 'the end.' Anyway, all those nasty technicalities aside, could I possibly get a robe beforehand? Oh, and some slippers. No man wants to die bloody naked and cold, especially in front of so many pretty ladies."

Then he grinned. Mischievous. Utterly delighted with himself.

Katie screeched her fury with a wail, high and long. It was eerie, one she'd heard often coming from the exotic animal park during the long nights she spent trying to sleep and forget why she'd come to this town to begin with. The mournful cry said she had a taste for blood—literally—and tag, Spanky was it.

Nina was the first to her side with the other women and Kaih shoving up behind her. She planted a hand like a vise grip, intrusive and annoying as hell on Katie's shoulder. "Whoa-ho there, Dances with Wolves. Get a grip. Let the kid be."

Katie, from somewhere primal and unknown, gazed up at Nina, her eyes narrowed, her breathing labored and hitching in a wheeze. "Take your hand off me."

Nina cocked her head in challenge, a strand of her gorgeous, wavy long hair falling from behind her shoulder. Her nostrils flared when she asked, "Or?"

Yeah. Or? Katie's anger at the audacity of this mere child's question about her hand evaporated like dew in the morning sun. She looked back down at Spanky, unmoving, his breathing steady and collected, his gaze pensive.

She'd just threatened to kill someone, and she'd done it after she'd launched through the air in a triple axel of deadly intent.

Katie's hands shot up into the space between them in a flash of movement. "Oh, God! I'm sorry. I'm so sorry. Are you hurt?" She let hesitant hands flutter over him, only to pull them back in a gesture of uncertainty.

He folded his arms, bulging with muscle, behind his head and cocked her a smile full of white teeth. A smile that seemed so strange, coming from a face so roughly hewn and carved from granite. "I have to guess I've been much worse off than having a pretty lady like yourself sitting on my chest. So please don't mock when I again make mention of the fact that the floor's still just as cold as it was before you came to your senses and opted out of your wish to annihilate me. Though, I suspect, if you keep sitting on top of me, I'll warm up rather nicely." He wiggled a raven eyebrow at her and winked, making the jagged scar at the corner of his right eye wrinkle in rakish fashion.

Nina took her by surprise and just in time to save Spanky's jugular by hauling Katie off him, yanking her upward so fast, her bones creaked in protest. "Kaih. Could we have something to, you know, cover his man-bits? They're dangling. Ingrid, quit hovering in the corner like some weird-ass voyeur and man up. Make yourself useful, and help Tonto here find a blanket to cover the kid with."

Kaih looked as though he might challenge Nina's stab at him until she gave him her special brand of the evil eye. He and a simpering Ingrid scurried out of the room to do Nina's bidding, wordless.

Nina held out her hand to Spanky, keeping her eyes on his face and pulling him to his feet. He wobbled, but Wanda came to stand on the other side of him, offering him support. He shook his head as though to clear the cobwebs that had surely formed in his tranquilizer-induced brain. His gaze fell on Nina. "Pump iron much?"

Nina's glance back was amused, judging by the tilt of her eyebrow. "Naked much?"

His handsome face went sheepish as he cast his eyes downward to his impressive southern regions. "That is rather problematic," he shot back. Very British. Very proper.

Kaih raced back in, Ingrid, less red-eyed now, following close behind. "I got your back, pal. Here." He shoved one of his old lab coats at Spanky while Ingrid hurled more towels at him and skid over to stand behind Marty.

Wanda helped him into the lab coat, and the stark white material against his olive-toned skin made Katie's breath hiss in and out once more. Rolling her head on her shoulders to work out her tension, she grappled with the slew of questions she had, forcing herself to ask them one at a time in a logical fashion. "So, Spanky," she drawled, "who are you, and how did you land on the front steps of my veterinary clinic?"

His eyes darted evasively from one woman to the next. "Uh, I'm Spanky . . . I guess, and I have no idea how I ended up on your steps—or in a cage—or in a room so full of such lovely women."

Marty preened, hoisting Muffin under her right arm and stroking the dog's snow-white head. Her sigh was long and wistful. "Did I mention I wish I'd been turned at twenty?"

"You did, Miss America. Now quit with the googly eyes because you're a long way from twenty, sister, and focus," Nina ordered. She approached Spanky the way a hunter approached their prey. Well, a hunter who wasn't even a little worried her prey would startle and make an escape, that is. "Lay off the charming, Kit and Caboodle, and start talking. Now, or I just might bite."

Spanky's eyebrow rose with an arrogant slant to it, the right corner of his yummy mouth tilting upward just a little. "You bite?" He mock shivered, shooting her a smoldering gaze. "I find that almost titillating coming from a woman of your beauty."

He was a real slick Willy, Katie noted. She also noted how charming and well-spoken he was for someone who appeared so young.

Nina leaned into him, letting her lips hover near his chin, covered in dark, sinfully-raspy-when-it-scraped-the-collar-of-the-lab-coat stubble. "I'll titillate you right into next week if you don't tell us who you are, and how"—she reached behind her, latching onto Katie's paw and lunging it in his face like some scary Halloween mask—"she got *this*. You've got three seconds."

Wanda flicked Nina's nose from over Spanky's shoulder with the snap of two fingers. "Back up, Sugar Ray, and give the child some room."

"Child?" Spanky repeated, his tone littered with surprise. Like he didn't know he was all of thirteen.

"Isn't that what everyone our age calls someone your age? You know, when you're prepubescent and we're not?" Katie muttered more to herself than for public consumption.

She sauntered up to him, all swagger and sashay, noting her head just reached the top of his shoulder. "Forget it. Your age has nothing to do with what you've done to me." She held up her hand. "Explain this. Do it fast before the urge to take your juice box away forever strikes me."

His sharp jaw clenched in what she'd label a brief moment of horror at the condition of her hand, then his face fell blank in confusion. If he was playing them, he was a better actor than Brad Pitt on his best day. "I'm afraid I don't understand your question. However, I hope you won't find me out of line when I ask, and please, don't by any stretch of the imagination consider me ungrateful for the use of your 'just like home' *cage* and down-home hospitality, but where the bloody hell am I? And how did I end up, you know, in the emperor's new clothes?" Spanky glanced down and back up at seven astonished pairs of eyes, meeting their surprised gazes dead-on.

Katie tucked her paw under her armpit, cornering him against the examining table. Her nostrils flared, his unique male scent tangible and fragrant to her nose. She didn't just smell him, she inhaled every aspect of his scent right down to the bead of sweat she was sure she'd find trickling down his spine if he were still naked. "Who are you?"

His jaw jutted forward, littered with dark stubble and full of defiance. "I find I'm not entirely in love with the tone of your question. I feel cheapened by your evident suspicion."

"Really?" she spat. "Well, I'm not in love with this!" She shot her hand upward right under his nose again, the rough pads of her paw grazing his hair until it swung back downward in a pendulum-like dash for her side.

Instantly, Spanky took on a look of contrition and winced. "I see your dilemma."

Her chest heaved while she fought a shriek of indignation. "*You* created my dilemma! Now, who are you and how did you escape Mr. Magoo's Exotic Animal Zoo?"

He appeared as though he was going to yell right back at her, but instead he paused, clearly in deep thought. Deep groves in his forehead formed in a frown. "You know, it's the strangest thing . . ." he mumbled, "I can't seem to remember my name . . . or anything."

"Maybe it was the tranq, Doc? I did shoot him up pretty good," Kaih offered.

Katie shook her head. "That wouldn't make him forget his name. I'm not buying it. Unless . . ." She turned to Wanda. "Didn't you all say when you're a paranormal being, your chemistry changes? Nina mentioned it. She said the anesthesia she gave her husband was a general anesthetic, yet he was affected much differently than a human because he's a vampire."

Spanky stuck his head between Kaih and Katie, a conciliatory smile on his ruggedly handsome face. "Well, then. It's clear there are much larger issues at hand here than my nakedness and some silly, old cage. You all obviously have your hands full. I'll just be on my way while you sort out your . . ." He waved a hand. "Paranormal whatever. Your hospitality was nothing short of grandiose. For that, I thank you kindly." He made a gesture as though he were tipping the brim of an imaginary hat and attempted to escape.

"No!" Ingrid shouted for the first time since she'd watched the women of OOPS shed their human forms. Her tired eyes began to water. "You can't leave!"

Spanky's eyes zeroed in on Ingrid. "Because?"

"Because I fucking said you can't," Nina interfered, pushing her way into the mix, poking a finger into his bare chest. "Dude, you ain't goin' nowhere until you give up this lame bullshit act about forgetting your name and cough up what we want to know. And trust me when I tell you, I will kick your ass from here to Botswana if you try. Now sit down, and don't move a single muscle but the one called your tongue."

Spanky's nostrils flared, and Katie wasn't sure if it was in anger at being challenged or with the sheer pleasure of being challenged. "Are your knickers always in such a twist?"

Nina shot him a devious grin. "I'll wrap my fucking knickers around your fucking head. Now explain. Because I'm beat, and I'd really like to clear this up so my friends here don't go all 'Oh, Nina, you're such an insensitive beast' on me. I'll hear that shit all the way home if we don't get this straightened out. You have no idea what it's like to have BFFs like this lame bunch nagging the shit out of you because you're the kind of chick who tells it like it is. So for the last time, speak. Speak fast. Like now, Snagglepuss."

With a haughty cross of his arms over his chest, he glared at Nina. "Maybe you're not the one due an explanation, eh? Maybe you owe me one. The one that explains how I landed here—in a cage—with not a stitch of clothing on." He gave them all a "take that" glare.

"You really don't remember anything that happened today? Anything?" Ingrid squeaked, the tremble of a quiver in her question.

Katie frowned, cocking her head in Ingrid's direction, only to find when she met her eyes, Ingrid looked away. "Okay. I guess it's time for the reality check you all gave me. Buckle up, and hold on tight. Here's how it went down, Spanky. You showed up on the front steps of my clinic tonight. We found you, Ingrid, my receptionist, and Kaih, my intern, after we all went to Ed's for dinner—and you didn't look like this." She swept her good hand along his bulky body.

"So you did take my clothes off. Naughty ladies, the lot of you, eh?" he teased, a raven eyebrow cocked arrogantly.

Katie sighed, ragged and exasperated. The day was beginning to take its toll, and it didn't look like it was going to end any time soon. "No. We didn't take your clothes because you didn't have any clothes because *cougars* don't wear clothes. Yes, that's what I said. *Cougars*. When Ingrid, Kaih, and myself found you, you were a big kitty cat who was passed out. We didn't know if you were injured, so we brought you in here to examine you. Because I'm a veterinarian, and that's what I do when I think an animal's in distress. I diagnose. We figured you came from Mr. Magoo's down the road because, really, where else would you have come from? Mr. Magoo runs the exotic animal park. All you had on was a collar that we took off so I could get a closer look at you. The collar identified you as Spanky." Katie went to the countertop and held it up, letting the big copper medallion swing in the harsh glare of the examining room lights. "Look familiar?"

Spanky squinted his eyes and pursed his luscious lips. "Sadly, no."

"Right." Katie gave him a curt nod. "So we dragged you in here and hoisted you up on the table. As we did, you jerked and your paw"—she held up her very own paw with a grunt for the effort—"one just like this, scratched my arm. We then put you in a cage to protect you from harm after sedating you, and but two hours later, I had a paw, too. Oh, and these teeth. Another two hours later, after the OOPS team of shifters showed up, we came back in here to check up on you, and hopefully figure this out. You *are* the man with all the answers. Instead, we found you were no longer a cougar. You'd changed into a big, strapping boy, er, man, er . . . whatever. In closing, *you* did this to me. That means you have to fix it. You're a half man, half cougar or shapeshifter, I believe is the terminology, according to the OOPS team. So I think the explaining part of this conversation is on you. Ball's in your court, *Spanky*," she grated.

Spanky's beautiful, unlined eyes grew hooded, clouding with suspicion. "I don't think I want to play whatever game your ball involves. You women are bloody mental. Now I suggest you all move out of my way and let me leave, or I'll move you myself," he growled, low and threatening.

"Hold on there, Zac Efron." Wanda stood in his path. "Here's how it's going to be, young man. You're not going anywhere, and I do mean anywhere. Don't test me. You do not want to try my patience. I'm ugly when provoked, and I'm not talking just my temper, pal. I don't know what kind of game you think you're playing by pretending you don't know *who* you are, or for that matter, what you are, but by all that's holy, I'm darn tired. It's been a long day and my feet hurt. If you rub me the wrong way, I can't promise you won't lose a limb. So if you don't want me to go all werevamp on you, sit *down*!" she roared.

"Ohhhh," Nina taunted close to Spanky's angry face. "It's on, brother. Werevamp versus cougar. Let the games begin. I love the scent of impending death in the air," Nina cackled, taking a deep, mocking whiff of him to display her threat only to frown in confusion. "Uh, Wanda?"

Wanda huffed, her chest heaving with impatience. "Nina?"

"Hold up on the smackdown."

"Reason?"

"Something's just not right. I can smell it. Lemme read his mind."

"Did you just say you were going to read his mind?" Katie squawked.

"Yeah, blondie, that's what I said. Just another magical, mystical vampiric power. I can fly, too. Crazy, right? Now just be quiet. I'm still learning this shit, and it takes concentration." Wanda backed away, allowing Nina space.

Nina grabbed Spanky's chin, tightening her grip when he attempted to defiantly pull away. Her eyes pierced his, making his jaw go slack and his blue eyes hazy and dull. Her own charcoal black eyes went wide. "Fuck, fuck, fuck."

"What's wrong?" Katie asked.

"He's totally telling the truth. He has no clue what the fuck we're talking about. Goddamn it. This is gonna take forever. I should have brought a change of underwear."

Katie's stomach sank with a sharp dive. "What do you mean he has no clue what we're talking about?"

Nina's eyes narrowed. "I mean, I can *smell* his confusion. Not to mention, I can read his almost-blank mind. He's got not a fucking thing up there but that he thinks you're hot, Doc Woods, and a nutter—his word, not mine—but still hot. Leave it to a man who has no idea who he is to have enough memory left to know what makes his Mr. Twinkie sit up and take notice. Anyway, he has no idea what you're talking about, or what his name is, or where the fuck he comes from, or how he got here, or what happened to your hand. Oh, but he likes your taters. He thinks they're the perfect size."

Nina chuckled when Spanky's face went from total agreement to chagrin. "I thought no such thing. It was breasts, not taters. I'd never use such a crass word to define such a fine pair of . . ." He cleared his throat, stopping short. "I assure you, I'd never use that word."

Marty nudged Nina with an elbow. "Jesus, Nina. You have no censor. Get out of his head right this minute and leave the boy some dignity."

Katie glanced at each woman. There was only so much bullshit she could contend with in one night. Her flip-out-ometer was growing jiggier by the second.

Okay, yeah. Nina, Marty, Casey, and Wanda had paranormal abilities. There was no denying what they'd shown her, but to believe that Nina could read minds, aside from her flying (hah!) capabilities would just be a hair shy of the ridiculous. Maybe they were all in cahoots with him? But to what end? "You expect me to believe you read people's minds? *Really?*"

Nina popped her lips. "Well, you've come this far. Why not go all the fucking way? Yeah, I read minds, and no, we're not in cahoots with Spanky here. And I can so fly, which is exactly what the shit I'll do, and soon, if we don't get the show on the road. Oh, and I'll show you 'just a hair shy of ridiculous.' Come shop with us at the outlet malls while Marty tries to squeeze her fat ass into a size-seven skirt. That defines ridiculous."

Katie swooned as Nina repeated exactly what she'd just thought. Casey was behind her in an instant, propping her up. "She's telling the truth, Dr. Woods."

"She is not," Marty scolded with a scowl in Nina's direction. "I can, too, wear a size seven, you thrift-store monger."

Nina snorted. "You and what crowbar?"

"Both of you pipe down! Can't you see you're only upsetting Dr. Woods more than she already is? I think next time we need to wait a little longer before we do the mind-reading thing. It's jarring and overall like having a case of the squicks from the inside out—especially when Nina's all in your head," Casey chided, running a soothing palm over Katie's stiff back.

Wanda's sigh was loud. "Look, this has been information overload for everyone involved, including the boy, er, Spanky. If what Nina says is correct, and Spanky has, for all intents and purposes, amnesia, we have a problem that won't be solved overnight. So we need a plan B."

Spanky, who'd quieted while the women argued, spoke up. He was working hard at keeping his composure so that only the slightest hint of panic shone in his eyes. "Did I mention how brilliant it was to meet each of you lovely ladies? If not, I'll do that on my way out the door. Again, thank you for your hospitality. You know, the drugs, the cage, the finest of clothing. All of it. Just brilliant. Good luck to you and your . . . your . . . well, just good luck, Dr. Woods. And remember, we'll always have Paris, or, er, wherever we are. I'll see myself out."

"Sit," Wanda growled, jabbing a finger in his chest until he plopped on the stool Nina chucked under his backend. "You're not going anywhere, and it isn't just because you hold the key to this mystery. We can't let you go out there in nothing but a lab coat. You don't even know who you are, let alone where you come from, or how you got to a place like an exotic animal park. We don't want to hurt you. We just want to help."

"Some of us more than others," Nina remarked in her acerbic tone.

Wanda rolled her eyes. "We're not crazy. Well, Nina's crazy, but I promise I'll keep a close eye on her so it doesn't rub off."

Spanky's gaze was unwavering when his suspicious eyes took in Wanda's. "After everything I've heard tonight—cougars, shifting, mind-reading, *crazy* never once crossed my mind." His tone was full of the sarcasm Katie herself had tinted her words with earlier.

Skater boy was in for a hella surprise.

"The word was *nutter*," Nina corrected. "That's what crossed your mind."

He held up a hand while shaking his head. "Right. Either way, and as kind as your offer is, I think I'll try and tough this one out alone."

"Look," Wanda continued. "I'm sure all of the information that's been bandied about tonight makes it seem as if we're all just one butterfly net away from the loony bin, but what we say is true. About you. About us."

Katie, tired and in need of anything alcoholic with the word *tini* tacked onto it, had had enough. If she had to be dumped into the river of acceptance headfirst, then so did the perp of the crime.

She slapped her good hand on her thigh. "You know what, ladies? I hate to ask you to pull out all the paranormal stops again, but I have a suggestion. Show him. At least he'll know the business about you all is true, and the possibility exists. Kaih, Ingrid, and I will wait out in the reception area. There are plenty of towels in the upper cabinets. You know, in case things get *messy*."

She was almost pleased by the nearly undetectable loss of color in Spanky's cheeks. Almost. She wasn't entirely convinced he was being truthful, despite Nina's mind-reading accuracy. If he really didn't know he was a cougar, that notion brought with it a whole new can of worms. How could he doubt their existence if he had no memory of anything other than her taters?

"Oh, please do. Show me, ladies," Spanky encouraged cockily. The smug tilt of his lips and that "yeah, right" expression reminded Katie of someone.

Oh, yeah. Her. The her of two hours ago when unicorns and trolls under bridges were still only mythological mysteries.

Nina laughed, holding her fist, knuckles forward at Katie. "You aiiight, Doc." She sighed with contentment. "Shit. I love this part. Twice in one night is pushing orgasmic."

Katie, giddy from the night's events, actually giggled like she hadn't in a coon's age. "I know you do. We'll be right out here," she said to Spanky. "In case you need tissues," she joked, letting the examining room door close behind her, blocking out his skeptically handsome face.

Wanda poked her head out. "Wait, Katie. He's been through a lot. He genuinely can't remember who he is. I don't know that it's wise to, well, to freak him out any more than I'm sure he already is."

Katie felt a moment of sympathy, but she let it pass due to the severity of her condition and the need for answers. "I think he's pretty tough, Wanda. I also think all's fair in love and the quest to rid yourself of teeth fit for a woolly mammoth. I need answers. I can't work like this, and I have an animal to care for with an owner who just wouldn't understand my paw. If Spanky doesn't have the answer, and you don't have the answers, then who does? If nothing else, he'll believe us when we tell him shapeshifters exist, and then maybe he'll see what's happened to me is very real. Or maybe when you do show him, whatever's keeping him from remembering will jog some memory of who he is."

Wanda's expression held doubt.

Katie sighed. "How about a compromise? Don't nail him with everything at once. Maybe just a little fang and fur—no fireballs or levitation. That was like an acid trip with Linda Blair as the tour guide."

Wanda chuckled and winked. "You got it. You're one tough cookie, Katie Woods. I admire that."

Yeah.

A tough cookie with an amnesiac man-cougar.

She shoots—she scores.

Silence.

There was nothing but nail-biting silence after the loud crashing of cages, Nina's wickedly delighted laughter, either Wanda or Marty's eerie howl, and one long, muffled gasp.

Katie put her ear to the door. Her hearing was oddly magnified and so crisp it almost hurt. Maybe she could get a listen at what was going on.

Nothing.

Guilt assaulted her. He was just a kid. She'd subjected him to an unimaginable encounter with creatures he probably thought only existed in the movies.

"You hear anything in there, Doc Woods?" Kaih asked.

"Nada. I'm concerned he's passed back out from shock."

"This has been some wild ride, huh?"

"For who?" She flashed her paw at him with a grimace.

"I know that part of this sucks, but can I just say something here?"

"Expression in the form of speech is always encouraged."

He jammed his hands into the pocket of his lab coat. "This has been the best friggin' night of my life. So totally beats kicking Skips on Water's ass at *Guitar Hero*. Seriously, working for you was cool. You're an okay boss, but this? This was a-mazing."

Katie turned, letting her back rest against the door. "You're not at all afraid, Kaih? After everything we've witnessed tonight? Ingrid may never be the same. Yet, you're acting like someone just gave you a ticket to ride on the starship *Enterprise*."

"It's probably just that cool," he joked. "No, Dr. Woods. I'm not afraid. Not of the OOPS team, anyway. They're okay. I can sense it. I'm more afraid of what you'll say when I tell you—"

"Dr. Woods!" someone bellowed from outside the door to the clinic. "Open this door now!"

Katie's eyes went wide when they met Kaih's. "Who the hell is that at this time of night?" she whisper-yelled, panic flaring in her gut.

Ingrid squealed from her fetal position in the corner, fat tears began streaming down her face. "OMG, Dr. Woods! I'm so sorry!"

Kaih threw an ACE bandage at Katie, instructing her to wrap it around her hand to hide her paw.

"What the hell is going on?" she asked, searching his dark eyes as he helped her tug the last of the bandage into place.

The banging of angry fists on the door mingled with the screech of the October wind. "Open this door. I know what you've done, and I'll prosecute if you don't open this door now!"

The examining room door swung open behind Katie. Nina popped her head out and yelped, "Who the fuck is making all that goddamned racket? My ears are sensitive and I'm nearly in a vampire coma. Shut whoever that is the fuck up now!" Nina stomped over to the door, flinging it open with an angry grunt.

Kaih tugged on her arm. "Listen, Dr. Woods, this is what I was trying to tell you—"

"Who the hell are you? Do you have any idea how late it is?" Nina asked an elderly man, his thick head of gray and silver hair windblown and mussed, his bifocals haphazardly perched on his nose.

Sharp clear eyes that matched his hair glared up at Nina. His wrinkled face was a mask of fury. He pushed past her, his bony finger pointed at Katie as the ends of his down coat, unzipped to reveal a plaid flannel shirt, flapped in the harsh wind. "What have you done?" he bellowed, so loud Katie's eardrums vibrated with the cavernous rumble. A batch of freshly fallen leaves skittered in on the howl of the breeze behind him, rustling and skipping over her waiting room floor.

Kaih grabbed her by the arm again when she made a move to approach the man. "Dr. Woods, listen to me! This man is dangerous—"

"Where is *he?*" the old man screeched, hoarse and high, the jowls of loose skin around his jawline trembling.

"Where is who, sir?" Wanda called, pressing her hands along her hips to smooth her skirt down. Her worried frown marred her beautiful face as she headed in the direction of the front door.

But the old man only had eyes for Katie, all his vengeance directed at her as he cornered her against the wall. "You crazy zealot! Do you have any idea what you've done? Always picketing us, making a ruckus. Now tell me where he is!"

Nina was instantly at Katie's side, towering over the squat man. "Whoa there, old-timer. I'm not big on taking down the senior shuffleboarders, but I'll do it if you don't catch your breath."

He huffed in her direction, spittle escaping his thinned lips. "She did this! You're responsible for this, and I'm going to the police. Do you hear me, Dr. Woods?" In a flash, one even Nina missed, he went for Katie, his hands, old and arthritic, latched onto her neck, wrapping around it with a strength that left her too surprised to react.

"Hookay!" Nina roared. "Time to head home for some warm milk and your Bengay rubdown, pardner." With that, she pried his fingers from Katie's neck, scooped him up by the back of his jacket, and planted him outside the door on the front steps, slamming the door with an angry grunt.

And she did it with only two fingers.

God.

Nina's lips were a thin line of pissed off when she surveyed the room. She crossed her arms over her chest, leaning back against the door and crossing her feet at the ankles. Her eyes zeroed in on Kaih and Ingrid. "So I got a hinky feelin' somebody's got some explainin' to do. And don't bother to lie to me, because if I gotta get inside your little heads to find out what you're hiding, I'll leave you praying for a lobotomy."

Kaih's angular chin lifted, his gaze met Nina's head-on. "That was some guy who works at the animal park."

Katie's eyes narrowed. "And he was here, screaming at me like some deranged lunatic because?"

Ingrid, her face wet with tears, cowered behind Kaih. Her reply bordered on a screech. "He was here because we stole Spanky!"

CHAPTER 5

Katie whirled around, brushing her tangled hair from her face. "You did what?"

Kaih held up a long-fingered hand to quiet the perpetually panicked Ingrid, tucking her behind his back with a protective hand. "I can't believe I let you talk me into this, Ingrid."

He sighed long and harsh before he began. "First, we didn't exactly steal him. Okay, we stole him. He was injured, Doc. At least when we saw him behind the fence he was. You know how Ingrid is. She's an animal lover just like you. She loses sleep worrying about them. She'd been down at the park, checking on the animals as best she could since the restraining order was placed on us. I told her those binoculars and that lame hat and sunglasses couldn't be classified as a disguise." He shook his dark head in disgust. "Whatever. The point is, when I went to investigate what she was so upset about, Spanky had a huge gash in his side. He was bleeding, Doc, and unconscious. We couldn't leave him like that. We also couldn't alert anyone inside the park—because, you know—"

"Restraining order," Katie supplied, her stomach a sea of nervous butterflies as Kaih let his story unfold.

"Restraining order?" Marty chimed in, her poodle lying over her shoulder now, exhausted from the commotion.

Kaih nodded. "Yeah, that. Long story."

"So long," Katie said with a tired sigh, biting her lip to fend off the outraged scream she wanted to holler at the top of her lungs at the injustice of anyone in this Podunk town placing a restraining order on her to protect an animal from her sinister clutches.

"Look, Dr. Woods, you know the care those poor animals get is on a par with crap. No one would've cared that Spanky was hurt anyway, and Ingrid can be pretty convincing when she's crying all those big, fat tears and fretting he'll end up with an infection. So we waited until sundown, and I picked that cheap excuse they call a lock on the gates. Then we 'borrowed' one of the animal park's golf carts, and me and Ingrid's retarded stoner of an on-again, off-again boyfriend, Clem, hauled him onto the cart and left him on the steps of the clinic. To be sure he wouldn't wake up while he was in the golf cart, I gave him a tranquilizer. Then we left Clem to watch him while we went and had dinner with you. We knew you'd help him without thinking about the restraining order and Sheriff Glenn, and it was a low-down thing to trick you into doing."

He glared at Ingrid, letting his dark eyes skim the floor with his guilt. "I did tell her, probably the entire trip back here, we were taking advantage of you and your good heart, but she kept saying you'd want to know, and if I know even a little about you, I know that much is true."

Katie's nod was in sharp agreement. Jesus. They knew her well. There was no way she could deny any animal in need of medical attention, restraining orders and the sheriff be damned.

She blew out a trembling breath. Shit. She'd done almost everything in her power to lay low since she'd left the city, but her lay-low powers were clearly on the fritz.

She'd done nothing short of take out a billboard with her picture on it to announce that Katie Woods, animal lover–slash-veterinarian, had arrived. "Do you have any idea the kind of trouble we'll be in when he goes to the sheriff's office and accuses us of stealing Spanky? We have a restraining order against us, for gravy's sake. That means we're not allowed within a hundred feet of the entrance to the animal park."

"Well, technically, you don't really have Spanky, now do you?" Casey said, her brown eyes sparkling. "You have a man. A gorgeous, albeit a little dazed man, but still a *man*."

Katie liked the way Casey thought. She'd labeled Casey a German shepherd. A quick thinker and always cautious and aware of her surroundings.

"I swear, Dr. Woods, I didn't know!" Ingrid cried, cutting into Katie's thoughts, her words jittery and disjointed. "How could I have known he was—a—a—man?"

Katie's mind raced like someone had hit fast-forward on the button to her brain. "I think the real question here is, does the old man know Spanky's a man? And if he does, how has he hidden something like that from everyone in town? For that matter, *who* is he? That certainly wasn't Seamus Magoo."

"I've only seen him a couple of times, and it was always with Spanky and the other cougars. I don't know what he does at the animal park," Kaih said.

Nina cracked her neck, the crunch of her bones popped and snapped. She aimed her gaze at Katie. "Didn't I fucking tell you there's always some drama? Never flippin' fails. I'd bet my newly built-up tolerance to a whole bite of a Twinkie that this is a fuckload bigger than just an old guy looking for his kitty cat."

Katie tended to believe Nina was right. Yet she chose not to panic. "Well, if he's in charge of making sure the animals don't escape, not only could he lose his job but if someone ended up hurt, he could be in much bigger trouble than just the loss of his paycheck. It would make sense he'd be upset."

Nina cracked her jaw, her skepticism clearly written on her face. "Oh, no, lady. Something else is goin' down. I don't know what. I don't know why. I just know I could smell it on him. He isn't just afraid he's going to lose his job because his overgrown kitty escaped and might devour a couple of eight-year-olds and a schnauzer. He said it himself. 'You don't know what you've done.'"

She'd forgotten that fact in the rush of words and panicked yelling. "Speaking of the overgrown kitty, how did Spanky take, you know, the shifting thing?" Katie fought a laugh. It was so wrong to laugh even a little at his undoubted shock and dismay, but if she had to be in this paranormal thing blind, then fair was fair. If he couldn't remember anything after the show these women put on, it would at least be point of reference.

Marty twirled her hair, setting Muffin on the floor. She scurried to Kaih's feet and nestled on his work boot. "Well, I don't want to debase his manhood, because don't get me wrong, he's super-duper manly, but he didn't quite take it the way you did, Dr. Woods. Of course, his circumstances are much different. He can't remember who he is. Add that to the shock of seeing us shift, and I'm willing to cut him some slack. So I'm not ready to play his 'girl card' just yet."

Wanda nodded with a sheepish wince. "He did squeal. But just a little, and to be fair, Marty did linger over him a little longer for true effect than she might have in an average shift."

"So he smells good, okay?" Marty defended. "I'm married, not dead. Unlike Dracula."

"He passed out like a little girl," Nina supplied with a dry yawn, stretching her arms over her head and cracking her knuckles.

"I'll have you know, this 'little girl' has a limit, and she reached it when the short one of you bunch set my toe on fire with her fingertip." Spanky drawled, coming out of the examining room, pale and quite obviously shaken, though he squared his broad shoulders like he was preparing to do another round of battle.

Muffin appeared to realize there was a new man in her midst and instantly abandoned the Kaih ship for the Spanky luxury liner. She slipped between his legs and placed a paw on his bare leg.

He chuckled, scooping her up and tucking her under his chin. Katie's heart picked up the pace at the sight of such a big, hard-looking man cuddling with a poodle. Muffin gave a sigh of girlish contentment, mirroring Marty's.

Casey patted him hard on the back, making his shoulders jolt forward. "Oh, I did not set your toe on fire. It was just a little warm, big boy. I apologized. I did tell you I have trouble with my aim sometimes. I'm still in the stages of perfecting it."

He came to stand near Katie, making her cheeks flush and her stomach jiggle. Her hope all this jiggling and flushing was simply an onset of the hormonal, perimenopausal variety gave her something to cling to.

She gave him a cursory glance, skimming his body as quickly as she could so as not to be called a jailbait-leering, old hag. "Quite the show, huh? You okay?"

"This is perfectly batty."

Katie leaned in with a giggle she couldn't contain. "Don't say that too loud. The mean, dark-haired one can be touchy, and she has the kind of hearing I thought only the Bionic Woman had."

"Tell a bloke about it," was his wry reply. "I make one little off-color remark about Count Chocula, and she's all teeth and testosterone."

While the other women talked with one another in a huddle about what to do next, Katie waffled. She couldn't very well let her only link to this cougar adventure walk out the door with no memory of who he was or why he'd been in the animal park to begin with, but what would she do with him?

How could she explain him to a town full of busybodies just looking to take yet another issue with her? She hadn't even begun to garner the trust of the folks here in Piney Creek. The slow trickle of patients she'd acquired were only those in dire need.

Should they find out her employees had stolen a cougar, they'd run her out of town on a rail. Her arrival here in Piney Creek was already under severe scrutiny. The town and its people loved the animal park, and they loved Seamus Magoo. He was a portly, red-cheeked man who vaguely resembled Santa Claus, and she'd found out the hard way just how beloved he was to the folks of Piney Creek.

Shortly after her arrival, while eating dinner at the local diner and overhearing how spectacular the new llamas were, Katie'd suggested the animals might not be receiving the proper care they needed. In the end, you'd think she'd suggested old lady Worsham was blowing for cash from the frowns and all the huffing and puffing over plates of chicken-fried steak with white gravy.

Katie rocked back on her feet in thought. "So what to do with you . . ."

Spanky nodded his dark head, muttering out of the side of his mouth, "Indeed."

"You'll need a place to stay."

"Preferably a place that doesn't have a water bottle and a bowl attached to the side of its bars. I don't want to be a demanding guest, but even we *girls* have our lines that cannot be crossed."

"How are you with animals?"

He cocked his head at the irony of that question. "According to the lot of you, I am one." Spanky hitched his jaw at Muffin for reference. The little dog stretched her head upward to revel in the rush of his warm breath ruffling over her hair. "How do you suppose I am with them?"

"Sorry. That was a dumb question. You can't remember how you feel about anything."

"But your taters. That I can remember," he said on a sexy chuckle, drawing out the word *tater* to give it a southern twang.

Katie's eyes fell to her feet to avoid his direct gaze. Good God, he made her cheeks flush and her heart race. "How do you feel about Muffin right now? Cougars are carnivores, if I'm remembering my training and my days of watching *Mutual of Omaha* right. Feel the tiniest bit like eating her whole?"

"She's not my type. I like them much less hairy."

"How would you know?"

"How would I know what?"

"Whether you like eating pampered poodles, hairy or not?"

Spanky frowned, the deep grooves of his forehead wrinkling. "I don't know. I can only tell you the moment you suggested it, the very notion of hurting a small, innocent animal—especially one with a pink T-shirt that reads 'Crazy Human Dog'—was instantly reprehensible."

"That's a big word."

"Which one confused you? Crazy or human?"

Her eyebrow rose at his sarcasm. "Funny. Reprehensible."

Spanky grinned. "I can haz big words, despite the fact that I'm just days away from my nursery school graduation."

"Ba-dump-bump," Katie acknowledged the slight full-on. "I deserved that. So, back to the original question."

"Which was?"

"How do you feel about working with animals?"

"Does it mean I'll work with you? You know, because you're a *cougar*, of course. That definitely classifies you as an animal." His words screamed the kind of doubt she understood.

"You'll work *for* me until we can figure this thing out. I'm partially responsible for what happened to you today, at least in how you ended up here. I won't take that lightly."

He smirked. "I heard. It was vague due to the fact that I was still in the girlish stage of my faint, but I heard most of it. Busy staff you have."

Katie gazed up into his youthful face with concern. "Did you hear that elderly gentleman when he barged in here? Did you recognize his voice?"

Spanky's face was blank. "I heard a lot of yelling, but I haven't a clue who he is."

No. That would be like asking to wake up and find George Clooney on the pillow next to hers shortly after he'd brought her poached eggs on toast and Earl Grey tea. Her sigh was defeated. "Right. Either way, letting you stay with me isn't totally altruistic. I need to know what to do next. You have the answer, even if you don't know you do yet. If you do something crazy like go out there alone, I may never know what's happened to me and how to learn to cope with it."

"And we couldn't have that."

Her temper flared in a red-hot bolt of tired irritation. "I'm not holding you hostage, but I'd think you'd want to know what's happened to you, too, and how you got into the animal park as a cougar but left it a fully grown man."

"You do realize I'm thoroughly unconvinced I did this to you, don't you?"

Katie bristled, tired and longing to be out of his close proximity and into the comfort of her big bed. "You can leave at any time." She had the Internet. Who needed a hot stud when the information highway was a costly Verizon bill away? Surely there was information about cougar people.

Surely.

"But who would provide you with endless skate-park fodder?"

Chagrin replaced irritation. "You *are* very young."

Spanky paused, but only for a moment. "I couldn't tell you if I was young, old, or in between. I can't get a clear picture in my mind of what I look like. I only know when the remark was made, it felt all wrong."

How horrible to not have an image of yourself in your own mind, even if it was always off by twenty pounds and its boobs were at least a good two inches perkier than your bra said they were. Worse, how horrible to not know your image was smokin'. "Well, there's nothing a good mirror can't set straight. I have several in my house. Let's go play eeny-meeny-miney-mo. Maybe it'll jar something of value."

Spanky barked a laugh. "And what will you do with your posse of paranormal?"

Katie looked at the women with concern. Nina's eyes had grown round with fatigue as she blinked back what she'd called vampire sleep. Wanda's clear, bright eyes were dull, too, and both Marty's and Casey's posture had begun to slump. "This clinic is the bottom floor of an enormous house I share with my aunt Teeny. She's partially deaf, a little outspoken—okay, a lot outspoken— and probably slept through this entire fiasco. These women came all the way from the city. They're tired. I'll ask them to stay here. It's the least I can do after all they've done. If the ladies are willing to double up, you can have a bedroom all to yourself."

His tone became playfully smoky-seductive and low. "And if they're not?"

"Well, the answer's obvious. You can share my bed."

"Really?"

"No."

"I *have* suffered a great many trials and tribulations," he said, giving her a comically tragic expression. One that made the grooves on either side of his mouth deepen and served to send an unfamiliar flutter of delight along her arms.

For self-preservation, Katie flung her hand, her growing-heavier-by-the-minute hand, in his rugged face. The ACE bandage Kaih had helped put on it flapped at the edges. "Yeah. Me, too. So either you're in or you're out. Your choice. I'm going to go upstairs now to get some extra sheets and ready rooms for everyone. Let me know what you decide to do."

She began to head toward the back of the clinic to the connecting stairs leading to the bottom floor of her aunt's when he stopped her by nearly shouting, *"Project Runway!"*

Katie whirled around. "Come again?"

"Either you're in or you're out," Spanky muttered, then smiled wide and luscious, clearly pleased with himself. "That's from *Project Runway*."

Marty cooed, smiling with a warm fondness directed at Spanky. "He watches *Project Runway*. I don't care if he's only twelve. He's a well-bred twelve with immaculate taste."

Wanda nodded, letting go of a yawn while her eyes rolled upward. "Nothing means more than your stamp of approval, Marty. Look, ladies, we'd better see if there's a Motel Six or something in this town. I don't think I'll make it back if I have to drive, and Nina definitely needs to sleep. You all know from experience, if she doesn't get her eight in some dark closet she turns into Vampire-zilla."

"You mean she gets worse?" Spanky blurted, then winced at his outspokenness, shoving his hands into the lab coat in amused contrition.

Nina's head shot up, her eyes pinning Spanky. "Crazy that, eh, Garfield? It gets worse times infinity," she grunted, her voice weary but still full of the ever-present threat she made everyone aware she imposed.

"Please," Katie interrupted. "Stay here. It's the least I can do, and I have plenty of room. It'll be much more comfortable than the motel in town. Believe me when I tell you, Motel Six is five star compared to the hotel run by Lurch."

"How lovely of you," Wanda said. "I, for one, am all in. I'm exhausted, and maybe some sleep is just what the doctor ordered for Spanky. Let's hope tomorrow he'll wake up and remember everything. Then we can leave you in his capable hands and still sleep at night."

Yeah. Maybe.

Ingrid slid along the wall of the waiting room in a crab-like walk as though to avoid the cooties that would rub off on her if she touched one of the women. "They're staying *here*? In the house?"

Katie flung the arm attached to her good hand around Ingrid's trembling shoulders. "Yes, and if Nina wants to suck your blood, just yell for me. I'll save you. Swear on my paw."

Ingrid blanched, even surrounded by the laughter Katie's comment evoked. As Kaih led the women to the living space she and her aunt shared, she held Ingrid back. "You know what I don't understand, Ingrid?"

"Everything? I don't understand anything anymore after tonight."

"First, you're some actress. You did a fantastically awesome job of pretending you didn't know how Spanky got on the steps of the clinic."

Guilt flew across her expression in the way of a wince. "I couldn't even look you in the eye. I'm sorry I lied, but I just couldn't stand to see him suffer. If I'd known what would happen . . . what he could do . . . I never . . ."

Katie was a firm believer in moving on. "Forget that, honey. I probably would have done the same thing if I'd seen him injured. But this is what I don't get. I don't understand how such a staunch believer in UFOs and alien life-forms and all that crazy sci-fi stuff you're always reading and spewing can be so frightened of these women and their abilities. If anyone would think this was beyond all out-of-this-world expectation, I would have thought that would have been you. It was you who found the ad in that magazine. You read them all the time. If your nose isn't buried in one of those magazines, it's buried in a romance novel, and the last time I caught a glimpse of the back of one of those things, they had all sorts of creatures as the main characters. So for all your interest in otherworldly beings and the conspiracy theories you're always spewing from those forums you follow online, what gives?"

Her breath shuddered as it escaped her lungs. "I've come to the conclusion that I liked the possibility of something like this existing a lot more than finding out it really does exist. It was fun to imagine it—with other people online—in my romance novels, but I don't know if I one hundred percent believed all the junk they write in those forums. I think deep down I just thought they were kooks who needed somewhere to belong like I do."

Just like Ingrid. Katie's heart swelled in sympathy for her receptionist. Ingrid sought acceptance in everything she did. The product of foster home after foster home, she'd managed to finally escape the system, but it hadn't escaped her. She put a cheerful smile on her face. "You belong here with me, and guess what?"

"The kooks were right?"

Katie popped her lips with a wink. "The kooks have merit. So let's get some sleep, and maybe tomorrow this won't seem as overwhelming."

"Do fangs and fireballs ever not overwhelm you?"

Katie tipped her head back and laughed. "Point."

"Did you see the things they did?"

"I did."

"That lady Wanda turned into a werewolf right in front of us.

Right there while I was sitting on a couch. And Oh-m-gee, the one called Nina is so strong, and—and mean. Cranky. Scaaaary. I can't believe you're not beyond freaked."

"Oh, don't get the wrong impression, kiddo. I'm not that tough. Of course I'm freaked, but we saw with our own eyes what's possible. It's the only explanation I have for my hand and my teeth. So what else is there to do but let them help me?"

Ingrid's eyes had lost some of their panic and were replaced with a solemn hue. "I'm afraid."

If Katie was about anything, she was all about owning her feelings. "Me, too."

"Me three. Strike that. Afraid might be a shade heavy. How does hesitant with a healthy dash of stimulation overload strike you ladies?" Spanky had hung back after the crowd had gone with Kaih. His sudden reemergence left Katie's heart thrashing as the unspoken question hung in the air.

Ingrid stiffened under the weight of Katie's arm when Spanky loomed over them. She tightened her grip around her shoulders in reassurance. "Tonight has been nothing if not eventful."

His raven eyebrow rose. "Which leaves me so jazzed for tomorrow."

Ingrid snorted, relaxing a little into Katie, though her eyes still had trouble meeting his. "I'm really sorry we took you from the park. I swear we only wanted to help you. You really did have a big wound on your side. I couldn't live with myself if I didn't do something to help you. I realize now it was impulsive and rash."

He tightened the lab coat around his wide, tanned chest, cracking a smile at her meek receptionist. Whether he was more attuned to Ingrid's wildly swinging emotions because he had the finely honed senses of a cougar, or he was just inherently a good person, Katie couldn't say.

Due to his amnesia, neither could he.

But it was clear, he'd read Ingrid and her lifetime of insecurities when, with a gentle hand, he tilted her chin up and forced her to look at him. His eyes, so brilliantly blue sent a million messages to a frightened young woman. "Thank you. I think I'm glad you were rash and impulsive, though the jury's still out. Anyway, Ingrid, I'm Spanky. The pleasure's all mine."

Ingrid beamed, two bright spots of red streaking her cheeks. "I think we need to find you a new name. Spanky makes me think of someone's pet hamster."

He held out his arm to her, offering to escort her down the long hallway leading to Katie's aunt's living room. "I'd be honored if you'd help me do just that. Maybe over morning tea? What say you and I go find a walk-in closet to lock that Nina up in to ensure the safety of our necks? There'll be no bloodsucking on my watch."

Ingrid's hesitation lasted but a second before she hooked her arm through his. "Oh, you're so on."

Katie watched until their backs disappeared into the dim lighting of her living room before she took another breath. The way he'd held out his arm to Ingrid with a question, coupled with his intuitive perception of her fear, and his obvious wish to ease those doubts, stole Katie's breath from her lungs.

In spite of his gruff exterior, he had a sensitive bone.

Well, yeah, Katie. He watches *Project Runway* and knows how to use *reprehensible* in a sentence.

Add to that, he was all sorts of sexy when he was in the act of being sensitive.

A thought struck her as she tried to at least make some sense of even a small portion of tonight.

Spanky was gay. He might not know it due to his memory loss, but his choice of television viewing said so. He was Tim Gunn approved.

If he was gay, that meant she could ogle every last inch of him till she turned blue in the face, and it would be as futile as her late teenage wish to create a love child with Ferris Bueller.

She blew out a sigh of relief. For all her heart palpitations, buttery knees, and stomach jitters, she found the idea that Spanky played for a different team left her with one less thing to worry about.

Well, then.

A reason to go on living.

CHAPTER 6

A sharp whistle startled Katie, who was deep in the midst of savoring a cup of coffee and distractedly doodling on her favorite morning ritual—a crossword puzzle. Though, she was stuck on a six-letter word for cat.

Katie had only five letters in it.

Yet her attention kept returning to the big bay window, overlooking the cement pathway that lead to the wide front porch steps of her aunt's house, while she swirled coffee in her mouth. Today the coffee had a heightened pleasure to it, likely due to her new taste buds.

Even with the added layer of flavor, there was nothing like Aunt Teeny's coffee.

With cream.

Yesterday, she'd liked her coffee black.

Today, she liked milk.

And apparently large game.

Huh.

Good thing at least her teeth had returned to normal, or she couldn't say for sure the deer in the backyard that had caught her attention earlier would be safe from her gnashing pearly whites. They had called to her in the way of delicious, warm blood coursing through their veins and the promise of some soft squishy . . . Katie shuddered, fending off the offensive images and forcing herself to greet her aunt.

She swiveled around on the wooden chair with the green-and-red-plaid cushioning to find her aunt Teeny in her customary floral housecoat, trailing across the floor in pressure socks and sandals. An unlit cigarette hung from her wrinkled lips.

Dozer, an old yellow Lab mix and their fourth stray dog in four months, followed close behind her, plunking himself down on the blue-and-green braided rug to bask in the shafts of weak, buttery sunlight coming from the bay window.

Li'l Anthony wasn't far behind, all five pounds of him. A pushy, arrogant, cranky, "hands off me, I don't need no lovin'" mixed breed with a painfully infected ear that she'd found in the surrounding woods while walking one afternoon a couple of months ago. He was confrontational, a total bully who barked at everything that moved, but a snuggle bunny at night when he curled up next to her in bed.

Katie scooped him up and checked his torn but finally healed ear, then gave him a dreaded kiss on the side of his black muzzle. He squirmed his displeasure. "Hey, cranky. Where're Petey and Paulie?" Petey and Paulie were the other two-thirds of what she fondly called the mob. They were a brother-and-sister pair of terrier mixes that had been abandoned out by the creek. Being younger dogs, they ganged up on poor Dozer at regular intervals. As a pack, their gang mentality was bark at high-pitched intervals first, pee on it later.

"Looky that, would ya? Nice-lookin' boy there," Aunt Teeny commented with approval, nodding her head in the direction of the opposite window where Spanky, in Kaih's borrowed jeans that were too short, and too loose around the waist, chopped wood. She went immediately to the bin of dog food they kept in the open pantry and filled the dogs' bowls. "You hire him to do odd jobs around the place?"

Katie's eyes fell back to her coffee as she set Li'l Anthony down, clamping the mug with her one good hand, and resting the other between her jean-clad thighs with a wince. She'd spent the better part of a restless night trying to figure out a cover story for her aunt and anyone else who might ask about Spanky and the women who were still sleeping soundly upstairs.

Of all the stories she'd come up with, declaring him the help, the simplest of all fabrications, had never occurred to her. "Um, yup. I hired him to take care of some things around the house and the clinic. Winter's coming. We need wood chopped and . . . and stuff done." Lots of stuff. Li'l Anthony gave her a strange glare of disapproval. "Well, we do need stuff done," she whispered to him.

"I can think of a coupla other stuffs he could do to me."

Katie rolled her eyes, tucking her chin deeper into her lace ruffled shirt with the matching navy blue turtleneck with a shiver. "Aunt Teeny! He's just a kid."

She shrugged her small, hunched shoulders with a cackle and a toothless grin of depravity. "Don't make no difference to me, Lady Jane. It all looks the same when you hit the sack. We all still got the same parts, just some of us come extra wrinkled. But I'd be willing to let him iron me." She dropped down in the seat opposite Katie with her mug of steaming coffee. "What happened to your hand?"

She averted her eyes to stare at Yancey, sprawled on the back of the living room sofa, without a care and, quite possibly, her kin. Katie winced, pushing herself to focus. "Sprained. From lifting some of the cages in the office. No big deal."

Teeny crinkled one eye at her niece's hand, the cigarette hanging from her sunken lips.

Katie set her mug down and snatched the cigarette from her aunt's lips. "Where do you keep getting these? I've scoured every inch of this house and come up dry. Yet every morning, you have another one. You'd better not have a stash, Aunt Teeny. No smoking. Dr. Gladwell told you you're one cigarette away from your grave."

Under the shed in a hole she had me dig.

Katie's eyes widened, then she frowned when she scanned the kitchen. Did cougars hear imaginary voices in their heads?

Teeny poked her hand, bringing her attention back to the table. "You take my smokes, I'm gonna flirt with your hired hand, and I won't wear a bra when I do it."

Her aunt's outrageous remarks weren't just the bane of her existence but one of the reasons she got up in the morning. Teeny made it possible for her to survive in this small town where scorn was dished out by the shovelful. "You don't wear a bra anyway. No smoking. No negotiation. No more back talk."

Teeny propped her hand in her chin, using the other to adjust the sound on her hearing aid. "Yeah, yeah. I don't see how it can make anything any worse. I'm seventy-two. I'm gonna die next week anyway. Why can't I just do it with my Camels, for Christ's sake?"

"Who'd protect me from Willard Brown if you up and die?"

"Willard's just a blowhard with a big piehole."

"And if not for you, his piehole would have kept Irma Rycroft from bringing Susie-Q in to see me. As I recall, he told her I was the devil and God would rain his thunder down on her in the way of famine and poverty if she brought that poor cat to me for treat-

ment. He told her paying me for my services was like paying the
devil to buy your soul."

Willard is a bad, bad shit of a man. He kicked me once.

Katie's head whipped around at the echo of words in her head.
What the hell was going on?

"He's a fruitcake, old Willard is," Teeny, oblivious to Katie's
concern, said. "He's been alone with his crazy thoughts for too
long. Best he stays out in that cabin of his and keeps his trap shut.
Don't you worry about Willard or any of the other old cronies in
this damn town. They're a suspicious lot who're too set in their
ways, thinkin' Piney Creek's gonna go all citified if they let out-
siders in. Not much's changed here because they won't let it. You
breathed new life into the town. They just don't know it yet."

Oh, she'd breathed and that exhale had brought with it not just
scorn upon her but her aunt, too. Add in her prior legal troubles
and it made for a whole lot of unease among the people in town.
Katie gave herself a mental shake—no more dwelling. She'd done
nothing wrong back in New York. "Has Magda-May invited you
back to the quilting circle yet?" The group of senior citizens and
one diehard thirtysomething Nazi-feminist old maid had booted
Teeny out the second they'd decided Katie had usurped Magda-
May's husband.

Dr. Cyrus Jules, DVM, the only veterinarian in Piney Creek
until she'd arrived.

It had happened completely by accident. She'd known Piney
Creek was small, but she hadn't been prepared for the kind of
shunning only a small town can give you until she'd "snatched the
food right from their mouths" like the greedy, city heathen she
was, as Magda and friends had described it.

Shortly after her arrival and quite by circumstance, she'd met
Lizzie Johnson and her old hound dog Roderick, sitting in Lizzie's
parked truck just outside the feed store.

She'd stopped to pet Roderick and noticed he had a rather raspy cough. One that, according to Lizzie, wouldn't clear up, no matter how many meds Dr. Jules gave her.

Katie'd suggested she bring Roderick by the clinic, free of charge, so she could run a simple test, and Lizzie had obliged. An X-ray revealed old Roderick had an enlarged heart, causing the coughing and gasping for breath.

You'd think she'd reinvented the wheel, if you listened to Lizzie tell the tale of Rod's improvement with the proper medication. Unfortunately, what had been a simple act of concern for an aging dog that was suffering turned into a redneck version of the Sharks versus the Jets, if Magda-May had the chance to tell the story.

Katie had tread on Dr. Jules's territory by *correctly* diagnosing Lizzie's dog. Nobody remembered the correct part of the equation or that Roderick was breathing better for it. That she was right didn't matter to the ladies in the Piney Creek quilting circle.

She'd taken business from Dr. Jules. Throw in her restraining order from the exotic animal park along with her checkered past, and she was a dirty bird from the city that'd come to milk Piney Creek residents dry with her highfalutin prices and fancy doctorin'.

Teeny snorted, smoothing the checkered tablecloth under her coffee mug with arthritic fingers. "Magda-May can bite my un-wiped rear end. I don't need her stupid circle or her ugly quilts. She always picks crappy colors for 'em anyway."

Katie cringed and chuckled all at once. Her aunt's reality television addiction had created a monster. "Aunt Teeny! Your language. Where do you get this stuff?"

Aunt Teeny snorted. "I'm just expressin' myself, and I get it from watching all that reality TV. Never let it be said Teeny's not in the know. As for Magda-May, she'll be sorry I'm not in on that stupid quilt making. I was the only one with any damn taste."

Remorse that it had taken her all of a week to leave her favorite aunt friendless and quiltless stung her gut. "I'm sorry, Aunt Teeny. I just couldn't stand to see Roderick suffer. I didn't mean to cause so much trouble."

Teeny gave her a confused look by way of a wrinkled frown. "What bubble?"

I love Aunt Teeny. She can't hear jack. I never have to worry I'm gonna get caught when I hump Dozer.

Oh, God. There were voices in her head. With Brooklyn accents.

That's 'cuz I'm from Brooklyn. I got dumped here on the way to Michigan. A family road trip to Michigan. Some family. The jerks.

Katie fought a frightened whimper, jamming her finger into her mouth as Li'l Anthony scampered off up the stairs. Maybe she was just tired.

"Hey, girl, you listenin'? What bubble?"

Now she fought a sigh. Her aunt's hearing, even with her hearing aids, was questionable. Today, as tired as she was, as worried as she was that not only did she have a paw but she wanted to thin the wildlife population by *eating* it, she struggled with her impatience. "Not a bubble, Aunt Teeny. Trou-ble," she said with a purposeful inflection to the word. "I'm sorry I caused you so much trouble."

"You? Cause trouble? I'd never believe it," a gruff voice called from the mudroom off the kitchen.

"He has an accent."

Finally a voice that belonged to someone who wasn't disembodied.

Katie smirked in her aunt's direction. "And look who's suddenly acquired the ears of an eighteen-year-old."

Spanky made his way into the big kitchen, extending a hand to Teeny, whose fingers immediately went to the pocket of her housecoat to pull out her pink bandanna with the skulls on it. She tugged it over her head, tying it in the back to hide her thinning hair.

Katie's nostrils flared when Spanky entered the kitchen. He smelled of the outdoors, fresh and crisp with a hint of pine and clean, country air. Katie fought the quickening of her heart at the sexy picture he made, even in ill-fitting jeans and a flannel shirt that was too short in length, reminding herself he was gay. He nodded cordially in her direction and said, "Eh, what's up, Doc?" in a sad, but distinguishable, Bugs Bunny voice.

"Ooooh-weee. Ain't you finer 'n a plate of fried chicken and gravy? I could just sop you up with a biscuit. I'm Katie's aunt, Bettina. Teeny for short."

Spanky let his dark head sink low when he took Teeny's hand. "A pleasure. I'm . . ."

Katie bit her lip, hoping Teeny's hearing impairment would kick into high gear when he offered up the name Spanky.

"Hey, *Beckham!*" Ingrid greeted, from the entrance to the kitchen by way of the clinic, wildly waving her hands behind Teeny's back and skidding in on white vinyl platform boots, screeching to a halt just short of Spanky.

"Beckham. I'm Beckham. Beck for short," Spanky repeated dutifully, the unfamiliar name rolling off his tongue without a hint of unease. "Brilliant to meet you, Teeny."

Beckham? Katie mouthed in Ingrid's direction, lifting an eyebrow.

Ingrid held up a ragmag with a picture of David and Victoria Beckham on it, giving her a wince and a shrug. She bumped shoulders with *Beckham* like they were old friends. As though last night hadn't been like seeing the Second Coming and Friday the thirteenth all rolled into one hair-raising experience for her. "So how's it going today, *Beck?*"

Katie rose, hoping to avoid any more explanations about Beckham. It wasn't like she'd discussed hiring someone to help around the place with Teeny. As though anyone in town would come to chop the devil's wood anyway—even if she offered to pay them.

He'd appeared out of nowhere; the less explanation about his circumstances, the better. "*Beck* was just chopping some wood, Ingrid. Something we sorely need for the wood-burning stove." She waved a dismissive hand at him. "So . . . you go, er, chop and I'll go see how our guests are doing."

"Bah," Teeny protested. "Where's your manners, Katie-did? Let the boy sit and have coffee to warm up that big body of his. We don't want somethin' that finger-lickin' good to get frostbit." Teeny rose, shuffling to the coffeepot, ignoring Katie's protest that it was only forty degrees out. Hardly frostbite weather.

"You like sugar in your coffee, Beck?" she asked over her shoulder with a wink.

He didn't even know his name. It was unlikely he knew if he liked coffee. Teeny's leering goodwill toward their new roommate ruffled Katie's feathers—which was ridiculous, petty with a cap on the *P*, and uncalled for. "Yes, how do you like your coffee, Beck?" Katie inquired, syrupy sweet.

"With teeth," he replied without hesitation, then stopped to ponder that admission by raising an eyebrow.

"Who's Keith?" Teeny asked, carrying the mug to him and plunking it in front of him with a toothless smile.

Ingrid must have recognized how frazzled Katie was and gratefully intervened for her. "*Teeth*, Aunt Teeny. He likes his coffee with teeth. Which I think means bite. No sugar, no cream, really strong."

Beck's nod was slow but the more he nodded, it was clear the more he'd become convinced that was indeed how he liked his coffee. "Yes. I like it strong."

Teeny snickered. "Me, too, big fella." She settled into her chair and leaned over next to him. She had a habit of invading your personal space in order to hear your words, and that was as good excuse as any to splay herself over the gorgeousness of Beck. "So what brings you to Piney Creek?"

They all looked at each other.

What did bring him to Piney Creek?

Guilt hung in the air like a helium balloon.

"Me!" Marty yelped from the top of the stairs where the bedrooms were located. She skipped down the wooden staircase, Muffin and Petey following close behind. She hustled into the kitchen, smiling bright and cheery, her makeup and accessories picture-perfect. "I brought him to Piney Creek. I'm Marty Flaherty. It's just so lovely to *finally* meet you. I've heard so much about you, Aunt Teeny. Katie has nothing but complimentary things to say about you."

Katie cocked her head in Marty's direction, a bewildered question in her eyes. Marty shot her an "I got your back" look when Teeny leaned forward and tugged on her dress while scooping up a willing Muffin who was thankfully, blissfully, silent in Katie's head. "Ain't you the smart one in your fancy clothes?"

Marty beamed and gave her a wink of her blue eye; never once considering Teeny was criticizing her apparel. "Thank you. So I see you've met, uh . . ."

"Beckham," Katie provided, letting the corner of her lips lift in a half smirk when Ingrid stuck her tongue out at her and Beck himself narrowed his blue eyes.

"Beckham! Right. Sorry. I'm groggy from all the clean, country air. Anyway, I can't tell you how grateful I am that Katie offered my *cousin* this job. He's from London. Poor thing would have been living in a cardboard box if not for Katie's generosity. I mean, with the economy in the toilet, you can imagine there isn't much call for Speedo designers these days—"

"Speedos?" Beck grumbled his displeasure.

"But thank goodness Katie mentioned she needed help around the house," Wanda added, sailing into the kitchen, holding Paulie in her arms and looking like she'd never shed her clothes and left them in a rumpled pile on the floor at her four paws. "We knew just the man for the job. Beck's so good at anything handy and DIY. Katie's offer was a blessing from right out of the blue." She turned her back to Teeny and the others briefly to drag her finger across her throat in a warning to Marty. She mouthed the word *Speedo* much in the way Katie had to Ingrid earlier, rolling her eyes at her friend in disgust.

Whirling back around, Wanda set Paulie on the floor with a kiss to the top of his head and extended her hand to Teeny, a wide, warm smile on her face. "I'm Wanda Schwartz Jefferson. So lovely to meet you."

Teeny's eyebrow rose over the rim of her cup before she set it down and took Wanda's hand. "You all friends of Katie's from the city?"

"Yes!" Marty and Wanda chimed in unison.

"Friends. We're all friends," Wanda agreed with a vigorous nod of her head. "Definitely, definitely friends—from the, uh, city."

Teeny nodded, chucking Muffin under the chin while she cast a scathing eyeball to Wanda's heels. "I should've known. The way you all dress like you're goin' to church and here it is only *Tuesday*."

"So she obviously hasn't met Nina?" Marty quipped with a grin.

Beck chuckled low, taking another sip of his coffee while he let this charade play out in the hands of the women who'd suddenly taken over his life.

Katie almost chuckled, too, until she realized, Nina was sleeping in the upstairs bedroom's walk-in closet. Shit. "Where's Casey?"

"There's more of 'em?" Teeny asked.

"Just two," Wanda informed her, holding up her fingers. "Nina and Casey are still sleeping. Must've been all that fresh air—

knocked them right out. We were all so excited about Beck's new job, we decided to make a day of it by getting out of the city and seeing some real fall foliage. It really is pretty here," she remarked. "And your house is fabulous. Thank you so much for your hospitality."

Katie held her breath. Teeny, suspicious by nature and clearly not as enamored of Wanda and Marty as she was of Beck and his wrinkle-free body, pushed away from the table with a grunt. "Didn't know I was bein' hospitable to begin with, but any friends of Katie are always welcome to hang their hats on my hook. I don't know what you girls have planned for the day, but I got some plantin' to do. Gotta go get my teeth." She clapped Beck on the shoulder and winked. "Lunchtime's noon. Save your appetite. I cook."

Teeny shuffled off to her bedroom to the collective releasing of pent-up air.

Beck leaned back in his chair, crossing his ankle over his leg, giving Marty an amused look. "Speedos? *Spee-dos?*"

She threw her hands up in the air in apology. "I know. I know. All I could think of was your mention of *Project Runway* last night, and I made the leap from clothing designers to Speedos. I'm sorry—it just popped out of my mouth."

Katie glanced at the two women and Ingrid. "Thank you. I was mulling over what to tell Aunt Teeny for most of last night."

"And another thing," Beck interrupted. "Beckham, Ingrid? Like David Beckham?"

Ingrid grinned. "It was the first thing that came to mind and it beats Spanky. I like it."

"Hands down, it beats Spanky," he agreed, his approval making Ingrid preen.

"You know the name David Beckham, but you can't remember your own? Why do you suppose that is?" Katie asked, a peevish tone to her voice. Petey and Paulie heard her tone of voice, usually reserved for asking them what they were doing digging in the trash, and cocked their heads in her direction. Blissfully, they were as silent as Muffin.

Beck shrugged. "I guess I know David Beckham's name in the same way I knew *Project Runway* and how to button my shirt. I just did. So I'll thank you to keep your skepticism to yourself, Katie Woods. Nina told you I had no memories in my head. Are you calling the scariest woman alive a liar? Were I you, I'd retract that statement instantly. My impression is she's killed for less."

"She's killed for just a nibble on a Twinkie," Casey said on a giggle, slipping down the stairs and heading toward the coffeepot Katie pointed to.

"The hell you say," Nina said gruff and bleary-eyed. She had a white stripe of zinc oxide over her nose and she'd wrapped a hoodie over her head. The sunglasses she wore hid her eyes, but Katie knew what lay behind them. "Who called me a liar? I'm damned tired, people. Don't make me take it out on you by way of my fist down your throat."

Ingrid's fear of Nina took hold once more as she inched her chair closer to Beck's. "Shouldn't you still be asleep? It's only nine in the morning . . ." Her face went from flushed to ashen. Her hands shook when they twisted the fabric of her miniskirt. "Omigod— will you turn to dust? Like right here in the kitchen?" That familiar tremble from last night in Ingrid's lower lip returned.

Nina let her head fall back on her shoulders to show her irritation. "Listen, lamebrain, if you'd paid attention last night, you'd know I can tolerate some sunlight with the proper protection. I don't like it, but it's doable, and if I had to spend one more second smelling all that girly soap and perfume up there in that closet, surrounded by all that lace, I was going to gak my cookies up. So I'm awake. Appease me." Beck rose to offer her a chair, but she waved him off and instead sunk down to the floor where Dozer lay, placing a hand on his rib cage to give him a scratch. Petey and Paulie, usually cautious around strangers, hovered at her hip.

Dozer stretched leisurely, letting her give him a good rub-down, moaning his appreciation while Muffin curled into her slim hip. "So what's on tap today, people? Did Felix the Cat remember anything, or are we still in the same fucking place we were last night?"

Beck leaned down, letting his eyes rove over Nina's face with leisurely arrogance. "Felix has a name now, thank you very much. You may refer to me as Beck. I'll thank you kindly to remember that and no, *he* didn't remember anything. But it certainly wasn't for lack of trying. I pondered this—this shapeshifting thing and the idea I created this feline havoc all night long while I was in a bed clearly made for one of the seven dwarves. I don't want to look the proverbial gift cougar in the mouth, but I believe the pink-and-purple ruffled spread prevented any clearing of the haze my thoughts are muddled by."

Katie winced. She'd put him in the room she'd once slept in as a child when she visited her aunt Teeny during the summers. A deep snort almost spewed from her throat at the visual of his long, lean body crammed into her bed with the pink-and-purple canopy.

Nina rolled her tongue along the inside of her cheek while she scooped both Petey and Paulie into her lap. "Oooo, look at you all cagey and full of fire this A.M. Which would be hot if it wasn't for the fact that nobody's allowed to be cockier than me this early in the morning. So let's get one thing straight, pussycat. I'm fuck-ing tired. I slept in a walk-in closet that smelled like the perfume counter at Macy's all in the name of some peace. I need to feed soon. Add to that, I don't like people—especially new people like A River Runs Through It and you, Chicken Little." She nodded her head in Ingrid's direction. "Being with all of you for the last twelve hours has been like some kind of 'new people' intervention by force. It makes me cranky. So can the cocky. Nobody gives me permission to do anything." She followed up her statement by reaching up and flicking his flannel collar.

"So sayeth Nina," Beck taunted out of the side of his mouth, stooping to run a tanned hand over Muffin's head and chuck Dozer under the chin as though he were letting Nina know she couldn't intimidate him.

Wow. She was right. He *was* hot. And not afraid of Nina. Hotter still.

Casey's giggle was light as a breeze. "I think he just told you to shut it, Nina."

Wanda was instantly between them, scooting the dogs off her lap and hauling Nina up with a yank to her long arm. "C'mon, bruiser. We have errands to run if we're going to be in town for a few days, and you're helping while Marty and Casey get in touch with Darnell."

Nina let her head fall back on her shoulders with a whining grunt. "Fuck you, Wanda. I don't want to run errands. I want to go home to my man and feed, not hang out in the town called Deliverance while banjos *da-da-ding-ding-ding-ding-ding-ding* in the background."

Wanda pinched her cheek and grinned. "Aw, then how unfortunate to be you today, Princess. You can't go home to someone who isn't there. Heath called me this morning from Pebble Beach. Hollis is with Keegan and Mara and Naomi are babysitting while the boys are on an impromptu 'the girls have stuck their noses into another mess' trip. He said they decided while we quote, unquote, save the noob paranormal, they might as well amuse themselves. But don't you fret your unforgiving tongue about blood, either. Darnell's bringing you enough to last a week. Now come. Put your best scary face on, Sunshine. You know you want to. I'll need someone to frighten off the unfriendly locals with just one grunt so I can shop in peace."

"Enough blood for a week? A flippin' week?" Nina griped, frowning.

Wanda cocked an eyebrow in reprimand at her as she gathered her purse, letting it slide to the crook of her arm. "It'll be for as long as I say it will. Now shut it and march." She pointed a finger at the back door with the colorful stained glass window.

Nina stomped out the door Beck obligingly held open for her with his self-assured smile. "Allow me, Nina," he cooed.

She flipped her middle finger over her shoulder at him as she slunk down the front porch steps, each heavy fall of her feet ringing with her discontent.

"Wanda, wait." Katie jumped up, putting her hand on her arm. "I've taken enough of your time as it is. I can't ask you to leave your lives for me."

Wanda's brown eyes were warm. "First, don't talk crazy. You're as helpless as a fetus in the womb. I couldn't live with myself if I left you in this semi-shift and didn't try to figure some way to help you. None of us knew what to expect when Marty was turned, but we all learned from each other's experiences. Second, there's something else, Katie. I woke up this morning with one thought after what happened last night. This *is* my life—or what I want to do with it when I'm not writing. Help people like you in paranormal distress. I decided no matter what the rest of the girls do, I'm going to try and make OOPS work. It makes me happy. So say no more," she chided with a cluck of her tongue.

"Now I'm off to stir up this sleepy town with my big-mouthed vampire. Marty and Casey will tell you all about Darnell. I pray he has some answers." She raised a hand in the air and with a wave she was gone.

Ingrid rose from the table, the glare of the multiple studs in her eyebrows glinting in the sunlight. "I'm going to go scour the Internet for shapeshifter info while I watch the front desk, Boss. How do you feel, by the way? You want me to close shop for the day? I don't think you should see patients this way."

Katie's chest lifted in a sigh of remorse for the practice she could have if only the townspeople would let her. Some days, she didn't know why she bothered to flip the sign on her door to OPEN. "Like we have many of those anyway, Ingrid? Or have you forgotten my right and proper shunning?"

Ingrid shook her finger at Katie just like she'd done a thousand times before when Katie had mourned out loud her lack of clientele for much else but the pet hotel/boarding she offered—something Dr. Jules didn't. "But you never know. I mean, who knew what happened last night could really happen? I've been telling you all along, it just takes one little shift in the cosmic wheel and poof"—she made a blowing-up motion with her hands that made her multiple bracelets jingle—"we have liftoff. Keep the faith."

Katie smiled with the optimism she knew Ingrid needed. "I don't know where I'd be without you, Ingrid. And for today, I agree. Let's close up shop. Though, really, I feel fine." And she did. In fact, she'd felt more alert and rested on three hours' sleep than she'd ever felt after eight.

Ingrid took her ragmag and skipped off to the reception area, satisfied she'd given Katie her daily dose of "go get 'em" while Marty and Casey lingered over coffee.

"Business is poor?" Beck commented, standing too close for her comfort, the heat his body radiated even in his ridiculous clothing making her pulse race.

"Business is nil."

"I can't imagine what with the superb cages and top-of-the-line cougar-wear. Do the townspeople find your accommodations lack that special something?"

Oh, she lacked all right. She now lacked a pristine record . . . "You'd be funny if I liked you today."

"Did you like me yesterday?"

"More than I do this morning, yes."

"More's the pity. But it's all right. I'm pacified with the notion that Aunt Teeny likes me enough for twelve of you. She cooks, you know."

"Oh, she cooks. I hope you like fish sticks and Tater Tots, and FYI, Aunt Teeny likes any man that doesn't need a penis pump."

"How flattering."

"But honest."

"So tell me, Dr. Woods, what else would you like me to do today aside from regaining my memory so I can teach you to hunt helpless mountain bikers all right and proper?" He mocked a southern accent with little success, almost making her laugh out loud at his absurd attempt.

But then she remembered she had the Claw for a hand because of him, and all thoughts of laughing flew over the cuckoo's nest. Her expression returned to its former frown. There were a million things to do. She and Teeny had made a list of them about a month ago, most of which escaped her now. "Can you hang shelves?"

"Your guess is as good as mine. Though, quite frankly, I was unprepared for the ease with which I handle an ax. Yet there I was, the epitome of grace and elegance in motion."

Oh, if he only knew how graceful his motion was . . . but his motion was gay. She nodded her head to agree with his statement. "It was almost like watching an Olympic event, you were so full of all that grace."

"I feel mocked."

"You should."

"You're a cruel taskmistress."

"I'd feel I failed you if your head got too big."

"I wouldn't fear that with you women in the mix."

"It's our instinct to mother and keep you humble."

"You don't look like anyone's mother," he purred, allowing his gaze to slide along her length in obvious appreciation.

Katie fought a flush of her cheeks and a ripple of pleasure by gritting her teeth. "Shelves—hang them, please." Before she got a noose and hung herself from the old maple out back. "Second room at the top of the stairs, the walk-in closet, all the hardware's on the floor. Hammer's in the toolbox in the laundry room." *Go. Away. Take your divine body with its scintillating, intoxicating smell a-way.*

"As you wish. Oh, and feline," he whispered in her ear.

"What?"

"A six-letter word for cat is *feline*," he chuckled before loping off toward the stairs, taking them two at a time with his long, muscled legs. Petey and Paulie followed on his heels, flying up the stairs in a tumbleweed of fur and yips, but thankfully, no voices in her head.

Marty stuck her head around Katie's shoulder and sighed, coffee in hand. "He's fucktastic, don't you think?"

"Fuck what?"

"It's one of the beast Nina's favorite words," Casey called. "It means he's fabulous and worthy of a good sheet shining. You have to admit, he's like a Blow Pop. One you wanna lick till you get to the middle."

The idea of licking Beck came in a hot rush and left in a gay one. "Aren't we all a little old to be gushing over a twenty-year-old?"

"It's what makes us unafraid to gush. We're secure in our womanhood, and every one of us happily married. We gush from afar, but we still gush. Lighten up, Katie," Marty chided with a grin. "It's not a crime to find a man of his age attractive. Whatever that age is, I'd bet it's at the very least legal. It looks like Beck's going to be around, at least for a little while, until he remembers who he is, and we figure this out. So enjoy the view. Especially the one from behind." She followed her words with a wink.

"Yeah, it's not like we're telling you to ride the landscape in your womanhood Hummer. Just appreciate it from afar if it makes you uncomfortable to *gush*," Casey reminded.

"He's gay. The point of appreciation then becomes null and void." Her response sounded so stuffy and snobbish. Neither of which she was.

"Oh, he is not either gay, Katie," Marty protested, snaring Muffin and hoisting her over her shoulder.

"Yes, he is." He damned well better be. It was her only hope for survival after the way just one word of his approval affected all regions womanesque on her body.

Casey clucked her tongue. "If he was thinking about your taters, I highly doubt he's gay."

"Maybe he was thinking about surgically acquiring a pair of his own that were fashioned after mine?" Transgenders had implant surgery all the time. Though any surgeon who took on the task of changing Beck's gender had his work cut out for him with all that hard, gruff exterior to work with. He'd make an ugly woman.

Marty chuckled. "You, as a veterinarian, know this already, but it bears saying the rule applies to the paranormal, too. Primarily, shapeshifters of the animal variety remain true to animal kingdom rules in their sexual behaviors. I can't say I've ever seen two male werewolves shack up, set up housekeeping, and make crème brûlée together in their nest of love. Not that I'd care, mind you. I'm every bit as progressive as the next person. I support love, period. I'm just saying it hasn't ever happened that I'm aware of. So if you hoped to fend off that growing attraction you have going on for him by telling yourself he's gay—I'd find a new distraction. It's okay to think he's yummy. We won't point fingers."

Noooo. Katie briefly rolled her eyes heavenward. *Please, please don't let that be true. I can't afford another attraction to a man that will only bring me trouble.* "But he likes *Project Runway*." Admittedly, a feeble defense if ever there was one.

Casey took one last sip of coffee before taking her cup to the big copper basin sink to rinse it. "And I like *Ice Road Truckers*, but I can assure you, I'm not a lesbian, and Beck didn't say he liked *Project Runway*. As I recall, it just sparked a memory for him."

Katie let her eyes slide closed when she leaned her hip against the counter. He had to be gay. Period. She'd accept nothing less.

"Katie!" her aunt yelled to her from the door. "Come out front, girl. We got company!" Teeny stuffed her gardening gloves into the pocket of her red-and-black-flannel jacket, her nostrils flaring, the air wheezing in and out of her lungs from so many years of smoking.

Katie grabbed her black knit hat and camouflage jacket before pushing her way out the front door to find Sheriff Glenn standing within the frame of the door of his police car. "Ms. Woods," he drawled, leisurely and slow, as though saying her name was more an accusation than a greeting. He tipped his big sheriff's hat at her, though his small eyes suggested disdain.

Not a look unfamiliar to her.

"Sheriff Glenn," Katie addressed him back, mirroring his tone as she took the front porch steps with heavy feet, pretending she had no idea why he could have possibly shown up. "What can I help you with?"

For sure, they'd been caught red-handed violating the restraining order. Surely, Sheriff Glenn had decided that was cause for their profiles to be placed on the FBI's Ten Most Wanted list.

He sucked in his large cheeks, resting his arm on the top of the police car door. "You got friends in visiting from the fancy city?"

Suspicion sent off a thousand alarms in her head. "And if I do?"

He smacked his thick lips together, then smiled cordially. "Visiting hours are between one and two and then again at five and six. You might wanna write that down."

Teeny grasped a garden rake between her two palms, planting it in a defensive stance in front of her. "Get to the point, for gravy's sake, Everett. Stop with all the mystery theater."

Everett Glenn's eyes snapped to Teeny. "Fine by me, Bettina. Your niece's fancy city friend and the one with the mouth the size of the biggest crater on the moon are in lockup. If she's wantin' to pay 'em a visit, you'd better be on time."

Katie's eyes widened, but not before Teeny swung into action, lifting the rake high over her head and charging the sheriff. "Everett! What the hell's gotten into you? Wha'd you do with those women?"

Katie lunged for her aunt, stepping in front of her and yanking the rake out of her hands with a force that surprised not just Teeny but her, too. The rake swung upward in a wild arc before she threw it, much like a javelin, across the lawn where it landed with a clatter against a rusty propane tank.

That feat brought with it an astonished silence until Casey and Marty flew down the steps in a flurry of heels and fashionable clothing. Casey's eyes zeroed in on Everett. "What's going on here? Katie? Aunt Teeny? Everything all right?"

The sheriff assessed the two women with critical small-town eyes. "More *city* friends?"

Katie's chin lifted as she set a spitting mad Teeny behind her. "It's none of your business if they're from the city or from an alternate universe, Sheriff Glenn. Now what have you done with Wanda and Nina?"

Everett clasped his hands together in a slow clench, cracking his knuckles, clearly deriving great pleasure from toying with her. "I arrested 'em." He let the words linger, smirking when Marty and Casey gasped.

"For?" Katie demanded.

The sheriff took his time getting into his cruiser, turning the key in a slow motion for effect. He leaned out the window with a smirk before finally saying, "For assault and battery on old man Green. He's in a coma, and your fancy friends are responsible for putting him there!"

CHAPTER
7

Beck eyed his shelf work critically, shoving slips of lace and silk out of his eyes. He inhaled the scent of lavender and musk on frilly lingerie neatly hanging in row upon row of satin hangers.

Katie's scent.

Delicious.

He'd noted almost everything she wore had some sort of lace on it, her shirt, the cuffs of her jeans. It only added to the allure of the curves he'd eyed and the swell of her shapely hips.

But here was the proof, hanging in almost every color of the rainbow in all shapes and scanty sizes. It brought with it hot, sweaty images of skin upon skin and deft fingers beneath short hems—heavy breathing—supple-smooth berries-and-cream skin—the sound of gasps of pleasure.

His ridiculous borrowed jeans tightened. He had no business lusting for a woman when he couldn't remember what his name was or how he'd come upon said woman.

But what a woman.

Beck frowned, forcing himself to focus on the shelves and not the scraps of silken temptations.

He found if he had something to focus on other than his predicament or what he'd seen last night, he could stand to be in this unfamiliar skin.

And his unfamiliar name.

He grimaced. Beck. For all he knew that could well be his name. Yet, he'd found, since this had all begun, he had a knack for getting a feel for what sat right and what didn't.

Beck felt wrong. But no more wrong than Spanky did. He only knew both names were wrong.

Now cougars and things that bloody well went bump in the night, sucked blood to remain upright, and set fire to inanimate objects via fingertips on the other hand, definitely had a strange, distant ring that lingered for a second or two then blew up into a cloud of disbelief.

Only to return with a nagging sense of urgency he could neither pinpoint nor find a shred of evidence to support. It was just there—ominous, dark.

While there was plenty of ominous and dark, there was also a sense of safety with these women and Katie. One he couldn't explain and was probably best left viewed for what it was worth. Borrowed time and a place to rest his head while he tried to figure out how he'd ended up here. A port in a storm. A sexy one, but one nonetheless.

The notion he was responsible for the fair Dr. Woods's peculiar condition made him not just cringe but determined to find a way to help her. A compelling need to right a wrong he wasn't wholly convinced he'd committed sat rooted in his gut.

And there it was. That nagging familiarity about this situation. Almost like he'd been here—done this. He just couldn't remember when or how.

Damned well frustrating.

Beck leaned against the wall of the walk-in closet, brushing impatiently at the wisps of nightgowns, and reviewed what information he did have.

He was British—a man—not entirely bad-looking, if the reflection he saw in the mirror wasn't distorted by his amnesia. Though, admittedly, Supermodel Ground Control wasn't going to be in any hurry to book him a print ad with Abercrombie and Fitch.

He was at least six-foot-two. When he'd weighed himself on Katie's scale this morning, he was two hundred point two pounds. And he liked cartoons. He'd caught an episode of *Scooby-Doo* on the television in his loaned pink-and-purple bedroom and had known exactly when Scooby would want a snack.

He also, apparently, liked *Project Runway* or knew of the show's existence.

Which he was sure had left at least one or two of those women believing he was light in his loafers. Unlike most heterosexual men who would find that particular bit of information disturbing and become defensive about it, Beck found he didn't much mind.

Sweet baby Jesus.

Maybe he was in fact a knob jockey.

He snatched a handful of Katie's lingerie in his palm and inhaled deeply.

Well then.

No. He wasn't gay.

Just secure.

He grinned.

"CASEY! S'up, demonlicious?" A man held his knuckled fist forward for Casey to butt.

Out of nowhere, a portly, enormously tall man with heavy gold chains around his neck, a NY Giants jersey, jeans that fell past his round belly, high-top Nikes, gold teeth, and the widest grin Katie'd ever seen had appeared.

Out of thin air.

One minute she and the women were all in Teeny's kitchen, worrying about how to spring Wanda and Nina while her aunt, angry to the point of fuming, had gone to lie down and take her heart medication. The next, a man who scooped Casey up in a bear hug, was standing in front of her, smiling and bringing with him an air of joviality.

Hooking her arm through his, Casey leaned her head on his shoulder and said, "Darnell, meet Dr. Katie Woods, DVM."

He cocked his shortly cropped head and held out his hand to Katie, who took it without fear. "She the one?" he asked Casey.

"Yep. She's it."

He groaned, rubbing his rotund belly. "Oh, lady. You sho went and done it, huh?"

Katie nodded, her head still whirling from his sudden appearance. Oh. She'd done. "It seems I've definitely overachieved here. Pleasure to meet you. Casey says you can help with my asperity."

Darnell shot Casey a confused glance. "Her who-ity?"

Katie smiled. "My predicament."

He ran his large palm over the top of his head, giving it a good scruff. "I dunno if I can help you. Don't know a lot about cats. Though don't you worry, I got me some feelers out right now 'bout your kind. But I sho can get those two women out the poe-poe fo they turn this into some paranormal hootenanny. So tell old Darnell what all happened up in here?"

Casey explained what Marty and Nina were accused of while Darnell's face went from one expressive state to the next. "Hoo, boy," he whistled when she was finished. "The men know what's goin' on right now?" he asked, and Katie assumed he meant their husbands.

Casey popped her lips with a wince. "They're golfing and the less they know, the better, don't you agree?"

Darnell winked. "Clay'll kill me, so yeah, I'm wit ya and never you mind. Darnell's got yer back. So where am I goin', and who I gotta take out when I get there?"

Katie blanched, but Casey placed a reassuring hand on her arm. "Don't worry. Darnell would never hurt anyone. He's just going to pose as Nina and Wanda's lawyer and post bail. We'll keep everything on the up-and-up so as not to arouse suspicion. That means no mind games, Darnell. Keep Vampira out of that sheriff's head, okay?"

Katie didn't mean for the eyeballing she gave Darnell to come off as quite so critical, but lawyerish, Darnell wasn't.

He chuckled deep, gurgling his glee. "It ain't like dat. I know what you thinkin', Katie. Darnell don't look like no lawyer you ever did see. But watch this." He looked over his shoulder to see if Teeny was in the vicinity before he simply rolled his broad frame, gave a shake, and instantly turned into the polar opposite of his former self.

He ran a now slender, dark hand down along the length of his dark gray suit to smooth away non-existent wrinkles. His grin was still just as wide. It was just on an entirely different face.

One that was no longer cherubic and reminiscent of Santa Claus, but instead, sharply angled and gaunt as though he'd spent many skipped meals fighting injustice in courtrooms.

Katie remained silent, taking in yet another paranormal oddity.

"Whacked, right?" he teased.

She shook her head. She didn't know what she meant any-more. Was nothing she'd seen in a movie or on television made up? Everything had become so *Twilight* only without the sparklies. "How . . . I mean what . . ."

"I'm demon, just like Casey," Darnell explained. "But I have the ability to shapeshift into different forms. Casey can, too, but she's just a little demon right now. It just takes time and practice to learn to take on different shapes."

Casey nodded with a chuckle. "Someday, when all this has passed, I'll tell you all about the time I tried to take on Megan Fox's form—and we'll laugh and laugh, because I can finally do that—now, anyway. Until then, Darnell, you go get the girls, and do me a favor. Whatever you do, zap Nina's mouth shut. All we need is for her to bend the bars on her cell like the Hulk because her temper got the best of her and she wants out of her cage. She'll just create more trouble for Katie than we already have."

Darnell eyed Casey with a concerned gaze. "Has Nina fed today?"

Casey shook her head. "No. Which means you need to hurry, or I can guarantee you that poor Sheriff Glenn won't be doing any local blood donation drives anytime soon."

Darnell nodded at the urgency of Casey's words. "Aiiiight. I'm out. We'll be back in no time flat." With those words, he was gone as swiftly as he'd entered.

Katie's head spun, her legs growing weak and limp. Marty swung an arm around her shoulder to steady her. "Don't worry, Katie. Darnell will get them out, and then we can figure out what's going on. Trust me. He knows what he's doing."

Two hours later and an unsuccessful nap under her belt, Katie let Marty guide her to the kitchen chair, plunking down in it with a depleted sigh. She was too tired to question her sudden trust in these complete strangers. Yet, there were things nagging her about this man Nina and Wanda were accused of putting in a coma. "Who is this old man Green?" she wondered, more to herself than to the people in the room, letting her head drop to the crook of her arm. "And how did he end up in a coma?"

"Daniel Green?" Beck asked, coming down the stairs, a hammer in his hand.

Katie's head shot up. "You know him?"

He let his fist, full of nails, drop to the railing of the old, oak banister, a frown lining his forehead. "I don't know where that came from."

Well, facepalm then. "Silly me."

Beck's eyes narrowed, glittering to fine, angry points. "Now don't you get all huffy with me, pussycat. I really don't know where that came from. I heard you use the surname Green and the rest just popped into my head and came out of my mouth."

Katie ran a thumb over her temple, a dull throb forming between her brows. "Well, whoever he is, he's in a coma, and apparently, Nina and Wanda have been arrested for it. Why or how Sheriff Glenn thinks they're involved is yet to be determined."

His wide chest expanded under his short shirt, his gasp, clearly one filled with anguish. "A coma?"

Marty nodded, her brows knitting together. "That's what he said. Did his name jar something loose? A memory?"

Beck slid down to sit on the wide step at the end of the staircase, dominating the surface. "I can't quite explain it, but hearing you say Daniel Green's in a coma pains me."

"But you don't know why, blah-blah-blah," Katie blew the words out of her mouth, her chest tight, her lungs suddenly in need of air, though her eyes were still in fine working order if the roll of them at Beck's answer was any indication.

He scowled when he stood up, sauntering in her direction in all of his sauntering yumminess. "That's right, Dr. Woods. I don't know why, but I promise to try harder to find explanations in the time you deem appropriate." His words weren't just filled with his frustration but underlying anger that she clearly wasn't coming to proper terms with his amnesia.

It wasn't his fault. Katie realized that even as she fought to catch her breath, becoming more labored and erratic with each gasp.

Beck was instantly standing over her, then kneeling in front of her to capture her gaze. "Katie? What's wrong?" He ran a hand over her forehead, the feel of his skin against hers welcome and consoling.

Remembering Casey's and Wanda's warnings about the animal kingdom and the laws of nature, she waved his hand away, struggling to move out of his close proximity and failing when she flopped back down in the chair. Each struggle for breath she took left her bones feeling like melting butter. "I feel so weak and out of breath all of a sudden."

"Oh!" Marty yelped. "I know what's happening." She moved out of Katie's line of vision to head toward the refrigerator. Reaching in, she handed the package she pulled out to Beck. "You need to eat. I'd bet you didn't have breakfast. Just some coffee, right?"

Right, she nodded with a weak bob of her head. Coffee and the gut-wrenching wish to eat some deer whole.

"Protein," Casey declared. "Meat, Katie. You need meat. You're now at least half carnivore. A carnivore that hasn't had a sufficient amount of protein to feed the changes your body's going through."

Beck held up the package and smiled devilishly. "What would you do for a Scooby snack?"

Marty grabbed it from him with a glare and slapped the package of deli roast beef in front of her. "Eat. Eat it all. Trust me when I tell you, I get this part of the change in your body. I was a vegan before I was turned. Now I'd eat a whole herd of cattle given the opportunity and some alone time on a grassy slope. You can't deny it, so don't bother. I'm going to keep my fingers crossed that while you're in this odd limbo you don't need to wax your legs twice a day like I did. But that's a story for another time. Right now, I'll look in the freezer to see if we can't find something else of more substance, but for now, this'll take the edge off."

Wax? Twice a day? Her hand would have immediately gone to her legs, which were lucky if they saw a razor once a month these days, but she was thwarted by the delicious call of protein in all its deli-liciousness.

The roast beef became an instant temptation, making Katie slide her fingers into the package and fight to keep from tearing it out in a huge hunk. Instead, her shaky fingers argued with one another to take only one delicate slice and not shove it all down her throat.

"Bread? Plate?" Beck inquired, lines of concern marring his forehead all while he kept an amused smile plastered across his lips.

Katie shook her head as the smell of the roast beef engulfed her every sense. Who needed cutlery? Oh, the aroma, redolent, rich with garlic and spices. It was all she could do not to bury her nose in the bag and inhale it all at once. She slid the slice into her mouth and buried a groan of instant satisfaction.

Beck dropped a paper napkin in front of her. "You know, for the carnage," he said with a snide smile.

"I'm worried about Wanda and Nina," Katie said out of the side of her mouth, renewed energy rushing through her veins with each bite she took. Her head began to clear while her veins hummed with blood.

"Hah!" Beck snorted. "I'd worry more for her jailor and cell mates."

Her stomach thanked her by way of a burp she stifled against her good hand. "I don't know the name Green, and while I haven't been in town very long, I know most everyone due to Aunt Teeny. I'm betting he was the guy who was here last night. That's the only connection Wanda and Nina have to me and someone here in town. So who do you think he is and how did he end up in a coma? For that matter, how could Nina and Wanda possibly be held responsible for it?"

A chilled gust of wind swept across her feet as the front door opened.

"He's the guy who was here last night. You remember him, right?" Nina inquired, stomping through the door, Wanda and Darnell, now returned to his former self, in tow. "The one who accused us of stealing whatever we're calling *him*?" She pointed at Beck with the snap of her finger and an accusatory glance.

Oh, shit.

"Yeah," Nina said in scathing tones, looking down into Katie's face. "That's what I said, too. So here's what the deal is. They hauled our asses in for questioning because of that dude. Wanna know why, Doc?"

No.

Nina made a face moments after Katie felt her rooting around in her head. "Well, too fucking bad, because I'm gonna tell you anyway. That geriatric nut gave our descriptions just before he fell into a coma. Do you have any idea what it's like to be in a jail cell with John-Boy and Bubba? Lady, I gotta tell ya, I'm not down with doin' time with the Beverly Hillbillies. I don't know what kind of bullshit you had going on before we got here, but I want out."

Wanda held her hand up in Nina's furious face, her own weary. "Quiet. It's hardly Katie's fault we landed in jail, and it isn't like they weren't amicable roomies. John-Boy did let you use the only pillow in the entire place. He was generous almost to a fault."

Nina tightened the strings of her hoodie with a harsh yank. "Was that before or after he blew his Hungry-Man dinner on my goddamned shoes, Wanda?"

Beck diverted Nina, taking her by the arm and leading her to the fridge, away from Katie. "Look, Dark Overlord—your friend, the one who came to rescue you, brought you a little snicky-snack. This should make everything right as rain."

He popped open the fridge to show Nina the blood Darnell had packed into the fridge in discreet brown wrapping she'd have to remember to move to the fridge in her office so Teeny wouldn't try to cook with it. He waved his arm with flourish like he was Vanna White, revealing *Wheel of Fortune* letters. Nina's face instantly lightened a shade.

"What happened?" Katie asked, struggling to focus on Wanda and not on the fact that Nina was preparing to drink blood. *Blood.* Like she was grabbing a Bud or a Pepsi . . .

Wanda squinted, pausing for only a moment. "We were in the middle of that dime-slash-feed store, Pappy's, shopping for some decent clothes for poor Beck and supplies, when the good sheriff of Piney Creek hauled us out of there like we were serial killers, guns drawn." Her words hitched and she paused, biting her knuckle to obviously keep from screaming her humiliation. She took another breath. "Ohhhh, the guns."

"Biiiig fucking guns," Nina drawled, leaning down to leer at Wanda. "Like shotguns or some shit."

Wanda reached up and clamped Nina's lips together to continue. "Anyway, he took us to the police station for questioning about this Daniel Green."

"So his first name *is* Daniel?" Beck interjected, his eyes searching Wanda's face.

Wanda nodded. "He was the man who was here last night and, according to the sheriff, beaten pretty badly when he was found by one of the janitors at the exotic animal park. Just before he slipped into a coma, he pointed the finger at Nina and me. The officer said he told them he'd been here at Katie's office last night and we were responsible for stealing Spanky, er, Beck. The. Cat.

He gave descriptions, though the sheriff did say they were disjointed and rambling, that matched ours. We, of course, are the obvious suspects. New in town, strangers etcetera. Clearly, after a gander around your town, we do look like we fell off the pages of . . ." She paused. "What was it the sheriff said Daniel claimed, Nina?"

Nina snorted. "*Good Housekeeping*. Like we fell off the pages of *Good Housekeeping*."

"Right." Wanda looked almost affronted. "Obviously, this Daniel Green's never seen *Cosmo*. Nonetheless, next thing I know, we're behind bars and in need of an outrageous amount of bail. It was dreadful."

Katie shook her head in disbelief. "I don't know what to say. If anything, he should have blamed me. So who would beat Daniel Green badly enough to leave him in a coma?"

Wanda pinched her temples. "Like I said, one of the janitors found him early this morning, and no one has any explanation for how he ended up in such bad shape."

"That led to a *coma*," Nina muttered. "If the dude dies, we could be up for manslaughter. So now you know what, Doc?"

Katie licked her lips in a gesture of nervous anticipation. "I can't wait."

"Me and Wanda here—we can't leave town until we're cleared of any wrongdoing. Know what else that means?"

"I should wash more sheets?" For whatever reason, Katie was reluctantly soothed by the fact that at least two of the shifter brigade would remain close.

"It means I'm going to be even crankier than I was when I showed the fuck up last night."

Beck chuckled. "Does this mean I should break out the band saw and plane some wood for the coffin so a good night's rest is in your future, milady?"

Nina gave him a playful jab in the arm. "No. It means you better hide your jugular."

Wanda waved a hand at Nina. "Go finish feeding. Shut up." She turned to Katie. "We won't trouble you. We can stay at the motel in town until this is cleared up."

Katie shook her head with vehemence. "No. I've discommoded you both. I won't have you staying in some flea-infested hotel."

Beck cocked his head. "What does this have to do with the commode?"

She waved a hand at him. "It means to put someone out. Inconvenience them. Sorry, it's all those crossword puzzles I do. I love words . . . Never mind." She shoved more roast beef in her mouth to still her tongue.

Wanda gave Katie's good hand a pat. "Hopefully, this will be cleared up soon, and we won't put you out for too long."

"It'd be cleared up if you'd have just let me get inside that sheriff's big-assed, hillbilly head, Wanda," Nina shouted.

Wanda shook her head. "Oh, no. No way am I going to let you mess around some poor soul's mind. You still don't have the ability to make your magic stick. No matter how misguided he is about our innocence, we're playing this straight for Katie's sake. From the grumblings we heard in town, she doesn't need any more hassles."

Nina snorted and tilted her dark head at Katie. "Yeah. It's like you have the plague or some shit. Every time we told people who we were staying with, they suddenly got hinky."

Katie stopped devouring the roast beef, her eyes unable to meet theirs. "I'm so sorry. The people in town, they . . . well, they didn't much like me setting up shop here. They think I've usurped the town's only veterinarian and taken business from him. They don't share well. Anyway, that's not the point right now. The point is, you've been accused of something wrongfully, and I'll go right down to the sheriff's and tell him so myself." She rose on unsteady legs, regaining her footing in time to wave off Beck's hand to her elbow.

"Wasted energy, Katie," Wanda replied. "The sheriff has an eyewitness to the crime—the victim himself—and while all he can do is question us right now, because this Daniel Green didn't accuse us of actually committing the crime, Sheriff Glenn can legally require that we not leave town."

Katie stopped in her tracks. She knew a little about the law—unfortunately, none of it was good. She'd once been ordered not to leave town . . . "You're right, but there's no way you'll be staying at that motel. You'll stay here. It's the least I can do after all the trouble I caused. If not for Ingrid's call to you, this never would have happened. So it's settled. No more talk of motels."

Beck leaned into her ear, sending a wave of delicious chills along her exposed flesh. "Shall I begin that coffin?" he teased, his breath warm, the heat of his body close.

Katie licked her lips, the savory roast beef still lingering on her lips. "I'd be very careful, were I you."

"Because?"

"I get the impression Nina isn't in love with our little town. Don't rile the vampire."

Nina scraped her chair away from the table. "Yeah," she agreed. "Don't. She riles easily. And save the stupid-ass jokes about coffins. I don't sleep in a coffin, Prince Charles. I sleep in a bed. With my man. A man I can't see because of you, pal. You started all this shit. If I were you, I'd start trying to remember something, or I'll knock your amnesia right the fuck out of you."

"Speaking of men," Casey said. "Marty and I have to go cover for Wanda and Nina. First and foremost, because we have children. Second, those men will want explanations when they get home tomorrow. If we're not there to provide them, you'll have far worse descending upon your quiet little town than four mouthy women."

Marty hoisted Muffin over her shoulder, giving Katie a smile and a quick hug. "But don't worry. Darnell's on it. If anyone can find any information about what's next, it's Darnell. And we won't be far. If you need us, all you have to do is call. I promise you, even though Nina's a bitch in secondhand clothing, and she's difficult and mouthy, she's got your back. No one's better at taking on a large, angry crowd than mouth here. Okay?"

Katie gulped, returning Marty's hug and giving Casey a quick one, too. "Thank you, both of you. I don't know how all of this will end, or what to expect, but I appreciate everything you've done."

"Don't you worry 'bout nuthin', Doc Katie," Darnell said, his grin wide, the beefy hand he placed on her shoulder kind and reassuring. "I'm gonna find you some info. Till then, if you need me, all you gotta do is think my name and I'm here." He pointed to the spot on the old wood flooring where he stood.

Casey chuckled at Katie's eleven-millionth surprised expression. "It's true. If you can't find one of us, think up Darnell. Just picture him in your mind—that's all it takes. Now be safe, and remember what Wanda told you. There'll be a day when you'll laugh about this. Promise. Beck? You take care, and I sure hope you figure this out. Nina? Shut your big, opinionated mouth, and try to remember you're a guest here. Wanda—call me and keep me updated. Love you both." She gave Wanda a hug and Nina a jab in her upper arm.

Darnell held out his hands to each woman. "Ladies, you ready?"

Marty blew Katie a kiss before taking the demon's hand. "Ready."

Casey nodded, too, before adding, "Say good-bye to Ingrid and Kaih for us."

They were gone in a shimmer of light and shade, as though they'd never been.

Beck stood silent for a moment, clearly taking in Darnell's ability to disappear with two women and a poodle in tow. "Do you suppose we cougars can disappear into thin air like that? I find it very amusing, not to mention useful."

"You mean for when you want to hurry home from the roller rink so you won't miss your milk and cookies before your nap?"

Beck cocked his head, dark and delicious, while he rolled up his sleeves. "Wow. I guess you are old. Aren't roller rinks extinct?"

Katie's cheeks burned two bright spots of pink. She rolled her tongue in her cheek and narrowed her eyes, forcing herself to remember she was his elder, and there was an example to be set. "How do you feel about laundry? Lots of it? We have guests who need fresh linens, and we need to move that blood to my office refrigerator so Aunt Teeny doesn't do something crazy like cook with it."

Beck cocked an eyebrow at her, his expression arrogant. "What if I told you I can't remember how to do laundry?"

"I'd tell you to read the instructions on the back of the laundry soap."

"Dooooc Woooods!" Ingrid hollered, skidding around the kitchen doorway. "Hurry! We have a patient!"

Katie crossed her arms over her chest, noting her ACE bandage was a little looser than it had been this morning. "I thought we agreed to close up shop for the day? Doesn't Dr. Jules take emergencies?" She fought the sting of his name on her tongue, but she couldn't hide the spiteful sarcasm saying his name out loud held.

Ingrid grabbed her arm, tugging her to the reception area. "She said she had to see you! Hurry, and Beck, you come, too, please. We might need help."

Katie stopped short just beyond her reception desk and realized who her patient's owner was.

Well, if people weren't talking before today's events, Daniel Green's coma, and her fancy New York friends who were arrested, they'd be wagging their tongues now at who sat on her waiting room couch.

Esmeralda Hunt.

The woman the warm, welcoming people of Piney Creek had labeled a modern-day witch.

CHAPTER
8

At this point in her week, after all the shifting, fanging, fireballing, and disappearing had come and gone, Katie began to wonder if the people of Piney Creek might not have some merit to their suspicions about Esmeralda Hunt.

Far be it for her to ever again in her lifetime say, "Fill in the blank doesn't exist." Because it did.

And it was in her kitchen.

Drinking blood.

Oh. God.

Katie made her way toward Esmeralda, hunched on her waiting room sofa with her bulldog Delray on her lap. Esmeralda had lived in Piney Creek for ten years now since the death of her husband, Nigel. No one knew a lot about her, and she didn't offer up much about herself—which was always an excuse for the Piney Creek residents to gossip.

She sure didn't look like a witch—not by one's typical definition. There were no warts, long, straggly black hair, or a pointy hat. If she'd come by way of broom, from the looks of Delray's stout body, it was probably in two pieces outside the clinic's door.

But then, aside from her hand and those crazy teeth that had sprung from her mouth last night, she didn't suspect anyone would brand her a cougar, either. Maybe by society's definition, but not by the animal kingdom's.

Esmeralda's coal black eyes were lined with fear and worry, her lips, colored in a cherry red that flattered her pale skin, trembled. Her gamine face, surrounded by a short fall of neat dark hair with threads of silver in it, screamed concerned as Delray moaned in her arms. Her legs were crossed at her ankles, her pristine white sneakers, digging into the floor to keep a grip on her overweight dog.

Delray, a red-brindle-and-white English bulldog lay flaccid in her lap, his tongue lolling from his mouth as he panted his pain, his black-and-white-checkered bow tie askew around his neck.

Ingrid quivered at her side. "You're not actually considering treating *her* dog, are you, Dr. Woods? I mean, they say she's a witch," Ingrid whispered with a hiss. "A witch who cast a spell on Doreen Panzowski. Everybody in town says Esmeralda made all of Doreen's hair fall out just because she denied her access to the gardening club. And that's not even the half of what they say she does up at that cottage of hers with all those plants and herbs she grows."

Katie's temper spiked. "Uh, Ingrid? Hello in there. Have you considered we're sort of in the same boat, Mrs. Hunt and I?" She held up her hand as a point of reference. "And no one in town likes me, either, but I'm certainly not going to turn away an animal in pain who clearly needs medical attention. For all we know, she really is a witch. It's not like we're making a huge leap into the fantastical after last night, wouldn't you agree?"

Ingrid paled at her admonishment. "Okay, you're right. It sucks to be labeled, but I'm telling you right now, if my hair falls out, you owe me the Hair Club for Men, at the very least. And I'm flying low on the radar with this one. If, in fact, we're going with the theory that anything is possible, then it's definitely possible Esmeralda put a hex on Doreen, and that's why she lost her hair. I like my hair."

Katie rechecked her hand to be sure it was properly covered before she moved toward Esmeralda. "Mrs. Hunt? What's the trouble with Delray?"

Her eyes caught Katie's, the eyes of a pet owner whose beloved companion was in distress. Delray moaned, low and mournful, his liquid brown eyes staring up at her. "I don't know," she whimpered. "He hasn't eaten at all today, and if you take one good look at my Delray, he doesn't miss many meals. I even tried tempting him with a can of soft food, but he just won't eat. Then about an hour ago, I couldn't even coax him into some of my chicken salad. Delray loves my chicken salad—especially when I make it with pickles. When he wouldn't move an inch, I knew something was wrong. I hauled his big carcass over to Dr. Jules, but . . ." She bit back the rest of her words, but her eyes welled with the tears of what Katie deduced were from Dr. Jules refusal to treat Delray. "I hope you take emergencies. I'll pay whatever the cost. Please, please help him. He's all I have!" Her sob tore at Katie's heart and ate a hole of resentment that Dr. Jules would turn any patient away for any reason.

Beck was at her side immediately, kneeling before Esmeralda and running a large hand over Delray's ears. "Why don't you let me carry him to the examining room, Mrs. Hunt? He's a rather portly boy, eh? Much too much of a load for a woman of your delicate frame to lug around. I promise to be very gentle with him," he coaxed, crooning to her in those honeyed British tones. He held out his arms, and the tune of Ingrid's sigh in her ears made Katie's spine stiffen.

"You know what he is, Doc?" Ingrid said on a sigh.

"What?"

"He's a four-letter word for salacious."

"Sexy?" she replied almost automatically.

Ingrid waved her hand while she stared at Beck's retreating back. "I don't know. He's just so everything," she drawled on another breath.

Yeah, yeah, yeah. Sexy, salacious Beck. It infuriated her. "Uh-huh, and he's so who did this to me and so who had your bowels making bricks all colors of the rainbow last night. How quickly we forget," Katie commented out of the side of her mouth, following Beck into the examining room.

What it was that made her resent Ingrid's sudden turnabout as far as Beck was concerned was something she'd examine more closely later. Maybe while she was brushing her paw and waxing her legs. "Bring Mrs. Hunt in so Delray doesn't become agitated, would you please, Ingrid?"

Beck settled the dog on a blanket he'd grabbed from the shelves and stroked his back. Katie washed her good hand and grabbed her stethoscope.

Ingrid seated a shaky Esmeralda by Delray's side so she could remain close.

Katie lifted Delray's back end to roll him so she could get a better feel of his abdomen.

Easy on the ass there, lady. It's killin' me.

Katie's head popped up. She eyeballed all parties present in the examining room. No one made a suspicious glance at Delray. In fact, no one stirred. The examining room was deathly quiet.

Except for the voices in her head.

Katie shook off what must be her imagination. It had to be lack of sleep. She'd only had one cup of coffee this morning, thus leaving her delusional. "All right, big guy," she crooned to him, feeling his sides for any swelling or irregularities. "I hate to tell you this, but I have to, you know, see what's going on down there. First up, we need to take your temp." Ingrid handed her the thermometer to insert, running her free hand over his wide head to comfort him.

Delray squirmed. *Tell your friend patting me on the head won't make me feel any better about you sticking that thing up my shitter.*

She closed her eyes and sighed a long release of aggravation. No. Seriously? Like really? No. It was her imagination. That's what it had been this morning, and that's what it was now.

Please, please, please let it be her imagination. Katie stared down into the chocolate brown eyes of Delray and decided, against her better judgment, to test her sanity. "I promise to be gentle, Del. Just hold still, buddy."

Is there any gentle when you have something shoved up your ass? And save the crazy-ass baby talk for somebody who's stupid enough to be cootchie-cootchie-cooed into some false sense of security by it. I been to this rodeo, lady. I know what the cutesy thing means in a setting like this. I'm gettin' it up the pooper. Don't let all those supposed dog gurus tell you any different, either. We might not be the smartest bunch in the chain, but we ain't total fargin' idiots, either. We know when we're being conned because something bad's about to go down. The bad being that thing shoved up my keister.

Her mouth fell open.

Oh, c'mon. Was there really any more crazy left to be had? Wasn't it all used up with werewolves and vampires and demons?

So are we doin' this? Or are you just gonna keep wavin' that thing at me like some kinda threat? Get it over with already. My ass is killin' me, and make sure you tell Esmeralda there better be some of that canned food in this for me, or I'll shit all over her bed first chance I get. When I can shit again, that is. I'm bound up like a goddamned chain caught in the spoke of a bicycle wheel.

Katie cleared her throat, rolling her neck from side to side. Was no one aware the dog . . . The. Dog. Was talking to her? Was she the only one who'd flown over this cuckoo's nest?

Beck eyed her from his stance against the far wall with a look of question, but thankfully, Esmeralda was too wrapped up in her worry over Delray to notice the disbelief Katie was sure she was doing a bad job of disguising via her bulging eyes.

Ingrid nudged her while shuffling her feet. "You got it?"

"Yes! Sorry." She aimed her apology at Esmeralda. "Long night last night. Okay, Del, here goes. Ingrid, if you'll just hold him still." She inserted the thermometer with care and frowned at the eventual reading. He had a temperature.

Katie leaned down to capture Delray's big head in her hands. If this was really happening, if Delray was really communicating with her, it could work to her advantage. She'd deal with the crazy of it later. In her best baby-talk voice, knowing it would incite him, Katie asked, "So what have you been eating lately, sunshine?"

Nothing . . .

"Aha! I see guilt in those eyes, pookie. C'mon, tell Dr. Woods what you've been eating." Katie almost snickered, but then she caught a shared look of Delray's shame on Esmeralda's face, too.

"Cheese! He loves cheese. I caught him stealing a whole hunk of it from my coffee table the other day. That binds, right? I can't think of what else it could be." Esmeralda's admission wrought one from Delray.

Oh, fine. She's right. I love cheese. Gouda, Roquefort, blue, Brie, sharp cheddar, goat. You name it, I'm down with it. But I swear, Doc, I only ate a little Muenster the other day. Definitely not enough to bind me up like this, and she's not tellin' the whole truth. She gave me the hunk of cheese.

All I gotta do is whimper and give her the pouty, sad eyes and she gives it up. She's the easiest mark on planet human.

Katie clucked her tongue, not entirely convinced. Her eyes held the dogs again. "How about foreign objects, Del? You know, like shoes, socks, tennis balls maybe?"

Esmeralda gasped. "Oh, Delray! I know what it was. It was my shoe. I'd bet my subscription to *Martha Stewart Living* he's been chewing on it under my bed." She gave Delray a frown of disapproval. "He knows I can't bend down to chase after him because my knees trouble me so, so he takes everything and hides it under the bed. I've been looking for days for that espadrille, Delray, and you know it. Shame on you!"

Katie eyed the dog, now tucking his chin to his chest, his eyes unable to connect with hers. "Oh, Del. Is that true, sweetums? Did you eat a shoe, you silly-willy?"

Whatev-er. I ate the shoe. Like that's a crime. It's not like I ate a cat, okay? She leaves them by the door all the time. What's a dog to do when all that tempting hand-stitched, straight-from-Spain footwear's sitting by the door, just asking to be consumed? I'm a dog, for pity's sake. Some people paint. We eat shoes.

Katie fought a chuckle. "As I suspected, and I have just the thing to take care of the blockage. It's not as serious as it seems. I think Delray's just very melodramatic because he enjoys the attention. However, aside from his discomfort, we really need to get his weight under control, Mrs. Hunt. Bulldogs are notorious for suffering from hip dysplasia. His hips will only pain him as he grows older, and you don't want that, now do you?"

Did you just say my ass looks fat in this?

Katie gave Delray's rotund belly a gentle squeeze in the hopes she could hush his interference in her head. She smiled at Esmeralda in understanding. "I know you love Delray, but I promise he'll still love you back just as much whether you give him chicken salad with pickles or not—"

Baloneyyyy, I call baloney! Scraps are what I love best about her! I'll retaliate, lady. I'll eat her stupid gardening gloves. No, wait! I'll eat her favorite lily. That one she's always coddling and giving special plant food to. I'll eat the shit out of it! Oh, please, Doc, don't take away my cheese!

Katie forced herself to ignore Delray's pleas. "So that means no more table scraps no matter how often he gives you his best sad face. No more cheese. No more hot dogs or chicken salad with pickles or not. I'm going to suggest a dietary dog food you can pick up locally and nothing else until his weight is under control. Also, walks. Two a day, thirty minutes each. Oh, and if you have a treadmill, it wouldn't hurt to put him on that as well. As to his constipation, I have just the cure . . . Ingrid? Could you, please?" She pointed Ingrid in a direction her faithful receptionist knew well.

Walk? You mean like outside on the pavement? With other animals? Oh, the hell! What kind of sadistic witch are you? Delray complained with a sharp yelp, his protest shooting around inside her head like Ping-Pong balls.

Leaning into his warm side, Katie whispered in his ear as Ingrid gave Esmeralda the directions for his care. "You know what this means, don't you, Del? It means suppositories. Big ones, shoe lover. Now, no more shoes. Ever. Or the next time you could end up with an intestinal blockage and that means enema, buddy, maybe even surgery, sometimes death. No joke. Now you be a good boy for Esmeralda and do as I prescribed. Your path to the patch of green regularity in Esmeralda's backyard will soon be blockage free." She dropped a kiss on his head and tweaked his ear.

Esmeralda gave her a quick hug. "Thank you, Dr. Woods. I can't tell you how afraid I was. I know they talk about me in town—

they say awful, awful things, but I'll never forget how kind you were to my Delray. Never," she repeated, her eyes glittering her newfound loyalty.

Yeah, me, neither. Color me all shades of grateful you've just made my life a special kind of hell, Delray muttered.

Katie gave Esmeralda a wink. "I won't pay a lot of mind to what they say about you in town, Mrs. Hunt, if you won't pay any mind to what they say about me. Deal?"

Esmeralda chuckled, sweet and bubbly. Her knowing eyes gave Katie a look of understanding. "Deal."

"Beck? Would you gather Delray up for Mrs. Hunt and put him in her car?"

Beck's silence drew her attention to where he stood, staring up at the locked medicine cabinet. His eyes were far away, fixated on something inside the cabinet she couldn't pinpoint.

"Beck?" she called. "You okay?"

He cleared his throat and turned, putting a vague smile on his face that didn't quite mask his disorientation. "Sorry. Say again?"

"Would you help Mrs. Hunt getting Delray to the car? Will you be okay getting him into the house alone, Mrs. Hunt?" Katie asked. "He's a heavy load of bulldog."

I am not fat. Lay off the fat, labeler. I'm husky.

Esmeralda assured her she'd be fine as Beck, strong, kind, and gentle, carried Delray out of Katie's office, but not before Del gave one last parting shot.

I got no love for ya right now, Doc, because you took away every guilty pleasure a pet owner can lavish on her most faithful companion, but you better be careful. I've been hearin' all kinds of smack coming from that exotic animal park. They got lots to say—none of it good, and lots of it has to do with the big dude here.

Smack? From the animals in the park? "Wait . . ." Katie stopped herself short. Damn. Somehow, having a full-blown conversation with her patient—a—*dog*—probably wasn't beneficial to not only repeat visits from Esmeralda but one's ability to suspend disbelief. But what could Delray possibly know?

"So, Dr. Woods, you wanna tell me what that was all about?" Ingrid asked while they watched Beck open Esmeralda's car door from the window in the reception area.

"What was what about? Do you mean taking Delray as a patient because Dr. Jules wouldn't?"

"No. I mean all that sweet talk with Delray. Usually, you talk to the pet owner to get the information you need, but it was almost like you were having an actual conversation with the dog. I can't remember the last time I heard you call any dog *sweetums*. Plus, it was the fastest diagnosis I've ever seen."

"I concur," Beck said, striding in the front door of the office to shoot her a handsome smile, his cheeks reddened from the chilly afternoon.

Katie shrugged, needing a moment to process what had just happened and Delray's warning. "Then that makes both of you just this shy of crazy." Deflect, deflect, deflect. At least until she had a chance to see if this was a one-time deal or a new, magical, mystical affliction due to her cougarlicious state.

"I'm going to go check on Mrs. Krupkowski's Chi. Ingrid, would you be sure Nina and Marty are comfortable?"

Ingrid nodded her multicolored head. "They stayin' awhile?" Her wide eyes held a distinct glimmer of hesitance.

"They are. I'll explain why later. For now, just make sure they have everything they need, okay?" Ingrid sidled off with a reluctant drag to her vinyl boots.

She turned to face Beck, keeping the memory of his tender hands and sweet demeanor with Delray at arm's length. "What was that about?"

His face unsuccessfully attempted to hide the reaction he'd had when he was caught up staring at the medicine cabinet. "What was what about?"

Okay, so he didn't want to embellish. At this point, as tired as she was, she would respect that. "Never mind. So, I hear a bottle of Tide calling you."

"Tide?"

Whether he was playing stupid or genuinely didn't know the name brand laundry detergent, Katie couldn't decipher. "Yeah, you know, the laundry?"

"Right. Heaven forbid the bloodsucker should sleep on sheets that smell of anything other than spring meadows."

"They're here to help," she reminded him, moving around him to head to the small guesthouse she used to board clients at the back of her aunt's property. His chest brushed hers when she scooted past him, sending a zing of awareness to her traitorous nipples, making her crankier.

If he just didn't make her girly bits sha-wing, everything would be so much easier. Even talking dogs.

He grinned, playful and full of his special brand of mischief. "You won't hear me say otherwise. In fact, I've decided that each day when I wake, I shall berate myself for creating the kind of drama typically only seen on television. Then I'll skip downstairs to prepare breakfasts fit only for the likes of the queen mother in order to remind myself of my place, and I'll do it with a smile on my face and a song in my heart."

Katie couldn't help the giggle threatening to spill from her lips. Hearing words like that, coming from a man so gruffly handsome had to mean he was gay. "Washing some sheets will do for now. I'll let you know about songs and smiles later."

Beck's chuckle, melodic and low, followed her out the door.

* * *

STUFFING the pink set of sheets into the washer, Beck poured the allotted amount suggested on the back of the laundry soap bottle into the water and slammed the top of the washer shut.

From where he stood at the laundry room window, he was able to allow his eyes to follow Katie as she ran the tiny Chi back and forth over the lawn, throwing a ball and encouraging the dog to fetch it and bring it back. He'd like to focus more on her backside. In fact, he'd like to focus on all of her, but there was a much more important question that needed to be asked.

Did this dog talk, too?

From the moment he'd scooped up Delray, he'd complained about his stomachache loud and proud in Beck's head.

At first, he considered the notion he was actually going crazy. After all, he couldn't remember his name, had no idea how he'd landed here, had been accused of being a predatory cat, and he was housed with women who could do things he assumed he'd only seen in movies.

However, Katie changed that notion. She could hear Delray, too. He'd known it the second she'd asked him what he'd eaten. She'd done a fine job of hiding it. He had to admire her for not running out of her office screaming, but instead, remaining the die-hard professional she clearly wanted everyone to know she was.

There had been a moment or two when Nina's accusation that he was indeed a girl had quite literally become a reality. The first thing he'd wanted to do was run the hell out of Katie's office and clap his hands over his ears to stop Delray's incessant jabber.

But he wasn't going to let some woman have one over on him. No matter how sexy she smelled, no matter how extraordinary she looked.

If she could take it, so could he.

And he had.

He'd also heard Delray's parting shot to Katie. Whatever was going on at the animal park had to do with him, and as an end result, Katie.

Which meant, when the coast was clear, some investigation was in order.

For now, he'd just fancy her pear-shaped backside from his position at the window.

Or maybe see if Yancey or Dozer or one of the other dogs in the house was up for a debate on the economic situation. Which wasn't good, if what he'd read on the Internet this morning with Ingrid was true.

Beck ran a hand over his chin, littered with dark stubble, in wonder.

He could hear dogs talk.

Jesus Christ.

"TINKERBELL, I have one more question." Katie held the small, fawn-colored Chi in her lap while she rocked the dog in a chair she'd handpicked for the boardinghouse play area. Toys suited for Tinkerbell's size were scattered at her feet on the throw rugs she'd flung casually to allow the dogs some warmth on the tile floor.

Knowledge was power, right? So instead of letting this latest round of surprises freak her out, Katie decided to use it to her advantage.

If she was the literal version of the Dog Whisperer, then so be it. If Delray could hear grumblings at the animal park from way over the hill into the outer lying country roads that surrounded Piney Creek, maybe an animal that lived in town could offer more information.

Unfortunately, her first test on Yancey and Dozer was unsuccessful. They'd merely mumbled incoherent strings of words that made no sense in her head, and she hadn't wanted to disturb the mob who'd slept peacefully beside Teeny. But Tinkerbell, Mrs. Krupkowski's Chi, was a wealth of words and pampered pet demands.

She scratched Tinkerbell under her chin, her soft fur a comfort beneath her fingers. "So that question . . ."

Like more? Oh-m-gee. I've answered like a million already.

"Well, like technically, it's only been two. But I can see how you'd lose count," Katie said, getting the hang of this Dr. Doolittle syndrome.

Tinkerbell sighed, leaning against her as Katie scratched her ears. *Fine, but if I answer a question, you have to totally promise you'll tell the old lady I hate, hate, hate the pink skirt she got from Prettypooches .com. It's soooo not a good color on me. And all that tulle is scratchy on my delicate skin. I'm much more a nice cantaloupe or even a honeydew. Everyone makes fun of me when I wear the pink tutu. I just don't think I can stand it one more day if that stupid papillon Lisette makes fun of me when we go to the park. Like it's all a crime to wear a tutu.*

"I promise to pass the message on. Cantaloupe tutus. Now the question. How did you know you could talk to me and I'd hear you?"

Tinkerbell tipped her tiny nose in the air. *Duh. I, like, smelled you.*

Katie held the dog up, letting her legs dangle while she captured Tinkerbell's gaze. "Smelled me?"

You smell like one of us. Well, maybe not totally like one of us. I so don't get how you can walk on two legs and not have six nipples but still smell like another animal, but whatever. We always know each other by scent. You don't think I'd, like, sniff butts just to sniff butts, do you? That's so barfy. It's for recognition purposes only.

"I don't know what I was thinking."

So is that all you want to know? I'm exhausted after that silly game of fetch. What makes you all think we want to chase after a dirty ball anyway? I'm much happier with a beef-bouillon-dipped bone, thank you. Now, I want to go back to my princess bed and nap. I can't be expected to be "mommy's pretty, pretty, precious girl" if I don't get the proper amount of pretty, pretty sleep.

Katie remembered Delray's words, ringing in her head before he'd left her office, and it prompted her to prod further. "Can you hear the other animals down the road, too? You know, the exotic animals in the park?"

Tinkerbell stretched her front paws out on Katie's lap, nuzzling her nose between them. *Oh, totally. I mean, like, who can't hear them like moaning all the time?*

Katie's pulse raced. "What do they moan about, Tink?"

I can't always understand them, but most of them just want to go home, wherever that is. They make me glad I have old lady Krupkowski, even if her breath smells like sardines and she wears cheap perfume.

Katie's heart constricted. She'd known all along those animals were suffering—now she had proof. Okay, so maybe it was the kind of proof only a psychiatric patient confessed at therapy, but it was proof. "Have they made any mention of a cougar named Spanky?"

Is that the new one?

A warning signal slinked up her spine. "I don't know if he's new or old. I just know he exists."

He hasn't been there very long. Like, maybe just a few weeks. I remember hearing something about him and something about some experiment or something . . . Tinkerbell's bulbous, round eyes began to drift closed.

Shit, shit, shit. They were using the animals to experiment on them? Those bastards. She'd always known it. A slow spiral of angry heat wove its way into her belly and burrowed there. "An experiment? What kind of experiment, Tinkerbell?"

Like I would know? Don't be silly. If they're not talking about how to keep your coat shiny and where to get the latest wee-wee pad, I tune them out. Mostly because they're loud and depressing.

Katie rose, her heart chugging with fear. "Can I ask you one more favor, Tink?"

Like, if I said no, that would stop you?

Katie placed the dog in one of the cages on her fluffy pink princess bed with the marabou trim. She leaned her elbows on the top of the cage to gaze upon a very tired Tinkerbell. "I am the key to your next treat, young lady. Helping me will only behoove you."

Be-what? Tinkerbell asked, groggy with sleep.

"Never mind. I mean, it's in your best interest to help me."

So totally like a human. Half human. Like, whatever. Always withholding so we'll do stupid pet tricks like roll over and dance. You kind of have me at cheesy-liver treats. So what else do you want?

"Keep an ear out for me, would you? If you hear anything else from the animal park, use those ears for the greater good and listen to what they're saying, okay? It's really important."

Tinkerbell moaned. *Ooookay.*

Katie rubbed the dog's jaw with a finger, and smiled at her. "Thanks, Tink." She closed the cage door, secured it and turned to leave.

"I knew it."

Katie whirled around at the sound of Beck's gruff accent.

Beck approached her with feet that clomped over the tile floor. He stopped but an inch in front of her, all with his too-short flannel shirt and sex-on-a-stick scent.

Katie's eyes narrowed. "Knew what?"

He pointed a finger under her nose as he gazed down at her. "I knew you heard Delray in that examining room, and you can hear Miss Fancy Pants here, too." Beck thumbed his finger at Tinkerbell's cage.

Excuse me. My pants are neither fancy nor pants. It's a tulle skirt,

*thank you, and if I were you, I wouldn't be tossing stones at my clothes. And
another thing, I like quiet when I nap. So could you two take this outside?
Please? I'm so not used to all this interruption. First it's Goldilocks with
all of her questions, and now you, with the funny talk that sounds like that
chef guy Gordon Ramsay the old lady likes to watch, and the shirt that
looks like it belongs on my neighbor's gross teenager. Can I get just a little
respect here? I'm a paying client. That means, there's a level of decency due
me.*

Beck's eyes narrowed right back at her, blue, deep, and glittering. "You heard that," he accused Katie, who had to slap her good
hand over her mouth to keep from laughing in snort-like fashion.

"So?"

"So I heard it, too."

"That's all kinds of awesome, Beck. You know what this means,
don't you?"

He jammed his face in hers and gave a low growl her body
responded to by unintentionally leaning into him. "More revela-
tions? I'm gobsmacked."

Gob-who?

"Quiet, young lady!" he seethed at Tinkerbell, shooting a glare
in her direction. "What the hell is going on here, Katie?"

"Like I'd have the answer to that? You're the one with the answers. I have no idea why I can communicate with dogs, and neither do you because of that amnesia you keep waving under my
nose."

Beck's flare of irritation went as quickly as it had come and was
replaced with a mixture of awe and vividly apparent confusion.
"This is absolutely barmey."

"I'm taking a stab here, but I'm guessing you mean crazy?"

"I do."

"Yeaahhhh," she said, fighting the irony of that statement. "You
don't need to tell me about the crazy. What we need to do is get

your memory back and find out what happened to you at the animal park. Remember anything about any experiments? Does that notion ring a bell?"

Beck frowned, the wrinkles on his forehead leaving a troubled frown in their wake. "Experiments? No. Nothing. I don't remember anything associated with the park but the name Daniel Green. Not at this point, anyway. I'm hoping that will change."

Katie tucked her arm behind her back. "Tink here says she hears the animals moaning. She thinks they're depressed, and she also mentioned experiments."

"Well, if Tink, a dog, says so, it must be true. Aren't Chihuahuas a breed well known for their ability to diagnose depression?" His look was disgusted.

Heeeeyyyy, Tinkerbell muttered a sleepy protest.

She heard his sarcasm and cocked her head in its direction. "You're disputing the validity of what I say? You wanna give that more thought? I'll wait."

He shook his dark head, his hair swinging down to fall over his stubble-riddled chin, giving him that sexy biker look. "Forget I said that. Okay, you're right. That I doubted even for a moment should have me drawn and quartered. So what next?"

"We go to the animal park and see if we can *hear* those animals, too. If we can, the mystery of you is potentially solved, and we go from there."

A shadow fell over his eyes, leaving a shroud of his hesitance visible. "You're under a restraining order. You can't go to the animal park without the possibility of arrest—most especially in light of Wanda and Nina's predicament."

Did he not want her to go because he was really concerned, or was he just stating a fact? Maybe what he didn't want was for her to find something. "We don't have a choice. If they were experimenting on the animals there, and those experiments had to do with you, we need to know about it. Tink says you only arrived there a few weeks ago, which is strange. Normally, when a new exotic arrives, they post flyers all over town so they can rake in more cash at the expense of some poor animal that's supposed to roam free. Why do you suppose you were there, and did Daniel Green know you were half human?"

"All this and more answered on the next episode of *Escape from Paranormal Island*," he muttered, mocking a narrator's voice.

"Joke all you like, but I'm finding a way into that animal park tonight."

"Not without me, you aren't."

A shot of pleasure zinged through her veins at the possessive tone of his statement. Her . . . Beck . . . the deep velvety cover of night, the . . . *the gay part of that equation, Katie.*

Her pleasure fizzled like cold water had doused her sunbathed skin. "Okay. So we wait until the staff's gone home and break in in the hopes we can find something—anything—that will give us a clue about what happened to you. We need to find out what's going on with you so you can, I don't know . . . get back to your life."

Beck assessed her from beneath hooded eyes, his next words devoid of any emotion other than empty and colorless. "My life."

"Yes. *Your life*. You must have had one before this. It will also mean I can get back to mine." Her big, fat life. Big. Full. Fabulous.

"Because it was so full," he remarked, giving Tinkerbell a scratch on the head before making his way to the door.

"Hey!" she yelped, pushing her way through the door he held open for her. "I was well on my way to making it full until you showed up. I just want to get back to normal. You know, the days where I do nothing but sit around and hope for patients? Those days held a certain kind of comfort in their quiet anonymity."

"And they all consisted of running away from something. That's why you take the piss when people in town treat you like their roadside rubbish."

"I do not."Though, admittedly, it was hard to be affronted. He wasn't far from the truth.

He took hold of her arm when they crossed the lawn, turning her to face him. "Of course you do, Katie. I'm not sure *why* you do, but you do."

Anger at his accuracy made the tips of her ears burn. She hadn't always been so willing to let life and the people in it trample her, but her shame was bigger than her will to fight back these days. Everyone in town knew the sordid events of her arrival. After leaving New York with the kind of shattered reputation she'd had, how could she expect the people of Piney Creek to see her in any other light but a tainted one?

Aside from her fancy city ways, their hatred of her had a great deal to do with what she'd hoped to leave behind her.

Forever.

Beck's eyes pierced hers through the fading sun, making her squint. "Want to talk about what keeps that sharp tongue from assaulting others besides me?"

No. Not with someone she barely knew, someone who didn't even know who he was. "Not even a little."

His thumb ran a maddening circle along the bare skin of her forearm. "I'm a good listener."

"How do you know?" she challenged, needing to get away from this man who, despite his appearance, was intuitive—even if it was intrusively so. If she kept distance between them, a dissonant distance, she just might survive his heart-pounding, womanly parts all agog, presence.

"I should think that's obvious. I've listened to you women babble all day. Quite patiently, I'll add. That's how I know. So, tell you what."

"Tell me."

"I'm here if you decide your backbone needs alignment."

Ohhhh, the thought of his hands on her backbone brought with it a vivid sensory overload. She shifted out of his grasp. It helped her to think more clearly. "My backbone?"

"Yep, you know the thing that thing you're supposed to use to take up for yourself? I'm happy to help you find it again should you ever want to use that sharp tongue on anyone other than me."

"I'll keep that in mind. We'd better get back. Aunt Teeny will be making dinner, and after this morning, she'd be disappointed if you weren't there to sample her Tater Tot hot dish."

His chuckle was easy, his hesitant glance filled with playfulness as he went from dark to light in a matter of a glance. "Should I ask?"

Katie smiled, inching further away from the delicious shelter his body offered. "You should *always* ask when it comes to Aunt Teeny's cooking. I'll see you at dinner."

Beck didn't follow her inside. Instead, she caught a glimpse of him staring off into the wooded area that separated her clinic from the animal park as she closed the front door and all but ran up the stairs to the safety of her room.

Running.

How ironic.

She'd done a lot of that lately.

There was no reason she should stop now.

CHAPTER 9

After a raucous dinner with the crew, Teeny, and some Tater Tot hot dish, she'd napped and taken a long, hot shower. She'd also spent a little time looking up amnesia online, and had left the Internet with little more than she knew already. Beck's amnesia was trauma related. His memory could return at any time or not at all.

With a sigh, Katie crossed the room to give each member of the mob a kiss on their sleeping heads.

After a brief conversation with Li'l Anthony about what Tink and Delray had offered, Katie'd given up. Anthony had no explanation as to why he could suddenly communicate with her but Dozer and the rest couldn't. Then he'd announced himself asswhooped and passed out on his favorite pillow with Petey and Paulie right behind him. They curled together in a mass of black and tan fur.

She sighed, glancing at the bedside clock, which told her she needed to move it.

She let the towel fall from her body but stopped short when she caught a glimpse of her breasts in the standing mirror under the light from her overhead fan.

Hmmm.

Was the word she was looking for *whoa* or *weeee*?

She knew her boobs like a man knew his trunk. They were intimate with one another. They had a relationship like no other and in that relationship, shouldn't they have notified her if they'd decided to go to the plane known as perky?

Obviously, someone from the Newly Revived Booby Society had forgotten to send her the memo.

Holy mother of hooters.

Maybe her eyes were on the fritz due to her cat-titude. She peered closer into the mirror, then raised her arms over her head just like she had a million times in the past years when she mourned her breasts' downhill slide.

She'd once joked that as a vet, if she didn't have to worry she'd lose the use of her fingers due to numbness, she'd just walk around with her arms in the air so her nah-nahs would be shelved where they rightfully belonged.

Oh, there was no denying this. The girls were upright and winking at her from high atop their youthful perches. Perches they'd staunchly refused to sit upon without the aid of a Miracle Bra for at least six years now.

Moonlight from her bedroom window streamed in, as though the heavens had opened up and were singing a chorus of joyous hallelujahs on behalf of 36Ds everywhere.

Katie cocked her head, yanking the towel from her waist to get a full-on view of her body.

Her eyebrows shot upward when she turned sideways.

Oh, Beyoncé.

Tell me, Miss Bootylicious? *Are you ready? Can you handle this?* Do you have a sad because my ass rocks?

Because it's high, round, and cellulite free?

Boom, baby!

How insane. It had to be a trick of the light—or dementia. Or . . . more cougar shifting characteristics? Katie made her way to the edge of her bed and sank into it. Her hand caught her eye—it was almost back to normal with only a slight deformity to the side of it. Caught between her human form and her cougar form, she supposed.

So when would this shift happen, and wouldn't it be a handy frickin' thing if it happened tonight—when she most needed to blend with her fellow mammals? Terror crept into her bones, leaving her immobilized. Had she just wished to shift?

She stole a deep breath, fighting the fear welling in her chest. This shifting thing could only be shoved to the recesses of her mind for so long before it had to be addressed. What if it happened in public? Could it be controlled? Did it hurt? Marty and Wanda didn't look worse for the wear when they'd shifted, yet maybe it was different for cougars.

The bedside alarm clock said ten of twelve. There was no time to spend wasted on even the slightest trepidation. Beck would be waiting for their animal park rendezvous at midnight. She rushed to find a pair of jeans and a top, resisting the ridiculous urge to locate something Beck would find appealing. Besides, it was too cold for cute.

Nabbing a thick, red turtleneck, she pulled it over her braless breasts and winked at herself in the mirror when she smoothed it over her waist with a smug smile, forgetting she was sacrificing a hand for the ta-tas of a twenty-year-old.

As she pulled her hair up into a high ponytail, the round lights surrounding her bathroom mirror shone on a much less desirable affliction.

Glancing up at the ceiling, she gave whoever was in charge a glare of discontent. Pointing to her chin, she asked, "Is this some kind of trade-off for the boob/butt job?"

With a disgusted sigh, Katie popped open the medicine cabinet and rummaged until she found her tweezers, plucking three coarse hairs that certainly hadn't been there this morning when she woke. She addressed whoever was in charge of the universe. "Look. I didn't ask for the boobs and butt, and I definitely would have turned the offer down if I'd known if meant chin hair in return. Maybe next time we could consult about the fair trades act?"

A knock on her door made her jump, making the tweezers fall to the ground with a clatter. "Just a sec," she yelled. She ran a hand over her chin to be sure she'd caught all of her little hairy enemies before popping her door open.

Wanda, fresh and smelling of lilies of the valley, smiled at her. "You ready?"

Katie grabbed her down jacket and threw it on, casting a glance at the dogs that ironically hadn't broken into their usual screeching barks when someone knocked on the door. "As ready as I can be, risking jail time and more hate mail."

Wanda's face went sympathetic, her warm, brown eyes gentle. "God, I had no idea, Katie. What a bunch of narrow-minded, backward-ass people in this town. To attack your living the way they do, especially when you're such a good veterinarian, is a sin."

Katie hooded her eyes to avoid contact with Wanda's. Somehow, she didn't think Wanda would understand that she and her very own brand of stupidity had brought some of that hatred on. "On the bright side, I did have a patient today."

Wanda giggled as she followed Katie down the stairs. "So I've heard—and he talks. I thought I'd seen it all, but I find I learn something new almost daily about this thing we call paranormal. Please tell me you can talk to Muffin. Marty's hair would stand right on end . . ."

"That's what's so strange about this particular nuance. There are some animals I can communicate with while others simply mumble incoherently."

Wanda's head bobbed. "Ah, the sweet mysteries of life, eh? Maybe it'll just take some fine-tuning. One thing about the paranormal, it's never predictable."

Katie stopped her at the bottom of the steps. "Do you . . . I mean, are you happy as a werevamp? Would you go back to being human if you could?"

Wanda cocked her head, but she didn't appear to hesitate. "Not without Heath, I wouldn't. Sure, there are things I miss about being human, but there are also things I'd miss if I wasn't a shifter."

"I miss fucking Twinkies, yo," Nina said from the interior of the darkened kitchen, appearing out of the dark confines, pale and beautiful. "I miss chicken wings and pizza and a damn Starbucks white chocolate mocha." Yet her smile was fond. "But Wanda's right. I'd miss Greg more. There are compensations. I mean, I can fly."

Her stomach dove hard to her feet. "But you'll live forever. That scares the hell out of me," Katie confessed, something that had been weighing heavily on her mind. "What if being a cougar means I'll live to watch everyone I love die—forever?"

Nina, almost incandescent in the dim kitchen, shot her a look of total understanding. Rare and fleeting, but comforting nonetheless. "There are downsides to this, no doubt, Doc. There's nothing I want to do less than watch my Granny Lou die and live with it forever, but it is what it is. I've accepted it. Don't kid yourself into thinking I didn't flip my nut when I found out, but it's been a couple of years, and I'm dealing."

Beck came in from outside, and the cold air he brought with him held a foreboding that left Katie shivering. "You flip a . . . nut, did you say? I'll assume that meant you went homicidal. I can't tell you how uncharacteristic I find that when relating that phrase to you. You're the most passive vampire I've ever met, Nina." He grinned, jamming his hands into the jeans Wanda had bought him in town before they were arrested.

Jeans that made her mouth dry at the way they hugged his ass and clung to his thighs.

His young gay thighs. Yes, there was that to comfort her.

"You, shut it." Nina pointed at Beck with a teasing smile. "Or I'll show you passive in a sentence that ends with my fist." Then she leaned into Katie and muttered, "Maybe young, but no to the gay. He's not Brokeback paranormal. I know that's what you were hoping for because it makes your drooling over him easier to live with. I hate to be the crusher of dreams, but well, I'm good at it." She shrugged as though to apologize when Katie blushed.

"Hey, matchmaker. Zip it." Wanda grabbed Nina by the back of her black hoodie and dragged her deeper into the kitchen.

"So, are we ready to do this?" Beck smiled at her in the semi-dark, bringing a small measure of secure warmth to Katie's heart that she fought with every fiber of her being. If he wasn't gay, then he was just way too young. There'd be no cougaring him up. And she was left sad by the notion but firm in her resolve.

"I'm petrified," she admitted, hoping the tremble in her voice wouldn't reveal itself.

On the other hand, Beck looked relaxed and confident. He'd shown more fear when Nina had threatened him than he did about going into the animal park and possibly running into unforeseen trouble. "I'll be with you."

"You're not at all afraid that first, we might get caught, and second, we'll be eaten alive by some ferocious carnivore?"

"You know, I can't quite explain it, but going to the animal park brings me a certain kind of peace. I'm not at all afraid of what's going on in there."

"Which could make you reckless."

His dark eyebrow cocked upward. "I prefer to think of myself as an asset."

"You would."

"Someone has to. My self-esteem could quite possibly end up in the loo amidst all you women."

Nina stepped in front of them to keep them from fighting their way out the door. "Listen, you two watch your asses. Neither one of you has the ability to save yourselves from some mad-ass rhino if he can't shift, and you still don't know how to—or even if you can shift at all. So lay low, dudes. See if you can't get into the office and that's it. If I have to come save your shitters from some hungry lion, I'll be pissed." She looked at Katie. "And I want you to know, I'm against you going alone with only Benny Hill here to protect you. I still say we should be going with."

"And risk getting caught? Not on your unlife, Nina," Katie said. "If I'm caught, I'm breaking a restraining order. If you and Wanda are caught, it's probably considered tampering with evidence. There's a police investigation going on, and you're both involved. You've already done enough where my predicament's concerned. I won't allow you to be hauled back to jail."

She threw her hands up in acquiescence. "You have a point, and if we're playing this clean to keep suspicion low so you won't have the Beverly Hillbillies beatin' down your door, I can't mess with any minds to erase anything. It wouldn't change the fact that the old man's in the hospital anyway. So do me this, make sure we're on your speed dial in case something goes down. Text me, call me, tweet, whatever, but don't think you can take on a litter of kitties alone."

"Wouldn't that be a pride?" Beck quipped, tugging a black, knit hat down over his head.

Nina grinned. "Get the fuck out of here before I steal your pride by kicking your ass in front of a bunch of girls."

"Be safe, and any sign of anyone, get out," Wanda warned. "I know you're the best candidate for this, Katie, because you're more likely to understand any medically experimental documentation, but I don't like it. In this case, I almost believe brawn is better than brains."

"Fuckin' A, it is," Nina agreed.

Wanda shook her head. "Forget I said that. Go. Be careful. We'll wait. If you're not back in an hour—we're coming to find you. No arguments." She gave Katie's arm a squeeze as she and Beck headed out into the cold night.

As they walked into the thick of the woods, the scent of wood-burning stoves in the air, it occurred to her that neither one of them had taken out the flashlights they each carried in their pockets so they'd be able to actually see through the thick pine trees separating her aunt Teeny's from the animal park.

Katie instantly stopped walking, a cold puff of air escaping her lips. "Do you see what I see?"

Beck came up short next to her, his shoulder brushing hers. "A star, a star, dancing in the night?"

Katie smirked at his Christmas carol reference. How many twenty-year-olds knew that song? "No. I mean, can you see as clearly as I can? It's pitch-black out here, but I can see everything as though the sun is shining and there's not a cloud in the sky. It's a little like having night-vision goggles on. For instance, that fern there." She pointed to her left at a log where a wild fern grew freely. "I can see every detail to it."

He glanced around the wooded area and nodded, putting his

hands in the back pocket of his jeans. "I didn't even realize it until you pointed it out, but you're right."

"Maybe you've just always taken it for granted—as a cougar, I mean."

"Maybe. It definitely didn't seem out of the ordinary at all to me."

Katie shook her head in wonder. "All these changes . . ." She thought of her breasts and wondered out loud, "I can't wait to see what happens next."

His teeth glowed in the dark when he smiled at that notion. The tufts of hair peeking out beneath his cap and curling against his neck made him more biker hot than ever. "The kid in me keeps hoping for wings and X-ray vision."

"That's all there is in you," Katie remarked dryly, again assaulted by a resentment she could only trace back to this wild attraction she felt to a man she'd known but a couple of days.

His sigh was gruff, filled with impatience. "Hold on there, lady. So tell me. What's up Katie's ass tonight?"

Well, in celebration of her new, younger ass, a thong, thank you. A lavender, frilly, satiny thong-tha-thong-thong-thong. She bristled at yet another shrewd observation from the eighth-grader. "Nothing's up my ass." Katie began to make her way to the steep decline in the hill that would lead to the parking lot of the animal park.

But Beck didn't budge. His work-boot clad feet remained immobile. "You're prickly. I can smell it on you. So what's the problem now?"

She kept her back to him, inhaling the chilled air, forcing back the urge to participate with more defensiveness. "I have no problem."

He stalked up behind her, grabbing her arm and whirling her

around. His nostrils flared and his eyes narrowed. "Oh, you've got one all right, and I know just what it is, Katie."

Hah. What did he know of *adult* problems? "I promise it has nothing to do with the rumor they're taking the marshmallows out of the Lucky Charms box."

He ignored her umpteenth jab at his youth by hitching his jaw in her direction. "You're conflicted."

"No. I'm *af*flicted. With a paw and the Dr. Doolittle syndrome." And whiskers. Jesus, what kind of sadistic Ruler of the Universe would give her whiskers before she'd even experienced her first hot flash?

"No, Dr. Woods. That's not the problem here, and you know it."

Katie rolled her tongue over her lips. "Did you also, in your amnesiac state, forget you have a degree in psychiatry?"

"It doesn't take a degree to see why you're so sensitive."

"I'm turning into a cat. A. Cat. You know, meow? I imagine there's a degree of sensitivity involved in losing parts of your humanity and gaining some whiskers and a paw. Not to mention the added thrill of canine communication."

"Whiner."

Katie's lips thinned in anger. "Did you just have the nads to call me a whiner?"

"That was me. All nads, resident amnesiac, and imposer upon your quiet, if not dull life."

The. Nerve. Her life wasn't dull. It was Zen, baby. A very quiet Zen. "Because?"

"Because despite the fact that you have a paw and a stray unwanted hair or two, you've also gained a reprieve from the dreaded middle-aged rack sag. Might I also mention, your back end has been given an enormous gift minus a surgeon's skillful knife? And yes, I noticed, though the first version I leered at was fine, too. Those two attributes alone are gifts some women would consider a more than fair trade-off. You just won't see the glass is half full."

He'd seen her whiskers and not said a word about them? What kind of gay friend was he? And he'd noticed her breasts . . . which excited her. Which made her even angrier.

She tried to shrug his grip off, but he wasn't letting go. The clasp of his lean fingers on her arm made her insane with two things. Lust and lust. Bad, bad, Katie. "Perky breasts and a firm ass are considered a fair trade for whiskers and a paw? What planet do you suspect you hail from?"

Beck's dark lashes fluttered against his cheeks while he looked down at her with that glare that saw past her angry platitudes. "I'd bet there are more than a hundred women who'd call that more than fair, and they'd take the deal in a New York minute." He snapped his fingers, long and lean, under her nose.

"Well I'm not one of those women. I was fine with the aging process. So if you thought gratitude was what I was handing out, you'd be mistaken."

Beck held up his hand, still keeping her in his grip with the other. "We've gone astray. That isn't why you're conflicted."

Katie rolled her eyes up at him and crossed her arms over her chest in a gesture of bored indifference. "Oh, then by all means, share your diagnosis."

"It has to do with me. I leave you on edge because you're conflicted."

"I'm on edge because I don't know what to expect next when I plant my foot on the floor tomorrow morning. I've been a cougar for two days—today it was the twenty-four-hour boob lift and bulldogs in my head, then it was whiskers and a perky ass. I'm not much for surprises."

"Really, Katie? Well, I have one for you."

She clapped her hands, mocking his statement. "Oh, boo and

yah. Please—please tell me it's another perk like maybe next I'll gak up a hairball."

"I'm not gay."

Wait, wait, wait. Yes, he was. She bit back a groan. No. No. No. She must insist he be gay. This wasn't an option he was allowed to take off the table. If he wasn't gay, she was doomed. So she bluffed. "Yeah? So what? Me, neither."

His smile was condescending and confident when he answered, "Thus the explanation for why you're so edgy."

Okay, now he was getting under her skin and burrowing there. "Wow. You're on fire tonight, Mr. I Can't Even Remember I'm a Cat. How do you figure you're being heterosexual factors into my edginess?" Damn, damn, damn. For someone supposedly so young, his insightful observations were not just mature, but killing her.

"Ah," he drawled as if he'd found the answer to evolution. "But now that I've told you I'm a heterosexual, your edginess will have a new facet."

"Holy circles."

"It's simple. Pay attention. You're edgy and conflicted because you find me attractive, Katie. It was easier to deny your attraction to me when you thought I was playing for the other team. Now that you know I'm not, you'll take issue with my age, an age that can't exactly be pinpointed with any accuracy, especially if the changes in your body are any indication to my own outward appearance. Maybe I'm not the twenty-two-year-old, skateboarding, candy-bar-eating teenager you thought I was. This presents a dilemma for you."

Hoo boy, did it ever. She continued on the journey she'd begun. Playing dumb. "That being?"

Beck's cheeks sucked inward, and then he smirked. "How to keep your hands off me."

Her hands were staying right where they were. That went double for her paw. "Funny how you can't remember anything, but you *can* remember how to be an arrogant egomaniac. Maybe you really are older. Only a mature man could have compiled that much conceit. It's a man gift, I think. One that even sprawls the great divide of amnesia."

Rocking back on his heels, Beck stared her down not even a little fazed, if his arrogant expression was any indication. "Call it what you will, it's the truth. I'm not gay, and that makes you uncomfortable. *Very* uncomfortable."

Oh, so the hell what? "It does not, teenager."

He made a mocking face at her. "Oh, it does so, *Grandma*. I can prove it."

"With your sage words of wisdom, Confucius?"

Beck lowered his head to her level, leaving an inch between their faces. "No. With this."

Those confident words between them in the chilled air, he gathered her up, pulling her to him with a hand to the back of her head and the other at the small of her back, plastering her length to his.

Katie's head tipped back, letting her catch a glimpse of his eyes seconds before his mouth swooped down to land on hers. They glittered with a self-assured amusement—a devilish glint of the hijinks he planned to embark upon.

Curling her hips into his, Beck slanted his mouth over hers, pausing but a moment to chuckle at her surprise before he parted her mouth. His hands splayed across her back, forcing her body to mold with his.

Hot fissures of pleasure were his instant reward, pricking awake each of her nerve endings like small ignitions of heat. She bucked beneath the smooth, heated feel of his mouth, the insistent pressure, the glide of his tongue when it touched hers.

If he was only twenty, they sure made 'em better kissers these days than they'd ever been when she was in college.

And then she found herself forgetting everything, succumbing to the swirl of hormones, racing and rushing to come out of their dark closet in a tumble of gleeful, targeted assaults on her body. The space between her thighs clapped imaginary hands of decadent joy. Her nipples, now crushed against Beck's sexy chest, newly revived and awake, cried out at the friction their bodies made pressed so tightly to one another.

Katie's hands gripped at his shoulders, feeling the rigid curves and planes beneath his thick, flannel jacket. They made her fingertips tingle with the need to discover his hot flesh naked, touch the place where his heart beat so fast, she felt it even through her jacket.

And an irrepressible need grew, spiraling from deep within her belly until her blood rushed through her veins and her heartbeat thumped in her ears like claps of thunder.

Beck's mouth worked hers, driving his tongue into it, the rasp of silky flesh making her entire body tremble with molten hot need. His kiss was wet, demanding, and so delicious, her knees began to buckle. The rigid press of his zipper against her abdomen drove her stand on tippy-toe to press even closer so she could explore the hard length of him.

A sigh fell from her lips as their tongues dueled. A sigh of delicious satisfaction. A sigh she hadn't sighed in a very long time. The sigh of a woman who wanted the pleasure this odd contradiction of a man wrought from someplace deep inside her.

Beck's groan, low and thick against her lips, and then his hand, large and hot, cupping her breast was what snapped her out of this bubble of wanton lust they'd created in the middle of the woods. It reminded her that she had no business kissing someone she hardly knew. Someone who'd wreaked havoc in more than just her loins.

Someone who was a kid. Despite his lip-locking skillz.

Katie tore her lips from his mouth with a ragged gasp, but he didn't loosen his hold on her. Instead, he forced her to look up at him by pulling her closer. Their chests crashed together, Beck's breath huffed in and out in puffs of condensation while his stare bore into hers. "Did that in any way feel like gay teenage boy to you?"

She shot him a guilty glance before finding a tree just over his shoulder to focus on. "We don't know how old you are. And I'm not kissing someone who could quite possibly be young enough to be my son. As to the gay thing, my only defense is you said you liked *Project Runway*. I know of maybe one straight man who does, and he's one pink shirt with the collar flipped up from gay."

"Correction. I never said I liked *Project Runway*. I don't know what I like unless you count cartoons. Which I saw briefly because I've been so busy doing household chores, I haven't had the chance to channel surf. I did recognize the tagline for *Project Runway*. That's beside the point. The point here is you find me attractive. I definitely, if the snug fit of my jeans is correct, find you attractive, too. That's the point. The other point being, you can't use my supposed homosexuality as an excuse to freely check out my arse anymore without some kind of guilt attached to it. Now you're just like me."

She was puzzled—horrified to have been caught, but puzzled. "Like you?"

"Checking out your sweet backside because it's sweet and I want it. Period."

That heat he'd fanned to a flame rushed back to her insides, making her chest tight. "I don't indulge in casual sex. With anyone. No matter their age."

"Well, maybe that's why you're so bloody tight-assed and tense. There's more to life than crossword puzzles and a marathon of *Hoarders*. Don't deny you watch it. I saw the look of dismay when you realized they had a new episode on tonight and you were going to miss it because we ate dinner late. And lighten up. Checking me out isn't a sin. I'm not opposed to you enjoying having a look at my body."

That's because Beck's body was hard and tight and sculpted to within an inch of his life. Oh, wait, hers was, too. Almost. Who knew if tomorrow wouldn't bring abs of steel and thighs like weapons that would need registering with the government?

And this was the second time in as many days someone had told her to lighten up. She'd once been light. Too light. No more light. Light meant you didn't pay attention, and when you didn't pay attention, bad things went on behind your back. Things you just couldn't convince anyone you knew nothing about. "I can assure you, I did *not* have a look at your body. And even if I did, that's still not a reason to . . ."

"Have one off? I think it's every reason. And here's another thought. Now that we've gotten the question of my sexual preferences out of the way, we *are* sharing the same space. You'll have trouble keeping your hands off me in such tight quarters," he said, following his bold, downright egomaniacal words with a boyish grin.

Oh, really. "Only a boy could make a statement so pathetically immature." *That's the way, Katie. Strike back at all those hormones he made scream in any old mature way you can.*

"We'll see who's immature when you can't stop your estrus."

Her who-us? Wait, she knew that word. It was Latin. She'd learned it in veterinary school, but she couldn't remember what it meant because she couldn't think clearly since this had all gone down. A frown wrinkled her brow. "My what?"

Beck's expression said he knew something she didn't know, and it was all too confident for her liking. "Huh. The lady with all those big words doesn't know what an estrus is. I'll give you a hint. It's a four-letter word for the opposite of cold."

Heat? She clearly wasn't making the connection.

His laughter at her failure to guess made her eyes narrow at him. "Your heat, in simpler terms. It lasts upward of possibly ten days, and it'll make you writhe with need." His words came out quite matter of fact, shooting from his mouth like he was narrating a cougar fact while reading a script for a *Nat Geo* program.

Katie's mouth fell open. Her heat? Like the kind where she was rubbing up against trees and lampposts while she howled, advertising her availability to any male within a hundred-mile radius heat? Flashes of the hundreds of animals she'd spayed and neutered in her career zipped before her eyes.

But wait again. How ironic that he could remember that part about being a cougar, yet nothing else sprang to mind? "It's funny how sexually selective your amnesia is, don't you think?"

Beck's delicious lips pursed and then he frowned, too. A frown that said he didn't know where that cougar detail had come from. "That just came out of—"

"Nowhere," she finished for him on an exaggerated sigh. "I've heard this song before. Look, forget it. Forget everything that just happened because it won't happen again. Ever. There'll be no slap and tickle with me to pass the time while we *Murder, She Wrote* this out. No way. Kissing me was a mistake. Don't make it again."

As she turned to leave him there in the middle of the woods, his big hand slapped her on the ass with a playful thwack. "That motherly tone of yours turns me on. Big, old lady."

Narrowing her eyes, Katie gritted her teeth. "You do that again, and I'll show you the meaning of the word grounded. Now let's hit it. If we screw around here in the Enchanted Forest any longer, Nina will come looking. You do not want me to tell her you had the nerve to touch my butt." She turned with a stomp to head down the hill, furious he took absolutely nothing seriously.

He virtually squealed with laughter, the clunk of his feet right behind her, his breath, hot on her neck. "Ooooh, no! Not the big, scary Nina. Please, please, anything but that."

Katie whipped around, her anger sizzling and spiky. "Are we going to take this seriously, or do you want to keep fooling around until we get caught?"

"I'm all for fooling around."

Her lips thinned in utter fed up.

Beck rolled his eyes with exaggeration, throwing up his hands and giving in. "Okay, fine, *Mom*. This is me serious and ready to storm the castle."

"Good. Now be quiet and let's go."

As they made their way down the steep hill leading to the parking lot, Katie fought the insane emotions Beck had dredged up in her. He'd made her feel like a living, breathing woman. Sexy, wanton, aware.

He'd also made it clear he wanted her in all of her estruswhateverthehell.

She'd made it clear that would go absolutely nowhere.

Watching his ass while he took the hill with sure feet, she had to ask herself why she'd done that?

"Are you looking at my ass, Dr. Woods?" Beck mocked over his shoulder with a chuckle.

"You are an ass!" she hissed in return, her face hot with embarrassment.

Dear Ruler of the Universe—I can handle paws and a frisky décolletage and even whiskers. I mean, what are razors for if not to shave your chin every day? But could we take a pass on the heat thing? I'll swap ya for hairy legs and an out-of-control hairball . . .

CHAPTER 10

Katie's heart throbbed in her chest. But it wasn't with fear. It was with utterly euphoric, *youthful* jubilation.

She hadn't felt this good in more years than she cared to count.

Beck stared up at her from down below just as she crested the top of the chain-link fence. He'd promised to catch her if she fell, but the confidence with which she'd climbed it left her unafraid to jump to the pavement below. What worried her was what her back would feel like once she made impact.

She wasn't twenty like Teen Cougar. If she hit that pavement too hard, there was some Icy Hot and a muscle relaxant in her future. Or a hip replacement. She swung a leg over, straddling the fence, her minor fear of heights as far off as yesterday's saggy ass.

"Mind making haste up there, Spider-Girl?" he whispered, giving a cursory glance around the all too well lit parking lot.

Katie stifled a giggle. She'd climbed the fence like she was an extra ape in *Gorillas in the Mist*. Hand over hand, she'd attacked the climb without much forethought and totally as though it was instinctual to crawl up a chain-link fence like she had suction cups on her feet and hands. When she hit the top, she felt like a young, athletic eighteen-year-old had possessed her body. No creaks, no aches, and absolutely no hesitation for what she was about to do next.

Without a qualm, Katie lunged to the ground, landing on all fours with a hushed thump.

Beck looked down at her with admiration in his eyes, his hands jammed into his jean pockets. "Impressive."

She rose as though her knees had springs, her adrenaline rushing and her cheeks hot with the flush of his praise. "That was awesome times a million."

His eyes held concern when he met hers. "I saw video cameras. We're going to have to skirt them if we hope to avoid being caught. I think it's possible, but better safe than sorry. We should use the ski masks."

Katie nodded, dragging hers out of her pocket and pulling it over her face. Somewhere between the woods and hitting the parking lot, this whole breaking-and-entering thing strangely excited her. Adrenaline pumped through her veins at warp speed and fire burned in her gut. "Ready?"

"Let's do it. Follow me, which won't be a hardship, I gather. You will have that view of my bum you so vehemently deny indulging in. But I think I've located all of the cameras, so I know where to go."

She rolled her eyes at him before falling behind his back.

They crept along the length of the fence, zigzagging in spots, ducking in others to keep from getting caught on the cameras.

Somehow, they'd found their way to the outer offices where the staff worked, passing huge outdoor waterfalls and trees designed for the cats to climb. There were faux caves and holes, a cougar's favorite place to hide and sleep, according to Ingrid's research online.

When they came to a padlocked door, Katie cursed at not having brought something to cut the heavy lock with, then shook her head in disbelief that this was all that kept criminals from getting in and dangerous animals from getting out.

"Shit!" Beck pulled up his mask and grabbed the lock in his hand, then yanked at it in angry frustration.

And then, as everything was wont to do in Beck's hands, the steel lock virtually melted away, clattering to the ground.

"Uh, Spider-Girl, meet Superman," she joked from over his shoulder.

Beck looked as surprised as she was when he stared down at his hands. "I just know there has to be X-ray vision in this for me." He popped the door open, peering around the corner before allowing her to follow him. His hand at her waist to prevent her from walking into a dangerous situation made her glow—then curse under her breath for even remotely considering a hint of a glow.

Katie's eyes went instantly to the corners of the ceiling. "No cameras? How can they possibly entertain ensuring the safety of these animals when their security is, at best, archaic?"

"Let's just be grateful it's archaic and get moving," Beck replied, heading down a long hall, taking her hand and pulling her behind him.

The walls of the corridor were lined with colorful pictures of the cats, elephants, a rhino, and even a camel in their performance costumes. Each was labeled with a name and the date they'd been brought to the park. Larry, Curly, Mo, Abbott, Costello, Alfalfa, Laurel, Hardy, Martin, Lewis . . . "Someone liked slapstick comedy," she remarked.

Then one picture in particular stopped her cold.

There was a framed photo of Spanky, sitting by a beach ball, a pink, fluted collar around his neck. In cougar form, he almost stole her breath away in the same fashion he did when he was in human form.

Beck let his chin rest on her shoulder, making a wild pattern of goose bumps scurry along her arms. "Me, I gather?"

"Definitely you. That's what you looked like before you shifted."

"I can see why you found me so irresistible. Though, I'm not sure I'm fond of the pink," was his dry remark so close to her ear, her nipples beaded when his hot, minty breath skittered over her skin.

She shooed him from her shoulder before she threw him to the ground and insisted he fix her estrus by way of wonk. "I think it makes you look approachable."

"So I was one of the animals who performed then?"

"You know, that's what's strange about all of this. Usually, when Mr. Magoo gets a new exotic, he slaps more announcements up all over town than Craigslist has. I don't get why he didn't do the same with you."

"Maybe I was untrainable—one of those diva performers who has to have only yellow M&M'S and Evian in a stemmed glass that's been chilled in the freezer for exactly two hours waiting for me backstage."

Katie fidgeted with the ends of her ponytail in thought. "Maybe. Or maybe that's not what you were here for at all."

"Maybe we'd better get looking so we can find out why I was here. Time is of the essence," he commented, pointing to her wristwatch.

A persistent vibration grew in her head when they stopped in front of a sanctuary, leading to glass enclosures filled with cats of prey. A cougar-topia of slumped, sleeping exotics all wearing identical collars to Spanky's, though none of them looked terribly undernourished to her physician's eye.

She rubbed her fingers over her forehead to assuage the pounding in her head.

Beck knocked shoulders with her as they stared into one particular glass window meant for the staff's viewing. "Aren't cougars nocturnal?"

"Asked the cougar of the cougar."

"Now who's not being serious here?" he accused.

"You're right. Sorry. From the little I know about them, not necessarily. They hunt from dusk till dawn, but are known to nap on their journeys. They like thickly wooded areas to hide in while they hunt, but I imagine, given their circumstances here"—she couldn't fight the disgust in her voice—even if the place was clean as a whistle—"it seems appropriate they'd adjust and sleep at night because there's nothing to hunt and nowhere to roam. Which makes my stomach turn, in case you were wondering."

His look of sympathy warmed her insides—whether she liked it or not. "Defender of animals without a voice, are you?"

She'd been called worse. Her heart melted when she gazed upon the fierce beauty of so much restricted mammal. "I love animals. I always have. I like them better than most people, which is why I became a veterinarian to begin with. I was always the kid who brought home the stray, stopped by the side of the road when I saw one injured, wanted to save them all. My heart aches for the abused and neglected. I take in as many as I can because I can."

"You're a good person," Beck said, his tone held admiration she heard but refused to wallow in. She didn't deserve his respect.

"But these animals"—she tapped the glass with a finger—"exotics who should be free to roam and let Mother Nature do with them what she will, are the ones I feel most sorry for. They're not meant to be gawked at through glass enclosures or paying for someone's fancy BMW by filling bleachers full of people who want to see some fool stick his head in a tiger's mouth. And while I realize some are in captivity to prevent extinction, or they can't survive in the wild, I don't agree with putting them on display, and Mr. Magoo knows it. That's why there's that restraining order." Her speech ended on a growl of pent-up frustration.

Beck brushed some stray strands of hair from her face with the tip of his finger in a gesture of familiarity she didn't attempt to shoo away for the comfort it brought. "Easy there, killer. Tell me about the restraining order."

She shrugged, the crinkle of her jacket harsh to her sensitive ears and her pounding temple. "It's not that big of a deal. I didn't break in here like Ingrid and Kaih did to help you. I came in as a paying customer. I did make my objections about what appeared to be some shoddy care very clear. Looking around now, I feel a little stupid. I only saw the one tiger, and he didn't look well to the naked eye. So I objected. Okay, so maybe I jumped the gun because I'm an animal rights activist, and maybe I was a little loud when I did it, but I offered free vet services as a way to ensure they were getting at least the bare minimum. I don't know a great deal about exotics, but I can handle simple things. I mean, I handled you, right?"

"You drugged me and put me in a cage with no clothes on."

"Exactly. Handled, no?" She chuckled, her grin genuine.

"I concede. So this Mr. Magoo turned you down?"

She paused, remembering the angry scowl and the ensuing insulted expression Mr. Magoo had given her. "Come to think of it, with a vengeance. The next thing I know, we're being served a restraining order like I'm some rabid zealot who pickets for PETA. I'm not against eating a steak or a chicken leg. I'm against puppy mills and . . . and . . ."

No, she wasn't going there. Not tonight. She'd revisited that nightmare on many a night. Tonight wouldn't be one of them.

With a shake of her head, she said, "Forget it. I swear to you, I left when I was asked to and I haven't been back since. I made it a point to stay put at Aunt Teeny's and never come back so I wouldn't have to see what was going on here. I even take alternate routes to town to avoid this place."

Beck nodded his head in understanding. The eerie glow of the exit signs showed off his angular face to its best advantage. "Ah. So, see no evil, hear no evil."

"Do no evil. But now, looking at their living conditions, they don't appear to be neglected at all, and I admit, I can be oversensitive."

"An understatement," he said on a laugh as they stood side by side, peering at the sleeping cats.

The moment struck Katie as peaceful, despite the still increasing throb in her head. They both noted movement coming from the dark shelter of the cat sanctuary. Katie cocked her head in awe when she realized she could actually identify the sound of soft paws, moving with stealth across the grassy terrain.

Without warning, a cougar had stretched upward to press its face and wide paws against the glass, making Katie gasp and startle backward.

But not Beck. He stared back into the soulfully deep eyes of the cougar, pressing a hand to the glass to meet the cat's outstretched paw, appearing almost mesmerized.

The cougar wore a collar, just as Spanky had, that read "Lucille."

Katie stared in rapt fascination when the big cat's head tilted as though in question, taking in Beck, languishing a long moment while they faced each other. The animal's eyes roamed over his face, scouring every inch of him, clearly savoring Beck's arrival.

Yet, there was no threat involved in its stance. No low growl of warning to caution him to back away. Only a sadness Katie felt to the deepest recesses of her soul. She leaned in, hoping against hope to hear something in her head, words, mumbling, something, anything like she had with Tinkerbell and Delray.

There was only a deafening silence.

The spell appeared to break for Beck, who placed his forehead against the glass, but then the big cat did the strangest thing.

Its long tongue licked the place on the viewing window where Beck's forehead was pressed to it. Its eyes were that of the wounded—deeply so, bringing a shiver to Katie's spine.

Finally, the cat jumped down, in a gesture so closely resembling defeated resignation, Katie almost sobbed.

Beck backed away, bumping into her when he did.

"What just happened?" she asked him, breathless with wonder after what she'd seen pass between them. The compulsion to touch him grew heavy and to such an extreme, she jammed her hands into her jacket pockets.

His face was a mask of emotion more in keeping with the hard granite of his rakish facade and in total dichotomy to his normally playful personality.

Katie sensed his discord. Understood it and couldn't identify with it all in one sweep of confusion. She couldn't stop herself when she placed a hand on his arm, an arm stiff and unyielding. "Beck?"

"I *don't know* what just happened, Katie," was the only offer he made in the way of explanation, and it was done between tightly compressed teeth. "I know my amnesia is a burr in your cute butt, but you'll damn well have to accept my answer. *I don't know*."

Instantly, Katie backed off. Instinctually, she knew she shouldn't push him to define where his head was. "Okay. I'm sorry. Let's get to moving so we can figure out where Daniel Green fits into this." This time, she took the lead in order to give Beck a chance to process whatever had just gone down between him and the cougar.

She stopped with a stutter of feet at a door with a name plaque on it. Daniel Green's name.

Dr. Daniel Green.

BECK let a hiss of a breath escape his throat when he came up short behind Katie. Staring at the name on the door, an image flashed through his head—sharp, and almost as though it was happening right before his eyes.

He saw Daniel Green, knew it was him without any other means of identification. He was a mussed mass of gray hair on his head, standing up on his scalp in some places. His glasses were tipped at an awkward angle to the left, and hanging by a thread on the right. He scowled as he entered what Beck was sure was his office, shoving a piece of paper into his lab coat pocket.

Beck's nostrils flared at an odor he couldn't place while his eyes caught a quick glimpse of stacks and stacks of computer printouts on a metal desk cluttered with what he assumed was laboratory paraphernalia.

The old man looked tired, frustrated, and woefully defeated. His white lab coat was covered in stains, and Beck couldn't tell if they were from fallen food or something he wasn't sure he wanted to classify.

And then he felt hands, warmly aged and gentle, run over his spine, moving to chuff him under the chin before he heard Daniel Green speak in a voice he knew—a voice that hitched and faded in and out while the speaker paused to think, then spat words at a rapid fire pace. "Shaw . . . I'm sorry. So . . . sorry, son. I promise you, I'll find the answers. I won't let them hurt you. We just need to keep you safe."

Katie broke the vision when she latched onto his arm, her weight leaning into him, limp, her breathing ragged. "Beck," she panted. "I can't . . . something's happening." There was panic in her tone, controlled, but identifiably frightened to his ears.

Gathering her up, he gazed down with rapidly growing concern, a concern he realized in that moment went far deeper than a man who'd just met a woman he wanted to sack. His hand went to her cheek, running it over her smooth skin, hot as an oven. "Katie! Talk to me. Tell me what's happening!"

Her voice grew breathy, distant, her words broken and jagged as she began to sink against him, sliding away, slipping to the ground with soft mewls no matter how hard he tried to keep a grip on her.

And then he realized what was happening.

Well, if he was honest with himself, he didn't realize exactly what was happening due to the nature of her state.

That nature was brief.

It was but a mere blip in time.

But it was.

Oh, was it ever.

And it was of the naked nature.

But he owed himself a paw to the back for getting it together so quickly, despite the searing image of Katie's lush, full breasts and the sexy swell of her hips encased in creamy flesh he wanted to devour.

Of course, that paw would have to wait until he knew what to do about what happened next.

Katie charged him, tackling him with a hard crash to the ground and an "oomph" of a grunt whooshed from his lungs.

Then she was there, hovering over him, standing above him like some she-goddess—proud, fierce . . . furry.

Really furry.

*   *   *

KATIE stared down into Beck's face, chiseled with disbelief, his eyes wide, his jaw clenched with tension from the brunt of the fall he'd taken.

His mouth was moving . . . all yummy and schmexy. Ahhh. Beck in all his Beckness. Insidiously delicious—totally off limits.

Then words shot from between his lips. Words she was at first having trouble processing.

Strangely, Katie noted, the words Beck spoke registered, but they took a moment for her to understand them. It was as though he spoke, and his sentences hovered in the air for mere seconds before coming together and landing in her ears with a soft glide of his accent. She cocked her head at him when she made out his question.

Did she plan to make him a snack? He wanted to know.

She'd smile—if she could. Instead, Katie opened her mouth and yawned, wide, so he could see her teeth, teeth that were like an entity all unto themselves. As snacks came and went, he wouldn't be a bad deal come time for a side of prime beefcake. The blood rushing through his half-human veins called to her with a siren song of a deep hunger, nestling in her belly with a growl.

Yet she had no desire to eat him like she had the deer in the yard today.

Nay, she wanted to do wicked things to him that had nothing to do with nourishment and everything to do with nekkid.

Forget the fact that she didn't have just one paw, but four. Forget the fact that her entire body had felt as though it would incinerate right in Beck's arms as this thing called the shift discarded her human form for a furry one. Forget that resounding crunch of bones still ringing in her ears—or the prickly pinpoints tingling all over her new body where the follicles of her new hair had sprung up in thick patches.

Forget the fact that she had whiskers and she was shedding all over Beck's flannel jacket.

Shit. He was going to need one of those sticky hair-remover rollers she bought in bulk, for sure.

It made her forget everything but Beck's delicious scent and his even more delicious body beneath her rigid stance.

All reason, all sanity left her. There was only the ability to *feel*. Everything.

As though she were a toddler—each new texture was exciting—each item catching her attention, nirvana.

There were no worries—no bills to pay—no ugly divorces—no angry townspeople who refused to accept her—no shameful past to run from.

She was like one, big raw nerve of nothing but sensory perceptions so exaggerated—each tendon she stretched was like a revelation. Each muscle flexed was sinuous and stealthy in its catch and release.

This—ohhhh, this thing called shift was euphoric—a rush of senses and enormous overloads of stimuli, followed by an overwhelming charge of adrenaline, pulsing, pounding through her veins until she thought she would explode from the freedom of it all.

She wanted to run—climb—shed all her inhibitions and experience the bliss this new shape brought her.

A finger tapped her left paw, drawing her attention once more to Beck's handsome face scrunched and red.

"Heavy," he wheezed, pointing to her large front paws on his shoulders and the other two on his upper thighs.

Instantly, she leapt off him, sitting beside his glorious length to stretch and adjust to this bizarre metamorphosis. The cool floor beneath her belly was as comfortable as any bed she'd ever slept in.

Beck sucked in some air and sat up on his elbows to take her in with eyes that no longer held disbelief but hesitant awe. Beck shook his head. "Bloody bonkers."

Katie reared her head back in agreement, only to find she had to temper that movement with caution. As a cougar, her flexibility beat any class in Pilates she'd ever taken.

Beck placed a hand under her chin, gazing into her eyes. "I can't explain it, but this—you like this—in this form—makes complete sense. I understand what just happened and don't all at once. No, don't say it. I know it chuffs you when I repeat that same refrain. Hold on—I'll do the grating sigh for you." Beck let loose a disgusted sigh for her, then grinned. "But you know, I just thought of something. You can't say anything about it, can you?" His chuckle was deep and satisfied to her ears. "I won't deny I feel a certain affinity for your inability to speak. The quiet is a nice change from your sharp-tongued sniper attacks."

She growled her disapproval, pulling her jaw from his grasp and rising on all fours to indicate they should do what they came to. Katie wanted to ask what had happened when they saw Daniel Green's name on the door—why Beck had appeared so far away in disconcerting thought, but that would have to wait.

Testing her hindquarters, she reared up to place her paws on the door of Dr. Green's office, scraping it with sharp claws against the smooth oak surface until she got her balance.

Beck rose, too, following her lead by popping the door open to an office filled with clutter. Stacks of computer printout paper lined the metal desk—a computer, broken, the pieces scattered, lay in ruin. Clearly, Dr. Green had kept some kind of records someone didn't want found if the trashed computer was any indication. Which meant the hard drive was probably long gone.

Damn.

Beakers, tumbled and strewn across the floor with unidentifiable substances, were everywhere. Gadgets Katie couldn't identify took up almost all of the tiny space Dr. Green called his office.

Yellow police tape surrounded a large stain of what Katie assumed was Daniel Green's blood. She shivered in sympathy, feeling the hairs on her body stand on end.

Beck knelt under the tape to gaze at the crusted, dark stain. Again, his eyes held sorrow Katie would chalk up to the sort of remorse one felt when hearing an elderly man had been beaten into a coma.

Yet Beck lingered, closing his eyes, his nostrils flaring, as though he were deep in thought.

She brushed against him to encourage him to hurry it up. Their hour had surely passed. The last thing they needed was a surly vampire stomping through what was already a hella mess.

Beck rose and began digging through the stacks and stacks of paper, frowning, mumbling, and cursing the disaster area while he sifted. "I have no idea what this means—any of it. It's all like reading a foreign language. Though it's a relief to know I can read," he quipped, ever optimistic. "I don't know what to take, Katie. Damn. Can you read any of this?" He shoved a piece of paper in front of her with what she supposed was Dr. Green's handwriting.

And it was in a foreign language.

Perfect.

Katie nudged the paper to indicate she didn't understand it. Now how to tell him to gather as much as he could carry so they could sift through it when they returned to the house.

Again he must have read her cougar mind. "I'm going to grab as much of this as I can, and we'll take it back to the house, but first, let's go through his desk drawers. Maybe we'll find something personal that will help."

Drawer after drawer contained absolutely nothing. Most likely, the police had taken whatever was once contained in the drawers as evidence. But then, why hadn't they taken the research Dr. Green was doing?

Her newly acquired large head butted sloppily against the top of Beck's thigh when he stopped short at a small TV tray with an array of pictures. She followed his line of vision, smelled his hesitation much the way she would if she were hunting him as prey.

Instinctively, she knew this would be the time to pounce were she on the prowl—when his defenses were down, weakened by whatever had caught him off guard.

Katie let her nose nudge his hand, telling herself it had nothing to do with the shiver that left her delirious along her spine and everything to do with asking him what was taking so long. They needed to get the hell out before someone caught them.

Beck swiped at the picture on the tray, holding it at an angle she could see.

Faded and torn at one edge, and yellowed from age, the photograph was a sketch rather than a picture taken with a camera. A woman, dressed in something out of the 1800s with a hoopskirt and a hat with feathers peered back at her. Her features were sharply defined, almond-shaped eyes, solemn and lifeless, bore into Katie's. The woman's high cheekbones led to a nose that worked perfectly with her face and lips that were wide, but only wide enough to add a sensual hint to them. It was her full mouth that made Katie look twice. She knew that mouth . . .

Beck rolled the sketch up and jammed it into his flannel jacket pocket.

Oh, no. They weren't leaving here until he explained his reaction to the sketch. She used her mouth to tug on the hem of his jacket, but he brushed her away with an impatient hand.

So she did what any good cougar with the strength of ten men would do.

Charged him again, tipping his big body over as though he were nothing more than some wooden blocks.

She'd smile in satisfaction at the surprised, then clearly annoyed expression on his face, if she could, that was. Instead, she flattened her lithe new form over his and opened her mouth wide to hiss her displeasure.

Beck narrowed his gaze and wrinkled his nose. "Breath mint?"

Okay. Enough. She reacted by digging through his jacket until she saw the tip of the sketch and managed to use her paws, awkward, awkward, awkward, and mouth to slide it out. She cocked her head at him in question and waited.

His eyebrow rose. "You could have just asked." Then he barked a laugh up at her meant to taunt. "Sorry. I guess your words are otherwise engaged."

Katie put her paw on his mouth and growled, leaning into him with a threatening lick of his jugular. Which was ever so yummy on her tongue.

He sputtered it back at her with a sharp blow from his lips. "Don't you threaten me, Dr. Woods. There's going to come a day when I can do what you just did, and I'd bet my eyeteeth, I'm a badder ass. Just you keep that in mind when you go knocking me around like some stuffed toy."

Frustration made her wrinkle the sketch with a clunky shove.

He sighed, forlornly and with great exaggeration. "So I suppose you want to know why the picture caught me off guard?"

Katie responded by pounding her paws on his chest with impatience.

Beck's face turned into a mask of stone when he grabbed at her paws with big hands to still them.

And then he dropped a bomb. "This"—he pointed to the paper—"is a portrait of my mother."

CHAPTER
II

Beck's mother was from the 1800s?

So did that mean his father was from the future?

How was this possible? Maybe he was mistaken. He couldn't remember a goddamned thing about himself, but he could remember something so crazy it should be on the SyFy Channel?

And then she paused, remembering at one time just how impossible she'd thought everything that had passed in the last two days was.

Did this mean cougars did have eternal life after all? Like vampires and werewolves? Her thoughts scattered so, she couldn't remember what Nina and Wanda had told her about their paranormal details.

How unfair was it that she could neither question him about how he knew who was in the sketch nor press him for details? Beck was probably feeling lucky, too.

And then a thought crept in—unbidden and unwanted.

What if she couldn't shift back to her human form, and she could never ask anyone anything again? Her nirvana took a nose-dive into doom.

Beck sat up suddenly, ramrod straight, placing a hand on her head that almost made her purr. "Did you hear that?"

A tilt of her head, the twitch of an ear, and she caught what Beck was hearing. Footsteps. Of the human variety. The soft fall of sneakers, padding along the corridor was distinct.

She was on her feet in seconds, creeping to the door of the office with Beck right behind her. They absolutely couldn't get caught. Aunt Teeny would have to break out the cookie-jar money to post bail.

Beck peered around the corner, holding his hand in front of her nose to keep her from moving. Despite imminent disaster, Katie yearned to nuzzle it, smell his skin, rub her face against his callused skin. Heat shot along her spine at the thought.

"Damn," he hissed, shoving the papers he'd gathered inside his jacket.

Yeah. Damn.

Damn what?

Her eyes followed his around the corner.

Oh, yes. That was a *damn*.

And a *what the fuck* all in one thought.

Why was Esmeralda Hunt at the animal park, and why was she heading toward Dr. Green's office?

Their intake of breath was simultaneous. There was nowhere to hide a cougar and a man the size of a skyscraper in this tiny office. Not to mention, try explaining a cougar on the loose with said skyscraper.

Just then Esmeralda veered off to the left and down another corridor they'd yet to explore.

Which meant they needed to bust a move while the busting was good.

Katie made a leap for the opening of the door, only to find she was awkward for a moment. Her brain registered two feet—not four paws.

She skidded out into the slick hallway and crashed against the wall, her paws slipping out from under her while she tried to get a grip on the floor. When she attempted to right herself, she flopped back down on her belly, her paws splaying in all directions.

Jesus Christ and a kitten.

But Beck was behind her, pushing her back end upward and whispering with a harsh tone, "Get it together, Dr. Woods—we need to get out of here now!"

His hard shove lifted her to her feet again and catapulted her into moving. Again she scrambled, but this time only momentarily before she began to successfully alternate her front and back legs into coordinated movement.

Beck ran toward the door they'd come in like he had wings on his feet, punching the door open and holding it for her. Katie zipped past him and made a dash for the parking lot, darting toward the fence.

The slap of Beck's feet behind her, heavy in their work boots, came to a stomping halt. He looked up at the fence with a grimace, muttering a curse.

Yeah, she concurred. How the hell was she going to climb a chain-link fence like this?

"Dude!" a voice out of the darkness whispered with fierce intensity.

Katie's big head swung to her left. Her eyes zeroed in on a big hole in the links of the fence and a round face, surrounded by dark hair poking through it.

Kaih!

Both she and Beck made a beeline for him, the pads of her paws crunching against some loose gravel.

"You better hurry it up! The vampire? She's wide awake, and she says you're almost ten minutes past the hour. Make it fast because I do not want to see what your dick looks like after it's been pulled out through your belly button."

Beck threw his forearm over his mouth to muffle his squeal of laughter. "Glad to see you, man."

Kaih pulled at the hole in the fence with two hands so Beck could climb through. "Better me than the Count. She's homicidal when she gets going. I don't know how I talked her into letting me come alone."

"You didn't, Runs Like a Ballerina."

Katie shuddered at the sound of Nina's voice.

"Stop doing that!" Kaih insisted.

Nina popped Kaih in his dark head with a snap of her finger. "I wouldn't have to do that if you'd have done what you were told. I told you to stay put."

Kaih fought a cower, and he was almost successful when he rebutted, "You did. But you're an angry vampire. Doc Woods can't afford to have any more trouble. Wanda said for sure your big mouth would create an unnecessary amount of noise and maybe even some property damage. I was just trying to keep everyone out of trouble."

Nina, possibly two inches taller than Kaih, leered down at him. "You think I'm angry?"

Kaih gulped, his Adam's apple bobbing under the light of the moon. He rocked back on his heels in a nervous gesture. "Sor . . . Sort of. Yeah." He puffed his chest out, gathering his bravado. "I think you're angry."

Nina chuckled. "Silly. This is me happy. You haven't even touched angry. Now move," she ordered. Her face, so pale in the half moonlight, all business and determination shifted expressions as her eyes widened when she caught a look at Katie. "Holy shift. Is that the doc?"

"Shhhheeeiit!" Kaih yelped, jumping back to fall on the hard ground, shooting fallen leaves up in his wake.

Nina knocked him in the shoulder with the flat of her hand. "Why don't you just fucking call the cops on that phone of yours and tell them we're here? Shut up, dipshit."

Kaih instantly clamped his mouth shut, backing away to let Nina pull at the fence and help Beck through first. He turned, taking Nina's place at the fence to help Katie safely through what was, due to Nina's strength, now a jagged metal hole.

Katie's fear they'd all be caught made her rush her exit, catching her side with a stinging tear to her side. Instead of a hushed "ouch," her cry of pain came out in a growl of discontent.

Nina looked to Beck while she bent the fence back in place. "Can she understand us?"

His nod was curt, his shiny, black hair brushing against his collar. "I think she can. We'd better get the hell out of here before we're found out."

But Nina was in no rush. Instead, she sat on her haunches in front of Katie and chucked her under the chin with a sympathetic grin. "Some crazy shit, huh, Doc lady?" Then she frowned, pressing her fingers to Katie's stinging side. "Dudes, she's bleeding pretty bad. Let's get the fuck out of here. You okay to make a break for it, Katie?"

Katie didn't bother to try to answer Nina's question with her body language. Instead, she took off at a jog. As her feet became surer beneath her, her sprint turned into a soaring run—free— without worry.

Trees passed by her in a blur of falling leaves and aged trunks. She hurtled over logs as though they were mere twigs in her path.

The light on Teeny's front porch beckoned her, guiding her toward home—and maybe a flea bath if that damned itch around her neck was a sign.

Katie made it back to the house and up the wide steps of the front porch, panting. The pain in her side now a dull throb.

She experienced a moment of inner, childish satisfaction that she'd beat everyone else back.

"Vampire beats cougar," Nina said on a chuckle from the direction of the porch swing. "C'mere and let me take a good look at that cut."

Katie sauntered over to her, turning so Nina could see the cut clearly.

Her arched brows met each other in concern. "We need to clean that up. I don't know if you heal like we do, but if not, you're gonna have some nasty gash in your human form."

She sank back on her haunches when Nina mentioned her human form. What if she was stuck like this? How did Wanda and Marty summon a shift at will? Or not shift when they shouldn't, for that matter?

Nina used her sneakered foot to nudge Katie's front paw. "I know what you're worried about, Doc. But Wanda and Marty tell me it's about concentration. At least when they first started shifting. You have to focus on your bones and crap—or something like that. Now they can do it by just thinking it. You will, too."

Katie let out what she hoped was a sound similar to relief, grateful for the comfort and astounded it had come from Nina.

"So what the hell? Did it just happen? Wait. Hoo, shit! Did you end up all nekkid in front of the teenybopper?" She threw her head back and laughed. When she tilted it back upward, her eyes widened.

"In fact, that was exactly how it happened, Nina," Katie remarked, dry and surly.

Nina was just pulling off her jacket when Kaih and Beck flew up the steps.

Kaih shrieked in horror just before Beck had the chance to throw one hand over his mouth and the other over his eyes. "Jesus. I just saw my boss naked," he struggled to say around Beck's hand. "How am I ever going to be able to look her in the eye again?"

Katie's eyes narrowed at Kaih's back. Oh, c'mon. She looked hella fine naked, according to the reflection she'd seen in the mirror tonight.

Yet Beck's eyes remained glued on Katie's awkwardly sprawled, naked body.

"Hey," Nina snarled, throwing her hoodie over Katie and tucking it around her. "Turn your ass around, pal. This ain't a peep show for pervs."

Beck immediately followed Nina's orders, but an amused chuckle escaped his lips anyway. Until his eyes fell to the drops of blood on the slate gray porch floor. "You're hurt." His eyes held concern, deep, blue, warm. "Let me look." He moved toward Katie, but Nina stopped him.

"I got this. You take the mouth inside and make some tea for her."

Beck went with a terse grunt, shoving Kaih in the front door, and letting it close behind them.

Nina helped Katie up, slipping her arms into the hoodie. "You need to take a look at that cut, Doc. You'd know better than I do if you're gonna need stitches, but it looks pretty deep."

Katie nodded, too dazed to answer. Whatever happened to your body when you shifted, it was exhausting. Her legs were like jelly rolls and her knees, butter.

Nina took her in through the kitchen and directed her straight to an examining room where she could see the damage, giving

Kaih and Beck the finger as they passed them. "One word from either one of you, and I'll snatch your fucking tongues out of your heads and beat you about the head and shoulders with 'em," she warned over her shoulder.

Nina flipped on the light and settled Katie on a chair. The glare made Katie wince. "Lift your arms so I can see."

Katie obliged, so tired, her eyes fought to stay open, despite Nina's prodding, yet gentle fingers. A brief knock on the door, and Wanda was there. Sweet, concerned, speaking softly to her. "Oh, Katie . . . You're injured." Wanda was like an Afghan, Katie mused at finally finding the right dog-to-human definition, regal and dignified in any situation.

Katie's head lolled back, but firm fingers gripped her chin, eyes brown and full of worry searched her grainy ones. "Katie, honey? Tell me what I need to do. I know you're exhausted. The first few shifts will do that to you, but you have to let me tend this wound. It's deep. Tell me what to do first."

"C . . . Clean it . . ." she offered, her throat sore and scratchy, her words dry and croaking.

"Right. Sorry. I don't know what I was thinking. Nina, antiseptic and cotton balls. Now, please. And one of those towels to wrap around her waist."

The sharp, cold sting of the antiseptic smarted, making her suck in a gulp of air.

"I'm sorry," Wanda fretted, running a hand over Katie's tangled hair. "You need to take a look at this. I don't know if you need stitches, Katie."

Katie's head fell forward like it was made of lead, forcing her eyes to focus on the placement of Nina's hands on her sore flesh mid–rib cage. The skin was puckered and pink, but it was a clean cut. Just a flesh wound, not deep enough for stitches, but very close. Her lips stuck together when she attempted to convey that, but instead, her head fell forward like some sad imitation of a lifeless rag doll.

Wanda forced her chin back up again. "Take my hand, Katie, and pay attention. Squeeze once if you need stitches, twice if you just need a bandage."

Katie felt Wanda's hand encompass hers, warm, soothing. She was like warm milk when you couldn't sleep. Tums when you had an upset stomach. Compassionate, kind—nuts to hang around a tight ass like Nina. Katie gave two weak squeezes.

"Get those big bandages, Nina."

"Anti . . . stuff to stop . . ." Everything was beginning to grow hazy. Her words slurred, fading in and out. She was aware it was happening even as her eyes warred with her brain.

Nina stooped down and scanned her eyes, reading her mind. "Antiseptic, Wanda. We have to put some on before the bandage."

Cool hands began a soothing ministration of cleansing and slathering a silky gel on her rib cage. She let out a whimper when the cold cream met her wounded flesh.

Vaguely, Katie heard Beck burst through the door. "What the bloody hell are you doing to her?" The worry in his gruff voice made her smile sleepily. Then she remembered he'd seen her naked.

Twice.

"Chill, Fancy Feast," Nina scolded, the sound of her feet shuffling ringing in Katie's head. "It's just a flesh wound. We're fixing her up. Shut it."

Beck's strong presence, one that apparently had the balls to defy Nina, came to warm her right side. He put a hand on her shoulder. "I'm not going anywhere until I know Katie's okay. Deal," he said, tight and tense.

Soooo sexy.

Soooo young.

Soooo.

Wanda's laugh was breathy and Katie was almost sure, giddy. "Quiet, Nina. He's just being a gentleman. You'd think by now you'd recognize the signs with Greg for a mate. Beck, if you could just get her to the table, we can lay her down so I can get a better look at what I'm doing."

Strong arms swung her upward, and Katie found her nose nestled in the crook of his sinewy neck. Her sigh was of contentment. Nice. Beck was super-duper nice.

Someone had considerately thrown a blanket on the cold metal where Beck set her down with a tender touch, his hands adjusting the towel and hoodie with such care, it made her sigh once more.

So yummy was the last thought she had before a drugged-like sleep pulled her into its velvety blackness.

So who was responsible for the freight train that had not just run over her body but had been put in reverse and had run over her again just to make sure she was in extra agony?

A groan slipped from her lips when Katie attempted to stretch her legs beneath the cool sheets on her bed.

Cougar might not beat vampire, but it damned well beat Shaun T's Hip-Hop Abs.

"You're awake," a husky, accented voice said, making her almost purr in appreciation.

Her eyes popped open to find Beck, head on his raised arm, lying next to her on her bed and staring down at her with those blue penetrating eyes always so full of deviltry. "You've slept 'round the clock."

She made a move to sit up but unsuccessfully flopped back on the pillows when her abs screeched a protest. Rolling her tongue over her teeth, she also realized she was naked beneath the thin sheet, and Beck was only mere inches from her. "What time is it?"

He grinned and pointed to her bedside clock. "Midnight. Almost a full day since we made our daring escape from the animal park yesterday."

Katie made another attempt to rise and remove herself from his freshly showered scent. "Tinkerbell. She has to be fed and at least cuddled. Jesus, she must be frantic."

Beck placed a solid hand on her bare shoulder, pushing her back on the bed and tucking the blanket back around her with the other. "Kaih, Ingrid, and I took care of everything. Tink is fine, if not still as vocal as ever. Everything's quiet."

She skimmed her fingers over the surface of the king-sized, rose-colored pillow above her head where the mob usually slept. "The mob . . . Where are they?"

"They're with Auntie Nina. I confess, hearing Nina coo at those three little yapping monsters while she throws a ball for them is a stark contradiction to the woman who threatened to break my *fucking* legs if I came up the stairs one more time to check on you. She's quite an animal lover."

Forget Nina—he'd checked on her? Katie ran a hand over her tangled hair to distract herself from the warmth coiling in her belly. "Aunt Teeny, is she okay?"

"In your stead, I took her smokes from her first thing this morning."

"How'd that go?"

"There was a struggle. She went left, I went right—we danced for a minute or two until she couldn't catch her breath—which I dutifully reminded her was due to her smoking. Otherwise, I have no doubt she could take me. She's one tough bird, Teeny is. But then I promised to have Nina rub her feet *and* soak her dentures. She folded like a house of cards."

Katie laughed, even though it hurt her stomach to. What didn't hurt was Beck's hand on her shoulder—warm, callused, distracting while he lay on a bed so utterly a dichotomy to the man he was. "I'm glad I missed the fireworks when you shared that with Nina. Did she ask questions about what I was doing in bed all day? It's not like me, and Teeny isn't known for her subtlety."

Beck's fingers began to lightly massage her skin. "She did. We told her you had a twenty-four-hour thing, and then we kept her busy all day long. We even let her make us creamed beef on toast for dinner. God-awful stuff, by the way. No worries. You're covered."

Then his face went from playful to serious. "How do you feel? I'd have been in a state of panic if not for Nina and Wanda assuring me that this kind of sleep after your first few shifts was normal. There were times when I couldn't visibly see you breathe."

Her heart sped up. He'd been panicked? Over her? The notion left her giddy. Then it made *her* panic. "I feel like someone ran me over, but otherwise okay. How do you feel?" As in, how do you feel about remembering a woman who's clearly not from this century just happens to be your mother?

His head cocked. "Is this the point in the conversation where I tell you about what happened at the animal park?"

The memory of last night and his reaction to that sketch came rushing back to her. She decided pressuring him, when his reaction had been so emotional and verging on angry, was unwise. Instead, she opted to nudge. "If telling me something personal is uncomfortable, then no. This isn't the point. But if it's something that will help both of us, then I'd appreciate whatever you know."

"Very PC, Dr. Woods."

She half smiled, sleep still making her eyes grainy. "I'd curtsy, but I think my legs would collapse."

His smile was brief. "It wasn't that I didn't want to tell you, Katie. I just needed to process it."

"Fair enough. So you've had twenty-four hours. Enough process?"

"I think my name is Shaw."

"You got that from a sketch?"

"No. I got that from Daniel Green's office. Just as we were about to become felons, I had the strangest vision. I think he was talking to me, and I think he was doing it while I was in cougar form. He called me Shaw."

"Does that feel comfortable? Or is it still a blank?"

"It does, in fact, feel comfortable. Much the way Spanky and Beck felt uncomfortable. It feels like putting on an old hat or a worn pair of faded jeans."

Now she rose on her elbows to catch a glimpse of his eyes, searching to see if he was hiding anything. "So you remember being a cougar?"

His gaze became distant as he looked past her shoulder and out her bedroom window, but his fingers continued making scintillating patterns over her skin. "That vision I had was so damn real. I felt Daniel Green's hand on me, but it wasn't me—not looking like this anyway. I heard him speak, and when he did, he apologized and called me Shaw. I can't be sure *I* was who was on that table in his office, but it felt like it was happening to me."

Shaw . . . For whatever reason, it fit him. It was strong and confident. Stately, but sexy. "Did he say anything else?"

"No."

"How do you know it was Daniel Green doing the talking?"

"You know, that's a valid point. I just assumed, because he was in Dr. Green's office, that's who it was."

Katie's look grew thoughtful while she continued to fight a sigh of pleasure at Beck's fingers on her now-heated skin. "Describe him to me."

Beck's description matched that of the man who'd come to the clinic the night this all began. "That's him. Did this vision tell you how you came to be at the animal park?"

"Not a single clue as to my origins. Though, Dr. Green apologized to me in that vision. He said, and I quote, 'I won't let them hurt you.' I can't get a clear fix on whether he knew I could do this shift thing or not. The only thing I do know is we know each other. Or rather, I know him. What our relationship is, is anyone's guess."

Katie groaned when his fingers dipped under the sheet, hoping to hide it with a disappointed look. "Did you look through those stacks of computer printouts?"

Now his face grew grim and dark. "All five of us spent a grueling eight hours trying to piece that mess together. We've come to the conclusion that those notes aren't in a foreign language; they're in Daniel Green's own special language. His handwriting is, in Ingrid's words, 'a hot mess,' and almost indecipherable."

Katie nodded. "I had a professor like that in college. A genius. A genius who couldn't spell and whose handwriting resembles that of a kindergartner. So nothing of any use? Damn."

"Maybe you'll see something we didn't, you being a doctor, but none of us could even make out two letters in a word to copy and Google. It was an incredibly frustrating process. I sent Ingrid to bed to rest and Kaih home, both exhausted. Nina and Wanda are watching John Wayne movies with Teeny and the mob as we speak."

Katie smiled at how unbelievably kind Nina and Wanda were, kind and obviously much more tolerant than she'd given at least Nina credit for. Watching television with Teeny was much like sitting in the epicenter of a tornado because of her partial deafness. "And the sketch? How do you know it's of your mother?"

"I just know. I can't explain how, and I already sighed a thousand of your exasperated sighs about it, so you don't need to bother.

Look, all I know was that when I looked at that sketch, I knew she was my mother like you know Teeny is your aunt."

"Did you happen to see the way she was dressed, Beck? That wasn't something from this era, or several gone by now."

"Shaw," he corrected with a smile. "I think, anyway. And I know that, too. I just don't have an explanation for it."

Her mind spun with the possibilities this created. "Do you think it's the eternal-life thing? Maybe cougars have the same gift of eternity vampires and werewolves do."

"That's what Nina and Wanda suggested."

"I just remembered something."

He nodded his head. "Esmeralda Hunt, right?"

"What the hell was she doing there? None of this makes a lick of sense," Katie said. "What could she have to do with the animal park, and why didn't Delray know about it?"

Shaw laughed. "He was too busy obsessing over cheese? We need to talk to her as soon as possible. She never mentioned a word about Daniel Green when she came in with Delray, and you'd think, with the way things spread like wildfire here, she'd know you and the ladies are involved. So she's either hiding something or at least knows something."

Sympathy flooded her veins at the look of aggravation he gave when his lips thinned and his brow furrowed. "This must be very frustrating for you."

His hand ran over his stubbled jaw with long fingers she imagined were on her instead. "I can't even begin to tell you."

"And it's not helping that I've done nothing but breathe down your neck about it."

"I don't mind the breathing on the neck. That was actually kind of nice. It's the hint of suspicion I find insulting."

Fuck the suspicion. Who cared about suspicion when there was neck breathing that was kind of nice. *Oh, you Flirty-McFlirt, Katie Woods.* "Kind of nice?"

Now his eyes glittered with amusement. "As old women go, yes. It was kind of nice."

"I'm not old. I'm older."

"I noticed."

"That I'm older."

"No. That you're not old. Naked, you don't look old."

Her face flamed with embarrassment. "I forgot about that."

Shaw pressed a fingertip to her hot cheek, leaving the flesh of her shoulder cold and lonely. "Me? Not so much."

"It'll pass."

Out of the blue, he asked another astute question. "Who made you feel this way, Katie?"

"What way?"

"That you're not young enough, attractive enough?"

Her eyes skimmed the top of his shoulder to avoid his gaze. "I didn't realize that's how I came across."

"Sure you did. You joke all the time about your age, and mine for that matter, but it's never without that sarcastic edge to it."

"That was hardly a joke. I am older than you, if we're counting appearances. Almost forty-one."

"And?"

Katie twirled the end of her matted braid. "And what?"

"Why is that such a deal breaker for you? What if I am twenty? Though I doubt it, not after seeing that picture of my mother."

"Who we don't know for sure is your mother—yet," she reminded him, "and there's no deal to break. I just don't date younger men—especially if I could have been the one responsible for setting their bedtime." But she might reconsider if he kept pressing his thigh against hers and filling up her frilly bed with his manly-man-ness.

"I'm going to go out on a ledge here. Have you tried dating younger men and had a bad experience?"

"It's never been my bailiwick."

"I have to tell you, if I were a lesser man, all these big words would intimidate me. But seeing as I'm a strong, self-assured, confident teenager, I'm just going to ask. Your who?"

Her eyes smiled. "My kind of thing—my territory. I've never dated a younger man because when I was still dating, a younger man was still jailbait. And as of late, I haven't dated anyone since my divor . . ."

"Teeny told me a little about that divorce today. Quite the dick, your ex, eh?"

A big, hairy dick—metaphorically speaking. That was George. And leave it to Aunt Teeny to tell anyone who would listen. "What did she tell you?" Katie cringed while she waited.

He paused in thought while he went back to distractedly drawing circles along her forearm. "Let me get this right—she said, and I quote, 'That good for nuthin', dipped-in-money bastard should be hung and shot for what he put Katie through during that divorce. He's the shit on my goddamned penny loafers.' Those were her words, I believe."

"And that's her description for him in polite company. You should hear how she really feels," Katie said on an uncomfortable laugh. This wasn't something she wanted to talk to Beck about. Shaw . . . whatever. The pain brought when remembering her divorce had eased some in the days since she'd moved in with Teeny. She had no desire to rip the scab off. She was fresh out of Band-Aids.

"You didn't let me finish. She said he should be drawn and quartered for what he did to your *career*. So what did he do to your career? I already know he's the reason you moved in with Teeny. I just don't know why. According to your aunt, you had a very successful career as a veterinarian in Manhattan."

She'd had many successful things in Manhattan, none of which were real—they were only delusions of what she'd thought she had—and they certainly hadn't been there for her when she'd needed them the most. "I had a good practice," was all she offered.

But Beck-Shaw wasn't having that. "And what happened to that practice that made you leave and come to Deliverance, as Nina so fondly calls it? Divorces happen all the time, Katie, as I recollect, and save the jokes about my memory. I can remember everything but the personal details about my own life. Anyway, divorces happen all the time. They don't typically affect your clientele. Teeny said your husband was some rich, influential lawyer. What does that have to do with you as a practicing vet?"

The pit of her stomach, once warm with his caress boiled now with rage she always had trouble containing. This was a subject best avoided. "I thought we were trying to figure out Dr. Daniel Green and your sudden appearance at the animal park, not the mating habits of the senior citizen who's pushing extinction."

"Ah, well here's the thing. I'm interested in you, Katie. I, unlike you, apparently have no inhibitions when it comes to age or expressing my interest. I'm uninhibited by baggage from past relationships because I don't even know that I had any. Baggage or relationships. I like you. In fact, I like you so much, I want to take you back behind the skate park and knock you up, but not before we hit the malt shop and share a chocolate shake."

Laughter bubbled from her throat and spilled out between her lips. "I'm not that interesting, and I can't get knocked up—I'm infertile." She gave him a mockingly forlorn sigh. "Thus ends our skate-park, chocolate-malt romance. And just when I had hope."

His expression went from teasing to serious. "You can't have children? Should I say I'm sorry?"

Katie shrugged. "Children were always a maybe for me to begin with. I was raised by parents who were pretty distant—definitely not an example of how I'd want a child of mine raised. That's why Aunt Teeny is so important to me. She taught me to bake cookies— even if they were like hockey pucks. She read to me. She encouraged my love of animals. She let me tend every stray I could get my hands on, and she kept them here at the house until I visited again. Teeny was everything my mother, her sister, wasn't. I spent all of my summers here with her in Piney Creek until I was fifteen while my parents vacationed in Europe or wherever."

His smile was warm. "I like Teeny more and more. So, children?"

Children were a much safer subject than her divorce. "When George and I finally did try without success, we did a few tests and found out my fallopian tubes were blocked. They flushed them out, and still nothing. We were both so busy with our careers; I can't see how we would have fit a child in anyway. Like I said, I had parents who left me with nannies, and butlers to take me to father-daughter dances. I didn't want that for my child. So I let it go. I have no regrets, but sure, I wonder sometimes what it would have been like. Though, after my divorce, I'm glad a child wasn't involved."

"You're still hedging. What happened in your divorce that made you run from a place like Manhattan to Piney Creek? You don't have to tell me, but I figure I should know something personal about you before I have my way with you." He wiggled his eyebrows playfully and in such stark contrast to his hard good looks.

Despite her protests, Beck-Shaw's suggestion about having his way with her made her heart race and her womanly parts throb. He was flirting with her, and without warning, she was flirting back by tilting her head at an angle that left her without a double chin. "Do you really want to talk about my divorce?" Because wow, she really didn't.

"Yeah, I really do," he said, tracing more maddening circles on her arms.

"Fine. George wasn't the man I thought I'd married. I knew that emotionally five or six years in, but I was too stupid to realize, morally, he was about as shallow as a dirty puddle. End of."

"Was he unfaithful?"

Shit. What was it about this man that had her in some midnight confessional? Words spilled from her lips like water flowing from a fountain. "Oh, he was, but even something as awful as that couldn't hurt me as much as he ended up hurting me."

"What else tears a marriage apart short of maybe, I dunno, murder?"

Katie's teeth clenched. "Murder's close enough."

His eyes widened, his fingers tightened on her arm. "Jesus Christ, Katie. He murdered someone?"

God, she so didn't want to go here, but here she was. It wasn't like he couldn't Google her and find out anything he wanted to know.

Katie gulped, the words thick on her tongue. "Not someone, no. He murdered animals, innocent animals, and I helped."

CHAPTER

12

Shaw sat upright, leaning over her by placing one arm along each side of her waist. "Say again?"

"George ran underground dog-fighting rings," she blurted, fighting the sob that threatened to escape whenever she said those words out loud.

Disgust shadowed his face, seeping into the lines of his frowning forehead. A disgust Katie knew well—had seen on hundreds of faces when George had been tried and gotten off with almost little or no punishment. "And you knew?"

A tear welled in her eye. Just one—a huge improvement on the thousands she'd shed over the last two years. The horrific nature of George's life outside their marriage still had the ability to make her heart bleed with pain for the animals she'd all but given him to abuse.

"No. I *absolutely* didn't know," she said with the fierce conviction she was so familiar with when she'd denied all allegations over and over. "I had no idea. George and I owned various properties. A house in the Hamptons—one in the Caymans. The cabin where this all took place was his before we married. It's in some remote region of Virginia. I knew of the cabin, but I thought it was where he went fishing with his lawyer buddies while they lived out their bromances. I was actually glad most times when he'd announce he was spending the weekend there. Our marriage had become stale. I knew it. I just didn't want to admit it. We were drifting apart long before I found out about what he was up to. Never, ever, in a million years did I think the cabin was where he participated and ran something so sick."

He stroked her cheek with his thumb, gentle, soothing. "I believe you. So how did that involve you helping him?"

Her chest tightened, constricting her lungs. "Whenever a client had an oops pregnancy that wasn't caught in time, resulting in litters of unwanted kittens or puppies, or if I found a stray, I always posted notes on my bulletin board in my office and on my website in the hopes the animals would be adopted by another client or someone surfing the Web on adoption." Oh, God. She couldn't breathe from the memory of the kind of betrayal George had inflicted upon her. Raw hatred for him resurfaced in a harsh shot to her gut.

Shaw sneered with narrowed eyes. "And the son of a bitch used those strays and unwanted litters of kittens and puppies as . . . I can't even finish that sentence. The fuck," he spat through clenched teeth.

Katie pressed a finger to her trembling lower lip before she spoke again. "It's worse than even that. He was having an affair with my receptionist, Danielle, who conned my clients into giving her the animals with the idea she'd found homes for them, and then she handed them off to George to do with as he pleased. God! It makes my stomach turn when I think about what he did not just to those animals but to the people who trusted me to help them find homes for animals they loved but couldn't necessarily care for."

"Now I see the connection. George gave you up as a sort of supplier, didn't he?"

Her fists clenched with the anger George's dirty dealings still summoned. "He's a slimy prick. Yes! Yes, he said I knew all about it and Danielle backed him up. It was my word against his and hers. The only difference being, they had proof on George and Danielle, but nothing on me. And still, after all this time, I haven't figured out why he was so determined to see me as ruined as he was. I don't understand the motivation behind it. Maybe he figured he would lose all of his possessions to me if he was convicted and I wasn't? George made a lot of money. I can only suspect he thought I'd get everything in the divorce he knew I was filing for." A sob shuddered, but remained silent in her chest. This had been a bad idea. Very bad.

But Shaw gave her a gentle smile. "So what happened to your practice?"

"I almost lost my license over it, but worse, I lost clients I'd had, in some cases, for ten years. I loved my work. I loved my life, even if I didn't really love George anymore. He took the respect I'd earned in the community and turned it into pickets and PETA rioting outside my office until I had to close my doors because my practice dwindled to nothing."

Shaw gathered her in his arms, wiping the stray tears that fell.

Katie's laugh was a harsh bark against the warm confines of his chest. "Kind of like it is now. Who wants a veterinarian even remotely involved with a dog-fighting ring? I was guilty by association. There was a trial, and George was fined and given community service, but I paid a steeper penalty in the end. I lost everything that was important to me, and I don't mean my apartment on the

Upper East Side or my Benz. I mean my patients. The clients I'd come to love and cherish."

"So not only did he decimate your practice, but he left you broke?"

Her smile was sly when she looked up at him. That was one front she'd been smart enough to cover, thanks to Aunt Teeny's advice. "No. Money's not an issue. I was smart enough to make investments through the years that had nothing to do with George. I was actually entitled to alimony, but I'd rather be flayed alive under the midday sun than take anything from that pig. He killed innocent animals. Babies." She sobbed. "Little, innocent babies, and he turned beautiful dogs into snarling, drooling beasts—some so twisted and unmanageable, they had to be euthanized. I just can't believe I didn't know. I just didn't know."

"He's a dick of much more epic proportions than even I gave him credit for. So you've been hiding here and the people in town aren't just afraid of your fancy city ways, they're afraid you'll turn their beloved pets into monsters."

Tears began to drip in stinging reminder of the scorn she just couldn't shake. "That's about the size of it. No matter where I go, that's what I'm up against. I've been officially labeled. Believe me, Piney Creek wasn't my ideal relocation hot spot. But it was the closest thing to home and comfort I know."

"And Tater Tot hot dish, I suspect."

Katie swiped at her tears with the heel of her hand. "Yes—even Teeny's Tater Tot hot dish couldn't keep me away. Had I known the Piney Creek people would shun her so severely, I might have reconsidered that hole I'd been digging."

Shaw rested his chin on the top of her head, smoothing his hands along her spine. "I don't think Teeny's sorry at all. I think she's just proud. There wasn't a note of bitter in her words when she called someone named Magda an overfed sow."

"Aunt Teeny plays the rejection off like she has no feelings, but I know it hurt her to have her friends taken from her. Or the people she thought were her friends, anyway. I just feel like I've done nothing but rain trouble on her since I got here."

"Ah, but you're family. Nothing's more important. The gospel according to Teeny," he said on a chuckle.

"Speaking of family—we were talking about yours."

"I say we don't talk anymore, Katie. You've had a rough few days, and reliving what brought you here, this journey you've been on, was very evidently painful, and I'm glad it was you who told me. I didn't want to have to wrestle Teeny for it."

"She'd so slaughter you."

"I don't doubt her ability to wrestle hungry alligators and come out the victor. Teeny's not the point right now. You are. But I have a cure that's sure to take your mind off Teeny and that ex of yours, whose neck I'd gladly squeeze until he was blue in the face for the shit he's put you through."

Somehow, the vision of Shaw wringing George's neck brought with it a deep feeling of being sheltered—protected, and it made her blush. "I say okay."

His lips grazed her hair. "Do you want to know what I think we should do instead?"

"Play *World of Warcraft?*"

The rumble of his laughter against her cheek made her body tingle. "Lay off the teen jokes. What I have in mind has nothing to do with video games. It's all adultlike, in fact."

"You wanna balance my checkbook, don't you?" She clamped her mouth shut, mortified she'd been so forward and flirtatious.

"Metaphorically speaking, I'd really just like to see your checkbook again." The smile that followed was lascivious.

Instantly, Katie was nervous. She'd had a semi-active sex life in college and before marrying George, but it'd been a long time since she'd engaged in something this spontaneous, and she'd never engaged in anything so forbidden. No matter how long his mother'd been around, Katie couldn't get past the part that quite possibly, when she'd been graduating college and drinking beer from a bong, he'd been riding Big Wheels and snarfing a Capri Sun.

She began to push Shaw away, even if doing so left her still wanting him. "We shouldn't do this."

He hauled her over his length, leaving them pressed together, their noses touching. "I can't think of one good reason not to. I like you, you like me. It's like that show Barney, but with some hanky-panky."

"Because we hardly know each other."

His mouth whispered over hers, making her nipples bead to tight knots. "In all fairness, you can't really know me because I don't know me. Therefore, the getting to know one another point is moot, which means we can skip right to the dirty without any residual guilt."

His lips against hers, light, caressing her mouth, left her breathless and as giddy as it had in the woods. "I ca . . . can't get past the idea that I could be old enough to be . . . your mother."

"Let me help you," he whispered, cupping her breast. A breast that was covered only by a sheet and now the heat of his hand engulfing it in flames.

Warmth spread to her belly, creeping along her thighs to settle between her legs. Shaw's mouth captured hers, hot, fierce. The slut in her, the one that wanted to clamp her thighs around him and never let go, just wouldn't stand up to the adult in her, who was going all sensible in her head right now. "We've known each other for *three* days. One of which I slept through."

His chuckle was thick. "I'll tell you all about today when we're done. Every detail. Promise."

Katie braced her hands on his chest, fighting not to dig her fingers into his hard pecs and indulge in this overwhelming desire to peel his clothes off. "That's not what I mean."

"Ah," he said on a laugh, placing his hands around her wrists. "You mean we should get to know each other. Do you want to know things like what my favorite color is? I'm sort of undecided between green and blue. Wanda tells me blue is perfect for my complexion and totally *in* my color wheel. Though, Nina said to fuck the color wheel and wear whatever I want. They left me very uncertain about myself and my fashion choices." He grinned and winked before rolling so he sprawled on top of her.

Shaw's heavy weight was bliss, hard, strong, pushing her into the cushy mattress with decadent pressure. "That's not what I mean, either. I just mean I usually don't engage in casual sex."

"Well, I don't know if I do, either. Oh, the dilemmas. But as crazy as this sounds, or maybe it'll just sound like I'll say anything, either way, I'm pretty sure that's not who I was. I watched an episode of *Jersey Shore* with Teeny. All that bed-hopping made me fear for their health," he teased while his mouth found the sensitive spot on her neck and began to nibble, driving her to a slow, mad descent into hell for what she was about to agree to.

Still, the responsible adult in her just couldn't let this bone go. No matter how luxurious his lips were sliding along her neck. No matter the rush of heat he created just by molding her to him, allowing the rigid outline of his hard shaft to grind against her. She had to at least look as though she had a misgiving. If she didn't, he'd think she was an easy lay—which certainly appeared to be the case today. Then there was the idea she could be contemplating sleeping with another woman's boyfriend.

"What if we do this, and in the end we find out you have a girlfriend? That's not okay, Shaw. It's called infidelity, and I won't be a part of hurting someone who could be looking for you."

He paused teasing her flesh, his gaze direct. "I've given that as much thought as anything else, and the only thing I can tell you is this—I just know there's no one else in my life right now. That fits. It makes sense, and I'm not saying that because I'm so desperate I can't walk away. I'm saying it because I *feel* it. Just as sure as in my gut I knew my name was Shaw."

His response was so quietly honest, Katie relaxed for a moment until another concern she needed to voice cropped up. "I don't have condoms, but I'm on the Pill to keep me regulated."

"You read my mind," he murmured.

Shaw's mouth was driving her to distraction, curving to her skin, nibbling in all the right places. Ground rules—always a good precaution. "This by no means is a commitment of any kind."

"Were you concerned I'd propose we hit Vegas?"

She arched her neck against the wetness of his tongue, rasping against her flesh. "No. I just don't want you to think—"

"That you'd be my prom date?"

Katie nudged his shoulder all while she arched into his exploration of her collarbone. "There's just no talking to you, is there? You take almost nothing seriously."

"I'm taking this bid to get in your panties very, *very* seriously," he husked, tugging at the sheet and pulling it to her waist. She might have protested, but her breasts stood proudly in an upright position instead of sagging to either side of her upper torso like in days of yore.

Win!

Shaw kissed his way along the curve at the top of each of her breasts, his breath hot and his mouth silky soft. Pinpricks of awareness sprung up on every square inch of her flesh, making a moan slip from her lips.

Heat raged in her veins, the slick feel of desire between her legs almost unbearable.

"So are we a go?" he rumbled, husky against her nipple.

Well, her nipples were giving the thumbs-up.

Katie dragged him to her lips, unable to fight the crazy roar of her hormones anymore. "Do me, cougar man," she demanded, sounding much more like the woman she'd once known—before George.

With that, Shaw tore the sheet from her, exposing her flesh to the cool of the room. Chills skittered along her flesh, followed by a molten swell of fire coursing through her veins at the hungry gaze he pinned her to the bed with.

His eyes glowed in the dark of the room, amber pinpoints shooting from beneath his long lashes as he consumed her with a long, hard glance.

Katie shivered—embarrassed and titillated in one fell swoop. She decided she wanted to see him sans clothes, too. The anticipation of revealing all that hard flesh made her mouth water and her heart crash almost painfully against her ribs.

Her fingers reached for the T-shirt he wore, pulling it up over his head. Her first glance at his abs, defined, sleek, left her fingers itching to touch each solid ridge.

He wasn't overly developed muscularly. In fact, his body was exactly what had always appealed to her—lean, smooth, with just enough muscle to glisten when sweat fell upon it.

Katie let her fingers drift to the belt at his jeans, pulling it, forcing herself to slow down so her fingers wouldn't tremble as though she were some inexperienced kid.

Shaw rose and yanked his jeans off, letting them fall along his thighs, thick with sinew and a sprinkling of dark hair. Her throat closed at the sight of his erection, pushing against his boxer briefs.

When he slipped those off, too, her heart entirely stopped.

Shaw, standing before her naked, could quite possibly be one of the most erotic sights she'd ever seen. He was male personified, every inch of him a treat to the eye. Every plane, dip, and valley on his long frame was worthy of some kind of praise she had no words for.

He sat at the edge of the bed, grabbing her thighs and hauling her over his lap to settle her there. Katie wrapped her legs around his lower back, waiting, her throat constricted, her stomach a knotted jumble of butterflies. His cock brushed her cleft, wet and aching, his hard shaft pulsing against her clit, throbbing and wet.

Shaw slipped a hand between them, using a callused thumb to stroke her clit, the stiff nub a mass of wet desire.

Katie groaned, so turned on, she was dizzy with need. For the first time in any of her sexual encounters, she wanted to skip foreplay and get right to the business at hand. Shaw driving his cock so deep within her, he ripped the breath from her very lungs.

This incredible ability he had to make her body smolder with frantic desire left her impatient. Uncontrollable shivers swept over her at the very thought. Never had she been this hungrily desperate, this hot for a man, not even in her untamed youth.

Shaw's eyes found hers in the velvety darkness, knowing, seeking, then looking deep into her most intimate thought. A thought she'd never voice, but hoped he'd intuitively respond to.

With his deliciously strong hands, Shaw lifted her hips, spanning them with ease, and drove into her, setting her back down hard on his thighs. Her wetness surrounded him, glided against the thickness of his shaft with ease.

Katie's head fell back on her shoulders with a gasp of such intense pleasure she felt it all the way to her core. His cock was hot inside her, filling her up, making her hands grip his shoulders for support. Her back arched when he drove upward, the divine pleasure rippling on an electric current. Katie's nipples scraped his smooth chest, the friction delicious and leaving her nerves raw and edgy.

Shaw cupped her breasts while he set a fierce rhythm of driving thrusts, forcing her hips to move in frantic circles.

Need clawed at her. Sharp, sweet, pounding, insatiable need. Her veins flooded with a new kind of heat when his lips finally captured her nipple, tugging at it, pulling it into his mouth only to let it go, then lavish it with his silken tongue. The scrape of his flesh against hers left a well of untapped desire in her belly.

Katie's fingers dug into his scalp, gripping his hair, driving her breast at him, demanding he satisfy this wild, raging passion.

Her clit scraped the crisp pubic hairs at the base of his cock, adding to the multitude of sensations she was already experiencing. She ground against his lap, driving down on him as though her life depended on it.

"Fuck," he groaned, thick and muffled against her breast, his breath coming in harsh gasps. "There's more, Katie. More I want to experience, but you're so damned hot and tight . . ."

But Katie didn't care about anything else. There was just Shaw's naked flesh, glistening with sweat, sliding against hers. There was only his scent, musky and clean, in her nose. There was only his length, buried balls deep in her, sending her to the edge of madness.

Frenzied hands pulled him close to her chest as she used her heels to garner the leverage she needed to drive him deeper inside her. Her whimper was of desperation, a cry to find relief from this place he'd taken her to.

Somewhere she'd never been.

Somewhere she didn't want to leave.

She clung to that thought until she was nothing but a shredded, hot mass of raw nerves, and as orgasm rose like a fiery swell, she couldn't fight it. Her head flung back, her scream was a hiss of total, blinding fulfillment.

Shaw's gasp filled her ears; his grip on her became almost painful. Yet she reveled in it, gripped his wrists so he'd dig his fingers farther into her skin as she came. She found herself deriving so much pleasure from his harsh grasp, it almost frightened her.

But that didn't stop her on her quest to wring every ounce of tantalizing, decadent sensation. When she contracted around his cock for the last time, Shaw jerked within her, jutting his hips upward for one final thrust.

She fell against the shelter of his chest, boneless and weary. Their intakes of breath mingled while he still pulsed within her. Shaw's hands soothed her flaming skin, damp and sensitive. He ran his hands all over her, along her arms, over the tops of her thighs, into her hair while they cooled down.

As her muddled thoughts cleared, she had but one notion.

This forbidden thing she'd been so hung up on? Not too shabby.

"Katie?"

"Shaw?" she asked from against his neck.

"Hot, huh?"

Like a fucking bonfire, baby. "Like lava."

"Regrets?"

"Not at this moment. But give me an hour, maybe less." She'd just had incredible, mind-blowing sex with a man who might not be far from the age of consent. That would have never happened with the old, adult Katie. The one who thought everything out, asked a million questions, asked a million more, and only then made a decision.

"No regrets. Something like that should never be regrettable."

"I'll work on that."

His chest brushed against hers when he sighed. "I want to say I've never experienced anything like that before. But my guess is you wouldn't believe me."

"You're setting a trend for disbelief."

His chuckle was deep and amused. "Clearly, I knew what I was doing."

"Should we knuck that statement up?"

"Are you going to start with the teen jokes again?"

Katie fought a grin. "Only if you make me knuck up your sexual success."

"That doesn't seem like something I'd do."

"Well, herein lies the glitch. We don't know for sure what you'd do or what you've done. For all we know, you brag about your conquests at the local pub while you have your eye on the next notch on your bedpost."

"I find the sound of that scenario distasteful. So I'm going to go with the notion I'm not that kind of guy."

"For all we know, you could be a serial killer. Don't corner the market on good just yet. I'd pace myself, were I you."

He laughed, his good-natured resolve firmly in place, pulling her closer while she used her biting sarcasm to push him away. "You know what the problem is here, Dr. Woods?"

"No. But I do know you'll have an answer whether I want one or not. So I'm prepared to ride this loose. Go."

"You're embarrassed by just how into me you are."

Was there a word bigger than embarrassed? Surely there had to be one for how totally into that she'd been. But the plan was to play it cool. She'd done it before, although, it had been a good fifteen years or so. Katie shrugged; game face in play, she leaned back and looked Shaw dead in the eye. "Maybe I'm just a nymphomaniac. Which means I'm into whoever my conquest is at the time."

"You're no nymphomaniac. You're definitely hot. Completely not the prude I expected, wearing all that girlish lace all the time, but I'll venture to guess you've had fewer lovers than you have fingers and toes."

"Point. Prudes don't do men they've only known for three days."

"Two. You slept through today."

"Thank you for the reminder. You're better than my iPhone calendar."

"I'm here to serve."

"Speaking of serving, I'm starving."

"You'd rather eat than talk about what just happened? Who's the man in this relationship anyway?"

"I haven't eaten since yesterday's dinner."

Running a finger across her cheekbone, leaving a tantalizing chill in its wake, he said, "I suddenly feel very cheap and discarded."

"Did you expect to feel warm and snuggly?"

Shaw's expression was mockingly grave. "I expected respect and understanding."

"You mean afterglow?"

"I mean any kind of glow that doesn't leave me feeling like a piece of meat."

"Well, that settles it."

"Settles what?"

"I *am* the man in this relationship."

"You're a mean one, Miss Grinch."

"I'm a practical one. We just had amazing sex. Yippee. Now let's eat."

She began to rise, but Shaw stopped her, throwing her down on the bed with a grin. "You're doing a fine job of pretending this meant nothing. I'm going to let you do that for a little while, but I'm certain I'll lose patience with you. Then you'll have to own this thing between us. Lock, stock, and my smoking gun."

Katie forced her expression to go blank. "I didn't say it meant nothing, and there's nothing between us but some good old-fashioned sex. I just said I was hungry." And she was. Ravenous, in fact. Those deer in her backyard better skedaddle or *Bambi Revisited* was a distinct possibility.

Refusing to allow her to dampen his spirits, Shaw ran a finger over her ribs and took a swipe at both nipples with his tongue before pulling her upward to stand and drape her arms around his neck. "I see how this is going to go. Okay, This Was No Big Deal, Dr. Woods. Have it your way, but when you can't look at me without seeing me in the buff, we'll just see if this isn't such a big deal."

He dropped her arms to her sides and strode naked to pull her lavender silk bathrobe from the arm of the chair in the corner of the room. He held it up for her with a grin. She followed suit by sliding her arms into it, fighting once again another swell of rising tingles he created when he nipped at her neck.

He was delicious. They'd had amazing sex.

The kind of sex she'd remember long after they solved his mystery and he was gone.

She hid her face in her tangled hair at the thought of Shaw leaving.

It left her stomach tied up in tight knots.

That just wasn't okay.

Shaw, who'd pulled on his jeans and shirt, leaned over her shoulder while she thoughtfully stared out the window. "I told you," he mocked with a light chuckle, like he'd read her dismayed thoughts.

He strode toward the door, stopping just short of it to shake his ass and roar with laughter before he slipped through it and closed it behind him.

Despite his blatant mockery, Katie let her head fall to her chest and she laughed, too.

Damn his infectious charm.

Damn his incredible lovemaking.

Damn *him*.

Just damn.

CHAPTER 13

A week had passed since that night in Katie's room. Though there'd been several nights just like it.

Fine. Every night was just like it.

She couldn't get enough of him, his hands on her, his lips devouring every square inch of her. Each time they made love, she cursed him and her own inability to resist him. There'd even been a night or two she'd found herself knocking on *his* door.

Which, Nina had slyly informed her when she'd caught her in the act, made her a cougar in every sense of the word. In fact, she'd be a cougar-MILF if she had children. Teeny, thankfully misunderstanding the laughter among the women one evening over after-dinner coffee, declared herself a GILF.

Aunt Teeny had decided Shaw had a crush on her because he held her balls of yarn for her while she knitted him a sweater and they watched reruns of *The Rockford Files*.

The sight of the two of them, ensconced in James Garner and

knee-deep in blue-and-green yarn had made Katie's heart literally shiver in her chest, awakening yet another emotion for Shaw she neither wanted nor needed. This could only end badly. What if he had a wife? Children? A life full of things she could never be a part of?

What if he really wasn't the child she'd accused him of being and instead, was like Nina and Wanda? Fully grown adults who had the youthful glow of teenagers, but lived responsible adult lives while trying to integrate into a human world.

They still had no new information about Shaw's origins, and according to Darnell, who'd kindly appointed himself watchdog, Daniel Green was still in a coma. After seeing with her own eyes the mess Dr. Green's notes were in, even Katie'd given up hope anything of use was in them. Ironically, there was no information online about Dr. Green, either. Kaih and Ingrid had searched tirelessly to find any information on him, but to no avail.

Mr. Magoo himself had closed the animal park until further notice, leaving a residual boo-hiss Katie heard in the averted eyes of the people in town when she'd gone to buy supplies for her guests, and pounds and pounds of beef to sustain her and Shaw's growing appetites.

Attempting to contact Esmeralda to gather an explanation about her appearance the night she and Shaw had broken into the park left them all scratching their heads. Esmeralda and Delray had left town. At least, according to her gloating neighbor Doreen, who'd cackled when she'd told them as she straightened her wig on her hairless head.

Katie hadn't shifted again since that night, either. Though Wanda informed her, shifting, when it first began, was as unpredictable as Nina's mouth.

Yet, they'd all found a strange, easy rhythm to their days, despite the limbo they were now in. Nina and Wanda spent a lot of time with Teeny, helping her lift heavy wheelbarrows full of dirt in the garden and laughing like they'd always been friends. Nina with a hat and sunglasses to keep the sun from burning her, and Wanda with the mob at her feet running frenzied circles, Dozer never far behind, sprawled in a patch of weak sunlight.

She and Shaw shared coffee every morning at sunrise—in a silent salute to their bedtime hijinks. She fought not to grin over the rim of her cup, and he made no bones about the fact that he felt no shame over their debauchery.

Katie spent a lot of time fending off girly sighs and dreamy gazes while she showered or put makeup on. Shaw was becoming a part of her everyday routine, and that, above everything else, even her cougarlicious status, frightened her. She didn't want to become attached to someone who was bound to have a life somewhere else, possibly far, far away from here, if his accent was any indication.

"You're thinking about me, aren't you?" a silky-rough voice whispered in her ear from behind. Shaw's hands went around her waist, sliding upward to cup her breasts beneath her UCLA sweatshirt, making her drop her book of crossword puzzles.

Katie gasped at the sting of pleasure he aroused the moment his hands touched her. Her nipples tightened beneath her bra, pressing against it with delicious friction. "I was thinking about whether we should give you a nap time so I can get some work done without you sneaking up behind me all the time and accosting me." As she spoke the words, she smiled, naughty and in anticipation.

Turning her to face him, he sipped at her lips while pushing her bra upward with aggressive, impatient fingers. "I'm always up for a nap. As long as it's naked and with you," he teased, backing her against the far wall of the boardinghouse and away from the windows.

"It's always about the naked with you," she remarked, keeping her tone dry despite the rasp of her zipper being dragged downward and the thrill his words brought her.

He drove a hand into her jeans, cupping her sex, spreading the lips to stroke her clit. "And it isn't for you?"

"It's not like you're easy to avoid," she said on a moan, biting her lower lip at the intense shot of pleasure he created between her legs.

Shaw nipped her neck hard, sending shooting volts of electricity through her veins. "I'm sorry. Wasn't that you knocking on my door just last night?"

Katie gasped when he forced her jeans over her hips to drop to her feet, leaving her in just the silky oyster white panties she'd put on after her shower. "I just wanted to be sure you didn't need anything before I went to bed."

"I need you. *Now*," he demanded, tearing off her sweatshirt and unclasping the front of her pink lace bra to shove it aside and encase a nipple between his lips.

Katie's arms rose above her head without thought, reveling in the hot pulse of his tongue skating over her nipples. He slid a finger over her still-clothed cleft with a hot moan. She groaned when Shaw slipped his hands into her panties and inserted his index finger inside her. He drove it upward, making her hips crash against his hand in urgent need.

"We could get caught," she huffed as her hips, adopting a will of their own, lifted upward, taking more of his finger, reveling in his callused skin scraping her passage.

Shaw's mouth left her breast to mutter, "I locked the door. Now be quiet. I've been thinking about being in you all morning."

Her whimper at his words wheezed from her lungs. She fought to slip her clogs off in order to allow him easier access, kicking them aside with sloppy feet.

The cold wall against her hot flesh only added to the eroticism when Shaw jolted her against it as he dragged her panties over her thighs and roughly shoved them to the floor.

"Hmmm," he hummed his pleasure at her nakedness in her ear, removing his finger and letting his hands explore her flaming skin. He caressed her hips, pulling them against the rough fabric of his jeans. "There should be a ban on clothes where you're concerned."

She groaned against his lips, lips that consumed hers. "So says the man who's still dressed." She flicked at the collar of his flannel shirt.

No more words were needed. Shaw's feet shuffled to kick off his sneakers and his hands dove for his jeans, unzipping them and letting them drop to the floor.

Katie drove his shirt upward and over his head, sighing in un-adulterated pleasure when her palms flattened to his skin. Each time their naked flesh met was like the first time, and it always wrought a hiss of pleasure from them both.

Shaw bent her backward over his forearm, strong and hard against her back. "Prepare to be ravaged," he said on a harsh gasp when she encompassed his cock in her hands, stroking the silken-hot flesh, tracing the veins that lined it.

He slid down her body with hot kisses strategically placed to evoke mini-groans from her lips. Centering himself between her thighs, he pulled her legs apart, leaning his head against the top of her thigh, the slide of his soft hair on her skin leaving her breath-less with anticipation for his tongue on her.

Katie bit her lip, her head thrashing when Shaw's hot breath grazed her sex. His thumbs spread her apart, and then he slashed his tongue between the lips of her swollen flesh, circling the hard nub of her clit with his tongue, nipping it with his teeth.

Her heart began the familiar staccato crash in her chest; her hands found their familiar place in his hair, driving her fingers against his scalp as he pleasured her. Her head thrashed back and forth, her teeth clenching as he drove his tongue against her swollen flesh over and over.

Katie's chest heaved, pulling him flush to her most intimate place, lifting her thigh to let it wrap around his shoulder.

Her first orgasm always began as a tightening in her belly, an almost unbearable tension she was desperate to find relief from. It swelled, slamming into her gut until it wrung every ounce of pleasure from her.

Shaw knew her body well enough by now to know the signs. He licked her until her fingers clawed at his shoulders and her knees were weak.

There was no rest when their lovemaking got to this point. Pulling her down to his level, he slid beneath her, lying flat on the braided throw rug. Katie straddled him, letting his cock rub against her clit while she stroked him hand over hand. His hard shaft sent her heart racing again; the buck of his hips made her wet her lips in anticipation.

She made a move to position herself between his thighs, but Shaw grabbed her upper arms with strong hands. His eyes, blue and hot with desire, pierced hers. "Not now, Katie," he warned in a sex-drenched lust of a grumble. "Right now I just need to fuck." He dragged her back upward, spreading her thighs to wrap around his waist, claiming her lips as he did. "I just want to fuck you— hard and fast. *Now, Katie.* Put my cock in you now."

Katie shivered her delight at his crude words. She'd never been much of a talker during lovemaking; now she wondered if that wasn't because there wasn't much to talk about. She groaned her compliance, lifting her hips and steadying the head of his cock at her entrance.

Shaw growled low and feral at her teasing. In contrast to his almost always calm, humorous demeanor, when it came to the bed sport, he was possessive, insatiable, and sometimes harshly demanding. And she was drawn to those demands like a moth to a flame, craved his words, longing for his slightest touch. "Don't toy with me, woman," he commanded, gripping the flesh of her hips with biting fingers and driving her down on his fiery shaft.

Katie screamed her pleasure, clinging to his neck by sliding her arms beneath his head. He drove upward, lifting her on his strong thighs so that she felt every muscle in his body contract and flex.

His hard chest scraped against her nipples, his hands dug into her ass, forcing her downward in a harsh demand for satisfaction. The pulse of him within her, thrusting into her silky wet passage, made her dizzy. Flashes of white lights screamed behind her closed eyes as their hips picked up a harder pace.

Shaw latched onto her earlobe, suckling it, whispering erotic words in her ear, encouraging her to come. Without meaning to, her teeth dug into the flesh of his shoulder, the pleasure was intense. Sweat glued them together, making their bodies glide in a decadent slip and slide of skin against skin.

"Christ, Katie," he said between clenched teeth.

Katie acknowledged the beginnings of his climax by nipping at his hard jaw, lifting her hips high, then jamming them back down, hearing the slap of their flesh.

Tendrils of electricity seized her, her every nerve screaming its need for release. It bit at her, clawed her until she could hear nothing but her blood rushing in her ears and the molten heat of orgasm.

Shaw thrashed his hips upward one last time, the strength of his muscles in full force, his climax jolting her.

Katie fell against him, letting her cheek rest against his chest while she gasped for breath. His arms went around her as they always did while they came back to Earth, stroking her back, running circles over her skin, still sensitive from their lovemaking.

"Woman, you'll break me like this," he muttered against the top of her head.

"Me?" Katie jabbed a finger into his chest. "I was minding my own business, cleaning Tinkerbell's cage and perusing my new crossword puzzle book. This is on you."

"My only defense is the notion you had on another pair of those silky wisps of underwear you call panties. Your fondness for naughty underthings will be my undoing."

His words made her heart skip a beat, and she found for the hundredth time in so many days, she had to tamp down her romantic notions. Shaw liked a good toss—developing feelings for a man who didn't even know his own telephone number would just be stupid. She pushed off him, rolling away to gather her clothes, refusing to snuggle against the warm cocoon of his chest. It always took all of her determination, but in the end, maybe when he returned to wherever it was he came from, it would hurt less.

Pounding at the boardinghouse's door startled them both into action.

"Yoo-hoo! Demi and Ashton!" Nina yelled. "Break it the fuck up in there. Jesus Christ, there's steam on the goddamned windows from all this cranking. Can't you two keep it in your pants until we're all asleep? Get back to the house now. Darnell's here with some shit about Dr. Green."

Both Katie and Shaw scurried to gather their clothes, making assholes and elbows to the door, clothes askew, hair mussed.

Just before they hit the front steps of the porch, Katie stopped and clutched the banister.

Shaw came up at her rear, tapping her on the ass. "You okay?"

What if Darnell held the elusive key to Shaw's mysterious life, and this was all over? There'd be no more late nights of fierce lovemaking. No more giggling at the thought of being caught by Teeny. No more watching Shaw as he swung an ax to chop wood, his muscles bulging and flexing in the late afternoon sun. No more ridiculous cartoon watching. No more. A tear sprang up in the corner of her eyes out of nowhere.

Shit. Clearly, those feelings she didn't want to develop were developing. Her heart fluttered at this new emotion, tight in her chest and uncomfortable in its newness.

"Katie?" Shaw said again, cupping her chin. "Are you okay?"

His blue gaze met hers. Sucking up her inner whine, she smiled. "Fine. Just a cramp in my leg, thanks to you and your yen for all things *Kama Sutra*–like."

"Blame, blame, blame," he said on a laugh, loping up the steps and holding the door for her with his charming grin full of white teeth and dimples. "Come now. Aren't you excited? Darnell has deets. I bet if you had confetti, you'd throw it."

Yeah. Yippee.

Katie forced her legs to move, taking the steps with the kind of exuberance Shaw expected of her, light and quick.

It was her heart that was heavy.

So fucking heavy.

"HEEEEY," Darnell called from the corner of the kitchen, Paulie propped against his wide chest. "Gimme some, brotha," he ordered Shaw, holding his fist forward.

Shaw bumped it with a welcoming grin. "Darnell. Good to see you."

Well, look who was all jazzed to up and leave her like some discarded mistress. Bet his bags were already mentally packed. Player.

Darnell's wide grin greeted Katie. "How you feelin'?"

Katie's return smile was reserved. She didn't want to shoot the messenger, but she wanted to at least wipe the infectious grin from his face. With the palm of her hand. Oh. Harsh, Katie. Harsh. "I'm okay, Darnell. How're you?"

He leaned back against the counter, crossing his feet at his ankles, the white of his Nikes glaring at her in all their cheerfulness. Happy, happy, happy. Darnell exuded it. And it sucked hairy ass when she was so unaccountably miserable. "I'm good, cougar lady. So, I got news. Not a lot, but some news that might help y'all, leastways a little."

Shaw's face was unreadable, yet the tension in his body was palpable—at least to Katie, who'd begun to read his body language in just a mere shift of his stance. "Have you seen Dr. Green? Is he better? At least physically?"

Darnell fiddled with the wide gold medallion on his chest. "Yep. I seen him aaiight. Doctors say he's comin' out the coma, and the bruises is fadin'. Least ways thass what I hear when I hover."

"Hover?" Katie asked, her eyebrows raising.

"Yeah. I don't just show up like me and the doc are homies. Hooo-wee, how'd that look? Me a big old scruffy bear and him a respectable doctor. 'Sides, they ain't allowin' him no visitors now. Police orders. So I lay low. I do it when I'm invisible. Hover. Ya know, like a UFO or a helicopter?" He held a wide, beefy hand up parallel to the floor to demonstrate.

Of course. *Hover, stoopid.* "Got it," she replied, her lips thin and trembling. "I didn't know you could be invisible. I'm still learning."

Darnell popped his lips. "I can only do it fo' a little bit. I'm practicin', though. Thass why I can only hear some stuff thass goin' on. But I heard the doctors say he might wake up." His face turned sour with distaste. "Shoot. He was some sight there, too. I dunno who took to him like that, but I like 'em to mess with old Darnell. Jack those shits up and make 'em cry fo their mamas, I would. Beatin' on an old man ain't right."

God. What a mess. Her heart constricted in pity for the confused, muttering man she'd encountered. He had to be at least seventy. Who would beat an old man almost to death?

"So what else do the doctors say, Darnell?" Shaw's words, cultured and inquiring interrupted her thoughts.

"Ain't heard much mo' from the docs, but that poor old man's been talkin' in his coma."

Katie swallowed hard, her throat almost too tight to speak. Yet she forced herself to find her words with clenched fists at her side. "What is he saying, Darnell?"

Darnell's wide face filled with sympathy. His chocolate brown eyes liquid in the late afternoon sun. "He says you gotta save them. Save Nissa. Save 'em *all*. Over and over. I don't know who Nissa is. I tried askin'. He got so riled up the other night 'bout it, I sat with him for a li'l bit. Held his hand till I knew the nurses was changin' shifts. He was bangin' around in that bed like he was gonna get up and go do what 'ere it is he seems to think needs doin'."

Katie couldn't help but smile, even in spite of Darnell's mention of this Nissa. He had a good heart and a gentle soul. How someone with such a good heart became a demon must have some story behind it.

Shaw frowned. "He said something similar in my vision, too. He said he'd keep me safe, but there was no mention of a Nissa."

"Is that it, Darnell? Did he say anything else?" Katie's eyes sought his, waiting, fearing his next words.

His face returned to usual, cheery and bright when he flashed his white teeth at them and blew in Paulie's face with a chuckle. "Nope. Thass all I got."

A breath of pent-up relief escaped Katie's lips. Okay. So Shaw and his life was still a mystery. She fought to contain her joy, especially when Shaw muttered a curse.

He shook his head, leaning a hand on the counter. "Damn. We're getting nowhere here. We're no closer to finding out who

I am. We just keep adding pieces to an already enormous jigsaw puzzle."

Yeahhh. Bummer that. Katie shot him a look of sympathy. She did sympathize. Really. She wanted him to know who he was just as much as he did. She just didn't want him to have a family or a nice English cottage by the sea with ivy crawling up the sides of it, and two-point-five children to greet him at the end of a day when he did it.

That was petty, but there it was. The truth. She liked his presence in her life, more and more with each passing day. She liked when he smiled at her in the dark of night after they'd torn the sheets up.

She especially liked that he was the one outside chopping wood when it was thirty degrees out. She liked. "I'm sorry," she offered. "I know this is frustrating for you." Well done. Appropriate disappointment displayed and noted, Katie Woods.

But Darnell wasn't done. He hoisted Paulie up over his shoulder to scratch his back. Paulie's eyes rolled back in his head while he nipped at the earring in Darnell's ear. "I got some other stuff, too."

Katie's hackles went back up. "About Dr. Green?"

"Nah. 'Bout you kitty shifters. Thought I'd seen prit-near ere' thing since I been a demon, but you cats is da shit. Hardly nuthin' out there 'bout ya. Usually, I can find someone who knows sumthin', but your world's like damned Attica. 'Scuse my bad language." Yet, there had to be some information given Darnell's pleased-with-himself expression. "So this is what I heard. I hear through the grapevine that you shapeshifting kitties are almost extinct 'cuz someone's been pickin' you off one by one."

Shaw's head bobbed upward. "What?"

"Uh-huh. Thass what I heard. Nobody of consequence told me, so don't think I got some important stoolie or nuthin'. Just a harmless demon thass been around awhile. There ain't any of ya that can make baby cougars to add to the breed, either, add to that the fact that there ain't been a baby cougar by a shifter in almost sixty years, and you all dyin' off. And somebody likes it that way."

Katie's sharp gasp filled the room. "But why?"

Darnell's wide shoulders shrugged. "I don't know whass gone wrong or why, but you all ain't reproducin' nuthin'. That just leaves the elders in your community—whoever they are—and now you, Doc, and Shaw here."

"Which means all that moaning and groaning coming from your room is officially considered safe sex, huh, Doc?" Nina said on a snort, Wanda hot on her heels.

Katie blanched.

"Nina Statleon! I told you to stay put, you eavesdropper. God, do you always have to be so crass?" Wanda yelped.

Nina gave her a blank stare. "Yep."

Wanda's eyes narrowed. "You are the ultimate heathen! I told you to give them some privacy, didn't I?"

She gave an embarrassed Darnell a playful shot to the arm. "I can't help it. Jesus, Wanda. It isn't my fault I have fucking super hearing. It's not like they were whispering. And it's true. They're all ridin' each other like that roller-coaster Hercules every fucking night, screamin' with their hands in the air to catch a wave. I'm nocturnal. I hear shit. Sue me."

Katie's face flamed red, but Shaw had the nerve to chuckle. *Chuckle.* "Ah, Nina. Ever honest. I find it, despite an almost always jaw-dropping reaction, very refreshing."

Nina grinned, tightening her hoodie around her head. "Thanks, Spanky-Beck-Shaw. So what's up with the chick?"

"The chick?" Darnell repeated, making cooing noises at Paulie, who responded by burying his nose in Darnell's Giants jersey.

"Yeah. This Nissa. I told you, Doc. There's always a woman,

and I'd bet my tolerance for two and half bites of Twinkie that that bitch wants your ass dead. Maybe she's Three Name's wife or some shit. I dunno. I just know it's always the way. There's always a woman, usually rabid and out-of-her-bird jealous. I called it. Just you remember that when we have to beat the whore down." She gave them all a pointed look.

Wanda's lips were turning blue from the clear effort not to slug Nina. Grabbing her by the back of her hoodie, she yanked her hard. "When will you realize you only make things worse? You're like some metaphoric spoon, always ready to hop into a pot of boiling pasta and stir. Go. Teeny needs help with her pressure socks." Wanda gave her a hard shove in the direction of the bedrooms upstairs.

Nina slunk off, but not without a parting shot and the flip upward of her middle finger. "Spanky-Beck-Shaw thinks I'm refreshing. So in your face," she muttered.

Wanda gave Darnell a hug. "I'm sorry. You know Nina. You all finish chatting, and when you're ready to tell us what you know, please do. I'll be upstairs beating Nina with a wire hanger until she screams, 'Please, Mommy! No more wire hangers!'" She laughed at her clever joke and followed Nina's path.

Katie'd had a moment to gather herself, and the questions had begun forming. "So maybe what Dr. Green was doing had something to do with the shifting population dying out? Maybe whoever tried to kill him knew he knew something? Maybe he was researching a cure? Or maybe he was using them as guinea pigs to find out why they can't shift?"

Now Shaw's typically tan skin turned pale. "Maybe when Daniel said we have to save them, he meant the other cougars at the park? Jesus Christ, Katie. Maybe they're shifters, too?"

Oh. Hell. "Do you think that's why that cougar jumped up on the glass? Remember, Shaw? I couldn't tear you away. Maybe, much like when I shifted, if the cougars at the park are half human, half cougar, they can understand everything we say, but they can't do anything about it because they're in cougar form?" Though she'd only experienced it briefly, it was painfully frustrating. Dear God, how awful.

Shaw began a brisk pace across the braided rugs, stepping over a sleeping Dozer. "There were at least five or six of them in that sanctuary, Katie. So why wouldn't they just shift and get the hell out?"

"Well, why didn't you? According to Tink and Delray, you were there for several weeks, and you didn't shift until you were in that cage here in my office. Maybe they can't shift? Maybe it's why you haven't shifted? Maybe it's why I haven't shifted since that night? I don't know. I haven't even twinged since that night. I had a horrible buzzing in my head that just kept growing worse, and then it felt like everything was falling away—out from under me—around me—off of me. But since then, nothing."

Shaw dragged a hand through his hair. "Fuck," he swore, clearly frustrated, as he almost never used a word so harsh. "I don't know. I just know I felt a connection with that cougar. It wasn't like she was talking to me in my head the way the other animals have. I just couldn't tear my eyes away from her."

Katie's eyes filled with tears, her anguish over her own dilemma all but gone. "We have to help them."

"That's gonna be hard to do," Kaih said, entering the room from the outer office.

"Why?" Both Shaw and Katie asked in unison.

Kaih jammed his hands into his lab coat, his face grim. "Because they moved them all today. Every last one of them and all the other exotics. They're closing the park, and everyone in town's blaming you and the 'city people' as they call them, for it."

CHAPTER 14

Katie let her head sink to her chest as she sat on the edge of her bathtub to steady her shaking legs. She stared at her red painted toenails, lost in thought.

"Katie Minerva! You okay in there?" Aunt Teeny knocked on the door with harsh knuckles.

She cringed at the use of her middle name. "Fine, Aunt Teeny. I'm fine." Fine. Fine. Fine.

"Why do you need time?" Teeny yelled.

Katie pressed a hand to her clammy forehead, pinching her cheeks for color before cracking open the door from her seat on the edge of the tub. "I said I'm fine, Aunt Teeny. I'll be out in a minute."

Teeny poked her do-ragged head in. She'd liked Darnell's so much, he'd given it to her. "What's a matter with you, girl? Break-fast's waitin' on you. I made some mush. Hurry up before it gets cold."

Her stomach roiled. "I'll be right there. Just finishing up," she managed.

Her aunt gave her a toothless grin. "Get to crack-a-lackin', young lady. We're all goin' pumpkin pickin'. You don't wanna miss that Nina stompin' though Guthrie's pumpkin patch like he owes her money, do ya? She's a card, that one. Then we're gonna do a hayride. So hurry it up."

She groaned as Shaw's head replaced Teeny's.

"Ahem. Katie Minerva, what seems to be the trouble? You're missing mush. *Mush*," Shaw emphasized with a grin, rubbing his hard belly in a circle on his latest flannel shirt.

Teeny gave him a lascivious grin and a wink before patting him on the shoulder and saying, "You see what you can do with her. She's been a persnickety little flower past few days."

He pushed his way into the tiny upstairs bathroom with its pedestal sink and avocado-and-yellow wallpaper. He pulled her head to his hip, stroking her hair. The comforting scent of his maleness made her sigh. Even feeling the way she was. "What's the matter?"

She closed her eyes and allowed him to comfort her. But it would only last a moment because she was on the verge of losing her mind. "I don't feel well."

"I can understand why. This bathroom's wallpaper is just this much away from vomit inducing. We'll have to see if we can't replace it."

Before he ditched her for this Nissa? Or did he plan to tell his maybe-wife he had to go help the old lady with her wallpaper as one last gesture of kindness for taking in his amnesia-riddled ass?

Since Darnell had dropped the "Nissa" bomb, and the whole extinction thing, and no one could locate the animals that had been moved, add to that the fact that Nina said there was always a woman involved made Katie an edgy, conflicted, upset, hormonal wreck. She'd wracked her brain and used the last two of the connections in the city she had who'd believed her innocence to find those animals to no avail. No one knew anything about exotics having been transferred anywhere. It kept her up at night, worrying for their well-being and their care. The possibility that they were trapped in bodies they couldn't escape.

And now she had this.

This. This. Thiiiis.

Shaw nudged her over on the small ledge and knocked her shoulder with his. "Want to talk about it?"

Yeah. "No."

"You do, too. Who wouldn't want to talk to me? I'm charming and witty and almost always in a good mood."

"And I'm what? A troll?"

He popped his lip-smacking-good lips. "You do have trollish properties, especially these past couple of days."

Five to be exact. "I'm tired."

"And mean."

And . . . Oh, she couldn't think it. "I'm not mean." Weak, but mostly true if you didn't count the ridiculous hissy fit she'd pitched because Shaw had moved the rib eye steaks from one freezer to another.

"Have you forgotten Steak-Gate? I thought you were going to produce chickens right there on the kitchen floor."

Katie winced. "I was hungry, and I like order. You changed the order of things." Which was also true. She just didn't like it so much she'd cry in gulping, sobbing tears over the loss of it.

"You're touchy and crabby. Do you think it's because we frolic like teenagers until all hours of the morning? I mean, I'm all for letting you get your beauty sleep, but you're an animal. There's just no keeping you away. I'm like your crack," he joked, slinging an arm around her.

She was in absolutely no mood to joke. "If I were you, know what I'd do?"

"What's that, beautiful?"

She gave him a hard nudge. "Back. Off!"

Shaw fell on the floor, leaving him awkwardly pressed up against the pedestal of the sink. He tilted his head backward to gaze up at her. "Is it your womanly time? Do you want me to make you some tea and rub your back? Maybe a hot water bottle to soothe those pesky cramps."

Oh-oh-oh! She was going to kill him. Anger, hot and spiky, hit her gut hard. Latching onto his luxurious hair, she pulled his head to her lap. "No. I *do not* want you to bring me tea or a hot-water bottle, and I definitely don't ever want you to touch me again! Ever, ever, eeeever." She dragged the word out, low and harsh. "Know why that is, *Shaw*?" She sneered his name, putting every ounce of pent-up frustration she had in saying it.

"Why would you ever want to give up all this?" he joked, running his hand along the length of his body.

"Because all that gave me this!" she shouted, pulling the pink stick from the pocket of her sweatshirt and let it dangle before his blue-blue eyes.

Which were now large with surprise.

His mouth fell open—so wide she wanted to ram the damn pink stick down his throat with the final destination being an exit from his ass.

Shaw forced her to let go of his hair and scooted back upward to the edge of the tub. "There's a song about this, right? Paul Anka, I think. Yep. That's the one."

"One more joke and I'll take you out," she seethed under her breath, gripping her fists to keep from right-hooking him. "You know what I'd like to know, don't you? How in the ever-loving fuck did I end up with child if us crazy cougar shifters are unable to procreate and I'm on the pill? What are you, super-sperm-Shaw?"

And then he did something strange, yet totally Shaw-esque.

He smiled. That smile turned into a wide grin. That wide grin turned into a bark of laughter.

Now Katie's mouth fell open as she pointed to her stomach. "*This* is funny?"

He threw his arm over his mouth to muffle the squeals coming from his throat.

"I'm pregnant, you sex maniac! All those nights you conned me into doing the wild thing in every available corner of our rooms and the shower, and you have the nerve to laugh at me being knocked up? How dare you laugh! I swear by all that's holy, if you don't stop right now, I'm going to make Nina look like a novice street fighter by the time I'm done with you!"

He gasped, wiping tears from his eyes with his thumbs, then trying to pull her into his arms. "I'm so—" He snorted, gasping again. Clearing his throat, he bit his top lip with his bottom teeth to fight for composure. "I'm sorry. I didn't mean to laugh-laugh. This is brilliant, Katie. I couldn't be happier."

Her eyes had surely found their way out of their sockets. "*What? Are you crazy? Happy?" Happy?*

He nodded his dark head. "Yep. That's what I said."

"Hey, coo-koo-ca-choo, have you forgotten everything that's happened?"

Shaw's stare was purposefully blank as he forced his face to go blank, too. "In fact, yes."

She made a face at him, full of disapproval. "I don't mean that, amnesiac! I mean have you forgotten that I'm almost forty-one years old and pregnant? High risk where I come from, buddy. I can't even go see an ob-gyn. How will I ever explain I'm going to have a *cat*? Oh, Jesus," she rambled with hysterical breathlessness.

"What if I have a litter? How does this work? Oh, forget it," she said, looking down at him. "You don't know. Perfect. This is so much awesome. Not only am I going to have a—a—whatever—we don't even know if it'll be human! Not to mention the fact that we have no idea if you should have impregnated me to begin with because this Nissa Dr. Green spoke of could be someone important to you—like—like—maybe your wife? Tack on your age, and I could well be impregnated by a man who's young enough to be my son. And let's not forget the thing about the cougar population becoming extinct and no babies for whateverthehell time frame that was!"

"Sixty years," he offered in a matter-of-fact tone, so calm, so together.

"Argh! Can you just please be serious for one minute, Shaw? This isn't something you can humor your way out of. I'm. Pregnant. Got that? With child. A. Baby."

His jaw tightened. "I heard you, Katie."

"Then could you do an old lady a favor and at least share in even half of my hysteria?"

"I'm neither hysterical nor upset."

"Why the hell not?"

"Because a child is a natural extension of my love for you. Be it a kitten or a squalling infant, I'm in."

Katie cocked her ear, tilting her head. Her surprise rang in her words, crystal clear. "What did you just say?"

His eyebrow rose in that arrogant way he had when he was making a point. "You heard me. I love you. Now, while you adjust to that statement and your newly out-of-control hormonal state, I'm going to go have some mush with the others. If you don't want to arouse suspicion, I'd beat feet to the kitchen. We have pumpkins to pick and carve. Teeny said she'd make pie with our booty. I don't want to miss pie if it's anything like her mush."

With that, Shaw rose, pressed a kiss to the top of her head, and left the bathroom.

Well, then.

Everything was better now that Shaw had told her he loved her, wasn't it?

It was like the icing on her baby-daddy cake.

Shaw stopped just short of the kitchen to catch his breath before facing the crowd that had gathered at the table for breakfast.

He grinned again. A warmth of emotions rushed to settle in his chest, leaving it tight with unexpected pleasure.

He was going to be a father.

And Katie was going to be a mother.

The mother of *his* child.

He hoped their baby would have her platinum blond hair. Hair he loved to watch her brush before she left his room. Hair he loved to see fall to the middle of her back when she'd taken it down from her braid before they made love.

Even though the circumstances were far less than equitable, he was simply gobsmacked. Period.

Yes, there were a million concerns. He had no idea who he was. He had no idea if he had a full life somewhere else. Though again, like the names Spanky and Beck, an involvement with another woman didn't feel comfortable. He had no clue how old he was or anything other than he was full of cartoon quotes.

He just knew he loved Katie. Much the way he knew he hated Teeny's chicken-fried chicken and gravy, and in the same way he knew he'd rather be outdoors doing something DIY than stuffed away in some office. Not to be forgotten, he knew he wasn't a twentysomething.

He just knew. Why or how was still left to be explored, but he knew.

Just like he knew he loved Katie. It had happened quickly,

without warning, and while she was giving him hell last week for making so much noise during their boisterous round three of lovemaking.

He. Knew.

And Miss Had Her Panties Bunched Up Her Cute Ass Cheeks was just going to have to adjust.

And if she didn't already, learn to love him right back.

So sayeth Shaw.

He smiled again, whistling as he greeted the women he was now coming to enjoy as a group and in single doses. If he had a family somewhere—he hoped they were even half as interesting, loyal, and ballsy as these women and Kaih were.

"EVERYONE'S staring," Ingrid commented, on edge and shifty-eyed when they passed a group of Piney Creek's biggest gossips at Guthrie's Corn Maze and Pumpkin Patch.

"Yeah," Nina grunted, stomping over the mucked earth. "And if they don't knock that shit off, I'm going to pop their eyeballs out and eat 'em like fucking malted milk balls."

Wanda was right behind her, tucking her chin into her tailored gray overcoat and looping her arm through Nina's. "Shut up, Nina," she said on a wide smile she shared with anyone who was huddled in a corner, gawking and talking about them. "We are going to do as we all agreed. Kill them with kindness. Not kill them, period. Walk. Walk swiftly, my friend. Smile. Smile a lot at the bigoted pigs, or I'll knock you into Tuesday. Today being Thursday. Now, no way are we letting these small-minded, arrogant know-it-alls get the best of us. Put on your happy face, sunshine. We're goin' in. I have a pumpkin to pick."

"Pumpkins are goddamned stupid, Wanda. Just like these people."

Wanda rolled her tongue over her teeth. "You care to share that with Aunt Teeny? I'll wait until she's done beating you with the shovel."

Nina's face instantly brightened, her fondness for Teeny trumping her agitation. "Fine. For her I'll shut up, but one wrong flippin' comment, and I'm kickin' some farm-boy ass. The hell I'll let some vagina in a pair of overalls insult Teeny."

Wanda pointed in the direction of the rickety stand that had been around since Katie was a child where you paid to pick pumpkins. "March," she ordered.

As Wanda navigated her way through the mud and small mounds of strewn hay, Katie hung back. There'd once been a time when she might have confronted these people who so hated her. Nowadays, she just wanted to crawl back to her cave and stay hidden while she made fires from the sparks of two rocks rubbed vigorously together, and drew pretty stick pictures on the wall of her cave.

Shaw caught up with her, grabbing her hand as they walked toward Magda and crew. He sucked in a deep breath. "It's a beautiful day. The sun is shining. The leaves are turning. Definitely crisp, clean, and—"

"Pregnant," Katie finished for him darkly, still reeling.

"I'll sing the song, if you don't stop being such a Krabby Patty," he teased, referencing *SpongeBob*.

Rather than fight his reach for her hand, she let hers slide into his like it had always belonged there. "If you sing 'Havin' My Baby,' I'll cut your tongue out and fry it for dinner."

"Which would probably be, in comparison to Teeny's fish sticks, a delicacy." He paused as they came within two feet of Magda and her cronies. "Afternoon, ladies. Brilliant day for pumpkin picking, yes?" He dared them with his eyes and British charm to say otherwise.

Magda blustered, her narrow face flushing, the tip of her nose red. "Indeed."

He tore his hand from a clinging Katie's. "Shaw," he said, giving them a wide smile and holding it in a surprised Magda's direction. "And you are?"

Magda's nose instantly tilted upward while the rest of the quilting circle twittered with sputters. "Magda. Magda-May Jules. What brings you to Piney Creek, son?" She sneered the implication that Shaw was young.

His grin grew secretive and more charming beneath the midday sun. "Money. As Dr. Woods's boy toy, I'm well paid. Brilliant to have met you all. Cheers, ladies." He winked before latching back onto her hand and pulling her in the direction of Teeny and the others.

"You do know you just made everything a million times worse, don't you?" Katie whispered as the women gasped.

"You do know I don't care, don't you?"

Suddenly, neither did she. The look lingering on those women's faces had been worth his boy-toy comment. Letting her head fall back on her shoulders, she laughed. Out loud. Hoping the gaggle of women would hear her. "Me, neither."

"Then shall we pumpkin pick before Teeny eats Mr. Guthrie alive?"

Teeny was in full Teeny mode, preparing to give Angus Guthrie lip if he even hinted at discord. Her gloved fists were clenched at her sides, and her mouth was pursed.

Shaw sidled up to her, capturing her elbow. "Problem, Teeny?"

Teeny tightened her rose-colored down jacket around her neck and spat, "Damn right, there's a problem. Old Angus says he don't do business with felons."

Angus Guthrie, so thin his Adam's apple bobbed when he simply stood still, narrowed his eyes from beneath the wide brim of his straw hat. He shot a knobby finger in Katie's face. "You heard right. 'Cuz a you and your fancy thug friends, I cain't take my grandkids to the animal park no more. Your friends here beat an old man till he was talkin' sideways. You ain't nuthin' but trouble, Dr. Woods, and I ain't havin' it in my pumpkin patch!"

Nina leaned around a cowed Ingrid. "You wanna be the next in line for a senior smackdown? I could always use another body to add to my growing pile of old people."

Wanda's leather-gloved hand snaked out, wrapping around Nina's neck and clamping over her mouth. She shot Angus a smile like butter wouldn't melt in her mouth. "She's joking, of course. We don't beat old men. That's work. We simply gut them like deer and eat them for dinner. That's just how us fancy people from the city roll."

Katie bit her lip to hide her laughter and at the way Angus took two leery steps backward from them, as though the lot of them would take him out in broad daylight.

Shaw placed an arm around Teeny. "You know what, Aunt Teeny? Angus's pumpkins look a little bleak, don't you agree? Sort of deflated and sad. I know of the perfect place just a few miles out of Piney Creek. Now those pumpkins? Big, round, plump, and they have apple picking, too. Oh, and doughnuts. Cider dough-nuts. I say we leave Angus to his scrawny pumpkins, and we take our business elsewhere."

Teeny nodded but didn't move before she had her say. Aunt Teeny always had the last word. "You're an old fool, Angus Guth-rie. I can't believe I ever let you talk me into bumping uglies with you. I was just curious to see if that enlarge-your-penis patch you say you been wearin' really works. But I got some news for ya, Angus, wasn't no bigger than my thumb any old ways. Better get a bigger patch. And while you're at it, you just remember who you treated like the crack of your wrinkly, old keister. I won't let you forget this, Angus. Mark my words." Teeny stomped off toward her old truck while everyone followed in stunned silence.

Well, almost everyone.

Nina was engaged in a full-on cackle, bent at the waist and squealing like a pig.

Wanda turned around and headed straight for her, taking her by the arm. "Let's go, Nina. Clearly, our fancy city money isn't good enough for the likes of these narrow-minded, cave-dwelling *dicks!*" she shouted, then cast a guilty glance at Katie, her face pinched and red with anger. "Oh, Katie," she muttered. "I'm sorry. I just couldn't stand it!"

"Penis patch! Ohhhh, Jesus, I love that woman!" Nina squealed her delight, aiming her mockery right at Angus Guthrie before strutting off with Wanda.

At the truck, Shaw held the door for her. "I had no idea, Katie."

"That Angus Guthrie bought the penis patch and slept with Teeny?" To tell the truth, neither had she. Teeny was all "I am woman, hear me roar." She'd always been as free with her opinions as she was her sexuality. Maybe that was why her declaration, in front of everyone, hadn't come as a huge surprise to Katie.

He brushed her windblown hair from her face with eyes that held sympathy. This time his words were neither teasing nor light. "No. How cruel they are to you and Teeny. I'm sorry I've only made things worse."

And he was sorry. She could sense it in him because of this ironic twist of fate. Emotions, especially those of weakness and fear, were easily smelled on another, heightened by her cougarness. She sensed his sympathy, his regret. As she climbed in the truck, she put a hand on his arm and said, "I'm not sorry, Shaw. Not even a little."

Once her tantrum had passed, and the pregnancy thing had sunk in, something else had, too. Shaw offered more than she'd given him credit for. He'd brought with his arrival respite from days that had begun to bleed into one another. He'd brought a reason to get up each day. A reason to smile again. A reason to want more than just a cave to hide in. And he'd punctuated that in this very moment.

"So you ready to pick those pumpkins?"

"Is there really another patch?"

"Strangest thing. As I was listening to Angus tell us we were unwanted, I remembered the road that led me here to Piney Creek. I have no recollection of how I got here, but I do know I passed a place on the way in here. They had a big sign advertising pumpkin picking and cider doughnuts. Which means I couldn't have arrived that long ago. I think I remember how to get there. If you left the house more often than to just pick up supplies, you'd know that." His reprimand was gentle but observant.

More memories. Hopefully, it wouldn't be long before he had a fuller picture.

Or not so hopefully.

Katie's smile was a wistful one. "Then let's do it."

Shaw climbed in behind her as Teeny took the wheel, covering her hand in his. Slapping the back of the driver's seat, he said, "Let's roll, Teeny."

INDEED, there was another pumpkin patch five miles down the road, and to Teeny's delight, they'd found plenty of pumpkins.

Shaw was loading them into the truck while Katie sipped mulled cider and watched him, in a deep state of lust from over the rim of her cup. Shaw was all the things little girls dreamed of when they giggled about their princes at slumber parties: considerate, sharp, kind, gentle. Sigh-worthy.

And he claimed he loved her.

Which was ridiculous, but so tempting to reach out and cling to. How could he possibly make a declaration like that when his life was in such turmoil? It was one of those disaster-time statements—like telling someone you owed them your life and never expecting them to come asking for payment. Their situation was shrouded in too much mystery to make such a life-altering statement. Maybe he was excited about the baby and his mouth had moved before his brain had fully caught up.

But oh, those words from his lips still made her tingle and smile.

"You like him."

Her focus left Shaw and the delicious way he moved in his jeans to settle on Ingrid. "He's likeable." And lickable, too.

"He's been good for you, Dr. Woods."

He'd undoubtedly been good to her lady parts. "How so?"

Ingrid's smile was sweet. "He makes you smile when you think no one's watching. He's funny and good to Teeny. He loves the animals, and they love him back. Even the mob likes him. He's handy. He's smart, and he's taken that frown full of worry off your face. You're super pretty when you're not back in New York in your head, letting that asshole stick it to you. I know your ex did some crappy things, and I'm sorry that, no matter where you go, people will always associate you with him and his shady dealings. But Shaw changed that. You smile more than you frown these days, and that's cool." She capped her statement off with a dreamy, wistful sigh.

Foreboding settled over her. Instead of comforting her, Ingrid's words reminded her that Shaw was responsible for many changes in her life as of late, and he'd take them all with him when he left. Which he was bound to do if he ever got his memory back. He belonged somewhere, and if that somewhere was far, far away . . .

"Doc!" someone roared from the truck, making both Katie and Ingrid look up and at each other.

Nina was at her side in a flash. "We got trouble. Ingrid," she ordered. "Put Teeny in your car—tell her Katie and Shaw need to borrow the truck—make something up. Just keep her busy. Take her back to the house and wait for us there. Doc? You come with me. Move it!"

Wanda came to a skidding halt in Teeny's truck, pulling up beside Katie as Ingrid made a dash for her car and a bewildered Teeny. Nina threw the door open, literally lifting Katie off her feet and shoving her in the truck on top of Shaw.

Her eyes went to his body, shaking and lying sideways on the backseat. His skin was hot to her touch, and his eyes were rolling back in his head. He jerked in small spasms, writhing as though something hurt.

Katie's frantic eyes sought Nina's who sat in the front passenger seat. "What happened?"

Wanda blew out a breath. "We have a problem," she said with such urgency, Katie experienced a cold stab of fear. Wanda gunned the truck out of the pumpkin patch's parking lot with a jolt.

"Why?" Katie asked, forcing back panic.

Nina's gaze compelled her to look deeply into her troubled eyes. "Dude, our boy is about to become a kitty cat."

"He's shifting?" she squeaked.

Nina nodded as Wanda tore off onto the side of the road about two miles away, spewing gravel in the wake of the truck's big tires. "I've only seen this once, Katie. So I need you to just let me do my thing, okay?"

Alarm shivered along her spine. "He's going to shift?"

"Like no tomorrow," Wanda muttered under her breath, throwing the truck in park and jumping out to hit the dirt road with a clap of her elegant feet.

Katie followed suit, fear rippling along her arms in waves of goose bumps. She flew around the truck, watching as Wanda lugged Shaw out, threw him over her shoulder as though he were a grocery sack, and headed into the thick of the pine trees.

"Wait!" she yelped, fear making her voice rise in terror. The wind picked up, screeching with a yowl as leaves whipped into the air. "What's happening? If he's shifting, shouldn't we just let him do his thing? Like we did with me? Just let it happen?"

Nina latched onto her shoulders, her eyes like two black chips of ice. "I need you to hear me, and hear me well. Doc, this shit ain't right. Shaw's not shifting like you. Something's wrong. I've seen this before, and I know what to do. Now we're going to take him into the woods. If you fucking have to follow us, do me a favor—no goddamned screaming like some Mary. Stuff your fist in your mouth, bite your tongue, do whatever it takes, but *do not* scream. It hurts my fucking ears."

Katie's heart began an erratic pounding she heard in her ears. Rain began to pelt at her face like sharp needles. She swiped at it as she grabbed for Nina's arm to stop her. "What are you going to do? I can't just let you take him without telling me what the hell's happening!"

Nina grimaced, gripping Katie's chin with strong fingers. Water dripped from her hoodie, soaking it within seconds, the ever-darkening skies casting an eerie glow on her pale face. "Shit's gonna happen. Not pretty shit, either. So get a grip. Pretend this is some medical doggie emergency where you have to keep your shit together. Keep. It. Together. Now back the fuck off, Katie. I've got to go. It'll take two of us to get 'er done."

The wind picked up with a roar, bending thick tree branches in a sway of leaves and bark as Nina took off so swiftly, she was like a blur of soundless motion.

She dove into the thick cover of trees with a rebel yell to Wanda.

And the wind howled, mournful and high.

Katie stood in the mud, a puddle forming at her feet—her thoughts frazzled and disconnected.

The only thing she could piece together was Nina's last words.

Exactly what, in the woods no less, had to get done?

OH, and snap.

Katie stood deep in the woods, rain dripping from her hair in streams of cold splashes that fell off her now-soaked jacket and plunked at her feet.

Watching.

In immobilized horror.

Terror kept her feet glued to the sticky mud of the woods' floor.

Fear, and Nina's string of harsh curse words, kept her in a rigid state of frozen shock.

Words flung between Nina and Wanda while they battled not only the elements but Shaw.

"Wanda Schwartz Jefferson, if you don't fucking hold his legs down, I'll beat you with that log so hard, you'll be a human again!" Nina screamed while wind slashed her face and the rain pounded her straining hands, locked around Shaw's neck in a grip he still managed to continue to escape.

"Goddamn it, Nina, STFU and just give me a minute! I have heels on, for the love of shit! How do you expect me to get any footing in all this mud?" she roared back, kicking her heels off, revealing her stocking feet.

Katie fought a gasp, watching Wanda's shoes soar in a perfect arc across the rain-swollen skies. Wanda almost never swore. Nina joked about how they all tried to get her to cuss. Which made the scene before her clearly very, very bad.

Wanda lunged her body at Shaw in a spray of rain-tattered clothing and shredded nylons.

Ohhhh. Katie shuddered a breath, leaving in its exhale a thin mist of condensation. She so wanted to help Nina and Wanda, but her feet refused to move in their direction. What they really wanted to do was head in the direction that was the fastest route out of Dodge. Then she wanted to hide beneath her covers forever.

Which made her a chickenshit baby.

Thus, making her frozen state that much more frustrating.

She was a physician. There shouldn't be any medical emergency she couldn't handle, now should there?

Yeah, but do tell, Dr. Woods, when was the last time you saw an emergency like . . . that?

True, true, she pondered. She'd seen some shit in her time as a vet. Lots of shit.

This was like no kind of shit before it.

Shaw howled—screeching his rage, the noise rocketing through her ears and making the surrounding trees echo his agony, tearing her from her reverie.

Remembering Nina's words, Katie stuffed a knuckle in her mouth as more waves of bone-numbing fear took over.

Lightning ripped across the black-and-purple sky just as Nina was able to pin Shaw to the ground. "Hold him, Wanda! For the love of fuck—I don't know how long I can keep up my end of the bargain!" she yelled over a clap of thunder.

Wanda's shriek of frustration was followed by a grunt when she clamped onto where Shaw's legs had once been.

If one was to reflect upon this situation, say, a week or two later, maybe when the utter terror had passed and relief had settled in while they partook of coffee and sugar-glazed doughnuts, one might actually joke about how *Gladiator*-ish the scene before her was.

Yeah. But maybe more *Gladiator* times ten million.

Except Nina and Wanda were no Russell Crowe, and they sure weren't trying to contain a tiger.

Because Shaw wasn't a tiger. He was a cougar.

Sort of.

When you had your human head, and one of your human arms, but the torso of a cougar and like three paws, that only sort of qualified you to be a cast member of the animal persuasion in *Gladiator*, yes?

Katie nodded to herself.

Yes.

Oh, he'd never do.

Russell Crowe would never find this acceptable.

CHAPTER 15

"Katieeee! Get your cell phone—call Kaih or Ingrid—tell them big drugs—*now!*" Wanda screamed out in her direction.

Her hands, chilled to the bone, fumbled in her pocket to find her cell phone. Shaking, Katie forced herself to concentrate on reaching Kaih.

He picked up on the third ring. "Doc?"

"Kaih, listen carefully," she ordered, teeth chattering. "Bring me needles and sedatives. A lot of sedatives. Drop them in Teeny's truck and turn right back around. Don't get out to come check on us. Do not ask questions. Just do what I say!" She followed up with directions to where Wanda had pulled off to the side of the road and hung up before he could hear the scream she was about to let loose.

One more deep breath was what she kept telling herself. One more and she'd be ready to jump into the fray.

Okay. Two more.

"Katie, get that shit now! Run!" Nina snarled, rainwater spewing from between her almost-blue lips.

In a flash, her legs were like a house on fire, zipping up the small incline and driving her way through the thick brush and trees, praying Kaih would drop the meds and wouldn't linger to check on her. Waiting in a small thicket of trees, she alternately willed time to speed up and prayed Kaih would hurry.

Ten agonizing minutes later the sharp screech of brakes and the slam of a door made Katie poked her head out, snaking her neck around the limbs. She huffed a harsh sigh of relief when she saw his taillights flash as his compact car took the sharp curve on his way down the road.

Lunging for the truck door, she yanked it open and found syringes and sedatives on the passenger seat. Shoving them under her arm, she slammed the door and lunged back down the hill toward Nina and Wanda, her sneakers slipping on the mud-soaked ground.

Shaw was writhing now—each crunch of his bones an absolute prison of agony he had no escape from. He heaved under Nina and Wanda, fighting them with the wild desperation of a caged animal.

Katie had to cover her mouth to keep from screaming her fear for him. What the hell was going on? Her shift hadn't been like this at all. Why wasn't he shifting fully? And what would happen if he couldn't go all one way or the other?

Nina's face was a mask of determination as she wrapped her lanky body around his torso while Wanda rode the lower half of his distorted body like a bucking bronco.

"Katie!" Wanda screeched on a ragged, hoarse cry. "Hit him hard, honey!"

Her hands trembling, frozen from the cold, she jammed the syringe into the bottle at full throttle, filling it while trying to decide on the dosage. If she went one step too far, if she gave him too much, she might paralyze him. Or worse, kill him.

There was no time to hem and haw. Shaw had become more rabid, more frightening than anything she'd ever seen in a movie. He snarled in Nina's face, growling his uncontrollable rage.

"Goddamn you, Three Names, when you come out of this, I'm going to fucking push you off a roof!" Nina gritted between her teeth.

"Katie, noooowww! I can't hold him anymore!" Wanda screamed.

What happened next would come back to haunt her in the way of Nina threatening to take her outside and beat the cougar out of her, but only after she pulled out every last one of her "purty blond hairs" from Katie's fat-ass head.

Dear God, if at all possible, could we swing this one in my favor? I really don't want to take the father of my child, and the best damned nookie I've ever had, out for good.

With that prayer, Katie went in for the kill, charging the three of them like a bull—the syringe poised and at the ready to take Shaw down.

She threw herself on him and fell onto a tangle of limbs and the harsh grunts from his chest. Nina's head butted hers with a painful crack when he bucked. Wanda's thigh clamped around her long braid at one point, yanking until her neck arched painfully.

Katie gripped the syringe, almost losing it due to the sheets of water that had begun to fall like someone was hurling buckets of water on them. Throwing her weight into him, fighting the constriction of her heart at his painful reemergence to cougar form and the race of her pulse, she jabbed at the first available pound of flesh she could pinch.

Katie winced when she looked up and was able to thrust her sodden hair from her eyes.

Oh and Jesus. Nina was going to kick her ass from here to Kentucky.

Katie only had a brief moment to ponder how her aim had become so fast and loose, and the quickest escape route from Nina's certain rage, before Nina slumped forward on Shaw, heavily medicated from the syringe hanging from her neck.

And then there were two . . .

The upper half of Shaw's body reared upright, knocking Katie back and leaving Wanda hanging onto his legs like she clung to the string of a kite. He roared his angry rage, a discontent so agonized in its wail, Katie fought a sob.

"Get the fucking drugs, Katie! We need more drugs!"

Katie scurried to her feet, scrambling to the spot where she'd dropped the sedatives and syringes. She tore the plastic from the syringe with her teeth, spitting it on the ground and jamming it into the bottle of meds.

Just when she was ready to go back in, she heard Wanda scream, "Don't let him get away, Katieeee!" before her slender form was sent flying across Katie's line of vision and slammed up against a pine tree with a crack so loud, it made her shudder.

And then Shaw, in all his deformities, began to rise. His face was a mask of fury, his eyes wild and glazed as he scanned the wooded alcove for an escape route.

His first attempt to stand on all fours was awkward due to his bizarre, misshapen shift. He used his human arm to push off, only to fall back to the ground with a heavy thump. His second effort had him up and preparing to bolt.

Oh, the hell.

Not on her watch.

Wanda had said they couldn't let him get away.

So there was gonna be no getting away.

"Shaw!" she screamed at him over the howl of the brittle wind. "It's Katie! Listen to me!"

He stopped cold for a moment, his beautiful face turning toward the sound of her voice.

Her breath came in raspy pants. She held up a hand in semi-surrender. "I just want to help you. Let me help you," she soothed, hoping the sound of her voice would comfort him while she rounded on him.

But Shaw's eyes filled with suspicion when they landed on her, and his heavy paws began to lift off the ground, clunky but still capable.

She circled him, speaking while she regained her breath in order to rush him. "Damn it, Shaw! Don't you dare ignore me!" She waved a finger at him, haughty and arrogant. "I will take you out! Do you hear me? Don't you think for one second, because you're the father of my child and a fine specimen of wonk, that I won't take you down like a ton of bricks!"

Once more, his eyes followed her movements, desperate to find a path around her.

And they circled, like some bizarre square dance, facing off, Shaw snarling, foamy drool dripping from the corners of his mouth, Katie moving from foot to foot, too fearful to even blink.

She made her move when a sharp crack of thunder rolled over their heads, distracting Shaw and making him look to the sky.

Katie landed on his back with a clap so solid it knocked the breath out of her. Still, she clung to his neck, raising the needle high and jamming it into his shoulder with a cry of success.

Shaw bucked like a mechanical bull, trying to shake her off; the force of him throwing his weight around was so ferocious, her legs swung in wide circles.

And then he fell to the ground, panting and gasping.

And she clung to him, whispering, "I'm here. I would never hurt you. I promise we'll figure this out." She stroked his hair, plastered to his head as he grunted one last grunt before succumbing to the tranquilizer.

Katie lay on top of him, half man, half cougar, sprawled on his back, forcing air into her lungs and clinging to this man she'd come to care so deeply for.

"Katie," Wanda said, kneeling down to brush the tears from her eyes. "We have to get you back, honey. It's cold and you're soaked. That can't be good for the baby."

Katie's chest heaved a sob. The baby. What kind of mother would she be if she didn't even take her pregnancy into consideration while she was stomping out rabid, dangerous cougars? "You know?"

Wanda's smile was gentle and filled with irony. "Well, you did just screech it. Plus, I smelled it on you. What can I say? It's a gift, and you're clearly disoriented. Now please, let me get you to the truck where it's warm. It's freezing out here."

She let Wanda lift her up, giving her a critical once-over. "Are you okay? You took some beating."

Wanda chuckled, her hair a soggy mess, her clothes torn and filthy. "No kidding, eh? That man of yours is quite the warrior, but we heal quickly. I heal in double time because I have two forces of paranormal nature running through my veins."

Katie found she couldn't leave Shaw, who lay in a crumpled heap of distorted limbs. "I can't leave him. He needs me."

"I'll get him to the truck. Nina, too."

Nina. That was someone who was not going to be singing her love songs when she woke up. "Oh, my God! I didn't mean to tranq her, but everything was such a mess, and I couldn't see."

Wanda hooked her arm through Katie's as they made their way to the truck. "A thought. Would you consider payment for some of that sedative?"

"Payment?"

Wanda laughed, light and carefree, like they hadn't just wrestled a saber-toothed cougar in the middle of a thunderstorm. "If I had a dart gun with a tranquilizer in it for every time Nina mouthed off—my world would be all kinds of shiny."

Now Katie laughed, too, and Wanda helped her into the truck and dragged a rough blanket they used for the truck bed to haul flowers over her legs.

While Wanda went back for Shaw and Nina, Katie sat. Wet, cold, determined.

This couldn't go on. She couldn't put off the inevitable. Not at the expense of Shaw's safety.

No matter what happened, it was time to stop stalling and find out where Shaw belonged, and how she could fix whatever had just happened.

No matter what.

"I don't fucking get it." Nina's comment made her turn her head at the sound of her voice. She tucked the blankets under Shaw's chin, smoothing them over his wide shoulders.

Yeah. Katie didn't fucking get it, either. She gazed in wonder at Shaw, who now lay on his pink-and-purple ruffled bed like he'd never been a rabid, half-shifted lunatic. "Something's definitely wrong. I'd bet that's what Daniel Green was doing—trying to figure out what was happening to Shaw. What I don't understand is why my transition was so much less traumatic. This was the scariest thing I've ever seen." Just remembering how horrifying he'd looked, how broken and confused amidst all that snarling rage, made Katie's stomach react with a heave and her heart ache.

Nina leaned into the doorframe. "Dude, that was some shit. That was worse than what went down with Wanda."

Wanda had explained about her turning. Due to her lack of response from Marty's bite, the women believed they'd done something wrong, and Nina bit her again to ensure the change and save Wanda from her ovarian cancer. Unfortunately, it sent Wanda's chemistry into overload, and she'd gone rabid. The only cure for that was the blood of a human. Thankfully, Heath, her husband, had been willing to sacrifice his life for Wanda's, and he'd allowed her to bite him.

Somehow, though Katie was still fuzzy, everything had turned out all right for the couple, and Heath had lived. However, Shaw's shift hadn't been complete, and it clearly, at least at this point, wasn't irreversible. "What if that happens again and he doesn't shift back, Nina?" The fear she'd lose him in human form forever overwhelmed her. Even if he had a life somewhere else, if she knew he was safe, happy, she could stand losing him.

Nina came to stand at the edge of the bed where Katie sat and placed a hand on her shoulder. "We'll figure it out, Doc. C'mon. You need rest, and so does Three Names. It's been a craptacular day. Plus, you're preggers. You need eight and a field full of cattle if you hope to keep up your strength. Wanda's cooking so come with, okay?"

Katie shook her head. Nina was a conundrum—a total contradiction at every corner. She rose, reluctant to leave Shaw, but her stomach rumbled. "So does this mean I'm forgiven? I swear I couldn't see who I was ramming that needle into."

Nina chuckled on her way down the stairs. "It means I'll have to wait to beat the living shit out of you until after Junior arrives."

The scent of steak and eggs made her mouth water. Wanda had set the table for her, waving her to a chair. "Sit, young lady. You need nourishment and bed. In that order."

Katie dragged a chair from under the table wearily, smiling gratefully at Wanda when she placed a full plate of food in front of her. "Where's Teeny? Is she okay?"

Nina plopped down on her right side. "Chicken Little took her out to dinner and put her to bed. I give the kid props for saving me from the pressure sock thing and *The Rockford Files*. I'm so over James Garner."

Katie giggled. "Did she wonder where we all were?"

Nina shook her head. "Ingrid told her you had a livestock emergency and you needed a few pairs of hands. She might be a pansy, but she's a quick thinker. No worries about Teeny. We got you covered."

Katie looked down at her stomach. "I can't tell you how appreciative I am of the two of you. I'm going to have a lot to explain to her very soon. I'm not sure where to begin."

Wanda sat next to her, dismissing Katie's compliment. "We're here to help, and thank God we were able to stop him. So, let's take one issue at a time. Speaking of, I'm just going to cut to the chase. How do you feel, Katie, about the baby?"

Her fork stopped midair. "I'm petrified. I'm no spring chicken, Wanda, despite this reversal of wrinkles and perky boobs. I'm forty-one years old as far as my biological clock goes. And then there's always the worry that we don't know what this pregnancy means. Will my gestation be normal, like a human's? Or is it going to be three months like a cougar's? And I can't even think about what's going to happen when I give birth. What will I have? There must be a reason no shifters in the cougar community have been born in sixty years."

Wanda took her hand and tucked it against her side. "You're afraid."

Katie toyed with the yolk of her over easy egg. "I'm scared spitless, and Shaw's behaving as though we're like any average couple, instead of a man who can't remember who he is and the woman he scratched who's now a cougar. It's all insane."

"Do you love him, Katie?" Wanda's glance was thoughtful.

Today had revealed many things. One of which was not just her attraction but her attachment to Shaw. She'd feared losing him. Feared for his safety and not just on a humane level.

On every level and some she hadn't known existed.

Katie dropped the fork and rested her forehead on the heel of her hand. "I'm so close I can't even tell you, but let's remember the circumstances. Me, us, we're all he has while he waits around for his memory to return. Doesn't it seem even remotely possible he'd latch onto us due to the epic nature of his circumstances? What if, when this passes, when Shaw gets his memory back, he finds out where he comes from, he realizes we were just a port in a storm for him? Somewhere to rest while he caught his breath and all the intense emotions we've experienced due to the craziness of this whole thing fade. There is such a thing as bonding over extreme circumstances."

"There's always that possibility, Katie, but anything's possible. Why couldn't it be just as possible that you're an addition to his life rather than a lifeline he clung to and can't cut loose from because he feels an obligation to you for taking him in? There's no doubting he loves you. Just ask Mouth."

"Yeah, just ask me," Nina cackled, running her feet over Dozer's back.

"Maybe he loves what I represent, something solid when everything around him is falling away. It makes sense he'd cling to me—you—us."

Nina came and sat next to her, nudging her thigh. "Yep. He loves that, too, but it isn't the motherly shit you keep thinking it is. I've been in his head a time or two these past couple of weeks. Just so I know he's not bullshittin' us about this memory thing. Like maybe hiding regaining his memory so he can milk us. His thoughts aren't like any teenager's head I've been in, Doc."

"Like you'd know an adult thought, Nina. Really," Wanda chided fondly.

Oddly, Nina didn't rise to Wanda's bait. "Look, I just know he's no liar. He's not thinking about how he's going to sell candy bars to feed this kid. He's trying like hell to figure out how to find out who he was so if he was really a big boy before this, with a big boy job, he can take care of Junior here. His plan is to get on the fucking computer, screwing with my tweeting time, so he can look at all sorts of ways to safeguard the house and strollers and crap. Teenagers, even kids in their twenties, don't spend a lot of time giving a shit like that."

Her heart rushed with warmth at the thought that Shaw was in so deep. So much warmth, a tear formed in her eye.

Nina wiped it with her thumb and forced Katie to look at her. "Either way, Doc, you're in this together. Kids do that whether you want them to or not. So how about you cut him just a little slack and let this play out. No guarantees, that's sure as shit, but maybe ease up on him. He's trying. Wouldn't hurt for you to try, too."

Wanda reached around Katie and pinched Nina's cheek. "My baby's maturing, right before my eyes. I feel like you've grown so much because of my influence."

"Fuck you, Wanda."

"One step forward, three hundred back," she said to Katie out of the side of her mouth.

Katie laughed a snort, feeling a bit of relief for speaking her fears out loud. While it brought some comfort, they were still valid issues.

Wanda gave Katie a pat on the back. "I say we talk to Marty about this pregnancy thing. Maybe she can offer insight to a paranormal pregnancy. I do know, her gestation was somewhere in between human and wolf time frames. But I think both Nina and I can tell you, it felt like a lot longer than the four and a half months she put in."

"Oh, Lawd," Nina commented, smoothing her hands over the

tablecloth. "Do you remember the fucking endless whine about how being such a whale wasn't in anyone's color wheel? Jesus. We should have taken her out right then and let me raise poor Hollis."

"Oh, definitely," Wanda agreed. "She'd have been cursing and knocking out preschoolers before she was even potty-trained. Who are you kidding here, Nina? You shouldn't be allowed to raise a hermit crab."

Nina stretched with a lazy smile. "Larry doesn't complain."

Wanda wrinkled her nose. "Larry can't complain. He can't speak. He's an unwilling hostage in your plight to make him submit to you."

Katie grew silent, her thoughts focused on nourishing the baby and saving Shaw.

Nina leaned in on her hand and eyed Katie. "I hear shit cookin' in your head, Doc. What gives?"

She took her last bite of steak before wiping her mouth with a napkin. "We have to figure out what's happening with Shaw. We need to see Daniel Green."

"And how is seeing a man in a coma going to help Shaw?" Wanda pondered out loud.

"Nina," Katie replied.

Wanda scoffed. "Oh, every man in a coma needs a Nina. Has the cougar thing addled your brain, Katie? Nina's the last thing a man who's in a coma needs. Did you see her bedside manner with Shaw when he was in that cage and wouldn't wake up?"

"Shut the fuck up, Wanda. I didn't hurt him—just shook him up."

"If you shake up Daniel Green, he'll break, Annihilator."

Katie found herself in the role of peacemaker. "No, no. That's not what I'm saying at all. Look, Nina can read minds, right? Didn't Darnell say that he was mumbling all sorts of things? Maybe if Nina can get in his head and read his thoughts, we can find out what he *isn't* mumbling."

Nina thumped her on the back. "You know, that would make sense if it wasn't for the fact that we can't go anywhere near Daniel Green because, oh, wait, we're wanted for *attempted murder*, brain surgeon."

Shit, shit, shit.

"We are most certainly not wanted for attempted murder. We're suspicious persons of origin," Wanda corrected with a peevish tone. "Big difference, miss."

"You say tomato, I say, fuck you. We still can't be anywhere near the wrinkly dude."

"But wait," Katie interjected, a plan forming. "Didn't you say you can fly, Nina?"

Her nod was smug. "Yeah. How do you think I haven't killed the lot of you? Because I've been holed up with you bunch of morons, well, except, Teeny, instead of home with my man? I have needs. So I hit the friendly skies every night for a couple of hours." Her grin was naughty.

"Hospital rooms have windows, right? Why can't Darnell hover, or whatever it is he does, open the window, and let you in? With me, that is. Your superior strength could hold me, right? This way, if he says something medical, say names a procedure, thinks about a chemical, a drug or whatever, I stand a better chance of knowing what it is, right?" Her adrenaline soared. This could work.

Wanda's face lightened a shade. "It could work."

Nina looked doubtful. "Are you a screamer?"

Katie's brow wrinkled. "What?"

"Like afraid of fucking heights, a crier, that sort of shit? Marty's a crier. The last time I let her put her fat ass on me piggyback style and took her up, she sobbed and screeched the entire time. I have sensitive ears."

"Oh, Nina, that's horse puckey, and you know it. You took off like Iron Man and you did it on purpose because you live to razz Marty."

"Like she doesn't deserve if for all the girly shit she drags me through? I'm sure you remember Nieman Marcus and the dressing room incident, don't you, Wanda? Fucking bullshit. The hell I'll let Marty do some fashion intervention on me with some fruity guy named Johan who wears pink ties and white shoes. I owed her."

But Katie wasn't listening to the women bicker. She was formulating a plan. "I promise not to scream, Nina. Okay, so let's call Darnell. Or summon him, er, think about him. Whatever, let's just do it. Wanda, you'll stay with Shaw? Check on him?" She was halfway out the door with Nina behind her.

"No worries," Wanda called. "I'll take care of the patient. Be very careful. Both of you. And, Nina? If you drop her, I'll suck you dry!"

Drop. Her?

Oh, dear God.

SHAW woke to the sound of rain against the windows. Soft, soothing. A dim nightlight shone from the corner of his purple-and-pink room.

His attempt to lift himself out of bed brought a wince of pain that shot through his ribs and wrapped around the muscles of his neck. Jesus Christ, he felt like hell.

Katie and the baby were his first thoughts after that. He needed to see to them—her. Something had happened to leave him so beaten down. He found himself praying she hadn't seen whatever that something was.

Again, he made the effort to lift his pain-riddled body, making it almost to his elbows before he gritted his teeth and fell back to the soft pillow.

"Whoa there, big guy. Stay put," Wanda ordered from the doorway, her arms crossed, her smile sympathetic and Wanda warm.

Shaw scrubbed a hand over his face. "What the hell happened?"

Wanda's sigh was jokingly tortured. "Oh, there was mud, wind, rain, just about every element known to man. It was me, you, and Nina locked in a death grip in a fight to the finish for supremacy. Kind of like cage fighting. Werevamp and vamp versus cougar." She huffed a breath on her nails and smiled at him. "We won, of course. There was no question, but it was a little dicey there for a minute or two."

His face was blank. "I have no idea what you're talking about. I only know I feel like I took a dive off a cliff and landed on some rocks. Everything hurts."

"You don't remember?" she inquired softly.

Define remember. "I don't know how I ended up like this." Which was honest, if not just this shy of shady.

Her head cocked, her soft brown hair glistening in the hall light. "You shifted. Sort of."

His ears pricked. "Sort of?"

"Something's not right, Shaw. You only half shifted. It was like watching a mythological creature, half man, half cougar, war with his two halves. I've never seen anything like it." She made an attempt to hide her shudder, but Shaw caught it all the same.

"So it was bad." If it was anything like he felt, bad was probably a minimalistic word.

"You want honesty?"

"Always."

"It was bad. We had to sedate you, it was so bad. We fought with you for what seemed like a lifetime."

He wanted to bolt upright and apologize, but his body just

wouldn't allow it. "I didn't hurt you, did I?" He'd never forgive himself.

"Hah! We're seasoned vets, baby. We've seen a brawl or three. It's like Nina says, there's always drama. No way you could have taken the both of us down, but I admit, there was a moment or two when I thought we'd need an act of God."

Shaw physically cringed. "Did Katie see?"

"She did. She's who sedated you."

Instantly, he wanted to protect. Find her. Hold her. "Is she hurt? The . . ."

"Baby? Yes, I know about the baby. Katie's fine. The baby's fine."

He craned his neck, scanning the hallway behind Wanda's slender frame. "Where is she?"

A shadow fell over her face, but she covered it with a faint smile. She just didn't do it quickly enough to hide it from him. Wanda was a horrible liar. "She's sleeping, which is exactly what you should be doing. Even if your shift wasn't successful, it still can drain you when it comes on so violently." She chuckled almost to herself. "Ask me, I know."

His wanted to ask what that meant. He also wanted his eyes to stay open, but they weren't cooperating. "I don't remember the shift, or half shift," he muttered, realizing his voice was fading.

"Then color yourself lucky. For this moment right now, you're safe and well. Sleep, Shaw. Tomorrow's another day." He felt the blanket being tucked under his chin with hands that soothed in a matronly fashion.

Tomorrow was indeed another day.

A day when everything would change for him. For Katie. But it didn't change how he felt about her.

And she was just going to have to like it.

CHAPTER 16

So.

She was a screamer.

Sue her.

"Doc?"

"Niiinnnaaaa?" she hollered as they soared over the landscape of Piney Creek while she clung to Nina's neck, her legs around her waist in a vise grip. Lights winked from down below, mocking her to remind her she was *flying*.

Fly-ing.

Nina tweaked her fingers, prying them apart, but no way was Katie moving an inch. "If you don't shut the fuck up and let up on my neck, see that pointy church thing down there?"

Katie gulped, but couldn't look down. "You—you mean a steeeeple?" she stammered.

"Steeple, people, banana-fana-fo-feeple. What the fuck ever. If you don't loosen up, lady, I'll drop your ass on it. Now shut up and let me concentrate. I'm still working on the finer points of this flying thing. I lose my concentration, you potentially need bionic limbs. So shut it."

Katie whimpered against her back, her hair whipping around her head in a tangled mess, her eyes shut tight. She shivered. Not just from the height, but from how much colder it was up here.

In the clouds.

God, oh, God, oh, God.

Her fingers clawed into Nina's infamous hoodie. Her teeth chattered and her heart raced so fast, she was dizzy from it.

"Doc, I think this is it. Now clamp it. Darnell said this dude's on the third floor. Help me look for his room. Which means you have to open your eyes, pansy."

Katie pried one eye open only to find her stomach lurched and heaved like it was in water. "Okay—I'll look—look—for Darnellll," she gasped.

"There he is." Nina pointed a finger to a corner room. "Now let's just keep our fucking fingers crossed that no one's looking out their window. Hang on tight, Doc. This is gonna have to happen fast."

In a shot they were at Daniel Green's hospital window where Darnell stood, waiting, his cheerful grin shining at them from inside the room.

Nina began to lose her hover.

Three stories up.

Oh, if they fell, she was going to be picking a carburetor out of her teeth for many moons to come.

"Open the fucking window, Darnell!" she yelped between clamped teeth, making an upward motion of her hand.

Darnell waved his fingers, spreading them then making a fist. Magically, the window popped open and Nina dove for it, thrusting them into the hospital room and smack into Darnell's big body.

He caught them both like baseballs, with flawless effort, losing only two steps backward and emitting a grunt.

Katie clung to his thick neck, letting her nose fall to his shoulder, inhaling his pleasant cologne and the sweet smell of safety.

"You aiiight, Doc?" he whispered, thumping her on the back and hoisting her up on his hip while letting the braver Nina slide to the floor.

Her teeth wouldn't stop chattering, so she simply nodded, reveling in Darnell's solid warmth. "Aiiight then, c'mon now. Suck it up. We got some work to do fo' that ratchety old nurse comes back. I swear she could smell a demon, always lookin' 'round the room like somebody up in here wantin' to hijack her. She makes me feel all dirty." He shivered, prying her legs from his waist with gentle hands, and coaxing her to let him go.

She took several deep breaths of air, reaching for the end of the bed to steady her wobbling feet. Wiping her sweaty palms on her jeans, she finally took in the comatose form of Daniel Green, and her heart squeezed painfully.

Fragile and thin, Daniel Green lay swallowed up by institutionally white sheets. Tubes ran into his nose and arm, and monitors beeped at short intervals. Her heart clamored in her chest. He was so frail. The bruises, scattered all along his body in more places than she could count, had begun to yellow and fade in some spots, but they were still there, big and ugly. Age spots covered his bare arms in a pattern that blended with the bruising and the blue of his prominent veins.

Darnell put a hand on her shoulder, his expression full of doubt. "He been quiet tonight, Doc. Don't know whatchu gonna get outta him."

Nina sat at the edge of the bed, surprising Katie when her chin fell to her chest, and she took Daniel's hand. "Dude," she whispered, her voice shaky. "You're in bad shape. Christ, who the fuck would do this to an old guy? If I ever find the shit eaters, I'll kick their asses. Just for you, pops."

Her sympathetic tone rang in Katie's ears. Nina, for all her mouth and fists of fury, hurt for Daniel Green.

She stroked his hand, crooning low and soft. "Okay, so I'm Nina, and here's the thing. I don't know if you can hear me, but I don't want you to be afraid. We need answers, Dr. Green, and we're running out of time. I'm here because of Shaw. He needs your help, and I know you want to help him. When you feel like someone's nudging your brain from the inside out, that's me. But I swear to Jesus, I mean no harm. I would never, ever hurt you. So help me on my Nana Lou's life. So relax, and just let me in."

Silence prevailed when Nina closed her eyes.

Katie held her breath while Darnell massaged her shoulder with a comforting hand.

Nina's head popped up, her eyes gleaming in the eerie glow of the machines when she turned to them both. "Nissa!" she whisper-yelled. "She's Shaw's . . ." She cocked her head as though to listen. "Mother. She's Shaw's mother? Yeah. I think that's right."

Katie almost wept with relief. Call her pathetic, or even insensitive for having this thought at this very inappropriate moment, but Shaw didn't have a girlfriend.

Yippee-kay-aye-a, motherfucker.

"She's in danger." Nina shook her head, confusion riddling her beautiful features. "Slow down, Dr. Green," she whispered in his ear. "Why is Nissa in danger? And from who?" Nina frowned. "From herself? I don't understand . . ."

Daniel became agitated in increments, his muscles flexing and tensing rigidly, and if his blood pressure rose, he'd set off the alarms, alerting the nurses. Katie came to sit on the other side of the bed, running a tender hand along his arm. "It's okay, Dr. Green. Please don't be upset. I'm Katie Woods. I'm a doctor, too.

Of veterinary medicine. Shaw's my . . . my friend. I want to help him. I can do that if you'll just talk to Nina. *Please*," she couldn't help but add, desperation dripping from her plea. "We'll do whatever we have to, to help Shaw. I swear it."

Nina cocked her head again, her long hair falling across her cheek, hiding her eyes. "Okay. Nice and easy now. Let's forget Nissa for just a second and move on to Shaw." She paused, biting her lip and nodding. "He's in danger, too. I get that. From what? Why?"

Katie held her breath, watching the blood pressure cuff and continuing a soothing stroke along his arm.

"The collar?" Nina asked. "What collar?" She gritted her teeth. Knowing Nina, even if only for a short time, Katie knew her patience had to be running out, but then she hissed again. "Wait, he'll die if he turns again? Do you mean Shaw? Please, please, please, Dr. Green! Slow down. Damn, I can't make out what he's saying anymore. His head's a fucking mess of shit I can't make out."

Daniel began to shift in the bed, his grip turning to steel when he clamped Nina's hand and sat upright. His eyes popped open, wide and unblinking, looking directly at them. His vacant stare penetrated everything and nothing. Alarms began to sound, piercing Katie's sensitive ears.

"Shoot," Darnell whispered fierce and low. "Those nurses are gonna be in here lickety-split, ladies. We gotta blow!" With a flash of his hand, Darnell blew the window open, but Katie ignored it and continued to cling to Daniel's hand.

"Please!" she pleaded, her professionalism and better judgment for Daniel Green's condition lost to the fear she smelled on him. He knew something, and if they could just make sense of it, maybe they could fix this mess. "How is Shaw in danger, Dr. Green?"

"Katie!" Nina hissed. "We gotta get outta here. Move it, blondie!"

Just a second more and maybe she'd have something else. "Just give me a second!" she cried, refusing to let go of Daniel's weathered hand.

"I said *now, Katie!*" Then Nina was there, grabbing her around the waist with hands of steel and lifting her off the bed to jettison out through the window like some kind of paranormal football player, heading for the goal post.

Katie fought a scream on the way down to the parking lot, closing her eyes and putting her fists against them. They landed with a jarring slap of Nina's feet to the ground. Nina set her down hard and Katie had to grab blindly at the air around her to steady herself.

Nina grabbed her up by the lapels of her jacket, her face an angry mask, her fangs out and shiny in the glow of the parking-lot lights. She gave Katie a hard jerk. "Listen, Bun in the Oven Barbie, didn't I fucking tell you if shit started to go down, we were out? Could you be any more selfish? Did you forget Wanda and me are in the shitter with the cops in this backward-ass town, you moron? Not to mention, that's one jacked-up senior in there who shouldn't be riled up. Even I, hardcore bitch that I am, am sensitive to that. I know you wanna help your man, and all that bullshit, but don't be so fucking free with my goddamned freedom and that old man's health, lady!" She gave Katie a hard shove, sending her backward and making her fight to keep her feet under her.

Horror and shame washed over her in waves of red-hot embarrassment. Nina was right. Nothing had mattered but helping Shaw. Not Daniel's dire medical state. Not the fact that Nina and Darnell could have been so much toast. Nothing. Her hands went to her face in embarrassment. Then she hurled herself at Nina, throwing her arms around her neck and hugging her tight just because Katie knew she hated it. "Nina, I'm so sorry. I got so caught up in—"

"Like our fair Nina doesn't know what it's like to be selfishly caught up in a moment," someone chided, someone *British*. "So what're we gonna do tonight, Pinky?" Shaw asked, looking down at her with amusement.

Katie whirled around to find Shaw, still weary around his eyes, but upright and mobile, minus three paws. "What the hell are you doing here?" Her hands instantly went to his face, checking for warmth, running her thumbs along his bruised cheeks to assure herself he was all right. "You should be in bed asleep."

"Yeah. So should you. But look at us." He spread his arms wide with a grin. "Not asleep."

Nina didn't bother to address Shaw's poke at her with a rebuttal. If Nina wasn't snarking, surely that meant her anger had reached a level none of them would wish to experience. "I'm going to let the doc tell you what Daniel Green told me because right now I want to bleed her dry. That poor man's head was in such a jumbled mess of panic, I could barely understand most of it, but I did get some info we didn't have before. Now take your woman away from me before I choke her medical degree the fuck out of her," Nina snarled with a flick of her wrist, stalking off to weave between cars.

Katie gave Shaw a sheepish glance, jamming her hands into her pockets. "She's *very* angry with me right now. Tonight when I say my prayers, I'm going to thank whoever's in charge for giving Nina the gift of restraint. I blew it and almost got us all caught."

Shaw pulled her into his arms, warm, safe, strong and gave her a shake. "Troublemaker," he muttered against her hair.

She breathed him in, the warm, clean scent of him comforting her. "But not a dead or jailed one. There's that to be grateful for."

Shaw set her from him in a loose grip and gave her a look of question. His eyes sparked embers of fiery anger. "Why the hell would you do something like this on your own, Katie? You're pregnant. Do you have any idea the million and two things that could have happened to you?"

"I wasn't on my own," she said defensively. "I had Nina and Darnell . . ."

"I wouldn't leave Nina to look after my pet rock, Katie, let alone the woman who's carrying my child," he chided, a hint of anger in his tone, so rare coming from the quick-to-make-a-joke Shaw. It sounded off all sorts of alarms in her head.

She scuffed her feet in guilt. "Oh, I dunno. I would. Have you seen her with the mob and Teeny? She might lead you to believe she's a bloodthirsty thug, but in all actuality, she's a gooey marshmallow of four-legged, denture-soaking senior love."

Clearly, from the simmering blue gaze he gave her, he wasn't amused. "You could have been killed, Katie. What if Nina had fallen?"

His protectiveness, the possessiveness in his voice left her all warm inside, but she couldn't let him see that. It would leave her open to her weakness for him. "Siberia would have called and asked me to keep the screaming down?"

He let go of her and ran an aggravated hand through his dark hair, his lips curling inward. "Not funny."

"Do you mean it's inappropriate to crack wise when a serious event has just occurred?" She rolled her eyes at him and made a face.

"Fine. I concede I'm the first to make a joke. You win, but, Jesus Christ, Katie. When I made Wanda, who's the worst liar in the world, by the way, tell me where you were and drive me here—"

"Wanda's here?"

Shaw pointed to the third row facing them in the parking lot. From Teeny's truck, Nina flipped her the bird and Wanda waved cheerfully at her before grabbing Nina's finger and bending it backward. "Anyway, when I found out where you were, I wanted to strangle you. Not only did you risk your safety but the baby's. What if someone had caught you? You'd be in jail and so would Nina. Is this what I have to look forward to in our future as a couple? You doing foolish things that put your life at risk?"

A couple. Those words left her excited and afraid. "Hey! I was just trying to help *you*. If you'd seen what I saw out in those woods late this afternoon, you'd want answers, too."

"Well, that's not entirely the truth now, is it, Katie?" was his smug question, followed by a dimpled grin. "You might want answers, but you also want to help me because you like me. I'd venture to say you're very close to falling in love with me. Don't lie. You know it's true, but all these questions surrounding me and my memory loss, plus the question of my age and potential inappropriate behavior on your part, had you just itching to go and do something damned well stupid in order to reassure yourself you weren't crossing this ridiculous line you have when it comes to age."

She totally refused to rise to his bait. Instead, she offered logic. "You couldn't have helped with Dr. Green. If he'd said something medical or research related, you wouldn't have been of any help. I'm the doctor here, remember? That's why Nina and Wanda went for this idea. Besides, helping you helps me."

He wasn't going to make her admit something she hadn't even come to complete terms with yet. Her emotions were too wiggy to be trusted. For all she knew, this insatiable lust for him would pass once her hormones stopped behaving as though they belonged to ten pregnant women, and they'd have nothing to say to each other. So, yeah.

"Liar."

"Look, you didn't see what I saw today. You don't even remember it, do you?"

His nod was short in the negative.

"See? God, Shaw, it looked like you were in utter agony." Katie fought ridiculous tears she wouldn't be crying if she weren't such an emotionally knocked-up train wreck. "It was horrible to watch you suffer. As a physician, I felt helpless. As a human being, I was immobilized by it. There was nothing I could do to ease what looked like incredible pain."

He softened a little. "I apologize for frightening you."

The shake of her head was brisk. "Don't apologize. It's clearly not your fault, but I never, ever want that to happen to you again. If it was brutal to watch, it had to be much more brutal to experience."

"I don't remember a thing."

"Then there's something to be grateful for, and if you'd seen what I saw, you'd have done the same thing I did if it meant there was a chance of preventing it from happening again."

"I probably would have, but I'm a big, strong man who can take care of himself."

"Who was as weak as a newborn when I left the house and resting, something I know you need after the experience of my shift."

"Okay, I get it. Just don't go around doing foolish things that put you and the baby at risk again, got that, Dr. Woods?"

His possessive nature almost made her preen, but then she remembered how she'd promised herself she'd use caution. "Got it."

"So what happened up there?" he asked, hitching his sharp jaw upward.

Her frustration became evident in her sigh. "We're not much farther along than we were with the information Darnell brought us. Except for two things."

He slung an arm around her shoulder, clearly passed his anger and right back to happy-go-lucky Shaw. He directed her to the edge of the hospital parking lot. "And they are?"

"We think Nissa is your mother, and both of you are in danger."

She couldn't tell him about the dying thing because she was still praying that was just Daniel Green's jumbled thoughts.

He nodded like he'd known that. Patting a picnic-table bench where patient's families could sit, he encouraged her to slide in by him. He surprised her when he said, "I know I'm in some kind of danger, but as far as I know, my mother's dead."

Her stomach did two things. It took a dive and danced with excitement. "You do? You remember?" She was almost afraid to say the words, but if she was going to stop hiding from this so Shaw could have the help he needed, and he'd never be subjected to that horrific shift again, Katie knew she had to hear what he'd remembered.

"Hold on. I don't remember everything. I remember up until the point I got here to the U.S. and met Daniel Green. Then it's all blank."

"So you are from England?" That so blew. Yet she fought asking the inevitable question. Like, how would his middle-school girlfriend feel about the fact that he'd knocked up someone old enough to be his mother? Would she refuse to sit at the cafeteria lunch table with him and deny him a carton of milk? Jealousy warred with reason in a mess of nervous anticipation.

"Originally from London, but now I live in a town called Diss."
"Diss . . ."

He chuckled "Diss. It's on a beautiful lake."

Where a beautiful cottage with ivy climbing up the side of it gave way to a vista of blue and green. And in that quaint cottage lived his beautiful wife and two children. Maybe he even had a dog.

Katie gulped. She'd known this was coming. Known. Now she was going to take it like the champ she was. But first thing was first. "Why were you here to begin with if you come from England?"

Dragging a finger across her cheek, he took her hands in his. "First my stats. My name is Shaw Sedgwick Eaton. I'm six-foot-three, two hundred and twenty pounds, before I left the mother-land anyway. Oh, and I'm pushing seventy years old. Your cougar status was just downgraded, fair lady. No more gummy bear jokes for you, young'un," he teased with a grin. "I'm older than you by almost thirty years. No"—he held up a hand with a smile—"don't thank me for dashing your high-school-boy fantasies."

"Seventy . . ." she murmured. He was older than she was? Oh, sweet mysteries of life. And yay. Yay. Yay. Yay. "How can you be seventy? You don't look a day over twenty."

"For the same reason my mother, the woman in the picture we found in Daniel Green's office, didn't look a day over thirty, and she's somewhere in her hundreds. At least, I think that was her picture. I don't know. My father never leaked much information about her. So I'm not exactly sure how old she is, and I'll get to why in a moment. We age very slowly because we're shapeshifters, Katie." His smile was ironic. "I've often thought eternal life was given to us as compensation for watching everyone around us die. So what applies to Wanda and the rest, also applies to us."

Holy cats. Her breath shuddered. "We have eternal life?" She'd given the notion a great deal of thought before she closed her eyes at night, but his confirmation still took her breath away.

"We do, though we're not quite as infallible as Nina and Wanda. We have our kryptonite much like Marty does. If someone were to take out a vital organ in just the right way, we'd most likely die without medical attention even with the power to self-heal."

Katie grimaced. Right now, she just couldn't wrap her brain around living for an eternity. "Okay, so why did you come to Piney Creek? I don't understand the connection to you and Daniel Green."

"Daniel is my grandfather. One I didn't know about until my father, *a human*, died just recently. It's probably why I was so distressed that he'd been hurt. Though I admit, I feel that on only a humane level at this point. I don't know him at all."

Her disbelief was evident. "So you're half cougar, half human like me. But wait, your father was still alive?"

Shaw chuckled with a nod. "Old damn coot. He was ninety-five and active up until the day he was mindlessly slaughtered." Now his expression went from fond to hard.

Katie gasped, her hands squeezing his in a gesture of sympathy. "He was murdered? Oh, my God. I'm so sorry. Please tell me it has nothing to do with whatever's going on right now." But apprehension stole over her. Of course it did, dummy. Darnell had said someone was taking out werecougars. Which totally didn't explain why, if Shaw's father was a human, he'd been murdered.

"I think it has everything to do with what's going on. My father was a research scientist—genetics, to be specific, as is Daniel Green, my grandfather."

Katie groaned, her eyes scanning his. "Are we going to some weird, sort of *Fringe/X-Files* place?"

"Like we aren't already there anyway?"

Duh. "Right. So I'm betting experiments and Bill Nye gone awry are in my not too distant future?"

Shaw's dark head shook in irony. "I know you're going to love this, but I don't know. I only suspect. Here's what I do know. My father, Alistair, owned an old converted apartment building. He rented the flats to a group who did nonprofit work for the homeless when he moved to his retirement home. When he was killed, they, purely by coincidence, made mention of some boxes in the basement that needed moving. I wasn't aware of them, nor was I aware my father spent many long hours in that basement well after he'd retired. Tinkering was what the one counselor said. I went to collect those boxes so they could use the space for group therapy meetings. I didn't think much about the contents for a few months because I was too busy mourning my father."

"So you two had a good relationship?"

Shaw smiled, his grin genuine and warm. "We did. We played chess every Tuesday over brandy and biscuits at his assisted-living facility where he was a champion shuffleboard player and quite the ladies' man. I often caught him wooing some woman or another with what he called his superior courting skills. He was quite the player for ninety-five."

Katie giggled. "Huh. Charming, you say? Clearly, a time-honored tradition in the Eaton family."

"He was also sharp as a tack right up until the day he died."

"You miss him."

"I definitely do. He was a good man who raised me almost to-tally alone."

Sorrow struck her in her heart, making her place a hand on his arm. "Where was your mother?"

"Dad always told me she died when I was an infant, and that's what I believed until I read some of his notes—notes that are much like Daniel Green's, and files, too. Daniel is my grandfather on my mother's side, but my father, when he referred to her, called her Lettie. I have to wonder if maybe that wasn't a nickname, not her real name? He always had a wistfully sad look on his face when he talked about her, but that wasn't often. She was just this big pot of secrets I was afraid to stir."

"So your mother was a shifter and so is Daniel Green?"

"That's my assumption. If Daniel Green is my mother's father, and that picture we found that night was a picture of her from the 1800s, what else could explain my grandfather still alive and kicking?"

"So what do these notes and files have to do with Daniel and your dad?"

"They worked together. On some project I'm still exceptionally unclear about."

Her spine stiffened. "I hear the theme to *The X-Files* playing . . ."

"Catchy tune, yes?"

"Not a good time to crack wise, funny man. Stay focused. So
what do you know from those files? Obviously you found Daniel
somehow, which was what brought you here in the first place."

"My father left me a red-hot trail right to Daniel—almost as
though he wanted me to find him. Though he never once mentioned him in all my life, he had his number here in the States and
his location very clearly printed out in emails they'd exchanged.
Nothing important in those emails but pleasantries, but they'd
kept in contact all these years. What I don't understand is why
Daniel never made any attempts to see me."

Her heart clenched again. Without Teeny in her life, Katie
didn't know what she'd do. To have missed out on a grandfather
had to suck. She caressed his hand with her fingers. "I don't know
what to say other than I'm sorry you missed out on Daniel."

"Here's the other crazy thing. I got on a plane and came here
because of something urgent that eludes me until I want to ram
my fist through a brick wall in frustration. All I can think of is Daniel had the cure for my problem."

There were more of those? God in heaven. She shivered. They
needed another problem like they needed an IRS audit. "Problem?"

"My shifting. What happened out in the woods this afternoon
happened twice before to me back in England."

Katie's eyes widened. "Wait, hold on. You've always known you
were a shifter?"

His smile was fleeting. "Yes. I've always known, and I've always shifted with the ease of Marty and Wanda. My father took
great measures to keep my paranormal abilities a secret from humans, and he did a terrific job of it. I was raised quite normally

despite them, lived an average life much the way the paranormal posse does. But I knew there was always a time and a place, and I can—or could—shift at will."

"Until recently."

"My last two shifts left me naked by the lake near my home, not knowing what happened to me or how I got there. I think feeling like I'd been run over by a cement truck when I woke up tonight was what brought everything back."

"God . . ." His somber words that he'd experienced this before frightened the hell out of her. "So did you ever ask your father why you were a cougar and he wasn't? How he met your mother? What led them to marry?"

"More times than I can count, and he had plenty of stories. When I was a child, he often told me I was a cougar because I was special. As I grew older and pressed him for answers, he explained that my mother was a shifter and he'd met her through his work as a scientist. She was one of the last werecougars on Earth besides me, and he'd loved her deeply, but she was killed. Now, knowing what we do about Daniel, it makes me wonder exactly what kind of scientific work was involved when they met."

Katie was incredulous. If what he said was true, Shaw and now she herself were pushing extinct. "How old was she when she died?"

His brow wrinkled. "One hundred and seventy-five or so, I think. Which leads me to believe the picture we saw at the animal park was hers."

"And that's it? Did you ever try to find anything else out about how you came to be? How she came to be? What she looked like?"

"Over the years, I've done more research than I care to admit behind Dad's back. We were very close, and I never wanted him to think I didn't believe him, but there was always doubt about my origins. Yet what Darnell says is true. There isn't much about us to be found. I know nothing about these elders Darnell told us about except for maybe Daniel, who I guess qualifies. I always thought my father's suspicious nature was what kept me from finding anyone else like me, but it seems that's not exactly true. As to what she looks like, Dad didn't have much in the way of photographs of her, either, something I asked about often and his reply was always the same. She didn't like having her picture taken."

Frustration settled back in. Knowing more about him only made their situation more complicated. Each time they took two steps forward, they took ten more back. She was almost afraid to ask, but he had said his father was murdered. Surely there was a basis for that theory. Her words were soft, her sorrow for what he'd lost seeping into her careful words. "Am I prying if I ask what happened to your father, Shaw? What the circumstances were surrounding his death?"

Shaw's gaze was direct, filled with blue fire and anger. "He was clawed to death."

CHAPTER
17

"Holy fucking shit, Three Names," Nina crowed from the darkness. "That sucks, my British friend. Condolences." She gave Shaw a slap on the back. "Man, you and Baby Bump Barbie just can't get a break."

"Oh, Shaw," Wanda said, right behind Nina. "I'm so sorry."

Katie couldn't comprehend it. Her hand went to his face to smooth away the lines of sadness. "Clawed to death?"

Shaw's nod was curt, his mouth a thin line of grim. "Yes. He was found in the woods behind his assisted-living facility."

"And how did the police explain something like that?" Katie asked.

"Wild dogs, which aren't uncommon in that area. However, he didn't die of the wounds, though they didn't help. The final coroners report claimed it was a heart attack. I never connected his death with anything having to do with me until now. Now I have to wonder if he died needlessly because of whatever was going on with my grandfather."

"Okay, lovebirds. No more gruesome tonight. Let's sleep on this. It's time to get back home. Katie's pregnant and needs her rest, and you're a shifter's nightmare, waiting to happen," Wanda scolded. "We don't need you turning into some whacky version of mythology's centaur out in public. We also don't need to alert the police, who'd love nothing more than to slap us back in that jail cell slicker than snot. Let's move."

Nina loomed over them, her face less tension-filled when she gave Katie "the look." "And now that I only want to scar you versus kick your stupid ass, I think I can ride in a car with you without driving you off a cliff. So get in it, and let's go home so we can figure out what the fuck this all means."

Katie popped up with a wince. "I said I was sorry. Wow, can you grudge." Nina's face darkened, but Katie was quick to pacify her. "It was a heat-of-the-moment kind of thing. I just got caught up. I apologize. Profusely. Which means a lot."

"I know what it fucking means. Next time you do that, you're gonna be caught up in my fist," Nina warned, holding that very fist under her nose.

Katie threw her hands and latched onto Nina's cheeks with a smile. "Got it. No more getting caught up."

"You know, Wanda?" Nina asked.

"What's that, oh, hot-tempered one?"

"I like Katie. She fucking listens. Unlike some other werewolf whose name is *Marty*."

"Speaking of listening—"

"Yeah," Nina agreed with Wanda. "We heard everything."

"Eavesdropping, Nina?" Shaw admonished with a teasing smile.

"I have super hearing, dude. Comes with the territory. And didn't I fucking tell you there's always a woman involved? Jesus Christ in a miniskirt. Never fails," she scoffed.

Katie shook her head. "But we don't know that Nissa, a woman who, if she's Shaw's mother and supposed to be dead, is involved. If she's dead, she can't be involved. I think whatever Daniel relayed to you via his thoughts was just muddled."

Nina began to walk toward Teeny's truck. "I dunno. I just know he said she had to be stopped. That she had to be saved from herself. That's enough evidence for me to believe she's lurking around here somewhere, and some big showdown's gonna happen. Always drama," she complained, holding the back door open for Katie.

Wanda hopped in the front driver's side and nodded her head, her lips thin in the rearview mirror. "I hate to say this. Nay, I despise saying it, but Nina might be right. Is there any way you can get your hands on those files, Shaw?"

Shaw slid in the other side and pulled Katie close to him. "For what purpose? They didn't have anything in them other than Daniel's information and notes that were as indecipherable as Dr. Green's were. Their emails to one another are how I found out Daniel is my grandfather."

Wanda slapped the flat of her hand against the steering wheel. "Darn. We just need one more dead end before I spork my eyes out."

They each fell silent on the ride back to Katie's, losing themselves in their thoughts.

One thing was for certain; Katie felt it deeply rooted in her gut. Something was going to blow.

Where, what, and how remained unclear.

But it was going to be big.

And in the psychically gifted Nina's words, probably involve a fucking woman.

WHEN they arrived home, Katie pulled Shaw to her side as everyone left to go to their rooms. Right now, right this minute, she needed him. She didn't want to sneak off to his room after everyone had settled in.

Stooping to give Dozer a quick stroke on the back, she gave him a coy smile. "C'mon, King of the Jungle. Let's come out of the closet and make a statement."

Shaw chuckled, following her up the stairs. "It's the senior thing, right? A real turn-on, huh?"

"If Teeny only knew, she'd be so jealous," she said on a soft laugh, pulling him into her bedroom and closing the door with a flirty smile. She leaned back against the door and cocked her head. "So, Shaw Eaton. How are we feeling this evening?"

His eyebrows wiggled when he sat at the edge of her bed and placed his hands on his thighs. "Oh, I dunno. It's been a long day, and there's always the chance I may have dislocated something. You know, being seventy has its brittle-bone disease issues."

Katie stripped off her jacket and began peeling the rest of her clothes off on her way to the bathroom. "I have a cure for those aching old bones," she said over her naked shoulder.

Shaw came up behind her, stealthy and soundless. He was naked, too, and pressing against her back, warm, solid, good. "You don't want to talk anymore? Who are you? My Katie wants an explanation for everything."

She let her head fall back against his wide chest, her eyes sliding closed. His Katie . . . "What's a four-letter word for quiet?"

"Hush?"

"Do that." Right now, she just wanted to forget all her fears and leave all constraints for the security of his arms.

Shaw spun her around and shook his head. "Not until we clear some things up."

She sighed, fighting to focus on his need to vent versus her nipples scraping against his delicious chest. "Okay. Clear away."

He planted a kiss on her nose, pressing her hips to his. "First, there is no other woman. I've avoided serious involvement most of my life with anyone due to my shifting. That's not to say there haven't been women, just no one serious. And in truth, for all this time, no one interested me enough to make me want to get serious."

So no sultry redhead that looked like Kate Winslet in his lakeside cottage making Yorkshire pudding for dinner? The gods had finally decided she was worthy. "I feel much better knowing I've not only not corrupted a child but that I'm not whoring around with someone else's husband." Relief was so swift, it made her knees weak. Shaw didn't belong to anyone.

"Second, I'm retired. Which means I can devote all of my time to you and the baby." He placed a possessive hand over her belly, now sporting a small bump.

"Retired?" Technically, that made sense. He was seventy. "What did you do for a living?"

Shaw pursed lips she wanted to kiss, creating dimples she wanted to touch. "You'll never believe it."

"A stripper? Oh, wait—Calvin Klein model. It's those abs. They say it all." She let her hand roam over them to prove it.

"First half of my life, you know, back in the days of yore, I did burlesque. Sometimes a rousing cancan. I had great legs," he teased, cupping her ass. "Second half, a veterinarian."

She gave him a playful slap on his shoulder. "Still with the funny."

"Nope. I'm not being funny. You remember that whole communicating-with-the-animals thing, right?"

"Like I could forget. It was like stepping into a Stephen King book."

"Goes a long way toward a lucrative practice when you can actually ask the animal what's ailing them. I love animals. I was a stray gatherer, too, much to Dad's dismay."

"Why didn't you say so earlier?"

"You were too busy telling me how much more qualified you

were to talk to Daniel and trying to convince me you wanted to help me because it helps you."

She had waved the doctor stick at him. Her heart warmed again. She liked Shaw with his memory more and more. "And you retired? Why?" If not for George's dirty dealing, she'd practice until her fingers fell off.

"People tend to get suspicious when you've been around as long as I have and you look like you're twenty when you're really forty. You can only use the forty is the new twenty for so long. I obtained not one, but two degrees in veterinary medicine in my lifetime and created two different practices on opposite ends of the globe to keep practicing. I was in the process of considering school in Germany and opening a third practice there just after my father died. Until this happened, anyway."

"So we can talk shop?"

"Do you want me to give you the first five steps to neutering as proof?"

It explained why he'd been so distracted by the medicine cabinet in her examining room, though. "Not right now. We have other pressing matters," she said on a flirty giggle, enveloping his thick shaft in her hands and running the length of it.

"Just keep in mind who has two degrees in veterinary medicine. Know your place, woman." He groaned against her lips.

"You know," she mused, her lips on fire from his nibbling, "this explains why the mob took to you right away. They're a difficult trio to inspire so much love so quickly."

"It also explains why you took to me, too. We have medical-like things in common," he said confidently, grinning down at her while he ran his knuckles along the underside of her breasts.

Katie reached up and wrapped her arms around his neck. "So a veterinarian with no girlfriend and nothing but animals to talk to must make for a lonely Shaw."

"Oh, lonely seems a small word in comparison to my deeply wounded soul." He chuckled, pressing his lips to hers. "Surely you can find something much bigger to explain the depth of my pain in your crossword arsenal."

"I'm all about healing wounded souls," she said, pulling away from him to flip the shower fixtures on, letting the bathroom fill with steam. She stepped into the bathtub, feeling his dark presence behind her, and it lit a fire, wild and free, in her. Katie turned to him, allowing the water to cascade over her. "Any thoughts on what would help the healing process along? You know, specifics?"

Shaw's raven eyebrow rose, his smile deliciously naughty. He grabbed a bottle of her favorite lavender-and-thistle body gel, squirting it into his hands and soaping them up. "I can name a few," he murmured, placing his hands on her hips and running them along her sides.

Katie shivered at his darkly intense gaze and his hot hands, roaming over her skin but avoiding anything more intimate. Placing her hands on his shoulders, she stared back at him, her eyes held a challenge. "Name them," she whispered, husky and thick.

Shaw dragged her to him, scraping his soapy hands against the swell of her hips, pressing his hard shaft against her thigh. "Kneel," he demanded, rough and hoarse.

Katie slid down his body, letting her lips glide over his hard planes, nipping at each ridge of his abs, caressing his thick thighs with her mouth.

Shaw adjusted the showerhead so the water fell behind her and reached for her shoulders. "Put me in your mouth, Katie. Do it *now*."

His forceful demand left her wet with desire. Her nipples beaded to tight nubs when she put her arms to his legs and pulled him to her mouth. Her first taste was light, exploratory, savoring the silky skin of his cock with her tongue.

Shaw's groan bounced off the walls, ringing in her ears and sending a shot of sharp pleasure up her spine.

Her tongue whispered over his length, licking him in short stabs until he groaned again. She cupped his balls, using gentle fingers to knead them before taking his length fully into her mouth.

His hiss was hot in reaction, thick and sweet to her ears.

Katie drew on him deeply, pulling him into her mouth with a hard suction, then dragging her tongue over him again and again. He bucked his hips, gyrating against her, digging his hands into her slick hair, driving into her mouth until he gasped with a grating breath and hauled her upward.

Shaw's mouth met hers, hard, demanding, his tongue driving between her lips, parting them and stealing her breath.

Katie clung to his shoulders, needy, the flesh of her most intimate parts swollen and aching. With powerful arms, he hoisted her up around his waist and climbed back out of the tub.

Wet feet slapped against the tile floor and made their way to the bedroom, where he dropped her to the bed and followed her, soaking wet.

He had the ability to make her forget everything, soggy sheets be damned. Katie wanted nothing more than his hard cock ramming into her with thick molten-hot strokes.

Yet Shaw drew back. "The baby," he muttered, with thick words of concern, letting his fingers trail a path of flaming heat between her legs. "Maybe we shouldn't."

She lifted her hips in invitation, relishing the sweet feel of cool air when he spread her lips apart, caressing her clit. "The hell we shouldn't." She groaned.

He took a nipple in his mouth, scraping his tongue over it. "I don't want to hurt you or the baby."

Katie's lower torso didn't agree. "Couples make love all the time, even as late as a few days before delivery," she gritted between clenched teeth, her heart full with his sweet, considerate words. "I promise you won't hurt me, Shaw." Her words came out as a plea for him to take her—now.

Rolling her to her stomach, Shaw let his lips slide over her skin, celebrating each inch of her.

Katie shivered at the wet trail he made with his mouth, gasping in anticipation when he lifted her hips and slid between her legs, letting his cock caress her clit. She reached between them, sliding her hands along his thick shaft, reveling in his hot moans.

He placed a hand between her shoulder blades, rocking between her legs, heightening her need until she begged him to enter her.

His entry was smooth and easy, making them both huff a harsh breath. Katie welcomed the invasion by spreading her legs wider, inviting him to drive more deeply. Scintillating slaps of flesh brought goose bumps to her flesh, rippling in waves of desire.

Her arms stretched upward, her fingers clenching the wet sheets. She panted, luxuriating in the stretch of her flesh, Shaw filling her until she almost couldn't bear to wait for climax.

Yet he took her to a new level when his strokes eased, and his hands kneaded her ass. His thrusts were rhythmic and hot, his hands big and forceful when they moved to her hips and ground against her.

The sharply sweet glide of his cock, the tightening of her belly could be denied no longer. Release was all she could think of, a driving force of need that wouldn't be ignored.

Shaw's grunt bounced in her ears, a familiar sign his release was near.

Katie strained upward, pushing against him until her knees ground into the bed, searching, needy for climax.

Her orgasm clawed at her, slamming into her with such force, she lost her breath. The combination of Shaw's sweet mutterings and his hot shaft in her drove her to madness. She thrashed upward, taking as much of him as she could, wanting him to consume every inch of her.

Shaw's breathing was rough and choppy when he fell forward on her, pressing her into the bed.

Katie smiled through her efforts to take air into her lungs, reaching for Shaw's hand and curling her fingers into it. She snuggled against him, a deep contentment, new and intoxicating, settling in her heart.

Shaw stroked her hair and chuckled. "Not bad for seventy, eh? I must be diligent about taking my calcium pills."

Katie rolled to her side with a giggle.

This.

This was the time she most treasured with Shaw, when they were alone in the dark, talking about nothing, and basking in the glow of their lovemaking.

If he went back to England, back to his life, she would miss this the most.

Her heart began that strange longing for him, and he wasn't even gone.

But for tonight, she wouldn't allow her dark thoughts to invade the utter bliss Shaw was bringing her in this moment.

Not tonight.

She gave him a playful poke. "Hey, Mr. All Caught Up in the Moment. Look what we did to the sheets."

He pulled her close, wet, cold sheets and all, barking a laugh. "Yeah, what kind of housekeeper are you, anyway? You'd better get on that."

Her grin against his chest was easy and unhindered by anything but the joy of being in his arms.

If only they could stay just like this.

If only.

* * *

"MORNING, ladies," Katie chirped to Wanda and Nina when she entered the kitchen. The warm smells of eggs frying made her stomach rumble. "Where is everyone?"

Wanda turned from the stove with a welcome plate of hash and eggs. "Sit—I know you need to eat after all that, ahem, *activity* well into the wee hours of the morning last night."

Katie flushed a hot red.

Nina cackled, her eyes on her BlackBerry. "Now don't be embarrassed, Doc. We approve of you gettin' yours. It's empowering. Makes us proud of our little girl, right, Wanda?"

Wanda swatted at her with the towel she had draped over her shoulder. "Shush." She directed her gaze toward Katie. "Teeny's still with Ingrid. They're having a long breakfast in the next town over and might take in a movie. Kaih's with them. Where's our favorite kitty?"

Katie flushed again. Last she'd taken a long savor-filled glance at him, he was spread-eagle on the bed, a slight snore lifting his chest. "Still sleeping," she fairly cooed, fighting a stupid grin.

Nina snorted. "Color me all sorts of surprised. Poor man must be delirious from all that wonking."

Wanda flicked Nina in the head. "Do I always have to play the role of your parent? Shut. Up. You're embarrassing her." And then she paused, narrowing her eyes. She peered at Nina's phone. "What exactly are you doing?"

Nina grinned. "Tweeting, tard. You said open an OOPS account to advertise. So I did."

Katie winced. If Nina's customer care was anything like the care she'd received, Twitter was going to ban her in the time it took to press the spam button.

Wanda snatched the phone from her and let out a sharp yelp

while she scrolled upward. "For the love of sensitivity, Nina! You know, I've often wondered if maybe you don't have ADHD. Why do you struggle so with the basic lessons of courtesy? Lessons I've all but beaten into your thick skull."

"Fuck you, Wanda. Dude was asking for it."

"Would you look at this?" Katie took a hesitant glance at the phone Wanda thrust in her face. She began to read the exchange and winced.

livesbythesea @OOPS is your ad for realz? R u people serious?

   OOPS @livesbythesea as a fucking heart attack.

   livesbythesea @OOPS WTF does OOPS mean?

   OOPS @livesbythesea Out in the Open Paranormal Support.

   livesbythesea @OOPS ?

   OOPS @livesbythesea Can u read, tard?

   livesbythesea @OOPS Hoo shit. U mean like True Blood and vampires and shit?

   OOPS @livesbythesea WTF is True Blood and yeah. I'm a vampire.

   livesbythesea @OOPS Do you sparkle like the vampires in Twilight?

   OOPS @livesbythesea I only sparkle when I'm getting ready to kill an asshole.

   livesbythesea @OOPS Sr'sly? u really think u r a vampire and can help other vampires?

   OOPS @livesbythesea I don't think. I KNOW.

   livesbythesea RT the crazy! @OOPS thinks she's a vampire. LOLLOL!

   Ingridbelieves @livesbythesea Shut up, stupidhead! You wish you knew!

OOPS @Ingridbelieves Back off, Braveheart. I got this.

OOPS RT you're fucking ball removal @ livesbythesea, you tard. Bet you should be @ liveswithhismotherinherbasement.

TonylovesChachi @OOPS why so testy w/@livesby-thesea? U have 2 admit telling people u r a vampire is whacked.

OOPS @TonylovesChachi U have to admit, hanging out on Twitter on a Friday night is whacked. Bet Chachi has a date tonight, douche.

"Nina!" Wanda slapped at her hands, shoving the BlackBerry into the pocket of her skirt with a scolding frown. "What have I told you about Twitter, Neanderzilla? We're professionals. If some-one is harassing you, block them, and stop involving Ingrid. The poor child's a neurotic mess because of you. How can we possibly expect to be taken seriously if you allow them to rile you? Ignore them, Mouthy McMouth! You are officially retired from the OOPS Twitter account, and that means Facebook, too!"

Nina rolled her eyes. "Fine. I'm going back to bed. After all that screeching from the two of you last night and my hours all fucked up, I need sleep." She stomped off toward the staircase and disap-peared in a flash.

Katie was grateful when her cell phone rang. She made a dash to her purse to dig it out, cocking her head when she saw it was Ingrid.

"Ingrid?"

"Heeeey, Doc! How's it going?"

"Okay. How's everything with you?"

"Little problem."

"Has Teeny beaten someone up? Lost her teeth?" Again. There was nothing like digging for Teeny's teeth in the Dumpster in the back of the Curl Up and Dye where she regularly found what she liked to call her "treasures."

Ingrid's laugh was shaky, which struck Katie as odd. "No. Teeny's fine. We broke down on the side of the road on the way back from the movies. My stupid car, you know. I should have never listened to Earl Hornsby when he said she was as good as new."

Ah. That explained the shaky in her tone. Ingrid and even a small crisis didn't go hand in hand. "I'll come get you. Where are you?"

"Over in Wainsburg—way out in the middle of noooowhere. Do you remember where the old train tracks are? You know, by the abandoned warehouse?"

Katie nodded to herself with a fond smile. When she'd learned to drive, that location had once been her favorite place to find strays. For some reason, it was a dropping off point to anyone who no longer wanted their animals. "I do. I'm on my way. Hang tight. I'm about thirty-five minutes out, okay?"

"Yep, Boss. Okay. See ya when I see ya. Which would be sooner if you put the pedal to the metal. You know, *hurried*?"

Katie grabbed her purse and frowned again. "I'll get there as quickly as I can."

"That'd be awesome. So much awesome. So hurry now. Quick like a bunny!"

The beeping tone in her ear signaled the call had been severed.

"What's up?" Wanda asked.

She put a hand on Wanda's arm, giving it a squeeze. "Ingrid's car broke down. I've got it. You rest, Wanda, and let Shaw do the same. You've had just as difficult a time as we have. Tonight we'll try to figure out if we can get Shaw in to see his grandfather. But for now, rest."

Wanda chuckled. "It's these hours that are killing me. I'm a night owl since my turn. Anyway, I'm going to take you up on that.

Keep your phone close, and if you need us, just ring. Or tweet," she joked. "Because, you know Nina's so ninja-skilled in gathering followers we'll have no one but each other to tweet soon, but it's a quick way to get us if need be."

Katie laughed on her way out the door. "See you in a bit!"

She hopped down the steps and jumped in Teeny's truck, turning the ignition and taking off.

AS Katie came to the abandoned railroad tracks, she sucked in a breath. Oh, Teeny . . . how had that woman managed to summon the military to come save her? She'd probably called the president himself and complained Ingrid's car had broken down, and all of the government was assholes and elbows at DEFCON 5 to save her.

She threw the truck in park and bit the inside of her lip at the sight before her. She mentally counted four military trucks in the clearing, surrounded by thick pine trees, but no one in sight. Ingrid's car wasn't anywhere to be found, either . . . "Hello? Ingrid? Aunt Teeny?" she called, only to hear her own voice echo as she climbed deeper into the clearing.

And then there was nothing but hands on her, something hard and cold slapped around her wrists, and darkness.

Oh, Katie-did. Why have your spidey-senses failed you so? she wondered even as someone grabbed her, throwing a burlap sack over her head and dragging her backward.

So much for all that cougar-rific sensory perception.

CHAPTER 18

"Shaw, my man! S'up? Where is everybody?"

Shaw ran a hand over his tired eyes and knucked it up with Darnell. "Wanda left me a note to say Katie went to get Ingrid, and she might be a while because she was in the next town over at some abandoned railroad tracks. Her car broke down. Wanda and the night dweller are napping, and I just woke up."

"Well, strap yerself in, cougar dude. I got good news!" he said cheerfully, his wide grin making Shaw smile, too.

Shaw cocked his head. "We could use some of that, Darnell."

Darnell nodded, kneeling to scoop up Petey, who'd run with abandon toward him when he caught sight of the brawny demon. He propped Petey on his shoulder and scratched the dog's head. "Doc Green's awake, and he's askin' for you."

His head whipped around from the coffeepot in surprise. "Did he talk to you?"

"He told the doctors. I heard him while I was hoverin'. Remember the hover? Anyways, he's eatin' Jell-O and makin' demands someone find you as we stand around coffee klatchin' like women."

He was of two minds about this information. Now, finally, he might be able to find out what was happening with him. But did he want to know? Did he want to leave the peace he'd found with Katie and the others to possibly find something more horrific than he'd already discovered?

Shaw realized he didn't have a choice. If he hoped to find out what was going on with his shift, there was a fat lady waiting to sing. She might be waiting to sing at his funeral . . .

Darnell slapped him on the back. "S'okay, man. I know you all hesitant to see him 'cuz some bad shit went down the other night and you afraid o' what he's gonna tell ya. But the doc says he got a cure for your problem. I heard him tell some lady who flew in them doors of the hospital like she was hittin' a Wayne Newton—Englebert Humperdinck concert. Name's Esmeralda. I think she's sweet on the old dude."

Shaw was dumbstruck. What did Esmeralda have to do with this? "A cure? Do you think I can get in to see him?"

"Thass what I heard. He told that cute little old lady he had to find you so he could give you the *cure*. I think it's aiiight to go see him, too. He is your grandpappy. Ain't nobody gonna say nuthin'. 'Sides, the police know it wasn't you and the ladies who took to him like some punching bag now. Means Wanda and the crabby vampire are in the clear, too."

His heart sped up. Maybe, if luck was on his side, he could clear all of this up and set about convincing a still waffling Katie to let him into her life.

Permanently. Even if there was kicking and screaming involved.

Shaw smiled, reaching for his jacket. "Good news, bloke. Let's go."

* * *

KATIE heard Ingrid's stuttering sobs and attempted to soothe her from beneath the rough cloth. "Ingrid! Hush. It's okay."

"Oh, no, Doc Woods. Nothing about this is okay! This is not okay!"

Katie couldn't wrap her head around what had just happened, only that they were bouncing willy-nilly in the back of a truck with hard metal floors. She didn't even have any idea if they were alone or someone was with them. Panic warred with rationale. "Where's Teeny?"

"Still with Kaih back at the movies!" Ingrid yelped. "They grabbed me in the bathroom and made me call you. They made me call you and lie," she sobbed. "While they had *guns* to my head. Huge guns. I felt them. I'm so sorry, Doc Woods!"

Guns? "Guns, Ingrid? Who took you?"

Katie could almost see Ingrid's chest heave in fear. "It happened so fast. One minute I was drying my hands in that fancy dryer they have. You know the one's where you stick your hands in and they suck the water off you like they might suck your skin off with it? And then everything was dark, and a cell phone was shoved in my face with the order to call you and tell you my car broke down."

Her stomach turned, revolting against her breakfast. "Did you see anything or anyone?"

"I only remember a flash of a man, a big, scary-looking man with scars all over his face, in green clothing. Military, I think, and then it's all blank."

Katie followed Ingrid's voice, using her hands, handcuffed behind her, and her knees to scoot closer to Ingrid. She bumped up against her, noting the scent of her favorite perfume. "Just sit next to me and take deep breaths, Ingrid. Please don't freak out. We need to stay calm and think."

There was no more time for talk when the truck came to a grinding, lurching halt. Her heart began to throb in her chest with such force, she thought it would fall to the ground.

The harsh metal slide of doors grated in her ears. Ingrid whimpered. "Shh, Ingrid. Just stay quiet."

Hands yanked her upright and gave her a hard shove between her shoulder blades, leading her to the edge of the truck's bed. One push, and she was falling to the dirt with a painful cry, hunching inward to protect the baby who'd only this morning moved.

"Doc Woods? Don't hurt her, do you hear me, you animals! You leave her alone!" Ingrid hollered, clearly summoning up all her bravado.

Someone hauled her upward. "I'm fine, Ingrid! Just stay calm," she ordered, even if calm was something she was sure she'd never experience again in two lifetimes.

Gravel crunched beneath her feet as rough fingers latched onto her arm and led her away. A sudden, persistent sluggishness invaded her body while she attempted to keep up the pace her captor set, stumbling and tripping.

In fact, if someone wasn't propelling her to a destination, she could easily close her eyes and sleep—on the spot and upright. "Who are you?" she managed, fighting the bone-weary tired. But no answer came, just another rough shove as she was propelled harshly again.

Then no movement, only a blanket of silence.

And then light, bright and glaring, drove a painful hammer into her head.

As Katie's eyes adjusted, her eyes widened in fear and surprise at her surroundings. The room was white and bare but for a metal table with restraints and a single chair on wheels.

Somehow, she didn't think the whole *Alias* décor was going to bode well for her.

A voice from behind greeted her. "Dr. Woods. You have no idea how I've anticipated meeting you."

Her ears pricked. It was a woman. British like Shaw.

Katie blinked, forcing her eyes to focus. "Where is Ingrid?"

"Oh, she's fine, I assure you. No harm will come to her as long as you do what I say."

Fuzzy, Katie attempted to shake the cobwebs from her head. "She's just a kid. Please, whatever this is about, don't hurt her."

"We don't know each other yet, Katie, but we have all the time in the world to get to know one another. A lifetime, in fact. I'd shake your hand, but"—she made a motion at Katie's painfully cuffed hands—"you're all tied up."

As Katie's eyes finally adjusted, she scanned the length of the woman. Short and round, with hair closely cropped to her head and pudgy cheeks, she had on a pink sweat suit with an embroidered teddy bear on the tip of each end of her collar. She looked more like one of Teeny's quilting-circle friends than some vicious kidnapper. "Who are you?"

Her smile round, almost cherubic, was totally in stark contradiction to her malevolent intent. "I'm Nissa Lithgow."

Oh.

Shaw's mother? Wait. Wasn't she dead? Now she was convinced Daniel Green's messages to Nina were just jumbled together.

Maybe this was some sort of bizarre cougar initiation into the family. Like a cat hazing.

But the stark contents of the room and the menacing gleam in the woman's eye said probably not.

What a way to meet the family.

"OH, Shaw," Daniel Green rumbled. "Son, thank goodness you're all right!"

Shaw entered the room with caution, conflicting emotions assaulting him in fits and spurts. He wanted to accept the man's embrace, yet he held back. "Sir, how are you feeling?" was the question he asked to stall.

The cute Esmeralda, sitting beside Daniel's bed with a lovestruck look on her face, chided him. "You silly, he doesn't even know you. Not in his human form anyway. Let him have a moment to adjust, Danny," she crooned, petting his arm.

Daniel blustered, dropping his arms, his wild hair bobbing in thick patches of gray and silver. "Certainly. Come. Sit. It's urgent we speak."

Darnell nudged him into the room, and Shaw obliged by pulling up a chair beside the old man's bed. "So you're my grandfather?"

"Indeed. This has all been a grave misunderstanding. Your friends, I'm told, were held responsible for this—my coma. Untrue!" he muttered excitably. "In my delirium, of which I mostly don't remember, I must have mentioned them because they were the last people I saw before someone took a bat to me. I went to Dr. Woods's clinic because she'd interfered before in what she deemed inappropriate care for the animals. Also untrue!" he shouted, his wrinkled fist raised. "All of the animals were given the finest of lodging and care. I saw to it myself. But I knew Dr. Woods must have had something to do with where you'd gone to. She'd brought trouble before with her meddling, so you understand why she was the likely suspect. When I realized you'd escaped, I knew where to look first. I had to . . . to make her understand the grave situation she would encounter in you."

Shaw nodded in understanding, worried Daniel would become more upset. He chose a soothing tone when he said, "It only makes sense you'd look for me at Katie's clinic."

"I was so distraught, but I do remember the lovely women who were with her. Friends of hers, I suppose. I especially remember the dark-haired beauty whose mouth rivals that of a foghorn." His voice rose in an uncannily familiar hitch and fall. One Shaw knew now he'd heard on many occasions.

Shaw found, though he didn't know this man, he was angry in a sudden rush that his grandfather had been so brutally assaulted. "Nina. That was Nina," he said on a grin. "So did this— your coma—happen because of me?" The notion had troubled him since he'd found out Daniel was his grandfather and was involved in some kind of research.

"Bah! No, son. This happened because of me. It's my own doing that you're in such danger, both you and Dr. Woods. You showing up was merely coincidental."

Shaw's eyes narrowed, his senses on red alert. "Danger? From whom?"

Daniel's remorse was a palpable thing. "From Nissa."

Shaw's eyes went wide. "My mother?"

"Oh, no, no, no, no, no!" Daniel barked, his thin chest heaving.

"Easy, Danny. You heard what the doctors said. You must take it easy." Esmeralda squeezed his hand.

His chest shuddered in and out before he said, "No, son. Nissa isn't your mother."

"SHAW'S mother?" Katie crowed.

The woman's expression grew sour as she circled Katie, her face turning harder with each perusal of Katie's face. "I'm not his mother. I'm his stepmother. An unwilling one, at that."

Katie gawked, her eyes wide. "That wasn't you in the picture in Daniel Green's office at the animal park?"

She sneered. "Of course not. That was Leticia Green. Mother to that bastard Shaw and daughter to Daniel Green."

Shaw had never mentioned a stepmother. He sure hadn't mentioned an evil one. There was a poison apple in this scenario, she just knew it. Her heart began to crash. "So what exactly do you have to do with all of this?"

Nissa slipped her foot under the chair on wheels and pulled it to her. She dropped down in it with a sigh, her lumpy form spreading, the teddy bears on her collar mocking Katie. "Daniel Green is responsible for not only ruining my marriage but throwing his whore of a daughter in my husband's face. That's what I have to do with it."

Ohhhh. Infidelity. A woman scorned. Yeah. Nina was right. It always did come down to a woman. "So you're angry that Shaw's mother, Leticia, stole your husband?"

She waved a pudgy hand in the air in indifference. "Oh, no. I'm long over that. I was angry. Very angry. In fact, so angry I killed Leticia."

Katie fought a gasp. Be gentle with the lunatic. "I could see that. I mean, infidelity is a crime of the heart. It really sucks. I think there should be a law against it, and anyone who participates in ruining a marriage should get their due. Total exoneration."

She smiled. Like some maniacal grandmother who'd just baked cookies with the blood of innocents. "You're lovely. Just lovely. I like you, Katie Woods."

Nice. Good. Friendships were forming. "In the name of liking me, could we loosen these handcuffs? They're a little tight and as a result, constrictive."

"No."

Okay, if she kept this up, BFF-dom was officially off the bargaining table. Katie nodded, ironically relaxed and calm though still so sleepy. "Understandable." She yawned. Not because she was bored. Nay. This was more exciting than an episode of *Supernatural*. She yawned because her eyes refused to cooperate, and despite her dire circumstances, she was exhausted.

"It's been a dreadfully long day, hasn't it, Katie?"

Sing it, sistah. "I'm so tired. Forgive me. It isn't the company. I'm sure you're nothing shy of stimulating."

"Oh, I know."

Katie's adrenaline began to flow again. "I'm sorry?"

"I said I know it isn't my company that's boring you."

Self-assured was probably an asset when you were a mindless killer. "As long as we understand each other."

"Do you know why you're so tired, Katie?" she taunted.

Her reply was one of caution. "Um, nope."

Nissa smiled again, her brown eyes twinkling. "It's the handcuffs. Do you feel the spikes on the back of them?"

Katie gave her wrist a small turn. Oh, yeah. "I do."

"As we speak, a sedative is seeping into your veins. It also immobilizes your shift, rendering you powerless. At least for now. I haven't quite figured out the antidote for a longer, more lasting effect. I was only able to obtain samples, which is, of course, why he's in such bad shape. If he hadn't caught me, I'd have saved his death until I was able to give him a more spectacular show. Like when I used the antidote on Shaw. That's why Daniel was so important. Because he knew the exact formula." She sighed and grinned. "However, my men are busy as little bees in the lab right now, dissecting the components."

Katie's legs turned to butter, and she was almost grateful for the matronly Nissa's help when she led her to the metal table. Her attempt to move her mouth met with no success. Definitely bad.

"You won't be able to talk, Katie. Soon, you'll be in a coma-like state. This ensures you won't interfere when we take the child, and kill you."

Hmmm.

What was a four-letter word for up the creek?

Oh, she knew.

Dead.

DANIEL waited, pausing as he allowed Shaw to assimilate the information. When he looked at Daniel again, he asked, "So Nissa wasn't my mother? Who was?"

His eyes grew wistful and teary. "Leticia. Your mother was Leticia."

That sparked recognition. His father had called her Lettie. "Lettie. That's what Dad called her. So who's Nissa?"

"Nissa is your stepmother. She was married to your father when . . . well, when something unfortunate happened." He cleared his throat, the loose flesh under his chin bobbing with a quiver.

Shaw ran his hands over his tired eyes, his body still sore from his extreme shift. "Okay. Let's back this up, sir. How did you know my father?"

Daniel's eyes filled with pride. "Your father was a genius. He attended the university I held tenure at. I was so impressed with his credits, I asked him to intern for me. I knew he could help."

"With?"

Now Daniel's weathered eyes grew sad. "With Leticia."

"My mother." Clearly, there'd been a whole lot of help where Alistair and his mother were concerned.

"Indeed, and my beloved daughter."

"What was wrong with her? Why did she need help?"

"To this day, I still don't know exactly what went wrong. Leticia was experiencing half shifts, much the way you were when you came to me. It was horrific, and painful, and after a time, left her exhausted to the point of incapacitation. Your father's genetic re-search was brilliant, even at such a young age. I spent a great deal of time investigating him until I brought him into what we called Project Paws."

Shaw's heart warmed remembering his father and his research, then grew cold when his father's infidelity settled there. "So if he was married to Nissa, he was unfaithful to her with my mother."

Daniel's eyes grew sorrowful, but there was a defensive fire in them. He lifted a gnarled finger and waved it in Shaw's direction. "Do not think ill of your father, Shaw. I won't have it. Even I, as upsetting as the whole matter was, couldn't fault him for loving my Leticia. She was bright as a summer's day, and as beautiful as any starlet. They spent great amounts of time together while we tried to understand why Leticia was affected by this anomaly when I, her father, wasn't. She was born werecougar, not manufactured and certainly not an accident. I still have no answer. I can only come to the conclusion that she had some rare defect. Your father was a geneticist—which was why I choose him to help me. One thing led to another with the two of them . . ." His voice lowered in that strange embarrassed way Shaw remembered from his cougar state.

"So you're a shifter, too?"

"One of the few elders left, yes."

"And I'm the product of an affair."

Esmeralda held up a glass of ice water with a straw and encouraged him to sip before speaking. "A torrid one, I'm afraid. Despite Leticia's shifting issues, your father and she fell deeply in love. He was going to leave Nissa when he found out about you. Your father was a good man, son. He took you as far away as he could from that horrible woman. He took a job well below his standards and genius, changed his name from Lithgow to Eaton—all to prevent that viper from finding you. He raised you well. But before that, on the night you were born, everything went horribly wrong."

"Meaning?" Shaw's voice came out sharper than he intended.

Daniel took a deep breath, placing his hand over his heart. "We secluded Leticia, watched her with eagle eyes while she carried you. Both your father and I. I'd never heard of a pregnancy in our community—not since Leticia was born. Werecougars were becoming sparse even back then. We were dying out because we couldn't reproduce. Yet when your mother became pregnant, she sparked new hope for the community. At one time, there was a strict law, forbidding all relations of the romantic nature with humans. But over time, and due to our decrease in population, there were those who weren't above committing despicable acts upon unsuspecting female humans in an effort to keep our breed alive. And there were those, like myself, who refused to participate and went into deep hiding." Grief lined his wrinkled face, making Shaw reach out to cup his shoulder in a sudden rush of sympathy.

"Those innocent women suffered debasing, painful deaths, yet no one was ever successful in their attempts to reproduce until Leticia. She was one of the first to not only mate with a human, but survive the mate and give birth."

And then he understood. "And if these elders could have gotten their hands on her, she would have become a vessel for reproduction in order to repopulate."

"I couldn't allow them to use her as their guinea pig—which is exactly what would have happened had they gotten their hands on her! They would have let any rutting male, human or otherwise have their way with my beautiful girl!"

Esmeralda gave him a chiding look, tucking the covers under his armpits. "Easy, Danny. Please. I'll have to insist you pace yourself or Shaw and his friend will have to leave."

Daniel shoved her hands away, placing them back in her lap and paused, almost as though he was reminding himself she was on his side. He patted her hand affectionately. "We hid Leticia. The long and the short of it is your father spent many, many nights away from home in concern for her. Nissa became suspicious. Ah . . . You know how it is when you finally put two and two together, don't you, son?"

"I wish I could just get two and two to put anything together."

"He has every right to be angry, Danny," Esmeralda warned when Daniel scowled.

"Nissa found out about their affair. She followed your father and me the night she gave birth to you." His face paled, his eyes darkening.

"So she killed my mother, Leticia." He didn't need to hear the words. He knew the answer.

"Nissa did, yes. Nissa was childless, and she liked it that way. She had professional plans of her own and they didn't involve children. Nissa was ruthless and greedy. Being married to your father, by then, one of the best in his field as a geneticist, was to her advantage. Oddly, it never occurred to her that your father was going to leave her for Leticia. Nissa was too pompous for that. But she didn't know about you. She only knew about the affair. At first . . ."

"And when she found out?"

Daniel shuddered, his IV line wobbling, the memory clearly disturbing. "She tried to talk your father into selling you . . ."

"And when that didn't work?"

"She killed Lettie, but not before she did something so odious, even I, knowing she was a ruthless monster, didn't think her capable of."

"Which was?"

"She took Leticia's lifeless hand and scratched herself."

"I know how that goes," Shaw commented, his tone dry and distant.

"Son?"

"I said I know how that goes. I didn't do it on purpose, of

course, but I apparently scratched Katie when she found me on the steps of her clinic."

Daniel's face grew ashen, his hands trembled. "She's turned?"

"Oh, like nobody's business. Big ol' paws, teeth, the whole she-bang." Darnell cackled, then grew somber. "Sorry. Din't mean to interrupt." He clamped his hands back over his chest and stilled his lips.

"Has she had trouble with the shift—like you did?"

He smiled at the mention of Katie, pride filling his chest. "She's better at it than I am."

Daniel's chest deflated. "Then there's still time."

"For?"

"To regulate her shift."

"Then you know how to fix this?"

"Yes! As long as we can get to Nissa and recoup the antidote, which Esmeralda tells me is gone from my office. She must not decipher the components, or she'll create something far worse! Tell me, son, were you wearing a collar when you met Katie?"

Shaw explained the circumstances surrounding how he'd gotten to Katie's clinic and nodded. "I was, with the name Spanky on it."

"I have a fondness for *The Little Rascals*."

Esmeralda chuckled in affectionate indulgence. "You're veering off topic, Danny."

"Of course. The collar you wore was what kept you from shifting so that in the meantime, I could find just the right amount of the antidote to give you to prevent the kinds of shifts you'd begun to experience." He shot Esmeralda another coy flirtatious glance that left her preening. "Esmeralda and her potions helped."

"So it's true what they say about you, Esmeralda, that you're a witch?"

She winked. "It's true. But I certainly don't ride a broom and

I definitely don't have warts. Though I have been known to exact small amounts of revenge on the old biddies from the garden club. Hair grows back," she muttered with a roll of her eyes, making Darnell chuckle.

"Why were you at the animal park just before they moved the animals, Esmeralda?" Shaw asked.

"To recoup the antidote, of course! I'd hoped Nissa hadn't found it, but I was sorely mistaken. Oh, the blood . . ." She shuddered, tears in her sharp eyes. Daniel smoothed a hand over her cheek she leaned into.

But Shaw was still suspicious. "When you brought Delray in to Katie, why didn't you tell me, us, you knew my grandfather?"

Esmeralda shook her head. "If you only knew how many times I've kicked myself today for not knowing you were Spanky, young man. I'd never seen you in human form, dear. Knowing I was so close just makes me want to scream. I'm so sorry."

"Which begs the question, have you shifted since you lost your memory, son?"

Shaw tensed, gripping the arms of the chair. "I don't remember it, but I hear it was a pretty bad deal."

Daniel nodded, his eyes alight with excitement. "Were you angry when it happened? Upset in any way?"

"I was infuriated by the way the people here in Piney Creek treated Katie and her aunt Teeny. So yes, I'd had enough."

"As was the case when you shifted in England. You were mourning the loss of your father. Your fury over his brutal death left you bereft. However, there are only so many shifts like that your body can withstand before you suffer a fatal episode. Each shift becomes more violent."

Fatal . . . He set that aside for the moment and continued to probe his grandfather. "And I was aware of this when I came to the States? I allowed you to put the collar on me?"

"Oh, indeed, son! You were a tortured soul when we finally met. And thank the gods you found me when you did. Had your father still been alive, and known about your trouble, he would have sent you to me posthaste. We were always very careful about communication. I never wanted Nissa to find you."

"Is it because I'm the product of a human and a werecougar that this half shift is happening?"

"That I don't know. There are so many factors I haven't been able to draw any solid conclusions. Age, chemistry . . ."

Shaw's mind went immediately to his unborn baby. "But it could be a possibility?"

"It could be a distinct possibility. I need time to research your DNA. Which was exactly what I was doing before that dreadful woman showed back up."

"Nissa?"

He shivered. "She's who did this to me. For the antidote, of course. Silly woman thought I'd be stupid enough to leave something like that on a computer." Daniel barked a laugh and then his voice went low. He pointed to his now-healing head. "But I keep it all up here in the old noggin. I may be almost five hundred, but I'm not the doddering fool they think I am. I've never left a trace of the contents of the antidote anywhere. What Nissa does have is the batch I made. I imagine she's experiencing shifts much like yours and she needs to control them."

"They?"

"Nissa and her band of thugs. Government blokes who want to turn your abilities to their advantage."

"A superrace? Soldiers?" How cliché.

"Something like that, I suppose. She'll sell it to the highest bidder, if I know Nissa, and it won't matter who that bidder is. Regardless, they want what I have. They think I have the key to creating more werecougars. They believe I gave something to Leticia to help her procreate, when, in fact, that's nowhere near the truth of the matter. But Nissa needs my research to prevent eventual madness. She's a manufactured werecougar much like your Katie. She wasn't born. She was created—with the worst sort of malice. Nissa wanted power, and she garnered it. However, all power comes with a price. I hear through the grapevine, she's experiencing half shifts. If I can keep her from getting her vile hands on my research, she'll shift much in the horrid way you did, her organs won't be able to stand the harsh change, and eventually she'll die. A fitting end to a legacy of filth," he spat.

But Shaw couldn't hear anything other than the fact that Katie's pregnancy was rare. "So no one in the werecougar community has been successful in breeding more werecougars?"

"No."

"What do you suppose was the reason my mother became impregnated?"

"Dear God. If you only knew how much . . . Again, I have no answer for that. At first, we thought it was because your father was a human, but results from the brutalization of several young, human women via full werecougars show that not to be the case."

"Which means Katie's in danger." He was already rising, but Daniel grabbed his hand and thwarted his effort to leave, his hand wrinkled.

"They wouldn't want her, son. She's no different than any other accident that's occurred, though accidents are rare."

"Would they want her if she was pregnant?"

"Dear God! Katie's pregnant?"

"She is." He still couldn't stop the deep sense of pride that he was going to be a father from seeping into his words.

"Oh, Shaw! It's imperative you find her! Nissa wanted nothing other than to stop her half shifts, but if she's aware that not only

can you reproduce but Katie's with child, she and her team of re-
searchers will brutalize her, and hunt you down!"

He was on his feet when the final warning from Daniel came—
ominous and ugly. "Son! Wait. You must be very careful when con-
fronting Nissa. Do not allow your rage to consume you. It's what's
been triggering your shifts. She'll taunt you, Shaw. With Alistair's
death—with the hateful things she wants to do to Katie and your
child. Do not take the bait. At all costs. If you do, this could be
your last shift before death!"

CHAPTER 19

So what was the hullabaloo about world domination anyway? It seemed like a lot of work, all that ruling a world. Katie was happy to just drift. Right here on the cold metal table. Even if restraints and bright, fluorescent lights were involved. Not to mention, they'd taken her clothes and put her in an itchy hospital gown.

But so far, there'd been no probe—so that was good, right?

"He'll come for her, you do know that, Dr. Lithgow, don't you?" a male voice said.

Nissa's chuckle was thin to Katie's ears. "I do know Shaw will come. Redemption is far sweeter when doled out in twos, don't you think? First, we'll find out exactly what Dr. Woods and that whore Leticia had in common, and then, we'll replicate it, using Shaw as our stud, so to speak. Until we're done with him, of course. Then he, too, can be disposed of."

Now hang on. Shaw was *her* stud, thank you very much. No one was using his studness without her consent. And that was never going to happen. So no studs and mares today. Yet Katie said none of those things. Instead, she weakly wondered out loud. "Ingrid. Where . . ." Jesus, whatever they'd given her was certainly an efficient way to keep her mouth shut. Shaw would probably dole out some hefty cash for it, in fact.

There was a pinch to her arm in sharp reprimand. "Oh, Ingrid's fine. In fact, we'll bring her to you. It might bring you comfort. Something you'll need when you begin the crying and begging."

Katie's stomach heaved while her senses reeled. She had to get to Ingrid. To Shaw. To warn them. Aware she was nearly immobilized, Katie struggled against the restraints with unsuccessful, weak twists of her arms. She felt the silver of the handcuffs, now on either hand instead of behind her.

Vaguely, she remembered her strength. As a cougar, shouldn't she be able to bust out of them like Superman? Again, she writhed but to no avail.

"Don't fight it, Katie," Nissa chided. "I told you, we've stripped you of every last one of your new abilities with those handcuffs, and we'll do the same to Shaw just as soon as he shows up. Shouldn't be long now, dear. According to my sources, he's been to see Daniel—who's awake, by the way. I thought I'd finished him off. Who knew the old curmudgeon was so bloody tough?"

Daniel was okay? Oh, that was good news. The not-so-good news? Daniel would tell Shaw everything and he'd storm the castle. If luck were on her side, he'd storm it with Nina and Wanda.

A roll of metal wheels on the cement floor brought another bed crashing against hers, the movement making her stomach heave violently. A door closed and then there was more silence.

"Dr. Woods?"

Katie felt a tear drip from her eye. Oh, Ingrid. She'd never survive this if Katie didn't find a way to help her. "Ingrid . . ." She drifted back off until she felt the sharp sting of another pinch on her hand.

"Dr. Woods! It's Ingrid. I'm right next to you. Stay awake, damn you! You need to stay awake."

Awake, awake, awake. "You okay?"

"Hell to the no, I'm not okay. I'm tied to a bed. You're tied to a bed. They want to hack you up so they can figure out why you can make babies. That is not okay, but listen to me. We can get out of this, but you have to pay attention."

Who was this woman? So strong and determined? Not at all the mild-mannered, meek mouse of a few weeks ago. Go, Ingrid. Yay her. "I'm trying, honey. I am . . . but I can't . . ."

"I know you can't, but you have to. You will. Look, my tongue ring—you remember it?"

How could she forget it? The very thought of piercing her tongue made Katie cringe. But Ingrid had been so proud when she'd come home from the mall with it, she didn't have the heart to balk at her. "I remember."

"If I can get the stupid back off of it, we can use the stud on the back of it to maybe unhook these restraints. I can lean pretty far forward. If I can spit the tongue ring into my hand, I can probably unlock these. Our hands are close enough together, and the hand-cuffs have just enough leeway around the bars."

Katie felt a warm finger latch onto hers. "Feel that? That's me. Ingrid. I'm going to try and do this, of all things, left-handed. So just hold tight, okay? Please, Dr. Woods. I need you to say a prayer. Throw it out there in the universe that I can get this one thing right. Just once."

Her heart swelled. All Ingrid needed was approval. Just a lit-tle. Katie cursed the bastards who'd dumped her in home after home instead of just accepting her for who she was. "Oh, In-grid . . . you're a goo . . . girl. I'm prou . . . proud. You've come

a long . . . place. A long place. No. Way. You've come a long way
since I met you—"

"Doc! I said throw a prayer out to the universe, not yak me to
death."

"Sorry, honey. Quiet. I'm like a . . . a . . . statue. Yep. Statue."

"Good. You be a statue. I'm going to get us the hell out of here,
but I can't do it while I'm talking. Even I'm not that good. Man, I sure
hope all those lessons my friend Gwendolyn gave me in juvie when it
was Monday Sundaes pans out. She was a whiz with a cherry stem."

Cherries were lovely. Big, fat red ones. Katie chuckled to herself. Whatever this drug was—it made everything better. Even
captivity in a hospital gown.

Katie heard someone spit and then her bed jolted again.

"Doc! I got it! Oh, thank the gods!"

Indeed. Thank them all. Generosity abound.

"Okay, Dr. Woods, you're going to have to help me here, which
requires opening your eyes. Please, please open your eyes. I know
you're drugged, but if you want to get out of this, you've got to
open your eyes and look at your hand."

Speaking of her hand. It was damned difficult to scratch your
nose when your hand was tied up.

"Dr. Woods? If you don't open your eyes now, and we get out of
this alive, I'm going to take all of your frilly shirts and give them
to the Salvation Army! I bet that old hobo Jonas Wiggs would love
that creamy confection from Anne Klein. Remember it? It's the
one with the silk ties in the front. Don't you think he'd do it proud
when he pukes all over it because he talked Wilmer Ford into buying him more booze at the Beer Bin?"

Katie's eyes popped open. Now, hang on. That Anne Klein shirt
had cost a fortune. Ingrid's face was distorted, almost comically
so. Her eyes were wide set like an alien's, and her forehead was
elongated to conical proportions. Katie giggled.

"Oh, that's gooood, Doc! Now keep them open and focus on your right hand. You have some mobility; just turn your wrist up so I can see the keyhole, and pray this stud is long enough to crack this puppy open. *Do not move*. If I drop this, we're meat."

Do. Not. Move.

"Dr. Woods! Turn your wrist."

"You said don't . . . don't something. Oh! Move. I'm not moving. Statue and stuff."

Voices from outside the door made Ingrid hiss. "Don't move after you turn your wrist upward. Look, if we don't do this ASAP, they're going to kill you, and Shaw, and the baby. Oh, God! I know you'd do whatever it takes for that not to happen. Please, we have to hurry!"

Every last nerve in Katie's body protested movement. Yet, she gritted her teeth as her mind whirred with the horrible things Ingrid had ticked off. No one was getting their hands on this baby. Maybe she hadn't realized it before—maybe because she'd been so caught off guard, but she wanted this baby.

Wanted.

And no one was going to take that away from her.

Sweat broke out on her forehead, her muscles tensed and wound tight as she moved just a fraction of an inch. Katie gasped, "Can you get it now?" Her head fell back on the hard imitation of a pillow in exhaustion.

Ingrid grunted, her breath's coming shallow and harsh.

And then miracle of miracles, she was free. The silver handcuff banging against the railing on the bed with a tinkle of joy.

Voices, gruff and authoritative, grew closer.

Katie moved her wrist, bending it back and forth to get the blood to circulate. Warmth rushed through her veins, making her eyes pop open. She turned to Ingrid, who smiled and lifted her hand the inch or so the handcuffs allowed. "I just lost an expensive tongue ring, Doc. Least you could do is hook me up."

Katie laughed. "You are brilliant! Hang tight and I'll get you out." Leaning to the other side of the bed, she yanked with force, but it took some doing before she was able to bend the bars and slip off the open cuff. The other still dangled from her wrist.

"As long as I live, Doc, this paranormal thing will never cease to amaze me."

Katie jumped off the bed, rushing to Ingrid's side to try to free her, too.

"Hurry! I hear them," Ingrid grated. "They're coming! Oh, Jesus. Forget me, Dr. Woods—get those bastards. You know, sneak attack?"

Something still didn't feel right. She'd come to know her body well since the turn, and she wasn't feeling on top of her game.

"Dr. Woods, what's wrong?" Ingrid's face had gone from relieved to fearful.

"I have to get this other cuff off—now! I can't hope to fight off all those men if I can't fully utilize my strength." Panic fought for supremacy. Think, Katie. Think. You're all about emergencies. "Do you have another earring?"

"Damn it all—no! I played down the piercings because of Teeny. It's bad enough I have four different colors in my hair. I didn't want to draw any more attention to Teeny than I had to. You know what she's like when she gets even a whiff of someone looking down their nose at me."

Katie looked at her left hand while the voices that had lingered in the hallway stopped outside the door. There was nothing left to do.

So she did it.

And Jesus. It sounded much better when you watched the

news report from the comfy confines of your living room. There, on your couch, with a nice cup of tea and a warm blanket, it was courageous.

Really doing it? Major ouch.

"DARNELL?"

"Cougar dude?"

"You don't have to do this."

"Riiiight. And let Wanda and that crazy-ass vampire get a load a me bein' a coward? Oh, no, sir. That shit would not go down easy. I'm in. All the way. 'Side's, you gotta have someone to keep yo head on straight. You can't see right when it comes to your woman. I'll make sure you don't lose dat cool. Cain't have you shiftin' to death."

Shaw ran a hand over his stubbled chin. "But you hate guns. They'll have guns."

Darnell waved a dismissive hand, shooting him an offended glance. "I didn't say I hate no guns."

"You did. You muttered it just as we left the hospital. You said, 'I hope they don't have no guns,' leaving me to believe you're afraid of guns."

Darnell bristled, rolling his head on his neck. "Shoot. I ain't afraid a nuthin' 'cept that nuttier-than-squirrel-shit vampire. She's one badass."

"So the guns won't stop you from what we have to do?"

Darnell's dark skin turned a lighter shade. "I don't like 'em, thass true, but the hell I'll let them get away with hurtin' Katie and the wee one, and don't get me started on the old man. I kinda got attached to him with all that hoverin' over him. You will, too. He's a little absentminded, but he got a good heart. So guns-schmuns, I say we take the mutha-effers down!"

They'd finally managed to reach Kaih, who was out of his mind with worry about Ingrid, but had Teeny safely with him. When Shaw told him what he suspected and the location Katie had claimed she'd gone to for Ingrid, Kaih had given them directions to the old railroad tracks.

"Why aren't those women answering their phones?" Shaw pondered out loud as the multicolored trees sped past the window of Darnell's SUV. "We don't have time to go and get Nina and Wanda. Can you talk to them in their minds or whatever it is that you do? Give them a heads-up?"

Darnell frowned, glancing back at his cell phone, perplexed, too. He gripped the steering wheel, covered in a leopard-skin print. "I cain't do that with ere'body, Shaw. They have to think me up."

"Damn it! We need more muscle than just us. There are only two of us. If what Daniel says is true, Nissa will be heavily guarded with God knows what. For all we know, she's turned these men and they're cougars, too."

Darnell threw his head back on the seat of his Escalade with a bark. "Hah! Shoulda seen the last hoedown I hit. Demons. Hundreds of 'em. Ain't nuthin' I cain't handle. I ain't afraid. You afraid?"

Yes. Yes, he was afraid for Katie. The baby. But the hell he'd let some woman with a grudge and an evil wish to create some sort of super soldiers take the two things he wanted most in the world away from him. Squaring his shoulders, Shaw let his lips thin. "I'm not afraid."

"Aiight then. You keep dat head on straight and less go get some super cougars."

Shaw gritted his teeth. One hair. That was all it would take. If there was one hair harmed on Katie's head, he'd chew the bitch's heart out with his own teeth.

"Cougar dude, I got an idea. Let's tweet 'em. I bet you my gift certificate to the Wing Stop, dat crazy vamp's tweetin', 'stead of payin' attention to her phone." Darnell grabbed his phone from the console and hit his Twitter account to send a message.

@OOPS In trouble. Need help. Bring crazy vampire for backup!

OOPS @Demonsarethenewsexy Call me crazy again, I'll mow your ass down next paranormal football game.

"Hoo, boy—it's the vampire. I sho did it now. She gonna kill me. Ain't never seen a lady take a guy out like she do. Boom! Like watchin' bricks fall. She plays for blood, man."

Shaw took his cell phone from him and couldn't help but laugh. "You're demonsarethenewsexy?"

Darnell's eyebrow rose. "Iss true. I'm all about the sexy. Now tweet that crazy lady!"

Shaw sent the next message.

Demonsarethenewsexy @OOPS Shaw here. Hurry. Big trouble. Railroad tracks. Ask Kaih 4 directions. We need your muscle, Mistress of Doom!

OOPS @ Demonsarethenewsexy Don't fucking tell me they have Katie!

Demonsarethenewsexy @OOPS Yes. Reinforcements needed. Baby in danger!

OOPS @ Demonsarethenewsexy one hair out of place on the sperm's head and I'll suck the fuckers dry! On my way w/Wanda!

Shaw took his first breath since they'd gotten in Darnell's SUV. As ridiculous as it sounded, he was grateful for the extra manpower.

Wanda and Nina were no joking matter when it came to brute strength.

KATIE'S limp, broken wrist hung at an awkward angle. She caught a glimpse of it as she glanced down at the guard she'd just taken out with the heel of her hand to his forehead.

Wow and wee. The element of surprise plus a bionic thwack to the face equaled the feeling of omnipotence.

"Nice shot, Boss—now get me the hell out of here!" Ingrid clanked her hands around, still tethered to the bed. Katie took hold of the first handcuff, putting two fingers inside of the circle and flipping it open while footsteps rushed down the hallway.

Katie gave a frantic glance to the door before popping Ingrid's other cuff and lifting her off the bed with one hand. She dropped her to the ground and yelled, "Bend your knees, Ingrid!"

The solid thunk of Ingrid's feet behind her left Katie rounding the backside of the open door in order to stay out of sight. "Whatever you do, stay quiet. I don't know how many of them there are, but if we can catch them by surprise, maybe I can take most of them out."

She looked over her shoulder, holding a good finger to her lips to quiet Ingrid. An Ingrid whose face was full of fierce determination and whose eyes were aglow with fire.

Footsteps crashed, screeching to a halt at the outside of the door. A head, shortly cropped and dark, peered around the corner. Katie swung around the door, grabbing his head and bringing it hard to her raised knee. He crumpled to the ground, his gun dropping with him.

Ingrid's hand snaked out, her fingers snatching the gun and dragging it to her side. Katie gave her a surprised look. "You don't know how to use a gun."

She shook her multicolored head. "Nope, but I've been listening to Nina. I know how to threaten," she whispered, pointing the barrel of the gun at the ceiling.

Loud voices grew closer to the room, barking orders, making Katie's stomach clench and her heart thump. "Okay, you be the brains. I'm the brawn," Katie said.

"How's your hand?" Ingrid asked. "You can't be a lot of brawn with only one hand."

Katie took a cautious turn of her wrist. "Better. Don't worry about me, Ingrid. Just do what I say. When they hit the doorway, be prepared. Ready?"

Ingrid gulped for the first time, allowing her slip in bravado to show. "I think so. May the power of Nina compel me."

The moment several pairs of feet stomped through the doorway, Ingrid acted.

Though she just didn't act in quite the way Katie had anticipated.

Ingrid threw her arm around Katie's neck, pulling her backward. "Don't shoot, or I take the bitch out!" she screamed.

Katie pulled at Ingrid's arm, struggling against her hold. "What the hell are you doing?" she whispered out of the side of her mouth, rearing her neck upward.

Ingrid leaned into her ear. Her words short and crisp. "Just trust me, Boss. Please. Play the game." And then in a harsh tone for everyone to hear, she sneered. "Shut up, you bitch!"

"Oh, Ingrid. You do know you're outnumbered, don't you, dear?" Nissa asked, entering the room, an army of unreadable, scowling-faced men behind her.

Ingrid's teeth clenched so hard, Katie heard them grind. "I know that if I kill her, you got nothin', bitch! So I guess there'll be no killing the quiet receptionist today, will there? If I go, she goes with me. That'd suck for you. She's the key to your whole dastardly plan. You fucking hear me?" She waved the revolver around for emphasis, and Katie hoped only she could see the tremor in Ingrid's fingers. "I'll take her ass out if you make one hinky move. Juuuust one. I'm hanging on to her until we're down that hall-way. One eyeball crossed, and she gets it in the heart. Now, all of you, move the fuck out of the way!" When no one moved, Ingrid yelped again, "Do it! Fucking do it *now*, whores!"

"What the hell kind of plan is this?" Katie mumbled, the heels of her feet scraping the floor as Ingrid dragged her toward the door.

"Trust," she growled in her ear.

The crowd gathered at the door began to move, but they were only shuffling their feet, guns trained on her and Ingrid.

"I said back the fuck off, you bunch of green-wearing ass-licking motherfuckers!" Ingrid screeched so loud, Katie's eardrums vi-brated. When no one moved, Ingrid cocked the gun and let a low rumble out. "Move the fuck out of my way, assholes!"

"Wow, Dirty Harry," Katie murmured.

"A lot on the eff word, Boss?"

"Oh, no. You say it with such flare."

"Thank you."

"You're welcome."

"Nina's got a point. It definitely works." As Ingrid shoved her toward the door, feet shuffled. Everyone's feet but Nissa's.

"Ingrid," she chastised. "You'd harm the woman who took you in when no one else would?"

Ingrid smacked her lips, not showing a shred of surprise that Nissa knew her circumstances. "She blows as a boss. The pay's for shit and the hours suck donkey balls. Need I say more?"

Katie coughed in rebuttal.

"Sorry, sorry, sorry. Just go with it," she whispered, then cleared her throat. "Now move, Granny. If you want this bitch alive, you'd better let me the fuck by!"

Katie was so shocked by Ingrid's ferocious words and award-winning performance, she played along, hoping to bypass the throng of men.

With guns.

Jesus. So many big guns.

As they passed hard faces chiseled from über-workouts and disciplined eating habits, Ingrid growled at them. "Huddle over there near Granny, you fucktards! Get where I can see you." More shuffling resulted in the men surrounding Nissa in a protective stance.

Ingrid whipped her around, her many bracelets digging into Katie's neck, scraping and burning her skin. She continued to drag her backward, pulling her to the end of the hall where she stopped. Her breath hitched, her mouth almost pressed to Katie's ear but a moment before she said, "*Trust,*" in a fierce whisper. "You want her, motherfuckers?" she screamed. "Come and get her!"

A hard shove with the flat of her hand sent Katie sprawling forward into the mass of men like she was the chum and they were sharks.

Katie had but one thought.

I goddamned well fed you Tater Tot hot dish, you ungrateful bitch.

CHAPTER 20

Just as Katie cursed Ingrid's existence, there was a loud roar—a mutinous screech—and Shaw was there, in front of her, picking her up and forcing her behind him.

He rounded on Nissa, hitching his jaw in her direction. "Nissa Lithgow?"

She smiled. Just like she'd offered him a fresh batch of cookies and a side of milk. "Look at how you've grown, Shaw. Strong. Handsome. *Fertile*."

Katie sensed something then, something she couldn't identify but made her nostrils flare. Shaw's muscled back rippled with rigid tension.

With fists clenched at his side, Shaw moved in on Nissa, unmindful of her band of thugs. "You murdered my father."

"Indeed. I eliminated him when I got the information I needed: Daniel Green's location. It took me a long time to find him. I waited many years for the moment I could taste his blood on my lips." She smacked them for effect. "It was just desserts. I owed him for ruining my life. For allowing your *existence* to ruin my life. He took everything away from me. I see no reason why you shouldn't suffer the same."

Katie tensed when she saw Shaw's fist jerk at his side.

Nissa reacted to his stance by taunting him. "He deserved it, don't you think? He was, after all, an infidel. A disgusting, rutting pig with a bastard child I certainly wasn't going to raise."

"A bastard child who has what you want."

Katie's head popped up. Why was Shaw so calm? She couldn't get a handle on where he was going . . .

"Whatever are you saying, Shaw?" Nissa asked sweetly.

"I'm saying, you let Katie and Ingrid go and I'll be your rutting pig. You can do whatever you like with me. I'm your test subject as long as Katie leaves safely."

"A thought," she responded.

"You have them?" he drawled.

"Why would I let a good breeder like your Katie go? How does that behoove me? She can clearly conceive. That's a valuable asset."

"Because you can have a hundred like her with me," Shaw responded, still calm. "She's old, pushing forty-one. While she may not age the way she once did, she was still turned late in life. By the time you're done with her, she'll be useless. She can only breed one baby at a time, and we don't even know if this one will be healthy. Clearly, you haven't thought this through, Nissa. Father would be so disappointed. Why impregnate one woman when you can impregnate several in one virile shot? Think big, Nissa. Besides, wouldn't *younger* females be more desirable?"

Katie's mouth fell open. What was a four-letter word for insulting, asshat shithead?

Oh, wait—Shaw.

Just when she was getting that warm, gushy feeling in her heart that he'd run in here on his white steed—he'd gone and blown it by calling her old. Forty-one was the new thirty, maybe thirty-five. Dick.

"While you have a point, she's still the only successful conception. We have no idea if the combination of the two of you is where the key lies. Thus, you can see why I can't honor your request."

Shaw's shoulder's slumped in defeat. "Well, okay. I figured I'd give it a try. You know, just for a test-the-waters kind of thing. I'd be less of a man if I didn't publicly offer myself up—so I thought it was worth a go. But I see your point now." His words were affable to the ear, enraging to Katie's brain.

What the . . . ? In Nina's words, what the ever-lovin' fuck was going on? They were just giving up? Just like that? Handing her over like she was some cougar to be trafficked and bred like a hamster? Where was the hot hunk who'd been possessive and sweet? The one who'd charmed her into all that hot lovin' like he was sexual napalm?

Nice. Oh, what a bastard. All that talk about loving her, and wanting this baby and how she wasn't old at all. If she got out of this alive, which was going to happen if it killed her, she was going to tear his heart out, but only after she ripped his forked tongue from his mouth with her razor-sharp teeth.

Katie raised a finger. "Um, pardon the interruption, but seeing as I'm the 'to be bred,' might I make just a small protest?"

"Shut up, Katie," Shaw sneered. *Sneered.* She'd have never thought it was possible for him to be ugly.

He shook his head. "Always with the mouth. Jesus, you're like a babbling brook. Why must you always be so negative? Can't you see there's no way out of this? Just shut up and accept defeat, you nag."

Her head cocked and her eyebrow rose. Tapping him on the shoulder, Shaw half turned to face her. "Did you just tell me to shut up?"

His eyes, blue chips of ice, stared back at her. "Ohhhh, you bet I did, lady. Want me to do it again? Shut. Up. Katie. There. Want more, Dr. Woods? You never know when to quit, do you? Gab, gab, gab." He pinched his fingers together, creating an imitation of her mouth constantly at work. "And to think I found you amusing."

A snicker from behind Nissa fueled an already hot fire in Katie.

Katie's eyes narrowed, her anger washing over her in a flush of uncontrollable rage. "You stinking son of a bitch! Amusing? I'll show you amused, you mendacious bastard. When I'm done, amusing and me will be like a distant memory for you!" she hollered, ignoring the pain deep in her heart. The one that said she should have known and focusing on the insatiable need to make a pâté out of his balls and serve them up on wafer-thin crackers.

"Mendacious." He turned to the crowd at the door's entry with a showy hand. "That means liar, for all of you who don't have the broad vocabulary the good doctor has."

"Fuck you!" she bellowed. "Is that easier for you to understand, simpleton?"

But Shaw only laughed, dismissing her with a callous snarl. Then his gaze returned to Nissa. He sighed a put-upon sigh. "Do you see what I've had to put up with? She's intolerable. Her big words, her stupid crossword puzzles. Oh, how I've suffered. I almost can't wait to live in a cage and yank my crank in a cup for you people. So take her. Please. I promise to send a thank-you card in return," he said, dry and distant.

Upon Shaw's words, the goons behind Nissa made a move to apprehend Katie, but a loud hiss from behind all of them had each one of them turning back to look at the opening of the door.

Katie's head sprang up and she noted, from some vague place, how incredibly interesting it was that fireballs the size of the planet Mars did make quite the ruckus.

Just when she was cursing the betrayal of not one loved one in her life, but almost two, the world tilted upside down with commotion and noise.

Shaw dove for her, scooping her up and rolling with her under the heat of the fire Darnell was shooting from his hands. A quick glance over his shoulder garnered Nina, Wanda, and her favorite demon evah, Darnell—en masse and noticeably enraged.

Nina was the first to grab two men up by their shirts and give them a hard shake. The rip of the material crackled even in the midst of the melee. "You fuckwits! She's preggers. What kind of animals are you?" she roared in their faces before hurling them to the ground and breaking their guns in half with her bare hands. "Aw, look. I broke your guns. Guess there'll be no cops and robbers for you today, fucktards."

With the cry of a seasoned samurai, Nina pounced on them, yanking them back up and launching them to the wall behind Katie. They crumpled, falling to the cement floor, lifeless.

Katie rolled away from Shaw, still smarting from his cruel words, but he didn't want to let her go. His hands snaked out to drag her back to him, trying to keep her from helping the others.

"You let me go, you snake in cougar's clothing!" she yelled, clawing at his hands until she got free, scrambling away, refusing to listen to his protests.

Wanda's cry of anger turned Katie's attention to the man she had by the ear, scolding as she dragged him to the end of the hall. Blood dripped from the side of his head in ugly, crimson drops, and his heels dug into the floor, but to no avail. "How dare you accost an innocent woman with child? What would your mother say, you heathen?" When she reached the end of the hallway, she leaned down and grabbed him by his ankles. Wanda leered in his white-with-shock face. "If you ever try and hurt my friend again, I'll rip that ear off and eat it *whole*, bitch!" Lifting him up, she swung him in a high arc, tossing him like he was nothing more than a foam Frisbee.

Brushing her hands together, Wanda squared her shoulders and took a running leap under a fireball and smack into the fray, where Nina was wrestling three more men.

Curses flew. Fists connected with flesh. Grunts of pain echoed in the sterile hallways.

Darnell fireballed his way to her, latching onto her arm and yelling, "Find yo man! No time to explain, but Dr. Green says if he gets mad and shifts, it could be the last time. You gotta keep him on the down low, Doc—keep him calm!" he shouted as another grunting lackey made a beeline for her. Darnell stopped him with one fist to his face.

Panic set in again—panic and another warm rush of joy. Shaw had been trying to stay calm—so he could help her. Of that she was sure now.

"Find Shaw!" Darnelle ordered.

And then Katie noted something. In all of the screeching fireballs and threats of ear a l'orange, Nissa was nowhere in sight.

No. No. No. Fear gripped her. Stay calm. Find Shaw. If Nissa had Shaw, she wouldn't stop until she saw him dead. No matter how valuable she claimed he was to her research, Katie knew the kind of jealousy he'd evoked in Nissa. One that had lasted more years than she could count.

In her mind, Shaw's existence had stolen her husband right out from under her. If she knew women, Katie knew Nissa would enrage him just to watch him suffer.

She had to find him.

Her eyes narrowed and her nostrils flared, searching for the woman's scent.

She made her way down winding hallways while the roar of explosions rang in her ears. With caution, she peered into empty offices, sniffing the air, stalking. The slap of her bare feet against the cement bounced off the walls.

"Looking for me?"

Katie whipped around, facing her captor.

Who held a big needle.

For all her years as a vet, she didn't mind giving shots. She did, however, hate receiving them.

And somehow, with the fire that burned in Nissa's eyes, she got the feeling that needle had her name on it.

But her anger, the sudden swell of a mother protecting her unborn child and her man, made her answer. "Oh, you bet I am!"

"You do know you'll die, don't you, Katie?"

"Maybe," she replied, coolly. "But it won't be before I make you look like so much meat. Now where's Shaw?" She had to find him. She would.

"Do you know what this syringe holds?"

"Let me guess. It's some sort of barbiturate?" Which, if she managed to inject it, would euthanize her. So not her idea of a party.

"You are a smart one, Katie."

"And you're incredibly unoriginal."

"Unoriginal maybe. But I've been called worse. So how does it feel to know you're going to die, Dr. Woods?"

NINA gave the last thug a kick in his gut when Shaw, an unconscious man slung over his shoulder like a sweater, approached her. "Where's Katie?"

Nina's dark head whipped around, her eyes scanning the corridors. "Shit, dude. I haven't seen her since we got here. Wanda! You got Katie?"

Wanda heaved another man on top of her army-man pile and

looked over her shoulder. "No! Oh, Jesus." She gave a frantic look in Darnell's direction as he tamped out a fire in one of the men's hair with his hand. "Darnell! Have you seen Katie?"

"Nuh-uh, but Ingrid's safe. I made sho a dat. We need to go huntin'?"

But Shaw was already gone, sniffing out her scent, running through the maze of halls. His heart pounded out a rhythm of panic he fought to keep at bay.

And then he saw them on the floor.

Nissa, on top of Katie, her hand around her throat, a syringe high in the air.

Katie fought wildly, thrashing against the heavier woman, scratching at her pudgy hands, her feet flailing wildly.

Her choking gasps sickened Shaw, making his gut rage with fury.

There was no stopping the wave after wave of anger that assaulted his body. He didn't even try. Katie and the baby were in danger—that meant Daniel's advice to stay calm would just have to go unheeded.

Without warning, he was in cougar form and launching himself at Nissa as though he were a missile, unaware that even though he'd shifted, it wasn't with the violence he'd come to experience in his last shifts.

He knew this form. He knew cougar. This was what was right. No matter the outcome.

Shaw's eerie screech pierced the air just seconds before he body-slammed Nissa, toppling her backward and cracking her head against the floor.

But she still held the upper hand.

Shaw saw the glint of the needle—realized this was probably where he'd meet his creator and had but one regret.

That he'd called Katie old and a nag.

He was sorry he'd miss the hell she'd give him for that.

* * *

Harsh breaths fell from Katie's mouth when she bolted upright to find Shaw in cougar form, sprawled across her in all his buff-colored beauty, and Nissa just seconds from jamming the needle of death into his body.

It took her only a moment to come to the conclusion that Shaw would die before she had the time to ream him a new one for calling her old.

No matter the circumstances.

No way was he leaving this Earth without a good, old-fashioned chewing out.

And only then would she tell him she loved him back.

Clawing her way to her feet, her hands bloody, her body one pulsing raw nerve, Katie saw red.

Her eyes zeroed in on Nissa, the woman's cherubic face a bull's-eye for her anger. How dare this woman have the nerve to attempt to kill the man who'd called her a nag before she was given the opportunity?

Hell to the no.

Katie sprang, high and long, tackling her, but it was too late. The tip of the needle hung from Shaw's lifeless neck.

And that was when enraged took on a whole new meaning. "You fucking bitch!" she screamed, grabbing Nissa's hair and dragging her down the hall, grunting and sweating as she went. "I—will—kill—youuuu!"

Footsteps clapped against the floor, squeaking and thumping, but Katie paid no mind. Instead, she threw her back into slamming Nissa against a wall and pouncing on her, straddling the older woman's body. She grabbed the front of her shirt and yanked her upward with so much force, Nissa's head fell back at an odd angle on her neck.

And then she began to take out every last ounce of fear she'd experienced in the past weeks, the terror for her child, and her anguish over Shaw by way of Nissa's head.

Taking two fists full of her hair, Katie began to slam it against the wall, huffing harsh gasps, perspiration dripping between her breasts. "You killed him! I'll kill you!"

"Katie! Katie stop!" Wanda yelled, but her haze of anger was so complete, she couldn't stop.

"That's my girl! Jesus, if I could shed a tear, I would. Look at her fucking go, Wanda!" Nina yelled in proud admiration.

Hands pulled at her, but her grip was so tight, her fingers were locked in place.

"Katie! You will let this woman go now! This instant! You're a physician. You took an oath! Stop, honey! Please stop!" Wanda screamed.

And then Nina was helping Wanda, muttering curse words and dragging her off a lifeless Nissa.

Katie fell back against Wanda, who wiped her sweat-drenched hair from her eyes, pulling her close and whispering against the top of her head, "Stop, Katie. Stop. Shhh, now. You have to know your own strength. Breathe, honey. Please breathe and think of the baby."

"Goddamn it, Wanda. You are, without a doubt, the biggest harsh to my need-for-death-and-destruction buzz. Why the fuck wouldn't you let her kill the bitch? She whacked her man." Yet Nina, for all her "kill the bitch" encouragement, ran soothing circles over Katie's back.

"Shaw," she whispered miserably, tears falling down her face in hot tracks.

Solid arms, warm and comforting, lifted her away from the scene of Nissa's prone body. "I got this, Wanda. We need to get her home and let her rest. She got the baby and all. You two do what needs doin' up in here, and I'll take the Doc and Ingrid back to the house, make sho they safe."

Darnell whispered soothing words into her ear, cradling her in his arms, and carrying her away from Wanda and Nina.

Away from Shaw.

Forever.

CHAPTER 21

"You got her, Ingrid?" Darnell asked.

A hand smoothed her hair back from her tear-stained face. "Oh, Dr. Woods. I'm so sorry. I tried. I tried the hardest I ever have. I would never, ever let anyone hurt you."

Katie lay in the back of a car she couldn't identify while Ingrid's tears fell on her hand. "Are you okay?"

"Jesus! I'm fine. Just rest, okay? We have to be careful with the baby."

"What was that about back there?"

"When I grabbed you, I did it to get us to the end of the hallway where Nina was. She motioned for me to get you to her. Taking you hostage was a distraction to get you away from all those guns pointing at you. I'm sorry I said all those horrible things. I love you, Dr. Woods. If it weren't for you, I never would have done anything with my life. But now, I want to be a veterinarian just like you. You made me care again. You took my love of animals and turned it into a reason for me to try and be a better person. You taught me. I would never let anyone hurt you, if I could help it."

Katie heard her words, but the deep sorrow in her heart made her response slow and sticky. "You thought on your feet, honey. I'm so proud."

Ingrid took her hand in hers and held it to her cheek, wet with tears. "I'll help you. I promise. I'll stay here in Piney Creek and help you raise the baby. We'll all help. I swear everything will be okay."

The baby . . . She raised a weak hand upward to caress Ingrid's cheek. "Shhh, Ingrid. Everything's going to be okay. Promise." But it would never be okay.

Shaw was dead.

That wasn't okay.

SHE woke with a jolt, suspended in the painful dream that had jarred her awake.

Oh, God, Shaw. Darkness settled over her soul, damp and riddled with despair.

"Dr. Woods," a husky voice with a British accent said.

Her eyes fought for focus, grainy and tired. It couldn't be Shaw. Somehow, while she'd slept, they'd captured her again and they were taunting her with someone who sounded like Shaw. "Are you another goon who wants me to breed babies? Because if that's the case, forget it. I'm old and a nag. Not good for breeding."

A chuckle, raspy and warm, hit her ears. And familiar. Wonderfully, butterflies in your belly, familiar. "I did a little community theater as a child. Good show, eh?"

Her eyes popped open to find it was Shaw, standing in her doorway with Nina, Wanda, Darnell, Kaih, and Ingrid. But she couldn't move. Though, if she could, she'd latch onto his ear and yank it. Hard. "You were a seven-letter word for jerk."

"Asshole?" Nina cackled.

"Ding-ding-ding," Katie confirmed dryly—so sluggish.

"But it did the trick, right, Doc? He distracted everybody so I could get to that room and catch 'em from behind," Darnell added. "Why didn't you think me up? I tole ya, all ya gotta do is think o' me."

She licked her dry lips, her tongue like sandpaper. "I was drugged. I couldn't think."

She heard Darnell's chuckle, so hearty, so welcome. "S'aiight. Yo man got yer back."

"See," Shaw said. "I was just looking out for you."

Katie lifted a weak hand to shoo him away while afraid to believe he was still alive. "Take your bromance elsewhere—he still called me old. I don't care if he saved me from some crazy scientist and her band of merry goons." But she did.

Shaw was alive!

Shaw chuckled. Slow and low. "I was trying to stay calm so I wouldn't shift. Darnell said he told you what my grandfather said."

God, he made her heart tremble. "So you had to stay calm at the expense of my big words and nagging qualities?"

Everyone laughed.

"Whatever gets the job done."

"Job well done," she remarked on a yawn, fighting the call of more sleep that even Shaw's miraculous recovery couldn't thwart. But wait. Before sweet oblivion called to her again, she needed to stay focused. "You died. After all those horrible things you said, you died and didn't give me the chance to find just the right big word for your fuckwittery."

"Hookay, everyone, this is where we vamoose," she heard Wanda demand. Though it was a shaky demand.

"Chicken," Shaw called on another laugh.

"I am no such thing," Wanda retorted.

"Oh, you are so, Wanda," Nina chided. "You know the kind of shit we could get into for doing what we did. Jesus Christ on a cracker. And you call me a troublemaker."

Katie fought the close of her eyes. She wanted to cling to him, wrap her arms around his neck, but not a muscle in her body was willing to cooperate. "What did Wanda do?"

"She saved me."

"Mouth-to-mouth? CPR?" Katie wondered aloud. Wait. No. He'd been dead. Nissa had euthanized him . . .

Nina snorted. No one snorted like Nina. "Yeah. CPR via we-revamp bite. And again, I say, fuck you for always calling me a troublemaker. All of you."

Wanda bristled. "No one has to know, okay? My goodness. You'd think I raped and plundered small villages. I saved a man for the woman he loves. Enough said. All of you get out of here right now and leave these two alone. Katie's exhausted and Shaw . . . well, he—"

"He's a cougar werevamp," Nina provided generously to the tune of feet shuffling. "Uh, we think. Look, I tried to tell Wanda this shit don't fly where we come from, but she's always reading those stupid romance novels, and the writer in her just couldn't let an opportunity like true love pass. So. Much. Bullshit. And the hell I'm getting a shunning for her googly-eyed love-rules crap. Got that, people? I was never there."

Wanda latched onto Nina's arm and dragged her out the door. "You just shut that mouth of yours and go back downstairs or you won't know shunning. Teeny needs help packing for her cruise. Only you know where her denture cream is."

Kaih planted a kiss on her forehead. "I'm so glad you're okay, Boss. Rest up, okay?"

"Yeah," Ingrid agreed, squeezing her hand. "Rest up. We've got everything covered."

As everyone filed out, Shaw, in all his yummy smelling, hard-bodied goodness sat next to her on the bed, taking her hand in his alive-and-well one. She so wanted to throw her arms around him—smile at him—kiss his lips, but sleep was a monkey on her back. "You're a cougar werevamp?"

"I'm not sure yet. I just know I'm still alive. That's all that matters."

God. He'd risked his life for her and the baby. How could she have doubted that he was capable of that? How could she not have the strength to beat him senseless for it? "How could you do something so stupid?"

"You mean ride in on Darnell's white SUV and rescue the heroine?"

"Yes," she muttered, groggy and drifting, but still gripped by the memory of the horror of his lifeless body. "I was so—so scared you were dead. Don't ever do that again. At least not until I have the chance to give you what for for calling me a nag—and old."

Shaw chuckled once more. "When tangling with death, I promise not to die before you can appropriately scold me. Noted."

"You risked your life for me . . . for the baby . . ."

"And it's over now, Katie."

Over. Yes. Finally. "Your grandfather?"

"He's fine and on the mend. The animal park is his. Mr. Magoo is only the caretaker. My grandfather led everyone to believe Magoo owned it so he could do his research in peace. He's been hiding from Nissa since my birth, hoping to find a cure to our breed's extinction."

"And the other animals? Shifters, too?"

"No. All of the animals were brought to him because they were rescues of some kind. Esmeralda and Mr. Magoo moved them when my grandfather was injured so someone qualified could take care of them while he mended."

"Esmeralda? She was there that night . . ."

"The town's accusations about her are right. She is a witch. A witch with one hell of an antidote for what ailed me and what ailed Nissa."

"Nissa . . ." She shivered at the thought of her.

"How about we talk about all of this another time, after you've rested, honey? We need to talk, but not now."

"Talk about what? How old I am?"

"Stop grudging," he said on a laugh, massaging her arm, making her sleepier.

"Why am I so tired?"

"Trauma, I believe. A good dose of shock, too. Not to mention, you're pregnant. The past couple of days' events have taken their toll. You need to rest, and then we'll talk about you and me and the baby, and Nissa, if we have to."

"You and me . . . maybe you should wait to make decisions about that. Heat-of-the-moment stuff." She forced herself to put those words out there. Because it was only right to offer him one last out. And if he didn't take it—he was SOL.

Forever.

"Let's wait on *everything*, Katie. You sleep." He pressed a kiss to her forehead and he was gone.

What did wait on everything mean? Did it mean that he wanted to wait to decide she was what he wanted? Did he want to go back to wherever he came from and do the waiting while he was deciding? But her eyes drifted closed, her mind shut down before she could make a protest or ask for his definition of wait.

And then there was peace.

* * *

KATIE sat alone in her kitchen a week later—miserable. A box of tissues sat on the kitchen table as the mob swarmed at her feet while Dozer and Yancey lounged in the living room. Ingrid and Kaih had left for the day, leaving her to simmer in her stupidity.

And she was really good at it.

She rubbed her swollen belly, wondering how long her gestation would last, and if it would indeed be half the time of a normal pregnancy like Marty had suggested.

If her belly was any indication, she couldn't afford another three months of this or she'd explode. With a sigh, she talked to her stomach, something she'd been doing a lot of lately since everyone had gone home. "So where do you think Daddy is, squirt?"

Yeah. Where was Daddy? When she'd woken two days later after the nightmare showdown with Nissa, Shaw had gone missing, breaking what was left of her heart.

Nina, Wanda, and the others claimed they'd woken up the next day to take Teeny to the airport for her cruise, and he was gone. Nina had offered to hunt his smarmy ass down, but Katie refused. She wasn't going to force herself and the baby on him.

She'd hoped all he needed was some time to assimilate. He was, after all, a whole new breed of paranormal. Add into the mix finding his grandfather, and the horrible showdown with Nissa, and Katie was left wondering if time to himself was what he sought.

And still, he was gone.

Why, her heart had screamed until she'd remembered her last words to him while she was shopping for maternity clothes from Omar the Tentmaker today.

It had hit her with sudden clarity—much the way bits and pieces of that conversation in her bedroom had. She'd told him to wait to make any important decisions.

Because she was just too bright for words. She'd pushed one time too many, and clearly, Shaw had had enough.

Her cell phone vibrated, and just like she had for the past week, she scooped it up, hoping against hope it was Shaw.

But it wasn't—it was OOPS, tweeting her.

OOPS @katieloveskitties Doc? You up and bawlin' your eyes out again abt Catdog?

And then a surge of new hope washed over her. Yes. She was bawling her eyes out again. But did she have to? How hard could Shaw be to find and stalk? Maybe this wasn't as hopeless as she'd once thought.

So enough sitting around and whining. Suck it up, buttercup, as Nina would say. Katie tweeted Nina back.

Katieloveskitties @OOPS Help! I've done something stupid.
    OOPS @katieloveskitties Is that you, Doc Woods?
    Katieloveskitties @OOPS Yes! Need help pronto.
    OOPS @katieloveskitties Do you want my surprised look?

Katie giggled through her tears. Nina. That had to be Nina.

Katieloveskitties @OOPS Don't beat me up. Help me!
    OOPS @katieloveskitties Are u gonna whine?
    Katieloveskitties @OOPS Have I yet? Even with a paw?
    OOPS @katieloveskitties Point. So shoot.
    Katieloveskitties @ OOPS. Can't in 140 characters.
Where's Wanda?

Wanda was definitely the better bet for sage relationship advice.

OOPS @katieloveskitties In Boca. On romantic getaway w/man. Just me. Sucks 2 b u. ROFLMAO. #Ninasefffinfunny

Katieloveskitties @OOPS You near a phone? #desperatetotalktoyou

OOPS @katieloveskitties Wanda took OOPS phone away. Said I was bad 4 customer care. Nazi. Call me on my private cell.

Katie grabbed her cell phone and pressed Nina's name. "Nina? Thank God."

Nina snorted in her ear. "Can't say I hear that often. So, s'up, Doc? How's it goin'? Any batshit-crazy stepmothers you need taken out?"

"I did something stupid. I told Shaw we should think about this relationship thing before we made any rash decisions," she said with a groan. Which was practical and adultlike, if not lonely and a black void.

"You sent all that hot back to England? We wondered where he'd gone. What the fuck is wrong with you, dipshit?"

Katie ran a hand over her swollen belly and winced. "I just remembered today what I said to him that night before I passed out. I told him he shouldn't make any rash decisions. I know what I meant to add to that conversation, but I couldn't seem to spit the words out. It all happened so fast, Nina. One day I was a veterinarian with a tainted past, the next I was queen of the cougars with a paw. Then I was doing things with a man I thought was half my age—"

"Yeah," Nina interrupted. "But they were good things, right?"

"Is that really the point?"

Nina paused for a moment, and then she said, "What is the point, Katie? I know it happened fast. I know shit got hot and heavy before you had the chance to wrap all of your fucking logic around it, but sometimes, there is no logic to falling in love or how fast it happens. Do you think you'd be so miserable if you didn't love him?"

Katie scoffed into the phone. "I never said one word about miserable. I'm a little sad, but nothing more." She gripped the box of tissues and hurled them into her kitchen sink, as if Nina would see them and catch her in a total lie.

"Oh, the fuck you say. You forget, I can read minds, and the whole time we were in Backwater Creek, you were worried Three Name had a wife or kids and he'd have to leave you and go back to his life. Don't bullshit me. As soon as the shit that went down was over, you got some hinky thoughts. Shoulda kept your mouth shut until the shock passed."

"I think I was just overwhelmed and afraid."

"That it'd all wear off once he got over the trauma of what went down. Because you were his life preserver when he had no one else. You figured once all of the unknowns about him passed, the way he felt about you would pass, too. Because we all know in dire situations, people do dire things. Like wonk until the entire town of Deliverance called to tell you to shut the fuck up because they couldn't hear their own banjos twanging."

"Ye—yes."

"Look, Doc. I get it. Totally. This all happened fast, but who says finding the person you want to spend the rest of your life with doesn't happen fast? Who the fuck says you have to know if they like brussels sprouts or broccoli before you decide to be together? Is there some kinda law or some shit that says you have to know every deet about the Lion King? Why can't you find out in a month just as easily as you can find out in a hundred years? You two worked. It was cool. From the sounds of the bedroom he was in, it was crazy cool."

"But that was sex—"

"Yeah, yeah—like that shit isn't important? Dude, you can go watch another TV if he likes stupid shit like the DIY channel and you wanna watch Animal Planet, but you can't make him turn you on if he doesn't. Sex is important. Especially if he's the only dude you're gonna have it with for a very long, long time."

Nina had a way of simplifying things with such crude honesty everything made sense. "But what if the sex is the only thing we have?"

"Then have a lot of it."

Katie barked a laugh into the cell phone.

"Here's the short of it, Doc, and it's gonna be short because you're getting on my nerves with the whine. Shaw loves you. You definitely love him. You're having a baby. Watch *Oprah* if you trip up on some relationship troubles you can't solve. She's got all the answers, right? It isn't like you have to mate for life with him like I did with Greg. Not that I regret that decision. Best damn thing I ever did. But just because you say you're willing to give it a shot, doesn't mean you have to wear white. Not that you're supposed to. Not if you listen to Marty. Because, you know, you're a tarnished woman. Whatever. Point is you can whine about it, or you can give this thing a shot. Either you're in or you're out. Love is love—even if it's only for a little while, that beats never. And here's something else to think about. We helped take care of him, too, you know. We were life preservers, too. But he didn't fall in love with me or Wanda or even Ingrid, did he? End lecture. Hurry with a response. I'm getting bored."

Katie grinned into the phone. "So I guess that means I'm going to England. Somewhere in England . . . I know he told me the name of the town, I just can't remember it right now."

"Tallyho and all that bullshit. I'll find him. Don't you worry. You want me to hook you up with reservations? I tweet with this guy who works for Expedia. Oh, and I don't like you goin' alone with the baby bump. I'll go with. Just so I know you're okay and the trio from hell doesn't give me agita with how insensitive I am, letting you go off to England alone and preggers."

Katie's heart clenched. All of her friends back in the city had abandoned her when those charges had been brought against her.

Yet these women, women who knew nothing about her a month ago, had become the ones she sought for advice. They were the women who'd set their lives aside to help her enter the paranormal world with greater ease. They were the women who had saved her from Nissa Lithgow without ever thinking about their own safety. They were her friends now. Whether Nina liked it or not.

"Nina?"

"What?"

"You're an awesome person. I'd hug you until you turn blue in the face if I could right now."

"Fuck you."

But Katie heard the grin in her tone. "I'll do that. In the meantime, while you make reservations, I'll pack. Call me when we're good to go."

"You got it. Oh, and pack cards or something. I need to keep busy. I fucking hate to fly."

"But you can fly, Nina."

"Oh, yeah. I say we can the reservations and fly Nina Express."

"Not for as long as I have breath left in me."

"Whiner."

"Yes."

"Fine. I'll see you in an hour or so, and don't pack a lot of bullshit girly crap. We go get him, drag his ass back here, and we're out."

WITH frozen fingers, Katie rapped on the door to her future while Nina gave the taxi driver hell. When the weathered door opened, Shaw let it flap in the cold breeze, crossing his arms over his chest. Gruffly sexy, rakishly hot. Her stomach clenched.

She took a deep gulp of freezing English air and rambled. "So I was wondering if you're in the relationship market."

"Really? Word travels fast. When Shaw Eaton speaks, the relationship market listens, eh?"

"Oh, you wouldn't believe the buzz you've created. Everyone's talking about you."

"So the pickings are good? Am I in for a bevy of beauties knocking down my cottage door? I should probably shower."

Not unless she was doing the knocking to the bevy . . . "Any second now, there'll be a line as long as the one I just left at customs. I thought I'd beat the rush."

"Very bold. I like bold. And what do you have to offer in the relationship market that makes you stand out from the pack?"

"Well, there's this." Katie pointed to her belly, rounding by the day. "And let's not forget, I'm an incredibly gifted crossword puzzle solver."

"Because every man needs a woman to find the five-letter word for insensitive. It's a staple in the relationship market."

"Crass."

"What?"

"A five-letter word for insensitive is crass. Which I've been."

"What's a six-letter word for meanie butt?"

Katie winced, not just at the harsh wind from the lake, but her most recent behavior. "Shitty?"

"That works."

"I've been that, too."

"You were, which certainly takes from your appeal on the relationship market."

"Ah, but, I'm awesomely skilled in the ways of bedside manner."

"You do know how to work a Band-Aid."

"Right! Not just that, I can tranq your ass in two flat."

"An uncommon skill, no doubt."

"I'm a good problem solver—logical—well, unless I'm with

child and in shock. Then I become irrational and over-the-top stupid. But minus the hormonal shifts, breasts that feel like they're preparing for homogenization, and the ever-present nag in my lower back, I'm pretty laid back."

His blue eyes glittered. "Your feet are huge."

"Thanks. The Abominable Snowman let me borrow his boots, but I have to return them next week. He has a rash of igloos to raid. Can't do that without boots, you know."

"Katie?"

"Shaw?"

"What made you get on a plane and come halfway around the world when you're so far along in your pregnancy?"

"You."

"Really? I'm open to expounding on that notion."

"You don't want to miss this, do you? I mean, c'mon. We're having a baby. There's all sorts of goodies to be had. Water breaking, dilating, screaming pain as Junior rips from my swollen, disfigured body. And afterbirth. I hear that's a kick."

"Katie?"

"Shaw?"

"You don't really believe I'd have allowed you to do this without me, do you?"

Relief, though fleeting, began to settle her jarred frozen nerves. "Now you tell me? *Now?* After I sat on a plane with Britain's answer to the Jonas Brothers wannabes, this according to them, of course, flew nine million miles and a hundred time zones with twenty layovers in places I can't even pronounce only to be served a crappy postage-stamp-sized bag of pretzels and a Diet Pepsi? With Nina. Did I mention the vampire's with me? I won't even go into the drive out here to the wilds of whatever the name of this town is with a cab driver that beat me up verbally because I had the nerve to tell him how to drive."

Shaw propped against the weathered door to his cottage, pointing to his suitcase. "I didn't get the memo that you were coming to my neck of the woods. I might have sent you a message via smoke signal and tom-tom, had I known. Don't you read your email? Or for that matter, the note I left you? I don't have a landline and I lost my cell phone when I first came to see my grandfather. I didn't have time to replace it with all that I've been trying to get done."

A tear stung her eye. Her smile trembled. "I've been on a plane too long to read anything but Wanda's romance novels. Which, I might add, are quite good. I don't understand all those mean reviews about them on Amazon . . ." She scratched her head. "Anyway, no. I didn't read my email, and I didn't get any note. Did you send me gushy love notes about how life wasn't worth living without me?"

He popped an eyebrow upward. "Um, nope. I just said I was coming back to Piney Creek, and you could suck it, if you didn't like it."

She gave him a flirty smile. "You and all that charm."

"It's an Eaton trait."

Katie moved closer to him, as close as her belly would allow. "So here was my plan. If you were going to be difficult, I was going to beg. But please, if you make me beg, and I have to do it on my knees, you'll have to help me up when the begging's done. I'm like some beached whale. If I roll on my side in bed, I need a strong captain and some anchors to roll me back over."

Shaw laughed. "You were going to beg?"

"I was going to do whatever I had to do to convince you that I'm the girl for you as your twilight years approach."

He trailed a finger along her cheek, brushing the strands of her hair from her face. "Will you push my wheelchair? Rinse my dentures? Cook me soft-boiled eggs and toast?"

"As long as you're down with putting my walker together. Teeny's was work."

"You were pretty dismissive—even in all that shock. I'm not sure I'm willing to suffer that kind of rejection again. That hurt." He made a mock face filled with pain.

"I was afraid. I was afraid we had come together in a dire situation and once the direness of it had passed, you'd realize what bonded us was a tragedy. You know, like disaster victims."

"Well, disaster isn't far off the mark, but it wasn't a disaster that's had me missing you since I left." He hauled her into his arms with a chuckle.

She placed her hands on his shoulders, right where they belonged. "About that."

"What?"

"The leaving thing. Reasons?"

"I told you in the no—"

Katie's cell phone jangled, she dug in her pocket for it and saw it was Teeny. "Hold that thought. It's Teeny. She's on a cruise. I worry she's bedded the captain and taken the male passengers as her sex slaves." She held the phone to her ear while Shaw drew her inside to sit by a warm crackling fire. "Hello?"

"Katie?"

"Aunt Teeny?"

"I'm not a weenie. I just made a mistake."

Katie looked at the phone, confused. "What?"

"I said—"

"No, I know what you said, Aunt Teeny. What mistake did you make?" she shouted, making Shaw smile.

"I forgot to give you the letter your big, strappin' man left you just before I left on my cruise. Oh, Lady Jane—did I ever blow it.

I remembered it when we were in the Mayan ruins. Let me tell you about boring, girly. My eyeballs near fell out of my head with boredom. Anyway, I was looking at some stupid statue, and it was lookin' me right back, square in the eye, I tell ya, and I remembered the letter."

Katie burst out into a fit of giggles. "What did the note Shaw left say, Aunt Teeny?" She eyed him from her place on the couch as he yanked her boots off and rubbed her swollen ankles.

"Said he had to go home to get his stuff, but he'd be back as fast as he could, whether you liked it or not."

Her heart soared, her smile broadened. "He said he was willing to be my slave for life, Aunt Teeny? How could I pass an offer like that up?"

"Whassamatter with you, girl? I'm the one with the hearin' problems, not you. The note didn't say anything about livin' in a cave for life. He said—"

"I heard you, Aunt Teeny," she shouted. "I'm with Shaw right now—in England."

"You ain't havin' that baby there, are ya?"

Katie shot Shaw a worried gaze. "You knew?"

" 'Course I knew, Katie-did. You were as mean as a bear caught in a trap who hadn't eaten in days. It runs in the family. Your mother was the same way as you. I know all the signs. So you comin' home to birth that grandniece or -nephew a mine? Or am I gonna have to come over there and getcha?"

Katie looked to Shaw, who reminded her of his packed bags and pointed to all the boxes in the sitting area. She grinned, her heart tight with joy. "Yes, Aunt Teeny! I'm coming home—with Shaw."

"Good girl!" she shouted. "Make sure he brings some of those tight jeans he's so fond a wearin' so's I got somethin' to ogle. Gotta go, girl—they're doin' the conga line!" The phone went dead.

Shaw knelt on the couch, pulling her to him and placing a hand on her belly. "I'd better pack my skinny jeans, no?"

Katie laughed, letting her lips finally touch his with a sigh of completion. "You'd better pack it all, cougar man. *All* of it."

EPILOGUE

Eleven Months Later—Five and Counting Freaky-Deaky Paranormal Accidents—and Not One but Two Additions to the Paranormal Neighborhood Fondly Dubbed "Mutual of Omaha" . . .

Shaw smiled down at Katie, who smiled up at him while burping a squirming Alistair Junior, now covered in the frosting his auntie Nina had snuck him on his pacifier. He was only eight months old, but he loved chocolate frosting, as did his brother, Daniel the Second.

Nina took Daniel from Shaw and cooed, swinging him high in the air while her mate, Greg, tickled his ribs. "Who loves his auntie Nina?" she asked, garnering a toothy drooling grin.

"Nina!" Marty gave her the evil eye from across the kitchen of Teeny's house where she and her pack mate, Keegan, rocked their daughter, Hollis, who was sound asleep after too many hamburgers, courtesy of Auntie Nina. "Stop jarring him by swinging him around. You'll make his tummy upset. He's not a toy."

"Oh, look," she said to Daniel. "It's Auntie Marty. The stupid Tummy Police." She held Daniel up to face him toward Marty. "See that face, squirt? That's the face of a meanie butt, buddy. You stick with Auntie Nina—she knows chocolate frosting."

"Give that child to me, Nina," Wanda demanded, leaving her husband Heath's embrace to take Daniel and cuddle him close. "Oh, the beautiful children the two of you produce. And thanks to me, you can *both* enjoy them." She shot her husband a pointed glare. When Heath had gotten wind of Wanda's spur-of-the-moment choice to save Shaw, he hadn't been happy. He was quick to remind her of the disaster she'd once experienced.

But clearly, he'd given up hope of ever quashing Wanda's romantic bone because Heath threw his hands up in the air. "I can't hear you, honey."

What Wanda said was true. Because of her, Shaw was indeed, a cougar werevamp—which made for some very strange, but overall successful, shifts. Though there was that shedding problem—in stereo.

"Hey, Wanda," Shaw asked, muttering under his breath to her. "How's OOPS going anyway? Still just a bunch of quacks tweeting you?"

Wanda chuckled. "You know, interesting you should put quacks and OOPS in the same sentence. Actually, we had a very promising tweet from someone today. Someone Ingrid knows through a friend of a friend—or something like that." She shrugged her shoulders. "I'm convinced," she whispered, "that there are more of us out there. Lord only knows what species, but I'm convinced more exist. So I'm not giving up. OOPS is alive and well and open for business."

"Here, here!" Marty said on a wink.

Teeny took the towel from her shoulder she'd been using to dry dishes after a late afternoon gathering of the paranormals she still didn't know existed, and that was just how Shaw and Katie planned to keep it.

What Teeny did know were men.

And she had her eye on every one of the OOPS women's mates.

She thwacked Clayton's backside with it and snickered when he jumped. "How come you never told me you had all these fancy friends with men who're prettier 'n I am, Katie?"

Casey threw an arm around Teeny's thin shoulders with a laugh. "Oh, Teeny. I wanna be you when I grow up."

"Then you'd better work on payin' closer attention when a pretty woman like me's flirtin' with yer man," Teeny joked, patting Casey's cheek. She reached out and grabbed Alistair's hand from behind Katie, nibbling it with a toothless grin. "Can you even believe how healthy these babies are after bein' premature?"

"That just goes to show you what a good mother Katie is, Teeny," Shaw said with a grin, resting his hand on Katie's shoulder, reminding her of the total completion he'd brought her life. The premature thing was the best excuse they could come up with for Katie's three-month gestation period.

Katie's heart filled with love when Alistair rubbed his blue eyes with chubby fists. Esmeralda held out her arms to Katie and smiled from the other side of the table where she sat beside her new husband, Daniel Green. "Give him here. I'll rock him to sleep," she offered.

Katie handed Alistair over with a kiss on his raven-haired head to the tune of a disgruntled moan, coming from Esmeralda's feet.

Can a dog not get even a little love here? I like to snuggle, too, Delray complained.

Katie hid her smile and reached down to scratch a discontent Delray's head. "So who's up for coffee?" she asked, her heart warming at all the smiling faces that now shared Teeny's kitchen. A kitchen that had once only held her, Teeny, and forgotten hopes.

Now it teemed with life—often.

"I'll get it, Boss," Ingrid offered. "I've gotten really good at brewing a strong pot since I have to get up at the butt crack of dawn to drive to school. I need coffee just to keep me from passing out. Not to mention it's what keeps me awake all day long while I deal with all this new clientele." Ingrid was studying for her degree in veterinary medicine and interning for Katie while taking part-time duties for OOPS, answering phones.

Katie's heart swelled at the mention of her booming practice and Ingrid's pending degree. The people of Piney Creek, once Seamus Magoo had put a good-natured bug in their ears, had finally decided she was worthy of more than just boarding their pets.

Oh, and Dr. Jules deciding it was time to retire hadn't hurt, either.

Month after month, the fine folk of Piney Creek began to bring their animals in. At first it had just been emergencies, but after a time, and the ladies' love of her handsome, charming foreign husband, she'd managed to earn their trust. Now their hands were full with the twins and animals in need of medical attention out the wazoo.

Daniel Green chucked his namesake under the chin with affection. "That was a wonderful brisket, Katie." He rubbed his belly, looking healthy and happy. Esmeralda had changed Daniel's life by bringing something more to his world than vials and lab equipment and his tireless research.

He continued to search for the answer as to why his daughter Leticia's shifts had become so violent, but with Esmeralda in his life, he now took the time out to enjoy some family gatherings and long walks around the animal park—which was thriving. The animals had been returned to Dr. Green's care, and he spent his days loving the animals no one wanted or had purchased with the mistaken idea they could care for them. They visited the animal park often as a family, and on one particular visit, Katie had learned that while Shaw was in his cougar state, Lucille, the cat who'd held him so mesmerized that night when they'd invaded the park, had a little crush on her man.

Katie knew, because Lucille had told her herself.

Daniel and Esmeralda had also come up with an antidote to prevent Katie from ever experiencing what Leticia had. The possibility that her shifts could go awry like Shaw's had Daniel and Esmeralda up late into the nights creating something to protect them from a potentially violent shift, taking into account that turning successfully was essential to their natures. It came in the way of matching silver bracelets, rich with some sort of herbs and minerals and a dash of Daniel's genius only he knew the secret to.

And she wore it around her wrist with an engraving on the inside that read, *Shaw, Katie, Daniel, Alistair—Always*, and the dates of the twins' birth.

Wanda and Nina had recovered what was left of the antidote that night—what Nissa hadn't consumed to keep her mad revenge alive and well.

They'd spoken of that revenge and Nissa's eventual suicide only once when Nina and Wanda had told her of the events of that horrible evening. According to Nina, it had been far worse than what Shaw had gone through in the woods that afternoon—and Nissa had, in a rage, thrown herself off the small cliffs in the wooded area just south of the compound she'd created. Nina and Wanda, along with Darnell, had buried her body with the kind of respect Katie still might not have been able to manage.

Nina had gotten into the heads of the thugs Nissa had hired, most of them mercenaries, and erased the events and Nissa's memory from their brains.

And then, they'd vowed to never speak of it again.

Several elders from the cougar community had revealed themselves to Daniel. They'd reconnected in their strong belief that if they died out, then so be the fate of their world. No humans would come to harm in order to prevent extinction.

Shaw came up behind her while she was deep in reflection. "Good day, huh, honey?"

She spun on her heel, wrapping her arms around his neck and pressing herself into his strength. "Are you happy? I mean, living here in the States with me and the boys? Teeny, too?" There'd been so many changes in their lives. So much tragedy.

He brushed his knuckles down her cheek with affection. "What kind of a question is that, Mrs. Eaton? Forget you and the boys. I'm bloody nuts over Teeny."

Katie let her head fall to his shoulder, resting it there, where it belonged with a chuckle. "She's really made strides with those fish sticks. We don't have to scrape them off the cookie sheet anymore. I can see why she's so appealing."

"Lest ye forget her latest dish, hamburger surprise. She's really stepped it up a notch. Though I worry about the surprise," he murmured, kissing the tip of her nose.

"Hey! You two quit that mackin', would ya? Me and the boy here's the only two single dudes in the joint. Why you all always gotta remind us?"

"Yeah, Boss," Kaih backed up Darnell. "You know what I think we should do, Darnell?"

Darnell draped his arm around Kaih's shoulder, dwarfing him. "Whass dat, little man?"

"I think we should hit Frannie's Four Corners and see what's in the corners." He gave Darnell a boyish grin.

Darnell fisted him with his knuckles. "I drive, you buy?"

"Deal."

"Then we out. Good eats, people. Good people, too. Let's do this a lot. Old Darnell ain't got nobody ta call family but you crazy bunch," he said, blowing a kiss to the babies and the women.

"Yeah," Shaw agreed, curving Katie to his side. "Let's do this a lot."

"I'll cook," Teeny offered, her toothless grin wide.

"You aiiight, Granny," Darnell said before planting a sloppy kiss on her cheek. "Peace out. You know what to do if ya get to needin' me." He and Kaih disappeared out the front door, slapping each other on the back.

Katie and Shaw lingered, as they often did, at the back of the kitchen, watching their friends and family from a distance so they could soak up the joy—together. "I love you, Katie Woods. You've made me happier than I ever hoped to be. Don't you forget that."

She sighed, raising her lips to meet his. "I love you, too. You, the boys, Teeny, our friends, our practice, our crazy life."

Cuddling closer together, they watched some more.

And Nina razzed Marty.

Marty covered Hollis's eyes and flipped Nina the bird.

Nina called Marty's behind bigger than the storefront of Macy's.

And Casey intervened by reminding Nina she knew nothing about the size of Macy's window anymore because she was no longer welcome at the establishment due to her verbal assault on the man with the pink shirt and white shoes.

Wanda cut them all off by threatening to extract their tongues from their heads and insist they all learn sign language as a form of communication.

Caught up in the fray, Daniel and Esmeralda rocked Alistair Junior, smiling, content.

While Teeny bounced Daniel, always awake long after his brother, she flirted with Clay, Heath, and Greg.

The mob, Delray, Dozer, and their latest stray Juan-Carlo, slept on feet beneath the table while Yancey purred from the interior of the living room.

And it struck Katie.

This was their life. Teeming, brewing, connecting with other lives, paths that might never have crossed if not for Shaw scratching Katie.

Precious lives that had entered unexpectedly but planned to stay for an eternity.

And she'd waited all of her adult life for just this. Her dreams way back when in New York hadn't been made of this stuff at all. They'd been filled with ambition and material things.

But tonight was confirmation that this was what her new dreams were made of now.

Shaw, Katie, Alistair, and Daniel—always.